"Rachel Lynn Solomon is becom_ _ _ _ of my favorite authors for contemporaries that blend insightful humor with unstinting emotion. . . . This book is intimate and unflinching."

—*The New York Times*

"Solomon's book is bawdy and hilarious, but it's also extremely emotionally resonant and smart as it tackles everything from abortion to mental health." —*Entertainment Weekly*

"Both wisecracking and wise, edgy and vulnerable, *Business or Pleasure* skillfully balances everything that makes romance great. Simply put, it is an unputdownable, sexy riot! Rachel Lynn Solomon is a romance virtuoso and her readers have the best seats in the house."

—Christina Lauren, *New York Times* bestselling author
of *The Soulmate Equation*

"Rachel Lynn Solomon's *Business or Pleasure* is a total delight. It's sexy, smart, and so freaking fun—I couldn't stop smiling! As always, Rachel's characters are rendered with tremendous love and care. You will fall hard for Chandler and Finn."

—Carley Fortune, *New York Times* bestselling author
of *Every Summer After*

"Rachel Lynn Solomon is an auto-buy author for me, and *Business or Pleasure* might be her best yet! Chandler and Finn's story is so vulnerable and hot, and the way Solomon weaves serious, important topics throughout a warm and engaging romance is truly masterful. I already can't wait to read this book again and again."

—Alicia Thompson, national bestselling author
of *Love in the Time of Serial Killers*

"*Business or Pleasure* is an absolute pleasure, full stop. This funny, delightful book will pull you in from the first page—a bighearted celebration of sex, consent, and love. Rachel Lynn Solomon knows exactly how to crank up the heat, and the chemistry between Chandler and Finn is hot hot hot. Solomon's voice shines in this sex-positive rom-com."

—Elissa Sussman, national bestselling author
of *Funny You Should Ask*

"Only Rachel Lynn Solomon could make a story about giving sex lessons to a celebrity feel this grounded and realistic. Chandler and Finn are equal parts smart and funny, charming and generous, thoughtful and endearing. Rachel takes the kind of risks that make romance as a genre so special and rewarding to read."

—Rosie Danan, author of *The Roommate*

"I can always count on Rachel Lynn Solomon to deliver rapid-fire dialogue, intense chemistry, and lived-in yet fresh characters that feel like your oldest friends. *Business or Pleasure* is delightfully addictive and downright red-hot spicy!"

—Amy Lea, international bestselling author of *Exes and O's*

"Rachel Lynn Solomon has a gift for looking directly into my soul and somehow giving me exactly the book I needed. *Business or Pleasure* is a perfect encapsulation of everything I love about Solomon's writing: depth, vulnerability, and thoughtfulness, topped off with laugh-out-loud banter and smoking-hot (and in this case, hard-won) chemistry."

—Ava Wilder, author of *How to Fake It in Hollywood*

"Rachel Lynn Solomon is back with her sexiest novel yet, and the pleasure is all ours. A love letter to self-empowerment, discovery, and intimacy of all forms, *Business or Pleasure* will fill your soul with everything readers hope to find in a phenomenal romance novel. Swoony, steamy, heart-wrenching, and healing, this story will hug your heart long after the last page. Solomon is a shining star."

—Courtney Kae, author of *In the Event of Love*

"*Business or Pleasure* transcends sexy into something almost radical in this honest, raw, fresh, and hugely fun romp under the sheets and across the country with Chandler and Finn. Romantic, hilarious, sizzling, and heartfelt, Rachel Lynn Solomon's latest has taken its place as my new favorite rom-com."

—Carlyn Greenwald, author of *Sizzle Reel*

PRAISE FOR

Weather Girl

"That feeling you get when you curl up on the couch on a rainy Saturday, with a great book in one hand and a spiked hot chocolate in the other: that's the feeling you get when you read *Weather Girl*."

—Jasmine Guillory, *New York Times* bestselling author of *While We Were Dating*

"A sexy storm of a book."

—Sophie Cousens, *New York Times* bestselling author of *This Time Next Year*

"A delightful romance. Perfect for rainy days and sunny days and everything in between."

—Helen Hoang, *New York Times* bestselling author
of *The Heart Principle*

"Rachel Lynn Solomon has crafted a magical story that celebrates hope, resilience, and love. My forecast: read it, and you'll be on cloud nine."

—Ali Hazelwood, *New York Times* bestselling author
of *The Love Hypothesis*

"A tender, hilarious, and heartfelt love story you'll read in one sitting!"

—Tessa Bailey, *New York Times* bestselling author
of *It Happened One Summer*

"[Solomon's] realistic portrayal of the internal struggles that come with the highs and lows of optimism and depression, and how it affects sex and relationships, is an important one."　　—BuzzFeed

"Humorous, captivating, and delightful."　　　　　—*USA Today*

PRAISE FOR

The Ex Talk

"A very funny book. . . . Rom-coms need tears the way bread dough needs salt, and here the mixture strikes a perfect balance between sweet and savory."　　　　—*The New York Times Book Review*

"*The Ex Talk* delivers. This book is quick, spicy, and sweet."

—Shondaland

"Forget fake dating . . . fake exes is where it's at! *The Ex Talk* has all the public radio nerdiness that you didn't know was missing from your life. An absolute delight of a read!"

—Jen DeLuca, author of *Well Met*

"This book gave me genuine butterflies. I fell in love with Shay and Dominic falling in love."

—Sarah Hogle, author of *You Deserve Each Other*

BERKLEY TITLES BY RACHEL LYNN SOLOMON

The Ex Talk

Weather Girl

Business or Pleasure

What Happens in Amsterdam

What Happens in Amsterdam

RACHEL LYNN SOLOMON

BERKLEY ROMANCE

New York

BERKLEY ROMANCE
Published by Berkley
An imprint of Penguin Random House LLC
1745 Broadway, New York, NY 10019
penguinrandomhouse.com

Book design by George Towne

Library of Congress Cataloging-in-Publication Data

Names: Solomon, Rachel Lynn, author.
Title: What happens in Amsterdam / Rachel Lynn Solomon.
Description: First edition. | New York: Berkley Romance, 2025.
Identifiers: LCCN 2024037574 (print) | LCCN 2024037575 (ebook) |
ISBN 9780593548554 (trade paperback) | ISBN 9780593548561 (epub)
Subjects: LCGFT: Romance fiction. | Novels.
Classification: LCC PS3619.O437236 W47 2025 (print) |
LCC PS3619.O437236 (ebook) | DDC 813/.6—dc23/eng/20240819
LC record available at https://lccn.loc.gov/2024037574
LC ebook record available at https://lccn.loc.gov/2024037575

First Edition: May 2025

Printed in the United States of America
1st Printing

The authorized representative in the EU for product safety and compliance
is Penguin Random House Ireland, Morrison Chambers, 32 Nassau Street,
Dublin D02 YH68, Ireland, https://eu-contact.penguin.ie.

For Sanne Zwart—
How lucky am I that you were my first friend in this country?
Hartelijk dank voor alles.

How fresh my memory of that time in Amsterdam is . . . how ridiculous the whole undertaking, how utterly foolish.

—VINCENT VAN GOGH, IN HIS LETTERS
TO HIS BROTHER, THEO

What Happens in Amsterdam

One

SOMETIMES YOU CAN HAVE THE CLEAREST MEMORIES OF places you've never been. Distant cities are familiar as old friends, either because you've seen them onscreen a thousand times or you've heard stories about life-changing vacations or years abroad. You can taste the sugar crystals dusted atop a pastry. You can see the lights of a famed monument shimmering bright with your eyes shut. You can hear the rush of water, but only if you're quiet enough to listen. The melody of a language you don't understand.

That kind of yearning is so specific, a dreamy ache that could be simple wanderlust or maybe something sharper, something that sits between your ribs and convinces you that's where you'll finally be happy. Able to breathe. The best version of yourself.

I fell in love with a place like that once, built it up until there was no way the reality could compare to my imagination.

As I sleepily pass the cabdriver a fistful of euros, I wonder if that place ever really existed at all.

I triple-check the address while my phone hunts for a signal. Somehow it's eight in the morning, a fact my body is protesting with every jet-lagged muscle. Anxiety kept me awake during the flight, worst-case scenarios piling up like Tetris blocks, and I only started nodding off when the pilot announced that we were beginning our descent. The low winter sun gives everything a haze of the surreal. A touch of the otherworldly.

That must be why I don't notice the basement unit at first. Concrete stairs on the steepest incline stop at a black metal door graffitied with a phrase someone tried to scrub off, leaving behind half an underlined word and a giant question mark. There's no apartment number. No window. I glance back toward the street, as though waiting for the patron saint of lost Americans to help me out, but there's no point. My cabdriver is gone. Everyone I know is on another continent.

For the first time, I am completely and utterly alone, except for an orange cat perched on the railing, tail flicking back and forth.

Before I left Los Angeles, my friends and family had plenty of questions. *Is this a real job, Dani?* and *Are you sure you can handle living on your own in another country?* and *Have you showered yet this week?* To which I replied: *Define "week."*

When your entire world implodes around you, sometimes the only option is to implode right along with it. Especially if that implosion takes you nearly five thousand miles away from home—or whatever that is in kilometers.

I will my nerves to remain at a low simmer and run a hand through my chin-length bob, a breakup haircut that doesn't suit my face the way the stylist assured me it did. I'm not sure I've properly exhaled since I got off the plane, not when I hauled my paperwork-stuffed carry-on through passport control or dragged my suitcases off the luggage belt. I do it now, letting my shoulders drop and my lungs relax. One deep breath of Amsterdam air, and then another. This is exciting. This is an adventure. This is not a catastrophe in the making.

The street is fringed with rows of crooked houses pressed tight against each other, most only three or four stories high, in shades ranging from light brown to dark brown. Some roofs are curved and some are shaped like bells, and some have intricate designs etched above the doors. Maybe the strangest thing is that it's so *quiet.* No cars, no traffic noises except the gentle *plink* of bicycle bells as commuters head to work, not a helmet in sight.

I'm so floored by this level of confidence that I don't notice a cyclist speeding toward me until he starts shouting in Dutch.

"I'm sorry!" I say, leaping out of the way as he nearly clips my backpack.

If I were halfway lucid, I'd have noticed that the street beneath my travel Crocs is painted red. Bike lane.

I assess my surroundings again. There's supposed to be a lock-box with a key inside, but I don't see it anywhere. Another mark for the catastrophe column.

That would track. A mysterious job offer, an interview process that seemed much too short, a free flight . . . Odds that this is a scam: getting higher by the moment. I would absolutely be the kind of person to fall for it, just like I fell for Jace promising me we were exclusive or my parents assuring me I'd grow into my ears someday.

Even the cat is judging me in that condescending way cats do, eyes unblinking as it lazily licks a paw.

"Hi there." I lift my hand, because long-ago warnings not to pet animals you don't know were never something I took seriously.

The cat hops off the railing and disappears down the street without giving me a second glance—revealing the little black lock-box it was sitting on. *Victory.*

I punch in the code from my email and the box opens up, pro-ducing a key that fits the industrial-grade door with minimal effort. A rush of adrenaline convinces me this is the greatest achievement of my thirty years on this earth. I am strength. I am power. I am—

—standing in a restored medieval torture chamber.

Basement apartment is too generous a description, I decide as I step into my new home, anxiety giving way to a shock of cold. A sliver of window lets in just enough light to cast grim shadows on every piece of dust-coated furniture: a couch with a gaping hole at the back, a kitchen table with two skeletal chairs. Walls painted dark blue, a dank musty smell hitting my nostrils and making me wish I hadn't swiped that extra packet of cookies from the galley when the flight attendants weren't looking.

None of that matters when it's clear the apartment's pièce de résistance is a gleaming white bathtub in the middle of the bedroom. Inexplicably. Mere steps from the bed.

An unhinged laugh slips past my throat. I must be delirious from travel if this is what finally sends me over the edge, because of course. *Of course* the apartment my company found and that I agreed to, sight unseen, looks like this.

A knock on the front door stops me on the verge of a panic spiral, but just barely.

"Hey—is that yours?" A girl who looks mid-twenties is peeking down from the stairs, motioning to the suitcase I left on the sidewalk. "I live next door," she explains with an accent I can't place. Not Dutch, I don't think. She's dressed for a run, long dark hair in a ponytail, one AirPod in her ear and the other in her palm.

"Sorry, yes," I say, embarrassed. "It is. Thank you."

It takes her an extra second to respond, one that I've gotten used to when meeting people for the first time.

Usually when someone sees my port-wine stain, they stare longer than they should and then make every effort to focus on a different part of my face to appear as though they're not staring at all. When I was a kid, I assumed people would be less obvious about it as I got older, but they've only gotten more awkward. Literal strangers have gone out of their way to assure me I'm "still beautiful."

The birthmark is a mottled pink that starts above my right eyebrow, drifts along my nose, and covers half my right cheek. My own little Rorschach test. I hid it under makeup in high school and used to think I'd try to get it lasered one day, but I made my peace with it years ago—mostly. Even if I still sometimes pose with the left side of my face forward in photos.

"You should be more careful," the girl says as she helps me carry the suitcase down the stairs. "It may be the offseason, but I've even seen phones stolen right out of people's hands."

Once it's safely over the threshold, I hug the dinged-up polycarbonate as though the bag and I have been reunited after an arduous journey. "I will. Thank you so much. I just got off an international flight, so I'm not entirely myself. I . . . live here now, I guess."

This makes her soften. "Rough time of year to move. Get ready for, like, eight hours of daylight each day."

I peer into the depths of my apartment. The sky was still dark when the plane touched down; the sun rose on my taxi ride into the city. "Love to live in complete darkness. I've been worried lately that I've been getting too much vitamin D."

"The summers are amazing, though," she says. "They make the winters worth it."

"You've lived here a while?"

"Almost seven years."

"And are all apartments . . . like this?" I ask with a flourish of my hand.

She takes another step down. Grimaces. "I think you got unlucky," she says, then gestures to her left. "I'm Iulia. I live right next door, if you need any help."

"Dani."

With a wave, she pops her AirPod back in, and before I can tell her I'm worried I might actually need quite a lot, she sets off jogging down the block.

I'm alone again, surrounded by disappointment and chipped dishes, my Crocs sticking to the floor.

Then, blatantly ignoring every piece of advice about how to adjust to a new time zone, I collapse onto the too-thin mattress and pass out.

UNTIL YESTERDAY, MY PASSPORT WAS MOSTLY BLANK, USED for a friend's bachelorette in Montreal and one regrettable college spring break in Cabo. This move wasn't a measured, calculated decision. There were no pro-con lists, no extended conversations with family or friends. There was just the implosion, where I lost both my job and my boyfriend—they say women are great at multitasking—and the jobs I drunkenly applied for because they weren't in LA. Some nameless fear urged me forward, convincing me I couldn't stay in the city that raised me.

Four weeks later, I packed my bags, sold my car, and moved halfway across the world.

When I open my eyes at three thirty in the afternoon, the apartment is somehow colder than it was when I got here. My head throbs with a dull, insistent ache, my throat dry. Groggily, I force myself into a sitting position, reaching for my phone on the nightstand before remembering it's tucked into the front pocket of my backpack on the other side of the room.

I grab my phone and the water bottle that was always a little too big for my car's cupholder and settle back in bed. Now that it's almost—I quickly count backward—seven a.m. on the West Coast, the Dorfman family chat is waking up.

Mom: How's your apartment? How's the weather? How's the food? We miss you already, send pictures when you can!

Dad: Is Amsterdam as charming as it is in photos, or are they all just a very well-crafted tourism campaign?

Mom: Be sure to make a doctor's appointment and refill your prescriptions! I read online that they might have different names in the Netherlands.

The messages come with a pang of homesickness I wasn't expecting to feel this soon. My parents have always regarded me with an extra sense of caution, as though I'm forever the micro preemie born three months early with lungs that didn't work properly. Severe asthma meant no contact sports, waivers from gym class, an urgent call to our family doctor if I experienced so much as a hint of discomfort. It's much more manageable than it used to be, but that never stops the constant check-ins. Sometimes I think they'd have plastic-wrapped me if they could.

I answer them with enough detail to put their minds at ease: **Extremely charming! Cold but sunny. Haven't eaten anything yet that didn't come from an airplane, will report back once I do. I have plenty of meds with me, but I'll make an appointment soon. Miss you too, will call when I'm a bit less jet-lagged!**

My father immediately replies, asking if I have digital copies of my medical records or if I need them to scan anything for me. And even though he's punctuated it with a handful of emojis—a doctor, a stethoscope, a grinning face—I can't help drawing the conclusion that they think I'm too fragile to do this on my own. I decide I'll reply to that one later, thumbing over to a separate thread with my sister, who's texted a much more rational **love you take your time but please know I want to hear everything!**

oops I tripped and fell into a dungeon, I type, sending her a few photos of the apartment.

Phoebe: noooooooooo
Phoebe: maya says dungeons are very in this year. perhaps an intentional design choice?

Maya, her wife, is an interior designer, while Phoebe owns an independent bookstore in Pasadena. I've always loved that they managed to turn their passions into careers, in part because it's something I've been chasing for years, never quite able to get there.

Maybe that's why it was so easy to say yes to this move—because I haven't put down the same roots.

Dani: that doesn't explain the bathtub in the bedroom
Phoebe: omg. go home amsterdam, you're drunk
Phoebe: also! don't forget to take those melatonin supplements I gave you for the jet lag

I track down the jar in my suitcase, position it lovingly on top of a pillow, and send her another photo.

We've always been close; Phoebe's only a year and a half older, and we've never lived more than an hour from each other, even in the worst LA traffic. But now that we're nine time zones apart and her wife is ten weeks pregnant, I imagine that's about to change.

They told us they were expecting during a dinner with my parents last month, Maya's hand easily curving around her stomach. I'd already committed to Amsterdam at that point and had to fight the urge to cancel all my plans—because what if I missed my niece or nephew being born?

That's still seven months away, I told myself. *Don't think about it right now.*

Compartmentalization works wonders on mental health.

Though I'm not exactly well rested, I know I shouldn't go back to sleep, so I head for the bathroom's tiny walk-in shower that sprays water . . . absolutely everywhere. There's no shower curtain, only a sheet of murky glass that does nothing to keep the water in. Because there's also no ventilation, I settle for mopping up the water as best I can before unzipping an oversized sweater and a fresh pair of jeans from the suitcase that also contains every product in my seven-step skincare routine, though I can't remember the last time I made it past step three.

The contents of my life fit perfectly into two checked bags and a carry-on, and while I'm not sure what that says about me, now's not the time to linger on it. So I shrug on a slightly wrinkled wool coat and step outside to explore.

I squint into the afternoon sun despite the mid-January cold. The street is more active now, kids scribbling chalk designs on the sidewalk and dogs pausing to sniff flower beds. Iulia's apartment is on the ground floor with a cluster of plants in the window, but I'm guessing she's at work.

I make sure to avoid the bike lane this time and feel irrationally proud, then completely expose myself as a foreigner by snapping photos of everything. The quaint brick architecture. The elevator contraption across the street lifting a couch through a third-story window. The orange cat I saw earlier, now sprawled in a sunbeam inside the basket of a parked bike.

"What is this place?" I mumble to myself.

My stomach lets out a low growl, a reminder I haven't eaten since I was somewhere above the Atlantic Ocean.

Groceries. I should probably find groceries.

I've never experienced freedom like this before—true freedom, no tethers or puppet strings. There was college, to some extent, where I experimented with boys and with alcohol because there wasn't anyone around telling me not to. But I was in the same state. The same time zone. Now I'm alone in a new country, with nothing on my calendar until I start work next week. There's a terrifying thrill that comes with it.

That connection I once thought I had, so distant now that it might as well have been another lifetime, wasn't just to this place.

There was a person, too—the first one to ever break my heart.

I try not to think of him often, but now that I'm here, it's unavoidable. For a fraction of a second, I panic about running into him, though the reality is that we're two specks in a country of seventeen million people. Still, he might be in the Netherlands somewhere, sketching the view out his window the way he used to do at our kitchen table.

Or maybe not. Maybe he left again with a suitcase of empty promises, the same way he left me.

The neighborhood I'm in is called De Pijp, a little strip of the city without canals but with plenty of bars and restaurants. Around the corner, something much better than a grocery store comes into view: a huge open-air market. The street is electric with activity, stands selling fruit and vegetables, freshly cut flowers, snacks from more cuisines than I can count. People shout in both Dutch and English above the hiss of the grills, enticing tourists and locals to come closer and to try something delicious. There are gigantic wheels of cheese and kitschy Amsterdam souvenirs. Multiple booths just for French fries, served in a cone and dripping with sauce. I nearly go dizzy from the scent of it all, savory and sweet and fried and perfect.

In my Burbank apartment, the only thing within walking distance was a car wash.

I stop in front of a cart selling miniature pancakes, where an older man is pumping batter into small circles on a griddle. POFFERTJES, says the sign above him.

"One of these, please?" I ask, and then try my best at the pronunciation. "Poffert-yays?"

"Poffertjes," says the man, the word sounding as light and fluffy as the pancakes themselves. *Po-fur-chess*. "With sugar or Nutella?"

"Both?"

I watch my little pancakes rise, darkening at the edges before he scoops them onto a paper tray, sprinkling them with powdered sugar and a healthy dollop of Nutella. The finishing touch: a toothpick with a tiny Dutch flag wrapped around it.

The first bite is all buttery warmth, the texture at the sacred intersection of pancake and donut. *Heavenly*. I've always had an incurable sweet tooth, and this is true comfort food for the jet-lagged.

As soon as I'm finished, I order another tray, every worry about this being a mistake instantly replaced with sheer dumb optimism.

I am in Amsterdam.

And then, an equally bizarre thought: *I live here.*

It sounds so absurd that my heart squeezes in my chest and a pressure starts building behind my eyes. And yet what's most absurd is that this could be my chance for a reinvention. Here, I don't have to be the girl whose parents consider too breakable. I don't have to be the girl who forwarded her ex's private, borderline-smutty emails to the whole company or the girl whose friends told her she was acting immature when all she wanted was for them to hold her hand and let her cry. The girl everyone is running laps around, mortgages and promotions and holiday cards with kids in matching outfits.

When are you going to figure things out?

Grow up?

Settle down?

And did you remember to refill your meds?

Maybe this is exactly where I'm supposed to be. Maybe it's a sugar rush or maybe it's the jet lag, or maybe it's a giddiness I haven't felt since I was a kid. I'm not sure I've ever possessed a true childlike sense of wonder—maybe jaded is in my nature—and yet here, in the middle of this market in a city I once wrapped in love and then in heartbreak, I finally feel it.

Amsterdam is going to change my life.

It has to.

Two

WHOEVER COINED THE PHRASE *JUST LIKE RIDING A BIKE*
had clearly never ridden one in Amsterdam. During rush hour. In
the pouring rain.

The Netherlands is the tallest country in the world and I am
only four-eleven, which I've just learned is 150 centimeters and
enough to make most bike shop owners recoil, as though outfitting
someone this short with a bike is a challenge they never received
the right training for.

"This is an omafiets," said the guy at the third shop I tried, a
rental subscription place with a monthly fee. "A granny bicycle."

Then it was my turn to recoil. Maybe this was a comment on my
biking ability or the dark circles under my eyes. Which, fair on
both counts. But the guy reassured me that this is simply the style
of bike here in the Netherlands. An omafiets has a taller curved
frame that lets you sit upright, which is more comfortable and easier to ride longer distances.

In theory, this sounded great. I imagined myself gliding through
the city on a charming pastel-pink bike, tulips I'd purchased from

the flower stand around the corner sticking out of my basket. I'd blend right in with the locals. Quintessential Dutch.

In practice, climbing on the thing feels a little like getting on a roller coaster with a busted track—I can see the way I die, and I've surrendered to my fate. The bike I rented isn't quite the right size, even after the guy lowered the seat as far down as it would go. My toes don't even skim the ground, and while this might be second nature for people who've grown up biking here, for me it feels completely out of control, like I have to trust my body to catch me every time I backpedal to a stop. My body has rarely proven itself trustworthy—not when I lived at the hospital for the first six months of my life, not when an asthma attack kept me from playing the lead in my third grade production of our teacher's original musical *Geology Rocks!*, not when I was so eager for my first kiss that I wound up biting poor Levi Moskowitz's tongue at Jewish summer camp in middle school.

The next few days are a blur of registration appointments. I get a residence permit, the Netherlands equivalent of a social security number, a bank account. I stumble my way through buying groceries, spending a full hour browsing the narrow aisles of Albert Heijn and translating everything with my phone. I learn that coffeeshops are not, in fact, coffeeshops when I try to order a latte before recognizing that earthy scent and realizing the menu is all joints and edibles with names like Lemon Skunk and Amnesia Haze.

Still, none of it feels real.

By my first day of work, I've mostly recovered from jet lag, having mapped the route to my office a few times by bike. I've been desperate for human interaction, and phone calls with Phoebe and my parents can only go so far.

"Oh, Dani," my mother said last night when I made the mistake of mentioning that I was not a natural on a Dutch bicycle. "Don't push your lungs too hard."

"You know there's no judgment if this ends up not working out," my father put in. "You can come home anytime."

And then I bit the inside of my cheek and changed the subject.

I try not to take the morning's steady rain as some kind of omen. Just like Iulia promised, it's still dark outside at eight thirty, and as a result of spending my whole life in a place without seasons, I don't have the right clothing for it.

"Water-resistant," I mutter as I shove at my bike pedals, rain dripping down my lashes and my joke of a jacket clinging to my shoulders, "is a fucking lie."

I yank the handlebars hard to the right when someone passes me on a bike with what looks like a wheelbarrow attached to the front. Inside are three kids in brightly colored raincoats, and there's even an infant strapped to the bike's smaller front seat. This, I gather, is an Amsterdam carpool.

"Sorry!" I yell out when the rider throws me an angry look, wondering if there's a limit to how many times I can apologize.

When I make it to the parking garage beneath the building that's just for bikes, I'm drenched and out of breath. I scrape my hair into a stubby ponytail and hit the buzzer for the third floor, squaring my shoulders and trying my best to project confidence.

The office is around the corner from Dam Square, the very center of the city, on a street parallel to international shops and tourist money grabs like Ripley's Believe It or Not! I've been so focused on settling in, I haven't had a chance to explore it much, but I vow to make some time this weekend. Everything is a clash of old and new: a KFC across from a World War II monument, an H&M next to the royal palace. I wonder if I'll ever get used to it.

CommerX is a startup that claims their new platform will democratize e-commerce like never before, and to be perfectly honest, I don't fully understand what that means. I'm also not 100 percent sure how to pronounce it.

The problem, I realized when I got to college, was that I had a lot of interests but wasn't particularly amazing at any of them. I'd always liked art, but I was too pragmatic to believe it could be a real career. The entertainment industry didn't hold the same allure for me as it did for a lot of my classmates. I liked history, math classes were fine, and there was even the year my parents gave me a fossil kit for Hanukkah and I told everyone I was going to become an archaeologist.

Every time I devoted myself to something new, I was certain it would expose some dormant untapped skill. Maybe I'd discover I had a talent for baking, though I burned all my attempts at brownies. Or I'd find that despite using SparkNotes every time we read Shakespeare, I had a knack for writing snappy dialogue. For about six months, I'd convince myself I was the next great chef or playwright, only to realize I didn't have a fraction of the talent needed to succeed.

UX design was a lucky accident. I'd taken too many intro classes and had to declare a major, and my advisor squinted down at my transcript and noticed I had the most credits toward either a BFA in art or an informatics major, of all things—which had included a class I'd signed up for because all my top choices were full. So I picked the more stable one and spent my twenties ping-ponging between different tech companies while my hobbies continued to spiral out of control, because if I could just find that *one thing*, then I could finally stop running.

This career has never been a true passion, not the way my sister and Maya love their jobs, and with astronomical housing prices, I couldn't afford more than the monthly rent on my one-bedroom apartment. Until Jace, I'd never had a relationship last long enough to have a conversation about living together, and in hindsight I'm relieved we never signed a lease.

Admitting I'm still trying to figure out what to do with my life prompted fewer eye rolls five years ago than it does now.

Which is why I've learned to keep that to myself.

Deep breaths. Fresh start.

A green-and-white logo is splashed across the wall behind the minimalist reception area. In fact, the whole place is minimalist: a couple rows of spare white desks, a conference room in back, too-bright lighting for the semidark sky. Aside from a few haphazard mugs, it doesn't look as though anyone's really made the space *theirs*. Even the fake potted plant looks droopy.

I step inside, wary of my jacket dripping onto the linoleum. "Hello?" I chance.

A man who looks like a stock photo for a startup bro in jeans and a Patagonia vest pokes his head around the corner, looking startled. "You're not here for the audit, are you?"

"Uh . . . no. I work here?" I say, hating the way my voice tilts into a question, distantly wondering if an impending audit is standard procedure or something I should be concerned about. "I'm Dani Dorfman. I'm supposed to start today?"

The confirmation that I am not an auditor seems to relax him. Which pretty much does the opposite for me.

A mid-thirties blond woman in a denim minidress that can't be practical for this weather speed-walks toward me with a grin that looks mostly genuine. "Danika?"

It happens again, because of course it does—her gaze lingers on my right cheek before she forces her smile even wider.

"Dani. Hi," I say, extending my hand. The bike ride wrinkled my black high-waisted pants, which I paired with a white V-neck and a striped blazer. I didn't know if business casual would mean something else on this side of the pond, and I'm relieved I haven't overdressed.

"Pleasure to meet you. I'm Charlotte in HR." Her accent is British. "Sorry no one was here to greet you! We lost our receptionist at the start of the month, unfortunately, and we haven't had a chance to replace him."

I love that the vagueness of "we lost our receptionist" implies he quit, died, or wandered into the woods where no one could find him. Charlotte does not elaborate.

"Totally fine. Is Yesenia in today? She's my recruiter."

Charlotte grimaces. Lowers her voice. "I thought someone would have told you. She . . . left last week." Her eyes grow wide as she realizes that in the space of thirty seconds, she's told a new hire about two employees recently leaving the company. "Very different circumstances, a new opportunity; you know how it goes. But not to worry! I'm here to orient you, and I think you'll get on with everyone just beautifully. It's a very international team."

"I'm glad to hear that. It's great to finally be here at, uh— CommerX." My mouth trips over the name.

"Lovely." Another broad smile, a flash of her teeth. Charlotte leads me deeper into the office, gesturing toward the rows of desks. Most are unoccupied. "We're big fans of hot-desking here. Modern office and all of that. You can take a seat anywhere that's free."

I follow her as she points out the conference room, the tiny kitchen, the bathroom we share with the other startup on the floor. Apparently—and thankfully—I showed up a bit early, and once others start to arrive, Charlotte introduces me around. I meet Natalia from Turin. Mehmet from Istanbul. Beatriz from a small town just north of Lisbon.

"The C-suite are out of town trying to secure more funding," Charlotte explains when we conclude the tour back at the row of desks. "You'll adore them. They're all brilliant, just brilliant—it's no wonder people are throwing money at them!" There's a slight strain in her voice, one I can almost convince myself I don't notice. "We're a small company, as you can see. Everyone pitches in. We actually thought we might start you doing something a little more administrative."

"Sure." I force my smile not to falter. "What did you have in mind?"

Being the receptionist, it turns out. Answering the phone that only rings once (a wrong number), working through some digital new-hire orientations, and making multiple coffee runs.

Midday, when there's a rush to the conference room, I close my laptop and start to get up.

"No need," Charlotte says breezily. "This is just a quick Zoom with the CEO."

My mind drifts between rudimentary PowerPoint trainings about payroll and core principles. There's a teeny window at the end of the hall allowing me a view of a Uniqlo. Clusters of tourists wait out the weather in line for Madame Tussauds. A tram glides by, but—as Charlotte took great joy in telling me—these windows are double-paned, nearly soundproof, so I don't hear any of it. A pang of something I can't name settles low in my stomach, and I try my best to force it away.

This is only day one. I couldn't have expected to be thrown into meetings right away, and even if I'm not really longing to be in that conference room down the hall, I'm not sure what it is that I'd rather be doing. Given how my previous job ended, I'm half convinced I'm the problem. I could call it a mistake, falling for a co-worker who was cheating on me, but my hand didn't exactly slip when I forwarded all those emails he'd sent me before I caught him. The subtle ones. The over-the-top flowery ones I couldn't read without cringing. The downright explicit ones, though there were only a couple of those. Spite may be petty, but it sure felt fantastic, and in those rage-warped moments, it seemed like the only way to regain some sense of control.

Until all he got was a slap on the wrist and I was the one kindly escorted from the building and asked, in the plainest of language, to turn in my badge and never set foot on the premises again.

"I don't get it," my friend Nora said when we met up for brunch a week before I left. Her toddler was screaming that he wanted more syrup while she rocked her newborn in a sling. "I thought you and Jace were talking about moving in together. And now you're moving to the literal weed capital of the world instead?"

"Also windmills," I said as her toddler flung a piece of waffle at my face. "And cheese."

This did not help her understand. Maybe even I didn't understand it, not really. I only knew that I felt *behind*, like everyone's lives were moving in these exciting new directions and I was trapped in amber.

But so far I haven't seen any windmills, and the only cheese I've had is the packaged kind, shredded and zipped in plastic.

Charlotte drops a stack of paperwork on my desk with an ominous thud. "If you have a moment, would you be able to organize these chronologically?" And because I know I should be grateful to be here, I tell her yes.

ON FRIDAY MORNING, I GET OUT OF BED AND STEP RIGHT into a puddle of cold liquid. I grab for the switch next to my bed, the pale beam of light offering just enough visibility to shock me fully awake.

The entire apartment is flooded, and there's really only one culprit.

"*Shit.*" I yank my phone charger from where it hangs lifelessly from a power outlet. "Shit, shit, shit!"

Last night I ventured into the bedroom bathtub because it had been a long week and I wanted to unwind. I'd almost made peace with the dungeon—I bought a couple new lamps and a cheap blanket to drape over the couch, where I eat all my meals because I don't trust the dining table. The water didn't drain very fast, to the point where I wondered if it was even draining at all, but I figured I could just leave it and it would drain overnight.

In a way, I guess it did. Onto the floor.

I snatch up yesterday's pair of soaked jeans, tossing them to safety before I beeline to the hall closet for some towels. The tub, still a quarter full, emits a defeated gurgle.

As quickly as I can, I stuff every article of clothing that isn't wet into my suitcase and urge myself to breathe. Inhale for four seconds. Hold it for seven. Exhale for eight. Just like that therapist taught me years ago during those few weeks I completely disconnected from the rest of the world. Then I fire off a message to the rental agency Yesenia connected me with before she left CommerX for her exciting new opportunity.

Or maybe she realized she was on a sinking ship, whispers a tiny voice at the back of my mind.

Preparing to grovel, I throw on a hoodie and knock on my neighbor's door.

"Hi—sorry—I know it's early," I manage when Iulia answers. "I hope I didn't wake you up. My apartment flooded, and I'm guessing this isn't what you imagined when you asked me if I needed help, but . . . I'm not sure what to do."

She clutches a robe around her pajamas, sleepy eyes growing wide. "You poor thing! Of course, of course, whatever you need." She opens the door, offers to hold on to my suitcase while I figure out my next steps. "I promise Amsterdam usually isn't this hostile to newcomers."

"Thank you so much. I owe you." I say it about a million more times for good measure as we exchange numbers.

I jam everything I need for the day into my backpack, getting dressed in Iulia's bathroom but unable to bring myself to ask if I can use her shower. The rental agency doesn't open until nine, so I grab a latte and croissant from the café—not coffeeshop—across the street and browse apartment listings. Just in case.

They are not cheap.

In fact, after ten minutes, I'm convinced that basement apartment was a hidden gem of the Amsterdam real estate market.

I send a panicky text to Phoebe, waiting for a response before remembering she won't be up for at least six more hours. I'm still not used to sharing only half the waking day with my sister, and I kind of hate it.

Bright side: after two weeks, the sky is no longer dark right when I wake up, even if today is another gray, rainy day. Like someone dipped a paintbrush in water and blotted out all the city's charm—because I'm struggling to see any of it right now.

My rental agency doesn't get back to me until after lunch.

"All our other properties are full at the moment," the guy tells me on the phone. "We can send a plumber tomorrow morning, but it's a very old building. You probably shouldn't use the water until next week."

"What do you recommend I use instead?" I ask, and maybe it's the language barrier, but he just repeats his previous sentence, slower this time.

Toward the end of the day, after another meeting I'm not invited to, I approach Charlotte's desk. I've had some shitty jobs—the time I dressed up as a Saint Bernard and passed out flyers for a mobile dog groomer for a summer during high school, the company that wouldn't let any two team members take PTO at the same time—but surely there's more to CommerX than this.

"I'm wondering if there's any product work I could be doing," I say. "Or if I could talk to the other designers on the team?"

They work remotely, Charlotte told me on Monday, and suddenly I'm not sure if that's the only reason I haven't met them yet.

Now I'm starting to wonder whether they exist at all.

"Next week," she says with a tight smile. "I promise."

As I'm leaving the office, Phoebe messages me with a few choice words and emojis for my landlord, asks if I'm free to talk during her lunch break. Ten p.m. in Amsterdam, and while that typically wouldn't be my Friday night bedtime, this move might as well have aged me forty years.

It's dark and damp, the resignation a heavy weight in my chest as I head out to my bike, where some asshole dumped a few empty beer bottles in the basket. Nope, I discover as I pick one up and liquid splashes across my sleeve—not empty.

Now Amsterdam's architecture seems to mock me. The buildings are all the same height, and there's nothing on the horizon. I'd gotten so used to the sight of the San Gabriel Mountains that I'm only just now realizing how much I took them for granted. Here the landscape feels sullen. Desolate. My fingers are frozen on the handlebars, cold biting at my face. If I were in LA, I'd be sitting in traffic right now, maybe on my way to dinner with Phoebe, or maybe I'd be back on the apps and waiting at a cocktail bar to meet a disappointing date. Even that sounds more appealing than biking home to a flooded apartment. I might be able to afford a night or two in a hotel—I just wish I could explain why that feels like giving up.

All I want right now is a sense of peace. Warmth and comfort and a garbage disposal, the things I left back in California because apparently the only solution to my problems was moving across the globe.

And it must be because I'm so deep in self-pity that I don't notice the light has turned red.

Because this time, I smash right into an oncoming biker, sending both of us toppling to the ground.

Something hard juts into my hip and I scrape my knee on the way down, rain-slick clothes on damp pavement. The other guy shouts in rapid-fire Dutch that I don't need to understand to know he's pissed, but I do catch a word that sounds like *tourist*.

"I'm sorry I'm sorry I'm sorry," I say, squinting through wet hair the crash plastered to my face, trying to ignore the searing pain in my hip.

More Dutch, some swearing in English, and then: "Danika?"

Three

Wouter van Leeuwen, my first love and first every-thing, is staring back at me, our bikes twisted in a heap between us. Broad shoulders fill out his raincoat, his gray Blundstones scuffed with age. He is almost the boy I remember—a swish of blond hair, darker at the roots, with far more stubble along his jaw than he had at seventeen. Deep hazel eyes, the kind he could render so beauti-fully in a self-portrait while I struggled to get their color just right. Round metal-rimmed glasses dotted with rain, slightly askew. The faintest freckles along his nose.

This can't be real life, and yet it's the only thing in the past two weeks that's made any amount of sense. Tiny Dutch pancakes and dogs in bicycle baskets? Completely fake.

Wouter van Leeuwen, with his soft mouth and baffled gaze, the boy—*man*—I've never been able to forgive?

So painfully, perfectly *real*.

He blinks himself out of the daze before I do, extending one large hand to pull me to my feet, then hauls both our bikes to the sidewalk with all the swiftness of a ball boy at Wimbledon.

"What are you doing here?" he asks once we're no longer block-ing traffic. Now his voice slips into the coziest memory centers of my brain. I should have recognized it immediately—even with thirteen years between then and now, I never thought I'd forget the sound of the first voice to utter *I love you*.

In English, and then in Dutch.

I hug my jacket tighter, but I can't decide if I'm too warm or too cold. "Trying to run you off the road, apparently." The joke doesn't have the right amount of humor to it. I'm too in shock, and my whole right leg is screaming with pain. "I'm—holy shit. Sorry. Try-ing to wrap my mind around this."

Wouter van Leeuwen still lives in Amsterdam. Wouter van Leeuwen is *here*, right in front of me, after the promises we made and his heartless breakup and before that, the relationship we couldn't tell anyone about.

Despite all the chaos I've caused in the span of five minutes, he breaks into a grin. Like he's *happy* to see me, when the feeling coursing through my body is more along the lines of panic and dread, with a sprinkling of unresolved conflict on top. "You look . . ." He trails off, as though realizing exactly how I look—like I was just fished out of a canal—and then blushes when his blatant assessment of me lasts a beat too long. "Wow," he finishes, and I'm not sure how to interpret that. "How long are you visiting?"

"I live here," I say. "I got a job at a startup. Just finished my first week."

Now the grin slides into an expression of pure disbelief. "You're serious? You live here, in Amsterdam? Holy shit is right. There's a café I like on this next street. Let me buy you a drink, and you can tell me all about it?"

He locks his bike to a rack and does the same with mine, and then I am following Wouter van Leeuwen down the block, limping on my injured leg while he shakes his head and mutters, "Danika Dorfman. I can't believe it."

The café is styled like a living room, with plush mismatched furniture, a bookshelf-lined wall, and mellow eighties rock playing in the background. Wouter asks the server for something in Dutch as we grab an empty table in the corner, and she returns with an ice pack, two waters, and a few bandages.

"I'm okay, really," I say, fully aware that I'm bleeding from at least three places, but Wouter just lifts his eyebrows at my shredded work slacks. I relent, holding the ice pack to my knee while I push damp hair out of my face with my other hand. I have a medium amount of vanity now that my birthmark and I aren't constantly at war, but every time I imagined seeing Wouter again, I looked much hotter than I do now. And I had definitely showered.

I've tested so many comebacks on him in my head, mentally cursed him out like I was casting a spell. A decade may have passed, but every relationship I've had, every time I've second-guessed myself—it all comes back to the year we spent wholly obsessed with each other.

And yet the words that leave my lips are "Are you hurt?" Because even if I'm bitter, that crash was absolutely my fault.

"A couple scrapes." He rubs his glasses lenses along his shirt to dry them. "I've had worse."

God, I'm still processing the absurdity of him sitting across from me, trying to reconcile this man with the boy I used to know. His details are slow to come into focus, a pencil drawing coming to life. Once I've started breathing again and sipped some water, I can properly take him in.

He was cute at seventeen, with a single dimple and glasses he was always forgetting to wear so he went without them sometimes, squinting down at his sketchbook. *You're going to get a wrinkle right there*, I'd say, pressing my thumb between his brows, and he'd grab my thumb and bring it to his lips. Now there's no denying it—he is *beautiful*, especially once he takes off his jacket, revealing a green button-up that brings out that color in his eyes. The rough hair along his jaw and chin is flecked with gray and, combined with the faintest lines at the edges of his eyes, makes him look mature, settled in his skin. I once dotted those light freckles with paint, turning his face into a work of art even though it already was. And his hands—I fell so hard for his hands.

Time has only been unkind to him in the way his hair is thinning in the back. I can't help wondering if he's self-conscious about it, but it doesn't seem to have affected his confidence. There's an ease to him I'm instantly jealous of, long legs spread as he leans back in his chair.

It's the cruelest thing he could do—have the nerve to look this good, this *comfortable*, after all these years.

My parents had always wanted to host a foreign exchange student, loved the idea of learning from them as much as they'd be learning from us. When I was seventeen and Phoebe was in college, they filled out all the applications and attended all the seminars, and then they were matched with a student from the Netherlands.

Wouter and I were the same age, and he immediately struck me as different from the boys I went to school with. Older, somehow. I tried to imagine living in the same place Van Gogh, Rembrandt, and Vermeer once did, captivated by all that creative energy in such a small country. The sheer amount of independence he'd grown up with floored me; he traveled everywhere by bike and had for years, often alone and never with a helmet. My parents couldn't get over that part, no matter how many times Wouter told them that's just how it was in the Netherlands.

The more time we spent together, the more I realized my feelings were deeper than simply finding him interesting. I couldn't stop thinking about his messy hair and soft accent and ink-smudged hands. His shirt hem would brush mine as we passed each other in the hall, and my heart would leap into my throat. I'd doze off on the couch in the middle of my homework, and he'd drape a blanket over me. It was torture, the fact that he was sleeping in the room across from mine, only a few feet away. Off-limits.

But I swore I'd never act on it. My parents would have grounded me until I was sixty, and I assumed Wouter didn't want to jeopardize his program by hooking up with his host parents' daughter. And yet—those feelings didn't go away. I wore my shortest shorts around the house, took him to my favorite places in LA, stayed up late watching movies with him. If we couldn't be together, I reasoned, then at least we could be inseparable.

One December evening when he was studying and no one else was home, I knocked on the door of his room. There were doodles in the margins of his notes. A sunset. A knight on horseback. "Do me," I said, summoning all my courage as I stood next to his desk, presenting my arm. He blushed, tapped the pen on his chin a few times before lowering it. The tip skated over my skin from freckle to freckle, curved lines forming the swell of the ocean. A ballpoint blue tidal wave.

"What do you think?" he asked as I gazed down at it. He was still touching me, his thumb moving in circles on my palm, and I was done for. The rest of the night unfolded in dizzy snapshots: my hand on his jaw, his fingertips skimming up my bare legs. We kissed until the garage door rumbled beneath us, and when I got into bed that night, I clutched my tattooed forearm close to my chest.

I knew we shouldn't—but for the next six months, we did.

"Wow," he says again now, after the server drops off a couple beers. "How are you doing? Aside from the crash, of course." His English still has that slight Dutch accent, giving his words round edges.

My stomach twists with long-buried frustration. Before he left LA, we'd made a plan. In all our starry-eyed optimism, we thought we'd do long-distance until we could reunite. Maybe I'd study abroad or he would, or we'd spend summer and winter breaks together. The geography was inconvenient, but we were determined to figure it out.

Then, a few days after he got home, enough time for the jet lag to settle his brain, he sent me the too-short text that sliced my life into a Before and After.

Now that I'm back, I've been doing a lot of thinking, and I'm just not sure it's going to work. I need to be with someone who has a little more ambition. I'm so sorry. Thanks for everything.

As though thanking me somehow made it okay. I'd be so touched by his politeness I'd forget what he was really saying.

Thanks for everything.

Six months of secrecy, and he didn't even have the guts for a phone call—I tried and tried, and he never picked up. He couldn't say it to my fucking face, which must have meant I didn't matter to him the way he mattered to me.

The heartbreak was a vicious, all-consuming thing. I remember bursting into Phoebe's dorm room at USC, tears dripping down my face, and she swaddled me in a blanket and slowly rocked me back and forth until I stopped crying.

I vowed I'd never let someone else control my emotions that way again. By the first week of school, I was dating a JV soccer player

I'd dumped by homecoming because I could sense him losing interest. To this day, I've always been the one to end a relationship before the other person can decide they're through with me. Anything to prevent feeling that hollow.

Wouter took the coward's way out—but he was exactly right. He was the one with all the ambition, buoyed by his parents' high expectations, while for my parents, sometimes it seemed like it was enough that I was alive. No pressure to achieve, a shrug and *you'll do better next time* when I got the occasional B-minus. I flitted from hobby to hobby and all they did was smile and clap.

I was adrift, and most days it feels like I haven't changed at all.

"I'm . . . yeah." Apparently, that's the best way to describe it. How do you catch up with someone when it's been that long? When they were this vital part of your life and then they were suddenly just . . . gone? I clear my throat and try again. "The past couple weeks have been interesting."

"You said you're here for work?"

With a nod, I readjust the ice pack. "I'm a UX designer at a fintech startup."

"What are the odds you'd end up in Amsterdam after all this time?" His initial excitement has worn off, replaced by something fidgety. Whenever his hands used to twitch in his lap the way they're doing now, I thought it was because he didn't have them wrapped around a Faber-Castell. Now I'm wondering if it's because he realizes how untidy our ending was.

Two baskets arrive at the table, and Wouter seems thrilled to have something to do. He gestures to the fried balls of dough in one of them. "Traditional Dutch snacks. Bitterballen, and these are kaasstengels—cheese sticks. I hope you like fried food." Then something seems to occur to him. "But you always preferred sweets, right? I can order—"

"This is fine." Even though it's true that I'd rather have dessert at any time of day, it's almost unsettling that he remembers this about me. He should have forfeited his right to those details, however trivial, the moment he decided it was over.

I bite into one of the bitterballen, and though it nearly burns my tongue, it's so good I don't care. Savory and warm with the perfect crunch. He nudges a small cup of mustard my way, and the next bite is even better, even if it's underscored by an awkward silence.

"I have to admit, I've spent all these years thinking you'd come at me with an axe if we ever saw each other again," he says.

"Nope, just a bike."

A groan mixes with a laugh as he pushes a hand into his forehead, jostling his glasses. "I was seventeen and an idiot. I would have deserved it."

I wait for more, surprised he's bringing it up, because *seventeen and an idiot* doesn't make up for anything. We were certainly old enough to call it love.

"Then again," he says, his eyes on his drink. "Clearly that relationship was not . . . what either of us thought it was."

I choke on a Dutch cheese stick, certain I heard him wrong.

Not what either of us thought it was.

He was the one who hurt *me*, and he's lamenting that the relationship didn't measure up to *his* expectations?

"That's just what happens when two idiots get together, I guess!" I say it as brightly as I can, even forcing a gritted smile, as though we're competing for whose heart shattered into more pieces. There's no world in which he has a claim to the title. Not when he's the one who swung the hammer. "But hey, that was a long time ago. Good thing we grew up."

I want so badly to press for more of an explanation, but I don't know how to do it without proving him right: that I'm still the unsteady, uncertain girl he knew back then.

"Exactly. No need to dwell on the past."

Okay, then. This was never going to be an excavation of our relationship when we haven't spoken in so long. We'll have a polite, superficial catch-up and then go our separate ways. I'll limp back to my dungeon, and he'll swagger home to a tall Dutch girlfriend who makes riding a bike look effortless.

Or wife.

Or children.

Jesus. He could really be anyone.

"So," I say, tugging the sleeves of my sweater over my hands, still cold from the ice pack. "What about you? What do you . . . do?"

He dunks a bitterbal into mustard, and it doesn't escape my notice that both of us are doing our best not to double-dip. "I'm a physiotherapist."

I almost have to ask him to repeat it—that's how much of a record scratch it is. If anything could interrupt my mental rewiring of Wouter van Leeuwen, it's this. Every other memory I have of him is wrapped in his love of art. One of the reasons he'd sought out the exchange program was to bolster his university applications, and it was clear his parents didn't think art was worth the time he spent on it. They wanted him in a steady career, something with a stable paycheck. They'd lived in Amsterdam for so long and rubbed elbows with the city's most powerful families, the ones that could trace their histories back to medieval times. They wanted to be able to brag about their doctor or lawyer or engineer, not their starving artist.

I was doggedly optimistic about it, so enraptured by his talent. If anyone could make it in an unpredictable creative field, it would be him.

"You went to school for that? Physiotherapy?"

"Both my bachelor's and master's." When I look impressed, he

adds, "It's more common to have a master's degree here. Very affordable."

"Affordable higher education, wonder what that's like." Another
forced smile. "Your parents must be proud. That was what they always wanted, right? Something important like that?"

I don't intend for the words to be wrapped in barbed wire, but
maybe that's how they sound to him, because he suddenly tenses,
his mouth forming a hard line.

"Right," he says in a strange hollow tone. When he glances
away, his lashes brush the lenses of his glasses. "They are."

I still have a million questions: *Why did you change your mind?*
and *Why did you give up art?* and *Did you ever miss me? Because I
missed you, for much longer than I'd like to admit.*

"You live nearby?" I ask instead. Keeping it surface. Safe.

"Just a few streets away, on the Prinsengracht."

"I want to say I know where that is, but . . ."

He laughs, but it doesn't reach his eyes. It's too polite, not one
of his pure and genuine laughs, the kind that would shake his
shoulders, make him hide his face because he didn't know if he was
supposed to find something funny. Me, dragging his chin up so I
could look at him, especially the dimple that only popped when it
was a true laugh. *Let me see you*, I'd say.

"The canals all have names here," Wouter says. "Prinsengracht
is one of the main ones—it means 'Prince's Canal.'"

"File that under basic facts I probably should have known
by now."

"It's a hard adjustment," he says. "I should know, given I did the
same thing in reverse. How are your parents? And Phoebe?"

I think about what my parents said on the phone earlier this
week. *You can come home anytime.* As though waiting for me to decide that Amsterdam is too much.

"They're all good. My parents have gotten really into kayaking, so that's how they spend most of their weekends. We all thought they were going to buy one and it would just sit in the garage, but they've proven us wrong. Phoebe's running an independent bookstore and loving it. She got married a few years ago, and her wife is pregnant."

"Happy to hear that. Congratulations to them." He watches me pick up the ice pack again, shifting it from my knee to my hip. "I could take a look at your leg, if you want." It takes a moment to dawn on me why he's offering: physiotherapist.

"No!" I say it so loudly that a few heads swivel our way. "You don't have to. I'm sure I'm fine. A bruise or two, nothing major."

An adult Wouter examining my adult body is not something I have the mental capacity for right now. Especially with the way he's grown into his long limbs, with hands that could probably soothe an ache the way they used to sketch out a landscape, right before he'd lick his index finger to turn the page.

They used to explore my legs, my waist, my hips, with the same careful determination. Thumb on my jaw. Palm on my stomach.

"I don't know if I'm destined to become a serious cyclist," I continue, fighting a blush that my brain in no way sanctioned. *These fucking memories.* "Actually . . . none of this has been what I expected so far, if I'm being honest. And not just the biking. I don't want to insult your city or anything, but . . ."

A frown deepens the line between his brows, just like I warned him about when we were seventeen. "What do you mean?"

"Well . . ." Before rational thought can intervene, all of it spills out. "My job has mostly been grunt work, and I'm not sure there's anyone else on my team. And—my apartment flooded last night."

He pauses with his beer halfway to his mouth. "Shit. Are you okay?" he asks. "And all your things? Well, they're not nearly as important, but, you know—they still matter."

"I managed to save most of them, but I'm not sure I can keep living there. I'm just wondering how anyone finds an apartment here. Some of these don't even include the *floor*, apparently?" Because I might as well get some advice, I swipe through my phone and show him a listing that says UNFURNISHED, UNUPHOLSTERED. "What does that mean? How is that possible?"

Wouter doesn't seem fazed by this. "Yes, that's not uncommon. Obviously there's something underneath you, but it's just concrete. People buy their own flooring—hardwood, laminate, carpet—and then take it to their next apartment when they move out."

"Do you have to bring your own toilet, too?"

His eyebrows shoot to his hairline as he barks out a laugh. "No, that's ridiculous."

"I'm glad my agony is hilarious to you," I say, dragging a hand down my face with a groan. "Because I feel like the most pathetic American. Just give me an Uncle Sam hat and a bucket of hot wings, because there's no way I'm ever blending in here."

The laughter stops, and he shakes his head. He's quiet for a while; his features look as though he's waging some inner battle. He places a finger on his beer glass, drawing a design in the condensation, keeping his eyes there instead of on me. "Danika . . . I might be able to help you out, actually."

Danika.

He's said it a couple times now, but for some reason, it's only this time that it truly registers. He was the only one who ever called me by my full name, whispering it into my skin with a sweetness that could crack me in half. *Danika, Danika, Danika. Ik hou van jou.*

I swallow hard, trying to push all of that away. The images are too vivid, those versions of ourselves still locked in time.

"My last tenant had to move on short notice, so . . . I have an apartment. My family owns the building."

"I couldn't—I couldn't stay with you," I say, unable to process what he's telling me.

"No, I rent it out." His finger, still inching up the glass. "Fully furnished, so most of my tenants end up being expats. I live upstairs. Entirely separate entrance."

I vaguely recall hearing about this. Back then, the Netherlands seemed this idyllic, fairy-tale place: tulips, windmills, Wouter. My parents occasionally talked about doing a family trip to Europe, but it took them years to pay off my medical bills, and then years after that to get stable again, which left me with a not insignificant amount of guilt.

Wouter slides his phone from his pocket, pulls up some photos of a charming ground-floor unit.

"There's no way I could afford that."

"I'll give you the pathetic-American discount." The dimple makes its first appearance. Slight, but it's there. "Although I don't think you're pathetic at all. Unlucky, maybe, but luck always turns around."

I'm inclined to keep brushing him off, because surely this is ridiculous, renting a room from the guy who lived across the hall from me during the best, then worst, year of my life. Then again, I'm low on options. None of my other ex-boyfriends are offering up lovely fully furnished apartments.

"And you'd be . . . my landlord?"

"Yes, that's how it works." Then his brow furrows with an expression I can't quite interpret—concern, maybe. It's been too long since I was able to read his face. "I wouldn't intrude on your privacy or anything. I'm fairly hands-off unless one of my tenants needs something." His eyes finally meet mine for a long moment, enough for a shiver to climb my spine that I could easily attribute to the slowly melting ice pack. "You'd barely even see me."

Something like hope hovers in my chest. "Well then," I say, downing the last of my beer. Fate or karma or simple coincidence— I'd be an idiot to say no without seeing it first. "I guess I can take a look."

Four

· · · · · · · · · ·

"AND THE AMAZING THING IS THAT THE FLOOR IS INCLUDED at no extra cost," Wouter says, completely straight-faced, after a run-through to document all the damage. There isn't much: some of the hardwood floors are scuffed, some of the crown molding cracked. "But that's an extra perk just for you. Don't tell any of my future tenants."

On the outside, this canal house looks like most of the others on the Prinsengracht—gorgeous, narrow, made of brick, and tipping forward just slightly—but inside, the space is bright and clean, with newer appliances and basic IKEA furniture. It was built in 1760, Wouter told me when we arrived, a year I could barely wrap my mind around, and his family's owned it since the late nineteenth century.

Here in the city's Grachtengordel—the canal belt—the facades of the buildings are UNESCO protected, with only interior renovations allowed. Even on the inside, plenty of the old-world charm remains: stained glass sliding doors separating the kitchen from the living room, a fireplace, tall street-level windows. Those windows are all over the city, and I can never stop myself from peering inside strangers' homes. I don't know how anyone can resist.

The combination washer-dryer may be under the bathroom sink—"we have to get creative with space here"—but even so, I'm grasping for reasons to say no.

I take a closer look at the stained glass doors. A ship is being tossed about the waves, serpentine swirls of blue and green. "This place really is a work of art."

"Indeed, it's very special." There's a clear reverence to the way he says it. I've always scoffed at men who baby their cars or their boats, but maybe I can appreciate taking pride in something beautiful, especially if it's been in your family for this long. "My grandmother owns the house, but she doesn't live in the city anymore. I've always hoped I'd inherit it one day and have the chance to make some improvements it desperately needs. You've probably noticed many of the houses here lean one way or another? Like a mouthful of crooked teeth."

I nod, tugging my sweater tighter around myself. The heat hasn't kicked on yet. "And it's not, I don't know, dangerous?"

"Nope. With the houses so close together, it's almost like they're all holding each other up, and the city is constantly surveying them to make sure they don't need reinforcements. The leaning . . ." He heads over to the window, drums a knuckle against the glass. "Some of it is because the houses were built on wooden piles, and they become unstable when the wood starts to rot. And you see the hooks on those houses across the canal, sticking out from the roofs?"

It's dark outside, but I can still make out the details with the help of a streetlamp.

"Most houses have steep, narrow stairs—including this one. Hundreds of years ago, it wasn't realistic for people to carry their possessions or merchandise up the stairs, since a lot of these homes belonged to merchants who sold their goods on the ground level and lived up top. So those hooks were attached so they could use a—" He breaks off, brow furrowing. "Sorry, I only know the word in Dutch. Katrolsysteem," he says, and makes two fists to mime the action.

"A pulley system?"

He nods. "Evidently not a term I've ever needed to know in English. They had a pulley system to bring their items up to the higher floors. And the houses were built to tip slightly forward so that they didn't bang into the building on the way up." When he turns back to me, I can still see the Prinsengracht reflected in his glasses. "Anyway. You didn't ask for an architecture lesson."

"I don't mind. I promise you're not mansplaining Amsterdam to me." Thirteen years, and I'm still enamored by the way he talks about this place. He's being much too nice, though, and I can't understand why. "Seriously, the apartment is perfect. Beyond perfect."

"And yet I can hear the hesitation."

I blow out a breath, every grudge-holding cell in my body telling me this is a bad idea. "You don't think it would be a little strange, me living here?"

He considers this. "It doesn't have to be. We can be adults, right?"

"My aching lower back would say yes."

"As would my thinning hair."

I try not to laugh. I don't want it to be this easy to fall back into conversation with him. Even when we tiptoed around our attraction, we never had trouble talking to each other. He'd wanted to see all the typical LA spots—Rodeo Drive and the Walk of Fame and Griffith Observatory—and my parents were always game to play tourist. But when it was just us, I designed my own itinerary.

"I have to warn you," I told him once as I started up the car, about a month before our first kiss, "this isn't going to be very culturally significant."

"As long as we can get In-N-Out afterward."

"That's a given. A cultural touchstone," I said. "What are you going to do when you get back to Amsterdam and you can't get a double-double?"

"Open my own franchise, obviously," he said. "It's time they expanded to Europe."

"You'll be an artist–slash–entrepreneur–slash–fry cook." I gave him a lift of my eyebrows. "Once you figure out how to make potatoes without burning them to a crisp."

He let out an exaggerated groan. "That was one time. *One time.*" He'd tried to cook dinner for my family, and it had ended in disaster: black smoke curling from the oven, the fire alarm blaring. In all fairness, I'd been distracting him, sitting on the kitchen counter and playing every Top 40 hit from the past five years to see which ones he knew. He kept shaking his head, laughing, telling me that the Netherlands was not in the dark ages and people still listened to Taylor Swift.

That night I drove us to Sunken City, the site of a nearly century-old landslide that had dragged houses into the ocean and left the neighborhood abandoned. My parents wouldn't have chosen it as one of their daytime destinations, and at night it verged on spooky, the air punctuated by coyote howls. With all the graffiti and jagged ruins, it screamed inspiration.

The risk of hopping the fence past the NO TRESPASSING signs was more than worth it when he turned to me as we sat on a rock, his mouth close to my ear. "You're the best tour guide," he said, and despite the warm autumn evening, I shivered all the way home.

This new version of him leans a hip against the kitchen counter, cream granite flecked with gray. Under the bright overhead lighting instead of the dim café, his eyes turn a glowing bronze. "You'd be helping me out, too. Now I don't have to take a chance on a complete stranger."

"Still, thank you. This is more than generous."

I watch him bite down on his lower lip. "I wasn't generous back then?"

The question is innocent enough, and yet I wrench my gaze away from his mouth, my cheeks burning with the memories.

He was. He always was.

"Maybe you could think of it as a peace offering," he continues. "A fresh start."

I don't hate the sound of a fresh start, especially since that's the refrain I've had in my head since I decided to leave LA.

Until it hits me, what this apartment might actually be.

Not just a peace offering—but an attempt to buy my forgiveness.

The realization is tinged with shame, a familiar emotion when it comes to Wouter. I'd been so embarrassed when it ended, thinking he was a once-in-a-lifetime kind of love. This is the man who broke my heart—and now I'm the one who needs his help.

But *fuck*, I really want this apartment.

I wander through the living room, lingering on a framed print where a swimming pool takes up nearly the whole canvas. Upon closer look, the figures in the pool aren't people but dogs. A dachshund lounges on an inflatable hot dog, and a human man sits nearby in a lifeguard tower. "I like this. Who's the artist?"

He shakes his head. "I got it in some local shop or another—I don't remember, I'm sorry."

"You're not still into art?"

It's the oddest thing to have known him so intimately when we were seventeen and not know the answer to this question. I get a flash of his palms grayed with charcoal, a smudge of paint on his thumbnail. There's not as much creativity in UX design as I'd like, especially when you're working for massive corporations. I hoped this startup would change that—and maybe it still could. This apartment makes me want to be optimistic.

Wouter joins me in front of the painting. I can sense his warmth next to me, his much taller frame; that barrier we once crossed so frequently might as well be made out of concrete now. We are washing dishes in my family's kitchen, splashing each other with suds, giggling but never touching. A domestic flirtation.

"I'm afraid I don't have as much time for it as I used to," he says.

"So the whole European work-life balance is a myth."

A hard crease of a smile as he leans against the wall. Broad shoulders swathed in green corduroy. I have to tilt my head upward to keep making eye contact, and suddenly I think the heat might be working just fine. "Not a myth. I guess I just have other hobbies," he says. "What about you? Still a . . . what did you call it back then?"

He absolutely knows, and he's just waiting for me to say it.

"A basic art bitch," I say, crossing my arms. "Yes, I am, and proud of it." I have a deep and abiding love for Monet's *Water Lilies*, Klimt's *The Kiss*, all of Degas's ballerinas. I even have a trio of Van Gogh's sunflowers tattooed on my hip. They might be some of the most commercialized pieces of art in history, and that's because they're magnificent. Every time I look at them, I see something new. "I had a massive Monet landscape in my living room in Burbank—beautiful."

"Oh, I'm sure it was."

If he were anyone else, I'd lean forward and swat his arm. The sleeve of his corduroy shirt looks soft. Inviting. But even if we can joke around like this, we are not close. "There's a reason they're so popular! As I'm sure I told you a thousand times."

He's laughing now, the dimple back. "I don't dislike them. There's just much more unique stuff out there."

This genuine laughter gives me such an endorphin rush that I can't help joining in—until he pushes back his hair with his left hand and I find myself searching for a ring.

Out of simple curiosity.

"So. Uh. Are you . . ." The sentence trails off, my face burning once again. ". . . seeing anyone?" I head for the kitchen and open up the cupboard—my cupboard, I suppose—for a glass of water.

"Ah—no, I'm not. And you?"

"Ended a relationship a few weeks before I left." I take a sip. Clear my throat.

The relationship had been fun at first, casual sex that became casual dinner dates and then a not-so-casual meeting of his parents. Jace was the kind of guy who swept effortlessly through the office, friendly with everyone, as confident in a one-on-one meeting as he was giving a presentation in front of a hundred people. When he said he wanted to settle down, I believed him. For eleven whole months, I believed him.

Until one of my sister's friends matched with him on Tinder.

"I just—didn't want to run into your wife or something in the hall and make anything awkward."

"No risk of that," he confirms, following me into the kitchen.

"Great. I mean, not great that you're single, unless of course you prefer being single, in which case, more power to you—but great in the sense of . . . now I know!" Surely some people are completely chill in front of their exes. I am not one of them.

Wouter just looks at me, and I can tell he's biting the inside of his cheek, trying not to laugh.

"You're making it worse," I say with a groan.

"You still get tongue-tied when you think you've said the wrong thing."

He's right. There was the time early in our relationship when I asked if he'd been with any other girls. Before he could answer, I rushed to tell him it didn't matter if he had—though I was relieved when he confirmed we had the same level of experience. And the time I told him I liked his accent, then worried maybe that was insensitive, and was I somehow problematic for saying it? So I over-corrected and wound up babbling about all the English words I'd ever mispronounced, until he cut me off and said he liked my accent, too.

"That's me." I place the glass on the counter and hold out my arms. "Between this and my taste in art—exactly the same as I was at seventeen."

His eyes rove downward from my face, taking me in almost the same way he did when we first met. Except this time, I feel the weight of his gaze more than I should. I caught a glimpse of myself when he showed me the bathroom earlier, my cheeks flushed from the alcohol and the cold. I looked dazed but hopeful. Happy, in a temporary kind of way.

"No," he says, a new roughness to his voice. "You've definitely changed."

Then he rubs his fingertips together, that telltale nervous habit. If he doesn't make as much art as he used to, he should probably reconsider that—his hands are clearly begging for it.

You've definitely changed. He might have meant it in a positive way, but the longer it sits between us, the heavier it is. Maybe only in the obvious physical ways, because sometimes I fear I haven't changed at all. This man, though—aside from his nervous habits, he has changed in more ways than I can fathom.

Once upon a time, Wouter van Leeuwen really knew me, more than anyone outside my family ever has. I gave him so much of myself, the parts I liked and the ones I was still trying to understand, the ones I was shy about and the ones I wasn't. And I thought that meant we would last.

An apartment and *I was an idiot* can't bridge the thirteen-year gap. What would a fresh start truly mean? That we erase all our history and move on? Even if I'd love a familiar face in the vastness of a new country, starting over isn't that easy.

"I want you to know," I start, choosing my words carefully, "that you don't have to babysit me here. Maybe we knew each other in a past life, but we don't have to make this complicated. You'll be the landlord, and I'll be the tenant. That's it. We don't—we're not going to be friends or anything."

His jaw tenses, that wrinkle between his brows making another appearance. For a second, I'm worried I was too mean and he'll snatch away this beautiful apartment before I've had the chance to unpack a single sweater.

Then he collects himself, features sliding back into neutral. "A past life," he repeats. Now his voice is purely professional. Distant. "Understood. I'll send you the rental contract tonight."

"Oh—okay. Great." I swallow, unsure why his words are hitting me like ice when I felt so certain I needed to make some rules. "I should go finish packing and bring my stuff over."

He reaches into his pocket and passes me the keys. "Of course. You want any help?" Then he pauses. Taps his chin. "Actually—and I could be wrong—but I don't think that's an official landlord duty. Forgive me for asking." The venom in his voice is subtle, but it's there.

"No, no. You've done plenty. Really." *And now I would like to disappear.*

I guess it could be a form of revenge, my shutting him down like this, but that wasn't ever something I wanted when it came to him. I only wanted answers.

I walk with him back down the hall, past the artwork he doesn't remember, and then I struggle with the doorknob, hating that I need his help yet again.

"Old houses," he explains, reaching for it. His hand brushes my wrist, and because I am too stupid to realize he's trying to show me how to open it, his fingers curve around mine for a moment. "You just have to give it a good yank."

Heat attacks my cheeks with such fervor, he might as well have suggested we go at it in front of the street-facing window. And yet he seems wholly unfazed by his word choice. I step backward to give him space, his body shifting in front of mine so he can do all the good yanking he needs.

This man was my entire sexual awakening, every first sigh and first gasp he held in the palm of his hand.

And I need to do my best to forget all of that if he's going to be living above me.

The door swings open on a creak. "Fijne avond, Danika," he says, and then he leaves me alone in my new apartment.

Five

AMSTERDAM OBSERVATIONS, WEEK THREE:

Every public toilet I've encountered—a toilet, not a bathroom, because here it's only a bathroom if there's a shower—has the tiniest sink I've ever seen with one tap for absolutely freezing water. The old buildings, the modern buildings, there's no difference. Always a tiny sink. Always cold water.

The preferred dipping sauce for fries is mayo, not ketchup, and it's impossible to go a block without at least three shops selling them in a giant paper cone. The proper way to eat them is with a miniature fork, which I believe scientifically makes them taste better. After I order them with mayo for the first time, I decide I might prefer it, at least until I order them "speciaal": with mayo, curry ketchup, and diced onions.

The city is more stunning than any photo or video could capture. The centuries-old architecture, the tilted houses—and *everywhere* in the Centrum is like that. I'll come across the most gorgeous building I've ever seen, and it'll be a Burger King. Especially living along the Prinsengracht, I can't help taking pictures every time the light changes, gazing out at the water where the·sun touches the surface, the houseboats moored on either side of the canals. *I am wildly lucky to be here*, I think every time. None of the photos has particularly great composition—in the never-ending hobby quest, my photography phase of '17 was short-lived for good reason—but that doesn't matter.

By the middle of the next week, I've begun to truly adjust—real, this-is-my-actual-home-now adjusting. I grocery shop every few days and bring home only what I can carry. No more weekly trips to Trader Joe's or overstuffed canvas bags jammed into the trunk of my car. Cashiers try Dutch with me when I'm checking out, switching to English after I mumble a *Sorry* and then *Dank je wel, fijne dag*, the paltry Dutch phrases I've picked up so far.

I'm too cowardly to try my bike again and decide to return it to the subscription shop, so I rely on a pair of Nikes and my OV-chipkaart, the Dutch transit card—because the public transportation here is *spectacular*. There are trams and buses and trains and a metro, and every time I slide into a seat on one of the sleek blue-and-white trams, I'm overcome with a sense of peace I never felt while stuck in LA traffic.

I hurry inside with the single bag of groceries I picked up on the way home from work, eager for a scheduled video call with Phoebe.

"Hi, hello, I miss you!" she says when she picks up, her dark hair piled on top of her head. She's wearing this crochet patchwork cardigan that's nearly part of her DNA—she made it ten years ago and wears it once a week; the thing is indestructible—and gives me an inordinate amount of homesickness. Her store doesn't open for another hour, and she's in her office there, surrounded by books, sipping from a mug that says I'M WITH THE BANNED. "Look at you in your cute Dutch apartment! With your cute sweet face! And your hair looks so much better now that it's grown out a bit, wow. I love it."

"I can't take credit for any of the design choices but agree about the hair, thank you for the validation," I say with a laugh, because my sister's voice has the power to soothe any amount of stress. "You want a tour?"

"Yes, please," she says, and I spend the next few minutes bringing her to each room and trying my best to remember all of Wouter's explanations. Then I settle at the kitchen table, propping the phone on a stack of Dutch cookbooks.

"How are you? How's Maya? How's the store?"

"Good, good, and good. We're collaborating with some local artists for Valentine's Day and hosting a bookish craft fair—it's going to be adorable."

Another pang. "I wish I could be there."

"I'll send you a valentine," she says, taking another sip of coffee. "Maya's been lucky with the morning sickness, and I swear she's already glowing. And I know it's probably too early to buy clothes, but Dan, everything is so precious. I found these tiny overalls at a flea market last weekend with manatees all over them—I'll send you a picture. It's criminal that they don't come in adult sizes." After I've squealed over them, her voice turns a little chillier. "And the question of the moment . . . How's Wouter?"

For some reason, hearing her say his name out loud makes my heart lurch in my chest, as though it's a confirmation that this is really happening. I told her the night I moved in, still trying to make sense of it all, and she was understandably cautious. Thrilled that I wasn't living in a dungeon anymore, but cautious nonetheless.

Half on instinct, I glance up at the ceiling. "I haven't seen him much since Friday, actually."

Just once, when he was locking up his bike when I got home

from work yesterday, and we exchanged awkward waves and *Can you believe the weather?* Sometimes I hear what sounds like a dog scampering around on hardwood floor, but I've never seen him outside with one, so we must keep very separate hours.

Despite all my unanswered questions, this can only be a good thing. Once I can afford a place of my own, I'll be gone, and he'll find another new tenant who's only a tenant.

I've even seen his upstairs neighbor more frequently, an older man named Hendrik who claims the stairs keep him young. Meanwhile, my LA friends have grown increasingly terrible at answering their texts, to the point where I'm not sure I can blame the time zone anymore—but then again, I haven't been making much effort, either. Truthfully, they felt distant even before I left.

A few times when the evening quiet turns lonely, I consider messaging Iulia but always stop myself. She seemed settled, seven years in the Netherlands and likely zero desire for an aimless American friend.

I also asked Phoebe not to tell our parents about Wouter. In the years after he left, they'd say they wished they'd done a better job of keeping in touch, though I think they were a little stung that he'd ghosted them. It was one kind of cruelty to end our relationship the way he did, but my parents had never been anything but generous toward him.

While I'm sure they'd be beside themselves that he's back in a Dorfman's life, I don't want them to view him as this Amsterdam savior.

"But he's been . . . cordial," I say to Phoebe after hunting for the right word, trying not to think about the way he stood where I am now and told me I still got tongue-tied. Even after severing our connection, he held on to so many details. "He's a physiotherapist now, which might be different from a physical therapist? I've been meaning to look it up."

"You know I can never forgive him for what he did to you. He lived with us for a *year*. He told you he fucking loved you."

I pull the sleeves of my big gray turtleneck over my hands. It's a habit I developed in college, when I studied in a library with AC that was always a bit too strong. "Do you think this is some way of trying to make it up to me? He feels sorry for me, and he saw an opportunity?"

Phoebe and I spent so much time trying to decipher that four-sentence rejection text, searching for meaning when there wasn't any. Maybe he'd met someone else, and this was his way of letting me down easy. Maybe he didn't think long distance would be worth it.

Or maybe he meant exactly what he said: *I need to be with someone who has a little more ambition.*

"I can't tell if that's nice or insulting. Maybe both," she says, still sounding uncertain. "Just be careful, okay? He's still half a stranger at this point, Dan. I don't mean this cruelly, you know I don't, but—you don't really know him anymore."

"Trust me, we're not going to have any kind of relationship that goes beyond real estate. I . . . made that pretty clear to him the other day."

Phoebe stretches in her chair, calls out hello to someone entering the office. "God, I can't believe you've been there almost a month. How's your Dutch?"

"Niet goed. I signed up for a class that starts next month."

"And your job is still sketchy as hell?"

"Two more people quit yesterday. The CEO's been out of town the whole time I've been there, and everyone seems to worship him, although no one can explain to me why he's supposedly so amazing."

"Maybe it wouldn't be the worst thing if you started looking around."

"Already in progress." From the little browsing I've done, I've found American companies with offices in Amsterdam that promise the exact same thing I was doing in Los Angeles, with a much slimmer salary, though most of them are looking for engineers. "Phee, please don't tell Mom and Dad about the job."

"I'm sensing a theme here," she says gently. "Of course."

I want to be thriving here—I want to learn the language, understand the customs. I thought I'd find myself in Amsterdam, but so far all I've found is a relic from my past.

Sometimes I think I can trace this aimlessness back to the beginning of my life. When my mother was rushed to the hospital for an emergency C-section at twenty-six weeks pregnant and her impossibly tiny baby later rushed to the NICU, our synagogue rallied around them. There were frozen lasagnas and casseroles, brisket and matzo ball soup. Then there was the fundraising for medical care. The stories on the local news. The prayers—of course, the prayers.

Naturally, I remember none of this, but I've seen enough photos of myself in an incubator, wires wrapped around me. When my parents finally brought me home six months later, after surgeries to repair my heart and my lungs, a camera crew followed us. Capturing my parents' tears and the wide-eyed curiosity on Phoebe's face.

Everyone swore I was destined for big things. As though that had been the reason I'd survived.

"The miracle baby," they said, though as I grew older, I started doubting how much I believed in God at all.

"What a beautiful family," they said, but they had no idea how long it would take me to feel comfortable in my skin.

"She's meant to do something great," they said. "We just know it."

And then I didn't.

The only remnants of my early foray into the world are my asthma and a lingering sense that I'm not living up to the potential everyone thought I had.

It's ironic how stunted I usually feel, given how I arrived in the world so early, as if the rest of my life was determined to make up for it. A self-fulfilling prophecy, maybe: my parents treated me like a kid, so I never truly grew up. I've spent so long searching for that Big and Meaningful Thing, watching friends find theirs with ease. Nora, a freelance photographer with two kids. Alexis, a talent agent who just started her second round of IVF. Madelyn, who got her dream job in New York and stopped talking to anyone back home.

For a while I even wondered if I was meant to work with books like my sister and spent a summer helping out at the store, and while I liked it, I didn't have the same knack for finding a customer the perfect recommendation the way she did.

Sometimes it seems like I'm the only one flailing. A late bloomer.

"Hold on, I'm going to start dinner," I tell Phoebe, reaching into the *New Yorker* tote I carry with pride despite never having read a full issue of the *New Yorker*. Inside is a box of penne, a jar of marinara sauce, an aspirational bag of lettuce. I hold a pot under the faucet—but when I turn the tap, no water comes out. Frowning, I wiggle it a few times with no luck.

I grab the phone and head down the hall to the bathroom, trying the tap there—that one works, but even if I'm going to be boiling it, bathroom-water pasta is not exactly appetizing.

"What is it?" Phoebe asks.

"Kitchen sink isn't working," I say after running back in and trying it again. With a groan, I set the pot back down on the counter. "I think I need to call Wouter."

"Ooh, leave me on in the background?"

"I thought we were still mad at him!"

"Yes, but I'm also dying to see what he looks like now. I contain multitudes. Is there anywhere you can secretly mount your phone to take a video?"

"I feel like that might be illegal?"

"Fine, fine. A sneaky photo. Final offer."

"I say this with only love in my heart: I don't know if you should be running a business."

Phoebe cackles. "Bye, love you. Go call your landlord."

Once I end the call, I pace the kitchen, as though the sink simply needs time to think about what I've asked of it. I wait fifteen minutes, and when there's still no water, I swallow down any remaining vestiges of pride and message him.

Not three minutes later, there's a knock on my door.

"That was fast," I say as I open it up, slightly out of breath from dashing down the hall. Maybe I tousled my hair a bit. Maybe I applied more tinted lip balm, but only because I was such a mess the first time he saw me. I want him to know that even if thirty-year-old Dani doesn't have her shit together, at least she can look the part.

Wouter's in a light blue button-up with a pen tucked in the pocket, jaw still dusted with stubble—and around his hips is an honest-to-god tool belt.

I draw a hand to my mouth. "*Oh.* Oh my god. You have a belt and everything."

"Is that not the easiest way to carry around tools?"

"No, no, I'm sure it is. Come in." Even though he knows where it is, I lead him toward the kitchen. "Sorry to bother you. I'm sure this is the last thing you wanted after a full day of work."

"Part of the job," he says, testing the faucet a few times. He doesn't make eye contact as he reaches into the belt for a wrench. "No point paying someone when I can usually figure out what's going on. I'd do it for any of my tenants."

There's an emphasis on that final word. A confirmation that this is all I am to him.

With that, he rolls up his sleeves and kneels to inspect the pipes beneath the sink. Then he turns so he can get on his back, head disappearing and long legs sprawled out on the floor.

"Do you just have to give it a good yank?" I ask in an effort to keep the mood light, shutting my eyes on a cringe the moment I say it.

He stills on the floor. "Something like that."

An uncomfortable stretch of quiet passes between us.

When he lived with us, I once asked about stereotypes. *The Dutch can be very direct*, he said, and I'd use it to force confessions out of him, asking how he really felt about a meal my parents made or what I was wearing that day. Even though he'd press his lips together and refuse to give me a straight answer, he was always direct when it came to his feelings for me.

Now that couldn't be further from the truth.

"It's kind of funny," I say, trying again as I lean against the counter across from where he's working, because I'm nothing if not persistent. Often to my detriment. "Flood in my last place and now the water won't work in this one. The universe had to restore the balance somehow, I guess."

"Then maybe you're secretly Dutch. We've always had a contentious relationship with water."

"Right—the windmills?"

"Yes. Most of them have been replaced by more modern systems, but hundreds of years ago, they were used to pump water back into the rivers to drain the land. About a quarter of the Netherlands is below sea level, and back then the country was mostly marshes. Uninhabitable. They were able to turn a lot of that into farmland, which is part of why the Dutch still have the reputation for excellent water management," he says, and god, that's a wholesome reputation. "This shouldn't be too bad. Last month, the pipes froze, and one of them in my apartment burst."

Surely a tenant and landlord can discuss water management. That's topical.

Also topical: that the bottom of his shirt has flapped open, exposing a section of his stomach.

Dark blond hair arrows down from his navel, his skin pulled taut over muscles he didn't have at seventeen. Ridges and valleys I never explored. I saw him shirtless so many times—late nights and stolen moments when I'd drag my hands along his chest, but also on trips to the beach or when he helped my parents in the garden. What's probably 4 percent of his naked body shouldn't bring this much heat to my face.

The light glints off his silver belt buckle, as though crafting a cinematic moment just for me. It feels wrong, getting this peek at him while he's under the sink, and yet right now logic and decorum are meaningless. Because there is a very tall, very attractive man on the floor of my kitchen, one whose body I used to know very well, and from this angle, I catch the slightest glimpse of a waistband beneath his jeans. A stripe of navy.

"You weren't kidding when you said this place needed work." I finally force my gaze away from his abdomen. "How'd you learn how to do all of this?"

There's a strange pause before he answers. "Probably a cliché, but I did some with my dad growing up." A clearing of his throat. "The rest—YouTube."

This brings back a memory. "Remember when we spent a whole day watching old Bob Ross painting videos because his voice was so mesmerizing? And then we challenged ourselves to see who could talk like him the longest?"

"Danika—" Wouter lets out a grunt of exertion, the muscles in his forearms flexing. "It's fine if we don't talk. You don't have to force it—I'm just here to do a job."

"Sure. Yeah. Sorry." My voice is high-pitched. Unrecognizable.

It's such a stark reversal from last week, when he was trying to be pleasant and I was the one setting boundaries.

This was what I wanted.

So I give him some space, attempting to keep busy in the kitchen while he works.

"Try it now?" he says after a few more minutes.

I have to step over his legs to get to the sink, and when I turn the tap, water flows freely. "Dutch water management in action. Thank you so much—I've never had a full-service landlord."

And because I am cursed, somehow it comes out sounding suggestive.

He's still beneath me, half in the process of getting up as scarlet attacks his cheeks, which only sparks another swell of memories: Wouter politely answering my parents' questions about our classes, becoming sheepish when they told him how impressed they were with his rigorous course schedule. Taking our notebooks to the Getty, sitting in front of our favorite paintings and sketching them for hours, him turning shy when he showed them to me.

Blushing in the back seat of my car, breath hot on my inner thighs as he asked me in a voice that was all desperate wanting: *Is this good? Do you like this?*

Good was too weak a word, but I didn't have the right vocabulary for any of it. How could you describe a feeling that split you open and snapped you together at the same time? So I stroked a hand through his hair, grazing the top of his ear, and gave him a feverish *yes*.

Just like we said the other day: a past life.

"No problem at all," he says, wiping his hands on a towel from his back pocket before readjusting the tool belt. His face is still hooded, as though he's making an effort to keep even the slightest emotion locked away. "Let me know if you have any other issues, but hopefully you won't have to see me again for a while."

"Right. Hopefully." Now my voice is the faintest scratch in my throat. I can't tell if he thinks I don't want him here or if this is truly how he feels—eager to get away from me.

It shouldn't bother me. Shouldn't make my eyes sting. I should be relieved that we're on the same page, even if it means we're stuck inside a book with a terrible ending.

Once he's gone, I drown my agony in sad-girl pasta night, wishing I'd said a hundred other things or maybe nothing at all.

THE THING ABOUT WORKING SOMEWHERE UNSTABLE IS that it's not actually all that hard to convince yourself the worst won't happen. It's what our brains do in most situations—protect us from the truth. CommerX clearly had the money to sponsor my move. They give us prepackaged sandwiches or salads for lunch every day. They can't possibly be on the verge of going under.

Then on Monday, two more people quit.

On Wednesday, I catch someone sobbing in the bathroom.

The end of the week brings more secretive meetings and hushed conversations, and on Friday afternoon, after another plastic-wrapped ham-and-cheese, Beatriz in accounting slowly packs her bag and slips out of the office. I probably wouldn't have noticed if it hadn't looked like she was trying to be sneaky about it, her eyes darting in every direction before she rounded a corner. Ten minutes later, Mehmet in sales does the same thing.

And then it's a free-for-all.

The twenty other employees are a flurry of jackets and paper and desperation. Mugs are snatched up, plants are inexplicably shoved into backpacks. Some people even break into a sprint as they head for the elevators.

"Get out while you still can!" Anjali in marketing calls to me before she makes a run for it.

I get to my feet, half-eager to flee with the rest of them but unable to make myself without an explanation. "What the—"

"Some unfortunate news." Charlotte rushes over to my desk with this massive understatement, her usually tidy blond ponytail in a state of subtle disarray. A messenger bag is slung over her shoulder, an extension cord spilling out of it. "The CEO might have made a couple . . . let's say unwise financial decisions. We've had investors dropping out left and right, and we've been trying to get them to stay, but there might be an investigation into some of his behavior. So . . ." She ends this with a little hiccup of a laugh, as though positive energy will trick me into thinking this isn't actually all that bad.

"But—but you said all the higher-ups were brilliant." Somehow my mind hinges on this. As though a brilliant person cannot possibly make a financial mistake.

Charlotte drops a sympathetic hand to my shoulder. "I'm so sorry."

Now all the confusion morphs to panic. "Maybe . . . couldn't someone else take over?" I ask feebly.

"There isn't any money, I'm afraid. There, ah, isn't that much of a company anymore." She scoops up some extra coffee filters and drops them into her bag. "I wish you the best, really I do. A shame this didn't work out, but I'm sure you'll land on your feet!"

By this point, we're two of the last people left. I half expect the roof to start caving in as I follow Charlotte to the elevator, where she passes a box of Kleenex to a crying colleague.

"Don't worry," she tells him. "I'm sure they won't be able to trace it back to you."

Maybe it's a good thing I'm getting out.

At least, that's how I feel until I'm standing dazed in the middle of Dam Square while tourists and pigeons swarm around me, trying to process the biggest what-the-fuck in a whole month of them. I could surrender myself to the birds. Let them peck out my eyes. It'd probably be less painless.

I have absolutely no idea what I'm supposed to do now.

I stumble past the line spilling from the TikTok-famous place that sells only one type of cookie, hugging my coat against the wind because of course I haven't adjusted to this weather yet. My lungs are too tight and I can't get a full breath, so I close my eyes and make myself pause for a second, rooting around my bag for my inhaler before remembering I left it on the kitchen counter. Not an asthma attack, I realize, just anxiety—although it's never really *just*, is it? Four breaths in, hold for seven, release for eight. For a moment I wonder if those doctors who operated on me as a baby didn't put me back together properly. Maybe my body was just waiting for a disaster before giving up on me, too.

This apparent dissolution of CommerX wasn't entirely unexpected, but I'm left with hundreds of questions. They sponsored my visa—what happens with it now? A quick google informs me I have ninety days to find a new job before I have to leave the country. In theory, three whole months sounds like plenty of time. But now that I've browsed some listings, I'm not so sure it's enough.

Holy shit.

I might not be able to stay.

"Excuse me?" A family of tourists is standing in front of me. An older grandmother, parents, two kids. The mother is holding out her phone. "Will you take our picture?"

Right. We're in front of the palace.

"Oh—sure. Of course."

They pose with broad grins, wind whipping their hair as they press close together, and the sad reality hits me: almost a month, and I have barely taken any of these photos.

I force myself to breathe as I pass back the phone. That ham sandwich isn't sitting well, so I buy a hot dog from the cart in front of the palace and proceed to spill mustard on my jacket. When I lost my last job, at least I knew I was the one responsible. I wallowed, but then I pulled myself together. I figured it out, even if *it* meant moving an ocean away from everything I knew.

Escaping.

Is that what I was doing?

In front of me, a pigeon snatches a fry out of a little girl's cone. She starts crying, and I feel this moment of kinship with her when we make eye contact—because yes, this city is brutal for all of us.

But it's beautiful, too.

Of all the ways I imagined this going wrong, I never thought being sent back to the US was a real possibility. And there it is. If I don't find another company to sponsor my visa, then I am fucked.

I allow myself to picture it: packing my bags, crawling to my childhood home because of course my parents would let me stay there while I got back on my feet. No—they'd insist on it. *You can come home anytime.* They'd fold their arms around me and assure me it's okay that I wasn't ready for something this big.

That nameless beast I thought I'd dodged by coming here, the heavy clouds that moved into my brain on my worst days—that would be back, too. Every good thing I imagined for myself when I arrived in Amsterdam would just be . . . gone. "I lived there for a few months," I'd tell people with a shrug when they asked about it. "It was cool."

Because what else could I say, even now? I've barely explored beyond the city center. I haven't been to a single museum, haven't tried stroopwafel, haven't *traveled*.

This can't be ending when it's barely begun.

I take a determined bite of my hot dog. If this really was an escape, then there's only one option.

I have ninety days to find a new job and to experience this city the way someone long ago told me I should, convincing me that once I did, I'd agree it was the loveliest place in the world.

Six

I SPEND THE NEXT FEW DAYS IN A FRENZIED STATE OF JOB hunting, scrolling through so many listings I start seeing them in my sleep.

We're sorry, but we just filled the position—

Recently had a round of layoffs—

Looking for someone with a little more experience—

I didn't expect the rejections to pour in so quickly, but there they are, glaring back at me from my inbox. Each one of them a ticking clock.

Late one evening, a message from Wouter drags me out of a self-pity-induced stupor, but only briefly. I haven't showered, and there's a pile of delivery boxes on the kitchen counter I swore I'd deal with before the end of the day.

Not trying to overstep, but if you haven't been yet, I have a free

ticket for the Van Gogh Museum this weekend, his text says, along with an attachment. **Best to go right when it opens to avoid crowds.**

It's enough to make me jolt upright in bed, wondering if he's also in bed in the apartment above mine. If the bedroom is even in the same place, or if he's on top of my refrigerator or shower instead.

I just got off the phone with Phoebe, who knows everything, and my parents, who know nothing. Yesterday I even talked to someone at immigration, who confirmed that I have ninety days—eighty-five, now—to secure new employment. Even if someone offers me an interview tomorrow, most tech companies have at least three rounds of interviews. That could take as long as a month, maybe more. Opportunities are slim, and though I vow I'll do anything, the jobs that aren't at international companies require at least a conversational level of Dutch.

There's little holding me back when I reply to Wouter.

Perfect timing, thanks. My company . . . collapsed? Laid me off? I'm not sure, but it seems as though I am no longer employed, so I would love a museum day. This is me as a tenant letting you as my landlord know that I already have a few leads on new jobs.

If I'm stretching the truth, it's only because my bruised ego needs it.

Regardless, he doesn't respond.

Clearly my reading comprehension skills could use some work—because when I show up at the museum Saturday morning, Wouter is parking his bike, his hair still damp from a morning shower and a bit ruffled by the wind.

I give him a puzzled look.

He gives me one back.

"Sorry, I'm just a little confused," I say as he approaches.

"It . . . was a two-for-one ticket," he says. "Didn't you get the attachment?"

Oh. The one I skimmed because it was in Dutch.

"It's a big museum," he rushes to say. "We don't have to—obviously—"

I nod vigorously. "Right. I'm sure we won't even run into each other."

Ten minutes in, I'm no longer thinking about my own sad circumstances but Vincent's, his lack of recognition while he was alive and the mental health care he desperately needed but wasn't advanced enough at the time. His close relationship with his art dealer brother always makes me emotional. Theo died only six months after Vincent, as though the heartbreak was too much to bear.

As it turns out, the museum isn't as big as Wouter claimed it was, or I'm too aware of him. I step closer to *The Potato Eaters*, one of Van Gogh's earlier works. A family of five huddles around a table with a single bulb illuminating their faces, the light giving them a hint of dusky warmth. And there's Wouter, approaching the painting from the other side, then making a hard right turn when he spots me.

I take my time reading the descriptions, listening to an audio tour, weaving around groups of excitable kids and tourists speaking different languages. But when I spot him in the crowd again near a series of sketches, I wait until he moves on to the next room. It's the most awkward game of espionage.

When this happens a third time, I don't even have to force the laugh. "This is a bit ridiculous, right?" I say. "We don't have to avoid each other."

Wouter visibly exhales, his shoulders softening. "You're sure you don't mind? I'd hate to make you uncomfortable."

"Not any more uncomfortable than what we're doing now." We can wander an art museum together. Nothing in our rental contract said we couldn't. "You've probably been here a hundred times."

"A handful," he admits. "But not since I was in school. That's why I was curious to go today, actually. They have a self-portrait exhibit that closes this weekend."

A salt-and-pepper-haired tour group passes us, a guide chattering in animated French.

"I might go slow," I warn, and he just shrugs, indicating this doesn't bother him. He doesn't shift his weight like he's eager for me to hurry up, doesn't check his phone, only watches me with a calm curiosity, the sleeves of his button-up rolled loosely past his wrists, one hand tucked in the pocket of his dark jeans.

The whole time, I'm aware of him in the space next to me, though I do my best to keep a couple feet between us. Occasionally the light catches the bald spot on the back of his head, and I remember how effortlessly he joked about it when we talked about getting old.

At one point, he leans in close. Whispers my name. "Danika."

Every molecule in my body becomes attuned to that low timbre of his voice.

When I glance up at him, and then behind me, there's a little girl with a sketch pad gazing intently at *Almond Blossom*, with its teal background and delicate white flowers. I give her a smile as I inch to the side, where I'm no longer blocking her view, and I wonder if Wouter is thinking the same thing I am.

We used to do that, haunt a museum for hours on end, circle back to our favorite pieces before finding a corner to sketch in. Sometimes we'd even just people watch, his head resting on my shoulder, my hand on his knee. We could be anonymous there.

"That looks great," I tell the girl when I get a glimpse of her rainbow-marker rendition of the painting. She gives us a toothy grin and says something in Dutch.

Wouter laughs as he translates. "She said he didn't use enough colors."

When we reach the self-portrait exhibit, Wouter's gaze lights up with recognition. "Ah, I've always loved this one."

Self-Portrait with Grey Felt Hat, 1887: one of his most well-known self-portraits. "*You* liking a popular piece of artwork?" I say. "What about it?"

"There's so much color, almost like he's in motion." Wouter gestures with his hands, mimicking the brushstrokes that make up Van Gogh's face, beard, jacket, all of them spiraling outward and drawing the eye right to the center. "He doesn't look unhappy, necessarily, but he doesn't look happy, either. You can see the sadness underneath all the color. The yearning. How badly he wanted to be seen as an artist in a world that didn't seem to have space for his style of art. No matter how beautiful, most of his work has that—that undeniable sense of melancholy."

I just stare at him. "But you don't care about Van Gogh." I even try to pronounce it the same way he does, the proper way: *Van Ghoff*, with a guttural *G*.

Wouter presses his lips together, trying to look nonchalant. "I never said that."

Our topic list has expanded: we can talk about the apartment, water management, and Vincent van Gogh.

We journey through each stage of his life, from the Netherlands to Paris to Arles, paintings interspersed with sketches and letters.

And then we get to the sunflowers.

Van Gogh painted them a number of times, and I've always loved that he was so captivated by them that a single still life wasn't enough. He wanted to be known as a painter of sunflowers, and the museum even has a Paul Gauguin piece depicting Van Gogh paint-ing them. When he died, mourners brought sunflowers to his funeral—a gesture he surely would have appreciated. This version of his sunflowers is from 1889, with a yellow background and an ornate gold frame, and we have to wait for a mass of people to dis-perse before we can get a clear view. I swallow down a swell of emotion as we move closer. There they are, shades of marigold and buttery yellow, brown paint thickly layered at their centers, splashes of green for stems and leaves. All that texture makes them look like they're swaying even from inside their vase.

"Your favorite?" Wouter asks gently.

I nod. "I took this art class freshman year of college where we had to imitate the style of different artists. When we got to Van Gogh, the teacher went on about how sunflowers weren't very common to paint at the time. They were rough and coarse, and other artists pre-ferred more delicate flowers. But that's exactly why Van Gogh liked them. And it's just never left me—the idea of creating something lovely from something that isn't typically viewed that way."

Now he's regarding me with a curious expression. "Why didn't you do anything with art?"

"We both know I wasn't good enough."

"That's not how I remember it."

There's an almost painful familiarity to the way he says it, though he's either just being nice or has holes in his memory. Be-cause it wasn't just art—it was every hobby I picked up hoping to excel at. The misshapen knitted scarves and the flute at the bottom of my closet and the half-built websites. I craved that ambition he said I didn't have. If only I found something that made me feel ex-traordinary, I swore I'd make it my entire world.

But Wouter and art always seemed meant to be, which makes it all the more perplexing that it's no longer part of his life.

Over my skirt, I touch my hip where the tattoo is. I never

thought I'd have the chance to see the sunflowers in person, which of course makes me think about all the chances I'll miss if I go back to California.

I try my best to push that away. Today is for exploring, and for sunflowers. Not for wallowing.

WHEN WE EMERGE FROM THE MUSEUM, MY EYES TAKE A few moments to readjust to the light. It's a gorgeous cloudless day, the rare midwinter sunshine turning Wouter's hair a rich gold, making him squint behind his glasses.

"So . . ." I say, just as he opens his mouth to speak, and then gestures for me to go first. "I sort of wanted to have a tourist day, since I haven't done much of that yet. And, well . . . maybe it wouldn't be the worst thing to be shown around by a local." I clear my throat, realizing he might have plans, or that maybe the peace we brokered inside the museum doesn't exist out here. "I mean—if you want to, of course. You obviously have free will to decide if you want to spend time with me or not—" I break off, fighting a grimace. *Tongue-tied*, he's probably thinking.

Instead, he gives me a quirk of a smile. "With that kind of ringing endorsement . . ." he says, but he's already motioning to a cart with the words FRESH STROOPWAFEL splashed across the side. I might have had sugary cereal for breakfast and grabbed a pain au chocolat in the museum café, but I'll never turn down sweets.

A grassy field sprawls in front of us, full of people even in early February. There's a market here, too, dozens of stalls lining the path to the Rijksmuseum, the national museum. Dutch souvenir paraphernalia is everywhere, Van Gogh paintings emblazoned on everything from umbrellas to water bottles to clogs. I even spy some tulip bulbs for sale, though they won't bloom until spring.

Wouter orders two stroopwafels in Dutch, and when the woman

hands them over, golden brown and perched on a napkin, my mouth begins to water. I'm no stranger to street food—there's a taco truck in North Hollywood I used to stop at once a week—but having to navigate traffic and parking always made the experience more stressful than I wanted it to be.

"Eet smakelijk," he says after we grab a bench, and I give him an exaggerated lift of my eyebrows before I take a bite. I expect it to have a crunch to it since it's so thin, but I'm delighted to discover it's soft and chewy, warm but not too hot, with a syrupy sweetness and hint of cinnamon.

"I'm in love," I declare, and Wouter finally bites into his with a grin, like his own enjoyment was dependent on mine. "Much better than the ones from Whole Foods."

It's only now that I'm eating one that I remember a stretch of time when he was living with us that he didn't seem like himself. He laughed less than usual, went to bed early, slept in on the weekends when he never slept in. "I think I'm a little homesick," he admitted when I asked if something was wrong. The next day, I scoured three grocery stores before I found something the label promised had been imported from the Netherlands: a package of stroopwafels in a blue-and-white-patterned box. I'd never seen his face light up like that, and I had a feeling it wasn't because he'd missed stroopwafels so dearly—and when he kissed me, he tasted like cinnamon.

"They got the job done," he says now.

An elegant gray heron surveys the market from a perch on top of a fish stall. I thought it was a statue at first, until it turned its head ever so slightly.

Once Wouter finishes his stroopwafel, he no longer seems certain what to do with his hands, jamming them into his pockets, zipping and unzipping his black windbreaker. It almost makes me wish I had a colored pencil to give him.

Finally he turns to me. "Danika . . . I'm sorry about your job." He still looks a little uncomfortable, but he pushes forward. "I didn't know what to say over text, but I probably should have started with that today."

"Thanks. Not exactly ideal, but I'll figure it out. I have to." I do my best to shrug this off, not wanting to drag him down into my panic. "I promise you won't have to lower the pathetic-American discount to unprecedented levels. I'll still be able to make rent."

His brow furrows. "Oh—I wasn't thinking about that at all." More twitching of his hands, and it's impossible not to look at them when he's doing this. The long lines of his fingers, the short, clean nails. The lack of ink or charcoal or paint. "It wasn't just over text. I feel like . . . maybe I don't know how to talk to you anymore."

My heart isn't sure what to make of that. Tourists buy souvenir tote bags and kids play catch in the park. The gray heron swoops off to some new destination. "You're doing it right now. Subjects, verbs, adjectives . . . it's quite impressive. Perfectly coherent."

He gives me a lift of his eyebrows, and I know I'm being petulant but it's easier than having the serious conversation. "The way things ended between us—I'm sure we both could have handled it differently."

There he goes again. *We both.* I'm not naive; I know that few conflicts are one-sided. And yet every time I replay the promises we made in the days before he left, I can't understand what I did wrong.

What I might have done to change his mind.

"We don't have to litigate it," I say, because the last time we attempted to discuss it, it did not end well. "You moved on. I moved on. And then I moved to Amsterdam."

He nods, taking his time before he speaks again. "It's still so surreal, seeing you here. I never imagined—I mean, of course I thought about it, but—and then you told me you didn't want to be friends, and I wanted to respect that . . ."

When he trails off, I can hear something wistful in his voice. His earlier chilliness was so jarring that I should be leaping at the chance for something normal.

Of course I thought about it.

Phoebe's words echo in my mind, almost to combat what he just said: *You don't really know him anymore.*

I want to, though. Even if it doesn't help me unravel the mystery he left me with. Even if it only means I have one other person in this country who doesn't want me to fail. He was mine during such a vital part of our lives, and that affection doesn't just go away. Years can pass, but certain songs and scents and pieces of art take me right back to seventeen.

"Unless you want me to just keep being your landlord," Wouter rushes to say when I haven't responded. "In which case, you'll tell me if you break anything else?"

A welcome laugh bursts out of me. "The sink was *not* my fault!" Then I sit up straighter, brushing stroopwafel crumbs from my wool jacket and finally becoming serious. "Maybe—maybe we should amend that part of the contract, too. Assuming I don't get sent back to the States anytime soon."

"You won't," he insists, and I wish I had that confidence.

Even now, I'm unsure what a friendship looks like between us. I should be cautious, the way my sister said, because he is still a semi-stranger.

Then again, I was supposed to be a new version of myself here— and this is something I've never done before.

"To fresh starts," I say, holding out my hand.

His whole face changes, eyes softening behind his glasses. His hand meets mine, warm and firm and solid. Thumb on my knuckle, the lightest brush. Even if he's no longer making art, I'm suddenly relieved he's in a field where he works with his hands—it would be an utter waste not to.

It's the first intentional beat of physical contact we've had since the bike accident, when he pulled me from wet pavement up to my feet.

"Fresh starts," he echoes. "And fresh stroopwafel."

A little dorky, sure, but when he smiles, I'm convinced it's the most genuine one I've seen from him so far. It's a time machine, that smile, lighting up his whole face, bringing out his dimple, and making too many long-buried memories rush back.

When I made that list of anti–tourist attractions, spending weekends taking him to the most bizarre places I could think of, he only ever beamed at me, like I was expanding his world in ways he'd never dreamed of. Ridiculous ways, and yet they meant something because it was the two of us. Sunken City at night. Clownerina at Venice Beach. The world's largest paper cup in Riverside. *I miss Amsterdam*, he said once. *But I'm going to miss all of this even more.*

I slide my hand from his.

"If I'm going to be a real tourist," I say, vowing to leave the past in the past, "then I think we should get high and go to the Red Light District."

Seven

WE DECIDE TO WAIT UNTIL DARK, FILLING THE AFTERNOON with more food tourism. I try kroketten, Dutch licorice called drop, and about a hundred samples of cheese. Then, when I declare I need more dessert, we stop at a gourmet bakery that sells all manner of pot-laced sweets.

Look at us, I want to say to everyone we pass on the street. *Look how evolved we are, former lovers who can casually stroll the streets of Amsterdam together. Look how mature.* Though we mostly stick to surface topics like work and the Netherlands, I realize I've been lonely. There's a comfort to this kind of connection after weeks of stumbling around on my own. A familiarity, of course, but a newness, too.

De Wallen, the official name of the Red Light District, has old medieval streets, much rougher than in other parts of the city, and it's easy for a shoe to get caught in cobblestone. Tonight's partying has already begun, people spilling from bars and terraces and lingering along the canals, shouting and singing and laughing.

"Amsterdam isn't just weed and the Red Light District," Wouter says as we pass the grand Oude Kerk, the old church, glowing bright against the darkening sky.

My head is already delightfully calm from the edible we shared, a slice of lemon cake, and I'm trying my best to keep away from cigarette smoke to avoid triggering my asthma. "Right, it's also tulips and windmills."

He rolls his eyes at this, but I get what he means. There's an interesting duality there. The Amsterdam stereotypes are this mix of wholesome—tulips, clogs, windmills—and indulgent—weed, mushrooms, the Red Light District.

"I just want you to know that I fully support tonight's mission, but people who live here aren't getting high like this on a regular basis. Most tourists aren't, either."

"I know, I know," I say. "But it was impossible to tell someone I was moving to Amsterdam without them making a crude, uninspired joke about it."

We dodge a group of a half dozen guys in full bachelor party attire, dressed in baby onesies with pacifiers around their necks. The groom is wearing a sash that loudly proclaims LAST NIGHT OF FREEDOM.

"Hey!" one of the guys calls out to us, cupping his hands around his mouth. "We're doing a scavenger hunt, and we get twenty points if we can nab a pair of women's panties." He leans closer, bats his lashes at me. "I happened to notice that you're wearing a skirt, which would make them very easy to take off."

I can barely contain my snort. "Yeah, good luck with that."

"We won't do anything gross with them!" the groom assures me.

Next to me, Wouter stretches to his full height, at least a head taller than anyone in their group. "Hey, let's move it along. And be safe."

They let out a chorus of boos as we pass them.

"She wasn't that hot anyway," the first guy says, loud enough that I'm sure he fully intends for me to hear. "Am I already pissed, or did you see that thing on her face?"

They burst into laughter, drunkenly stumbling their way down the street.

Wouter's head whips around, a muscle leaping in his jaw, and for a moment I think he may actually go after them.

"They're not worth it," I tell him, even if I'd love to see them fall into a canal.

"Fucking assholes." He blows out a breath as we fall back into step. "Your face—"

I hold up a hand, not needing his pity compliment. "I'm fine. Really. More than used to it."

"You shouldn't have to be. I feel like I need to apologize on behalf of, well . . . men."

"Then I think you might be apologizing for a very long time."

Fortunately, the night air is cool enough to combat the rising heat on my cheeks, even if I'm regretting the long skirt and the breeze climbing up my legs. My high is peaking, and yet my mind won't quiet down.

Your face is fine. Your face isn't that bad.

Your face is beautiful.

Surely, trying to finish his sentence isn't the best use of my time.

Aside from this interaction, the Red Light District is far less scandalous than I thought. Spread across a handful of streets and alleyways, the area may be packed on a Saturday night, with a few police officers to regulate traffic, but it seems like plenty of people are here to simply observe. All along the canal, neon lights advertise erotic shops, coffeeshops, and bars with names more groan-inducing than suggestive, nothing so risqué that it would make even my parents clutch their pearls.

"Sex show! Live sex show!" yells a man in a tuxedo T-shirt standing outside a theater. When I make the mistake of eye contact, he lifts thick brows at me. "A bit of fun for you and your boyfriend?"

"Oh—no, thanks," I say, fighting the urge to correct him, because this stranger doesn't care if Wouter's my boyfriend or not.

The man looks us up and down with a genial grin. "I can make you a deal. Ninety euros for both of you."

We shake our heads and keep walking.

"Eighty-five!" he calls after us as Wouter tells me in a low voice, "Complete rip-off. The least sexy thing you can imagine. Went with some buddies in school and we left after ten minutes. If you've ever wanted to watch two people have mechanical, emotionless sex in an auditorium packed with a few dozen drunk people, all while loud electronic music is blaring, then that's where you'll find it."

"You don't know my kinks," I say with mock offense.

Wouter lifts his eyebrows. "We can go back, if—"

"No!" I say it too quickly. Because even if it's mechanical and emotionless, the idea of watching two people stripped naked, their bodies tangled with each other, with Wouter next to me . . .

It doesn't *not* sound sexy.

And that's exactly why we shouldn't do it.

We weave through the crowd, turning down a narrow street where sex workers pose behind windows with a red light on overhead, indicating they're open for business. Although not all the lights are red, in fact—Wouter informs me that a purple or blue light indicates a trans sex worker. The windows are framed with red curtains, the majority of them open but a few of them closed, indicating a client is inside. Every block is plastered with signs that say NO PHOTOS OR VIDEO, and none of it feels seedy or unsafe—there are too many people around.

At first I stare straight ahead, not wanting to appear as though I'm gawking at anyone. When I finally let myself relax, I make eye contact with a few of the women, most of whom offer friendly smiles. They're dressed as though to appeal to every fantasy: plenty of lingerie but some sweats and pajamas, too, some costumes. A few of them are even sitting and texting, passing the time between clients.

Two guys are bartering with a girl in a white negligee, long hair curling past her shoulders.

"What can I get for twenty bucks?" one of them asks.

"Hmm . . . a high-five?"

They let out a groan as she shuts her window, laughing.

"Have you ever—" I start, which is not a question I'd ever ask sober, but it's impossible not to wonder.

Wouter shakes his head. "As you can imagine, a lot of people come here for stag nights," he says as we round a corner. "Like our friends back there. Most Dutch people I know stay away from this area because it's so crowded, and if they're partying, they're usually partying somewhere else."

A hard elbow lands between my shoulder blades. Someone pushes past me, throwing off my balance, and as though on instinct, Wouter reaches for my arm. Holds me upright.

"Does it make me a local if I want to go somewhere quieter?" I ask.

As though looking for a reprieve himself, Wouter's quick to steer us in the opposite direction, his hand shifting to the small of my back, this protective gesture that squeezes my heart just a bit. Like he wants to make sure no one else can mess with me.

Those six months we were together, we so rarely felt comfortable being affectionate in public unless we were certain there was no risk of running into anyone we knew. Sometimes I even considered telling my parents; after all, they loved him, they loved me, maybe there was the smallest chance they'd be happy for us. Supportive. But then I asked about going on birth control to help with acne and they overreacted, and I remembered why we decided to keep it a secret in the first place.

Now the way he touches me is almost second nature, and I wish it didn't make me ache for all the times he didn't.

ONCE WE'RE ON A QUIETER, CAR-FREE RESIDENTIAL STREET, Wouter visibly exhales, his shoulders softening. I can't believe people are still biking at night, but then again, it's how most of them get around. The canals are still, serene, the houses bursting with tangerine light reflected in the water below.

It feels almost mystical that a place like this exists.

"Thank you," I tell him. "For all of this. I'm a little mad I didn't explore sooner."

"I had fun, even if you refuse to accept that our licorice is superior to yours."

"It's so salty! Calling that dessert would be a punishable offense in America." I've paused on a bridge to snap a photo, and he leans against it next to me.

"So . . . thirteen years." He lets those words hang between us, drums his hands on the bridge. "Tell me, what have I missed? Besides everything."

I blow out an exaggerated breath. "Where to start? Let's see . . . I went to USC, like my sister, and majored in informatics with a minor in user experience. I've worked for a few different tech companies, but nothing's ever felt like the right fit, I guess." I'm not used to talking this much about myself outside of a corporate interview, but I'm guessing he wants more than my résumé. "Hmm . . . I like all the popular music I pretended to hate in high school just because it was trendy. I spend a lot of time with my sister. For a while I was really into acai bowls, which is probably a legally mandated phase for everyone who lives in LA, but fortunately for my bank account, that's over. Until about a month ago, I had a studio apartment in Burbank that also served as a shrine to Monet's water lilies, as you know."

"Of course. Very tasteful."

"And I've always wanted a dog, but none of my building managers have agreed with me."

At that, he lights up. "I have a dog," he says. "George. He's perfect when he isn't being a little menace."

"I thought I heard something from upstairs that sounded like scampering. Assumed it wasn't you." Then I give him my guiltiest look. "I stalked you online a few times over the years," I admit. "I've always been curious."

"I did, too. You haven't always been the easiest person to find, though."

"I deactivated everything a while back."

I don't tell him the reason why: that the updates from friends and acquaintances made me feel so far behind. Logically I knew social media was a highlight reel, but that didn't make it any less crushing to look at.

"What about you?" I ask. "Where did physiotherapy come from? And is it different from physical therapy?"

His smile tightens for a moment, so slight in the darkness that I almost don't catch it. "It surprised me, too. And there is a difference, yes. A physiotherapist is often more hands-on, with more stretching, more massage. A physical therapist does some of that, but there's a bigger exercise component. I also considered studying occupational therapy, which revolves around how to perform tasks in daily life, while physio is about the ability to move your body in general. I like that I get to really use my hands."

It's nothing like what I expected for him, and yet somehow it makes perfect sense.

"And I love developing relationships with my patients, getting to see them improve. When they come to me, sometimes they're in a great deal of pain, and being the person to take that away? It's a privilege for them to trust me with something that significant."

"That's really lovely," I say, meaning it.

He asks about Phoebe's bookstore, and I tell him it's the cutest little oasis in Pasadena: bright colors, beanbag chairs, bookish products from local artists. "You and your sister, Roos, were close, too," I say, trying to pronounce her name the way he taught me to, not *Rose* but *Rohss*, with a rolled *R*. "You still are?"

He nods. "She lives near Vondelpark, only a short bike ride away. Works in marketing. We probably see each other once a week, although I'm not sure how much of that is her wanting to spend time with George." When I make a pleading face at this, he laughs and says, "You'll meet him, I promise! Anything else to help me update my Danika Dorfman file?"

"There's a whole file?"

"A whole cabinet, even." Then he clears his throat. "You said you broke up with someone right before you left? If it's okay to ask about."

"Sure. Yeah." I tighten my hand on my purse strap. "My ex, Jace. We were together for about a year, and I thought we were going to move in together . . . until I found out he was cheating. Such a cliché, it's embarrassing."

But there's a hard slant to Wouter's brow. "You shouldn't be embarrassed—you didn't do anything wrong. I hope *he's* embarrassed."

"I'm not sure he is, but thank you."

I'm hesitant to share any details that might make me seem immature, the way my friends were so quick to judge. Just like every other relationship, I made sure I was the one ending it. On my terms.

And maybe I went too far, but I only want Wouter to put the best version of me in that Danika Dorfman file.

We're rebuilding something, the two of us, and I don't want to dredge up the past. Even after today, there's still plenty I don't know about him: his past relationships and why they ended. Why he's living alone in that beautiful house instead of with a partner.

If someone gave him a pencil, what he'd sketch.

Maybe I'd forgotten not just how handsome he is but how *kind*. My standards dropped so low over nearly a decade on the apps, and here he is, offering me a place to live and showing me around and putting his hand on my back to make sure I don't stumble.

Before I got on that plane, I imagined Amsterdam as an escape. An adventure.

I never thought it might feel like trying to regain something I'd lost.

Again I feel that ache in my chest for the naive versions of ourselves who thought we'd be able to make a relationship work by sheer force of will and heady teenage desire, despite the thousands of miles between us. The fact that we're in the same place again after all these years . . . well, it's something that might make me believe in fate.

"I really like it here," I say, gazing out at the water. At first it feels safer than looking at his face, but even this canal makes some new emotion take root in my stomach. "Three months feels like it could go by fast."

"You'll find something," Wouter says, sounding more certain than I've ever felt about myself. His deep hazel eyes meet mine, so pure and focused behind his glasses. "I remember you always put your whole self into everything you did. I haven't seen your work, but I have no doubts that you're good at it. That startup wouldn't have brought you over otherwise."

"Maybe. Or I could do a hundred interviews but never make the final cut, or I could get let go again, or—" I'm so surprised by the waver in my voice that I have to take a moment to collect myself. But when I speak again, it's still there. "This is going to sound stupid."

"I promise you, it's not."

A shaky breath. "It wasn't just my boyfriend cheating. After I found out, suddenly everything about my life seemed . . . wrong."

How after years of casual relationships, I didn't know I wanted something serious until it was over.

How I looked through my closet and realized I'd spent too much time in clothes that didn't make me feel like myself, but I also didn't know what "myself" was supposed to wear.

How despite being let go, I didn't miss anything about the day-to-day work.

All these ways I thought I was supposed to act felt like some grand performance, one where everyone else had learned the choreography and I was stuck stumbling over the basic steps. I don't know how else to vocalize it without exposing my deepest fear, the one about all my wasted potential.

I push my hands into my eyes, not wanting him to see me like this. Fragile.

"That doesn't sound stupid," he says softly. "If it makes you feel any better . . . I'm really glad you're here." Then, before I can linger on that: "And I don't feel like I have my shit together, either."

"I don't know, the tool belt really communicated something else entirely."

He cracks a smile at that.

"I think maybe I'd gotten so complacent in LA that I didn't even realize I was unhappy. And now that I'm here, I have a chance to do things differently. Maybe that's a drastic way of looking at it, and of course I miss my sister, and my parents, and burritos, but . . . I like it here. A lot. I—I'm not ready to leave."

Wouter turns quiet for so long that I wonder if he heard me at all. "What if you didn't have to?" he finally asks.

"I don't want you to think you have to rescue every distressed American you come across."

A twitch of his mouth. "No," he says. "Just you." Then he turns pensive, schooling his features back to neutral. "I've been thinking about this since you texted me last night, and there might actually be a solution to both our problems. But . . . fair warning, it's pretty outrageous. Extremely unorthodox. Once you hear it, there's a good chance you'll never stop laughing."

"Now you're making me nervous." I reach out to give his arm a nudge with mine. I mean it to be a friendly tap of encouragement, but I'm not expecting the rigidity of his triceps or the way his eyes close for a brief second, as though processing the physical contact. Now that the Red Light District isn't monopolizing my senses, that single touch feels drawn out, somehow, as though it happened in slow motion. *Friends*, I remind myself. *We are friends.* And new ones at that.

"There's no need, I promise. Really, you're probably going to find it hilarious. Or horrifying. Or both."

Swallowing hard, I force myself to keep my voice light. "You already have me convinced it's something not quite legal."

His grimace deepens.

"Holy shit. It's not legal, is it?"

"Well . . ." A look I've never seen crosses his face, along with all the other new Wouter expressions I've tried to categorize. There's an uncertainty mixed with something else as he runs a hand down his stubble. "Do you remember that I mentioned inheriting my building?"

"Yes?"

"My grandmother still owns it, and the rest of my family has no interest in it. But I love the place. It's where I grew up, and no matter how crowded the city gets, I can't imagine living anywhere else. It's just—it's *home*," he says. "My grandmother won't sign it off to me unless I meet certain conditions—well, just one, actually. She wants me to be married first."

I hold up my thumb and forefinger, my pulse kicking into a frantic new rhythm. "Just a touch old-fashioned?"

"I think the hope was that I would raise a family there. Unless . . . there was a way around that. Something that would benefit both of us." His gaze is expectant, eyebrows raised, as though he's waiting for me to put all his hints together.

It dawns on me a moment before he says it, his words an unholy blend of serious and absurd:

"We could get married."

Eight

. . . .

I HAVE TO GRIP THE BRIDGE RAILING TO MAKE SURE I DON'T tumble into the water. The ground beneath me is buckling, the charming houses blurring together. Those mouthfuls of crooked teeth morphing into something sinister.

"Dani," Wouter says, a touch of concern in his voice. His rare use of my nickname makes this sound serious, somehow the exact opposite of when anyone else uses my nickname. "Are you okay? Do you need your inhaler?"

He sounds far away, as though he's speaking to me from somewhere deep underwater.

When I blink myself out of the daze, I'm surprised to discover I'm still standing. That the world is not, in fact, caving in on itself.

And then, just as he warned, I burst out laughing.

"I'm so sorry," I say, swiping at my eyes. "Maybe that weed was stronger than we thought, because I think you just asked me to marry you? Or—I guess it wasn't a question, but more of a statement?"

Wouter looks entirely too logical. "I'm not high. I only had one bite of that cake. I—I wanted to be able to look after you." There's an uncharacteristic pang as this settles in my stomach, this quiet bit of caretaking. "You need a way to stay in the country. Marriage to a Dutch citizen would certainly accomplish that."

He says it so simply, as though it's basic math. One plus one equals visa. He isn't wrong, of course—except for the tiny inconvenient fact that a green-card marriage must be a crime here the same way it is in the US.

A green-card marriage. I didn't know this was something that happened outside of movies from the mid-2000s, the kind where the unfairly attractive leads end up falling in love and no one gets in any real trouble from the government.

"Should it be more formal?" Wouter asks. "Do you want me to get down on one knee?"

The postcard-perfect scene in front of us turns claustrophobic. Dizzying. Suddenly I wonder whether I've recovered from jet lag after all, because it feels like I left all rational thought on another continent.

My brain focuses on all the wrong questions.

Should my ex-boyfriend and current landlord get down on one knee?

To propose?

To *me*?

"I—no, you don't have to." With shaking hands, I fumble with a button on my jacket. My molecules are jittery, like someone stuck me in an electric socket and then hurled it into the sun. I probably won't need caffeine anymore—Wouter van Leeuwen asking me to green-card marry him each morning would do the trick.

How did we go from tentative friendship to marriage proposal in just a few hours? What's next—tomorrow we're setting up a joint bank account? Adopting triplets?

He gestures to a bench at the edge of the canal, and I'm grateful because I may not be capable of standing much longer. "It wouldn't be permanent," he says once we're seated. "But it would give you some time to figure out your next steps. It would only have to be on paper, of course, and in front of my family. Aside from that . . . no one would have to know."

The way he's talking about it . . . it sounds like something we could actually, legitimately *do*. For one reckless moment, I allow myself to consider it: the extra time to figure myself out. To explore. To travel.

To do whatever the "something big" is that everyone thought I was going to do all those years ago.

"Right. Your family," I say, unable to believe I'm entertaining the idea. *No*. Not entertaining it. Just poking holes in his logic. "I'm sure they'd love the idea of you marrying some random American."

"We could tell a convincing-enough story." He runs a hand down his stubble, a streetlamp catching a few flecks of gray. "Maybe we kept in touch over the years, and as soon as we saw each other . . . all those feelings came back.

"And you're not some random American," he continues. "We have history."

I let all of this hang between us. Try to absorb it.

Marriage. A ring on my finger and some kind of official document stating that we're legally bound.

I'm dizzy again, leaning over to balance my elbows on my knees, chin in my palms. Deep breaths.

A boat pierces the stillness of the water, a group of people bundled up and drinking, singing along to a pop song blasting from their speakers. It's a welcome distraction, and the sight of it tugs at something in my chest. Ever since I was a kid, I've loved being on the water. Ferry trips to Catalina Island that made the hours in the car more than worth it, summers at Santa Monica Beach and rushing into the waves as my parents yelled at me not to go too far but loving the spray of the ocean too much to stop.

Here I am, in a city that was quite literally pulled from the depths of the sea.

The truth is, I do want to stay here. I don't know if I can go back home with the knowledge that I barely even fought for it.

I sit up straight again. "Then—and I'm not agreeing to it yet—there's the whole issue of, you know, breaking the law."

He bites down on his lip, turning sheepish. I wish it weren't such an endearing look. Maybe it's because he's over six feet tall that this giant showing any amount of shyness has always made me soft.

"Actually . . . a friend of mine did it after university," he says. "So I have a bit of secondhand experience. Her boyfriend was from Australia, and his student visa expired when he didn't find a job after graduation. So they got married, then divorced a couple years later."

"And they're still together?"

The sheepishness turns to a grimace. "Well—they broke up before they got divorced—"

"Of course they did."

"—but they stayed married until he could get a proper visa! And it would be much easier for us, since we're not dating." The breeze has pulled some of his hair across his forehead, and he reaches a hand up to push it back. "Even after they broke up, it was fairly drama free. No one's going to be banging on our door, demanding proof that we're really together."

I lift my eyebrows at him. "Didn't realize you'd become such a rule breaker in the past decade."

He gives me a smirk to match my sarcasm. Nudges my knee with his, sending a shock of electricity up my spine. "Guess I've changed, too."

I think back to his palm on my skin. That whisper of touch that now makes me wonder whether I've just been starved for human contact these past few weeks. Then I urge myself to stay rational in this thoroughly irrational situation. If I say yes, whatever glimmer of attraction I might have felt even an hour ago cannot become more than that. I'd have to douse those feelings in cold water—far more willpower than I ever had when he was living across the hall from me.

What he's really offering here, with this proposal, is the gift of *time*. The ability to find the right job, to do all the exploring I want, to discover whether this place could truly become my home.

If I let feelings get in the way, I'm not sure I'd be able to forgive myself.

"You don't have to decide now," he says. "It's just an idea. If you hate it, I'm not going to push you. I promise."

Maybe I don't actually hate it, though. "How long would we be doing this for? Hypothetically?"

He thinks for a moment. "A year? Enough for my grandmother to know that we're serious. Just until the deed is transferred over to me and you have a steady job. And then we'd have a quick and simple divorce. No legal ties to each other, nothing uncomfortable."

A year. I didn't think far enough ahead to imagine myself living here long-term, but I certainly didn't imagine I'd be fake married during that time.

"And I'd keep living downstairs?"

A blush tinges his cheeks. "It might make the most sense if we lived in the same apartment. To keep people from asking questions, since we'd need to put the same address on all our forms."

"Right. Of course."

"We wouldn't have to—we wouldn't be sleeping together," he manages, the blush turning a deeper scarlet. "I mean, we wouldn't be in the same bed. Obviously. You'd have the guest room."

I want to make a joke about him being the tongue-tied one now, but the way he trips over his sentences drags forward the memory I've been trying the hardest to suppress.

The one that hurts the most, if only because I didn't know how fleeting it was.

Once we started sneaking around, sex seemed like an inevitability. Neither of us had much experience beyond kissing, but keeping the relationship a secret made us even more desperate for each other when we were finally alone. I never found myself wondering, *How far do I want this to go?* From the beginning, I had simply wanted all of him. And even then I wasn't sure it would be enough.

My friends had talked about how disappointing their first times were, and I'd prepared myself for it—that it wouldn't be fireworks. That it would be awkward and messy and maybe wouldn't even feel that great.

The thing was, most of those things were true.

And yet I loved every second of it.

My parents were gone for the weekend, and I lied that I was spending the night with a friend. Wouter and I cooked dinner together, the two of us laughing and blushing more than usual, even when I oversalted the pasta and he underseasoned the green beans. We lit too many candles and set off the smoke alarm—*Why does this keep happening to us?*—and I had to hop onto the table with a broom to turn it off.

Even with all those mishaps, I'd never felt so *adult*.

Then I led him into my room, and he kissed me up against the wall before we moved to my bed.

We'd figured it out together, how to make each other gasp, and here we were about to chart another brand-new first. I remember thinking I didn't know wanting, *true* wanting, until that moment, Wouter hovering above me with his mouth on my collarbone.

"I'm nervous," he whispered in that accent I adored. "I want it to be good for you."

I burrowed as close as I could. "It already is."

The way he looked at me afterward should have been too tender for how cynical I sometimes felt at my core. He toyed with a strand of my hair, fingers stroking up my bare back. "I love you," he said against my forehead, and that ignited a whole new emotion. Three words I'd held close to my heart because I didn't want to expose a too-soft piece of myself. "I love you, and I'm so scared of what's going to happen when I leave."

"So just don't leave. Because I love you, too." I kissed along his chest, where his skin was the warmest. His neck, where I could smell a hint of aftershave. "How do you say it in Dutch?"

"Ik hou van jou," he said, and when I repeated it back to him, he held me tighter.

That love felt like a precious, delicate thing, like we were two kids let loose in an antiques shop with signs everywhere declaring DO NOT BREAK.

And yet: we broke.

"How do I know you're not going to change your mind?" I ask him now. Because he did it once before, took something I thought was serious and turned it into *I'm just not sure it's going to work. I'm so sorry. Thanks for everything.*

He swallows hard. "I think you'd have to trust me. I—I understand if you don't."

"I guess I just don't get why you'd do this for me," I say in a small voice, feeling both seventeen and thirty at once, wholly unprepared for any of this. "You've already helped me out so much. There aren't any ex-girlfriends you'd prefer to ask? Or friends, even?"

He's quiet for a moment, as though the thought never occurred to him. "This way, you get something out of it, too," he says. "Nothing about our daily lives needs to change."

"Except the fact that I'd be living with you."

A half smile. "Except for that."

"And you could charge whoever moves in downstairs full rent."

I'm starting to get dizzy again, imagining this life, picturing how it might feel to be Wouter's legal spouse. If we ever spent time with his family, we'd have to *act* married. Newlyweds head over fucking heels for each other.

And my own family . . .

If my parents found out I'd run away to Amsterdam and gotten married, they'd be on the next flight out of LAX, ready to drag me home and back to my senses. *You're not thinking clearly*, they'd say. *This isn't like you.*

Maybe that's exactly why I should do it.

"I'm not really an impulsive person." I'm not sure why I say it—a last-ditch effort at common sense?

His knee taps mine again. "You packed up your entire life and moved to a different continent. A country you'd never been to before."

When he says it like that, I can't help wondering if maybe there is some hidden bravery inside me, something he can see but I can't. Maybe this is sheer idiocy, or maybe it's just a means to an end. Either way, by the time we get divorced, he'll own his building and I'll have figured out what I'm doing with my life.

Quick and simple. Nothing uncomfortable, just like he said.

Inside my coat pocket, my fingertips graze a scrap of paper. I pull out the straw wrapper from an afternoon iced latte and give him a lift of my eyebrows as I pinch the ends together, tying them in a knot.

He's grinning when I hand it over to him, and I can find his dimple even in the dark. I used to sketch that smile over and over, never able to do it justice. His lips would be too thin. Too crooked. Eventually I gave up and watched him draw me instead, with a focused intensity I was never sure I deserved.

His fingers shake as he reaches for my hand again. With his thumb, he traces the slope of a knuckle. Up and then back down, like he's trying to soothe me or himself or maybe both of us. Promising, with those strokes of his finger, that this is a good decision.

"I always imagined I'd be a little more suave when I did this," he whispers.

God, he's nervous, even giving me this paper ring.

"You're doing great," I tell him, trying and failing to keep the tremor out of my voice. There's a giddiness there, too, the feeling that comes with doing something that goes against all rational thought—and yet we've found a way to rationalize it.

If I went searching for a new version of myself in Amsterdam, I think I've found her.

"What do you say, Danika?" My name in his accent shouldn't be this irresistible. His questions shouldn't be this earnest. "Do you want to be impulsive with me?"

Somehow it's the sweetest thing I've heard in a long, long time.

"Yes." The word is trapped inside a laugh, a tiny, incredulous thing. He slides the wrapper ring onto my finger so carefully that for a moment, I can convince myself it's made of gold. "Yes, I do."

Nine

THE FIRST TIME WE LIVED TOGETHER, THERE WERE RULES.
Foreign exchange students had to attend school every day and help
out with chores around the house. They weren't allowed to drink,
drive, or get a job, and Wouter's program strongly discouraged dating.

"We're supposed to treat him like a member of the family," my
mother said. "Not like a guest."

Wouter became our newest family member two weeks before
junior year started. And I was completely unprepared.

In the beginning, we were overly polite. My mother brought out
a stack of board games we hadn't played in years, and my father
tried to incorporate every major food group into our dinners. Then
slowly, we let out the real Dorfmans, who weren't bad by any
means—just a little less polished. We traded Monopoly for Netflix,
grain bowls for pizza night. We stopped brushing our hair before
going downstairs to breakfast.

I was used to sharing a bathroom with my sister, but now her
familiar scents and sprays had been replaced with all these products
that signaled Very Boy, Much Man. The guys I sat next to in class

were always overcologned and underwhelming. Observing one in his natural habitat—or as natural as it could be, an ocean away from home—turned me into a scientist. Every discovery unstitched me a little more: body wash with a label in Dutch, aftershave with a hint of cloves that made me dizzy in a way I instantly loved. Then there were the clothes Wouter wore just to lounge around in, a pair of soft gray sweatpants and a faded Ajax T-shirt for Amsterdam's football team. A smiley face drawn in the condensation on the shower glass, and later, a heart.

Here we are thirteen years later, about to share another bathroom.

"Third home's the charm," I say as I haul my backpack up the steepest, narrowest flight of stairs I've ever seen. I'll never make fun of anyone on *House Hunters International* again.

With far too much ease, Wouter nudges my suitcases over the threshold. A tiny dog clambers toward us the moment the door opens, nails clacking on the hardwood floor. He's deep brown with long tufts of hair on his head and chin and above his eyes, maybe a dachshund mixed with a terrier, absolutely adorable. His tail goes wild as I kneel to try to pet him, but he's leaping around too quickly to catch, such a flurry of activity that I can barely take in the apartment. He wants love from his human, but he's also out-of-his-mind delighted that Wouter's brought him a new friend.

The dog zips from the hall over to the living room, does a lap, and races right back to us. And again. He carries something into the hall and drops it at my feet—a sock?

"Are you calm enough for a proper introduction?" Wouter says, and the dog seems to understand exactly what's being asked of him, plopping down on the floor and tilting his head. "Danika, this is George Costanza. George, this is Danika."

"Sorry, your dog is named . . ."

"George Costanza. After the character from—"

"*Seinfeld*. I know."

We spent so much time watching old *Seinfeld* episodes when he lived with us, my parents on the sectional, Phoebe curled up in the armchair, Wouter and I cushioned on the floor with a couple of pillows. A wholesome family activity, something all of us could do together. Wouter found the show hilarious in its Americanness. We made our way through two and a half seasons, shocked by the number of plotlines that could be resolved with the simple presence of a cell phone.

All these years later, he named his dog after a character from a show that had to—in some small way—remind him of *me*.

"Some of my fondest memories from the States," Wouter says, bending to pick up George and giving him a kiss on the head. "Guess I have a weakness for American sitcoms."

I needed only a couple days to pack everything up again, during which time I replayed our bridge conversation over and over. I spent hours researching green-card marriage horror stories, convincing myself we could really do this without getting caught. I half expected he'd get cold feet and I'd wake up to a message asking if we could talk. More than once, my own fingertips hovered over his name on my phone, debating the same thing.

And every time, I stopped myself.

Now that I'm in his home, I realize I didn't spend enough time contemplating the reality of not just marrying Wouter van Leeuwen but *living* with him, sharing this space from morning until night, seven days a week. I've only ever lived with my family, my sister, and a handful of female roommates. Never alone with a man—and the rational assumption was that if and when I did, it would be out of love, not pragmatism.

This man is about to become your husband, I think as he explains that George is around seven or eight, a rescue brought over from Hungary a few years ago. The dog's little pink tongue darts out to lick Wouter's cheek. I squeeze my eyes shut for a moment. *Four.*

Seven. Eight. The breathing technique that always sounded much too simple to work, and I'm still surprised when it releases some of the anxiety from my body.

Four. You're not going to get caught.

Seven. It's not permanent.

Eight. This is the best option.

It's not an instant cure for every spiraling thought, but at least I can breathe a bit easier.

When I imagined his apartment, I expected it to be covered with art. The reality is that it's lovely if a little stark, with modern built-in shelves, a coffee table with a single book on it, a blanketed bench by the windows with that unbelievable canal view that looks like the perfect reading nook. A basket of dog toys in one corner, though Wouter says George was probably never socialized as a puppy and doesn't understand the meaning of fetch.

"The only things he ever plays with are my socks, so you might want to keep a close eye on yours if you don't want holes in them."

There's a kitchen table that seems used mostly to store mail, a couple barstools at the counter, a balcony. Some of the original details remain, like the tiled fireplace and those cursed stairs, but aside from a few family photos, there's nothing that screams *this is where Wouter grew up.*

Then something becomes apparent that I should have noticed right away.

"Wait, is the floor . . ."

Wouter turns sheepish, rubbing at the back of his neck. "It's not level, yes. The house is tilting." He grabs a pen from the kitchen table, sets it down on the floor. Both of us crane our necks as it slowly starts rolling.

"I didn't notice it downstairs," I say.

"It's more pronounced on the upper floors. We need to level it off, but it's not cheap." Another shrug. "My parents always loved the floors, so we never got around to fixing them, although the angle wasn't quite as pronounced back then." He pats one of the walls. "I painted a couple years ago, but that was the last major change I made. I love this place, though. Maybe too much. Almost makes me feel guilty that I can't devote more time or money, but it feels like a separate full-time job."

I linger on one of the photos hanging above the sofa. Wouter and his parents, sister, and grandparents at what must have been his high school graduation. They're posed in front of this apartment, the Dutch flag behind them with a backpack hanging from it—a Netherlands tradition. His sister's grin is the widest; she's hugging her brother like he's her favorite person in the world. His father has his arm around his mother, his grandmother—*the* grandmother, the one I'm going to have to impress—next to her. The boy in this photo is so close to the Wouter I knew. Ganglier, maybe a bit more self-conscious, with the kind of thick-framed glasses that were in style back then, contrasted with the thin circular frames he wears now.

The house is almost three hundred years old. It's staggering to imagine all the people who lived here before the Van Leeuwens, all the milestones and heartbreaks they endured within these walls.

Wouter leads me down the hall, tapping on the first door. "My bedroom," he says, and then in front of the second, "and yours. Hopefully it's okay?"

I peek inside the tidy minimalist space, dropping my backpack on the bed while Wouter leans in the doorway, as though now that he's christened it mine, he needs permission to come inside. The duvet is a neutral paisley pattern, and everything else is white: lamp, sliding wardrobe doors, slim dresser.

And there's a small print of Van Gogh's sunflowers on the wall.

"Did you—was that here before?" I ask, somehow already knowing the answer.

He bites back a sheepish smile. Runs a hand through his hair. "Wanted to make it feel . . . a bit more like home for you."

"It's perfect, truly. Thank you." Then I wander into the bathroom across the hall and let out a bewildered laugh, grateful to move past the way that Van Gogh print tugged at my chest. "Still with the tiny sinks with cold water?"

"What's wrong with our tiny sinks?"

"Why are they that small?" I ask. "And what if you have big hands?"

Now he's laughing too, eyes turning bright behind his glasses. "That's just how it is here," he says. "Maybe your American sinks are too big."

"That was what you took away from your life-changing year abroad? That our sinks are too big?"

"And your bread is too sweet." Then, as I unzip a suitcase: "Can I help you with anything?"

"Sure. You want to open this mystery box with me?" I take out the package that arrived from the US yesterday. "A care package from Phoebe."

Wouter returns to the kitchen, where he rummages around in a drawer, then reappears with a box cutter. George is making himself at home on my bed, jumping onto the duvet so he can get closer to me, wagging his tail as I bend to scratch him.

"It's his only fault," Wouter says, mock-solemn. "Anyone else he meets—he instantly gets more attached to them, even though I'm the one who supports his lavish lifestyle of canned food and fleece blankets."

"I don't think you have any faults at all," I tell George, because I am already in love with his little face and perfect ears and the way he rolls over so I can scratch his belly.

My sister's box is full of treasures: Trader Joe's cookie butter, a few boxes of Annie's white cheddar macaroni and cheese, a Costco-sized pack of NyQuil.

"You can't get that here," Wouter muses.

"Leave it to Phoebe to unknowingly smuggle me drugs."

His hand dives into the packing peanuts. "What's this—*oh*." And he drops a lavender vibrator as though he's just unearthed a tarantula.

My reaction is twofold.

One: complete and utter mortification.

Two: gratitude, because I tossed my old toys before moving, thinking this would be a good time to restart my collection.

"Not sure why she felt the need to include one of these," I say quickly, even as I clock the brand as one of my favorites. "Obviously you have them over here. I mean—the general you, not *you* specifically, although no judgment if you do! Of course they can be enjoyed by—by anyone."

Wouter's face is a brilliant red, and I think he might be trying to hold back a laugh. "I don't have one," he says. "But now you're making me think I'm missing out." He nods his head toward the package. "Wow, twenty different vibration patterns."

"You know, I don't think I need help after all."

On the bed next to the box, my phone starts buzzing, and the sound is so jarring that at first I think the vibrator somehow got switched on.

But it's just a call from my mother, as though she knows exactly what's happening, a garage door lurching beneath us just as I was about to drag him down onto my bed. The two of us splitting apart, Wouter darting to the room across the hall and pretending he'd been studying the whole time.

"I should answer that." I've been avoiding my parents ever since Wouter's proposal, as though they'd be able to tell just from the sound of my voice that something unusual was going on. I've never kept this much from them.

I wait until Wouter leaves to walk George before I pick up the phone.

"Danibear!" my mother croons, an old nickname that makes me feel ten years old again. "Is that really you? Our long-lost daughter?"

I fight rolling my eyes. "Hi, Mom. How are you?"

"Good, good. Your father's out in the garden. The lilies are looking beautiful, but unfortunately the rabbits think so, too."

My parents are two other people whose jobs seem perfectly suited to them: my father teaches high school math, and my mother works in public health for the county. Solid jobs. Jobs that give something back.

Even if no one said it, I knew it would have delighted them if I'd gone into a similar field, but I always felt awkward in front of kids, and spending so much time in hospitals when I was little left me with zero desire to go back.

"We haven't gotten any photos from you in a while," my mother continues. "You haven't been updating the family album."

"Oh—I haven't?" I feign surprise. "Maybe something's off with the connection. I'll check once we hang up."

"Loved the ones from the Van Gogh Museum, though. You must have been in heaven, seeing all of that in person!"

At that, I let myself smile. A rare moment of connection between us. "I really was. It's still a little surreal to be here, but—I like it. I do. And before you ask, I'm taking all my medications." Wouter's out with George, but still, I say this quietly.

"What about a therapist? I've heard that with universal healthcare, sometimes it can take a long time to get an appointment to see someone . . ."

"Haven't looked into it yet," I say, in part because I hadn't been seeing anyone regularly in LA for a while. "But I will."

"You just want to make sure you have someone *before* you need them," she says. "What about friends? It breaks my heart to think of you feeling lonely out there. Have you made any yet, maybe some people from work?"

It's hard, gritting my teeth and telling her half truths. I hear Wouter come back inside and move around the kitchen, opening and closing cupboards and setting a pan on the stove.

These secrets have to become easier to keep.

AFTER A DINNER OF SOME STORE-BOUGHT GNOCCHI AND a salad, I clean up while Wouter opens a cupboard on the other side of the kitchen. "Tea?" he asks. "Unless you prefer coffee—I'm happy to make it."

"I want the tea," I say, which marks the first time I've uttered those words and meant them literally.

He places a ceramic kettle on the stove, showing me his various boxes of loose leaf so I can pick one out. Then he meticulously measures out tea leaves and pours the hot water over the strainer.

I wish I could tell heartbroken seventeen-year-old Dani that one day Wouter would be making chamomile hibiscus tea for her in Amsterdam.

"I love the ritual of it," he says while the water turns a warm caramel color. "If I'm having an awful day, making a pot of tea always seems to help. It's probably a bit more complicated than it needs to be, but loose leaf has so much more flavor than tea bags. They're essentially tea dust."

"No, this is cool." And it is—there's a reverence in the way he talks about it.

"That's the first time anyone who owns five different teapots has ever been described as cool."

We bring two mugs over to the couch along with a small plate of cookies, and George lifts his head from where he's nestled in a blanket to sniff the air, just in case. I hold the mug to my face and breathe it in, letting the aromatics soothe some of my anxiety.

Wouter turns on some classical music as he sits down next to his dog, who instantly hops over to my lap. "See? No loyalty." He crosses one leg over the other, leans back into the couch. This is more relaxed than I've seen him look so far, his posture less severe, sleeves rolled to his forearms and exposing a dusting of strawberry-blond hair.

The whole scene is so domestic, it could mess with my brain if I let it.

"You're not regretting this yet, are you?" he asks. "I know it's a lot of change in a short period of time. And if there's anything in the apartment you don't like—I'm not attached to any of the decor."

I have a feeling he's just being nice; I'm not about to redecorate his entire apartment. "Surprisingly? I feel calmer than I have since my plane landed."

"I'm glad," he says. "I think there are a few things we should discuss before the appointment."

Appointment: the most accurate way to discuss our impending nuptials. We had to declare our intent to marry two weeks before the appointment itself, and in the end, that's all it is, really. A time slot at city hall.

I alternate between petting George and sipping my tea. "Right. Getting our story straight for your family?"

"That's what I wanted to talk to you about." He brings his mug to his lips, waits a while before he speaks again. "It's just my mom, my sister, and my grandmother. My dad passed away a couple years ago."

The words are a punch to my stomach. "Wouter, I'm so sorry. I had no idea."

A couple years. That's hardly long ago at all.

"I've been waiting for the right time to tell you," he says. "But I suppose there never really is one. He had a stroke my first year of university. He was in the hospital for a few months, first for recovery and then for rehabilitation—it took a while for movement to come back. My mom made sure he exercised and ate as healthy as he could, and we really thought he was going to be okay after that. But a few years later . . . he had another one. And then he just wasn't the same."

I picture a Wouter not much older than the version I said goodbye to, all that fear and uncertainty twisted up inside him. That brow wrinkle he'd get from squinting down at his sketchbook, now a permanent fixture on his face. He would have been only eighteen or nineteen when the first stroke happened. A kid in so many ways.

Your parents must be proud, I said the day we first met, and he didn't correct me.

Without even second-guessing it, I reach out and brush my fingers against the hand that's resting on his jeans. I run my thumb along his knuckles in what must be only a marginal comfort, and yet his eyes fall shut for a moment.

"He needed a lot of help. His speech and mobility were impacted pretty significantly, and they weren't coming back the way they had the first time. He was adamant about not wanting to leave Amsterdam, but the stairs weren't possible anymore, so I moved with him to the ground floor unit. Helped him with his medications, exercises, eating and drinking. I'd been in De Pijp at the time, in a one-bedroom, but that felt much too far."

"You took care of him," I say softly, and he nods, not meeting my gaze again.

"I wanted to. It wasn't what he wanted for me, I know that, but

Roos was still in university, and my mom . . . I could tell it was harder for her. Not that it was easy for me, but I think, because of my work, I could compartmentalize sometimes. So I thought—no matter what, if these are the last years I get with him, even if he's different from the father I grew up with . . . then I want to do it."

I try to imagine this, Wouter at the bedside of the man in the photo right above me. Holding his hand as he grew frail.

"You should have had more time."

In this moment, he's clearer to me than he ever has been: a man who puts other people before himself. Who cares so deeply about his family, he'd do anything for them.

He nods again, mouth pressed in a firm line. If our thirty-year-old selves knew each other better, I wonder if he'd let himself show more emotion. "My mom's in Culemborg now, a much smaller city. My grandmother moved there a while back because that's where her husband was from. They debated selling the Amsterdam house, but I couldn't handle the thought of losing it when we'd already lost so much. I wanted to keep all those memories intact. So I suggested we renovate, convert it from two units to three so we could rent out two of them, and I'd gladly take over the landlord responsibilities. I couldn't live downstairs again, but—but I could live here." As though aware he might be needed, George lifts himself from my lap and drops his head into Wouter's, and Wouter absentmindedly strokes his fingers along his back. "This place comes with a lot of tradition. And with this marriage . . . it might seem counterintuitive, but I want them to think I'm happy."

Are you? I want to ask, but we're certainly not close enough for that.

"Of course, I know marriage isn't a requirement for that," he continues, hand buried in George's soft brown fur. "But it feels worth the lie if it means they won't worry about me. Because—I think they do sometimes."

"The people who love us really can't help it." As different as our families are, I can understand that piece of it. "And they'll be okay that you got married without telling them?"

"Maybe at first they won't quite get it. But it'll be easier because we knew each other as teens."

"Then we'll just have to sell it harder," I say. "Whatever we need to do—I'm all in."

"Thank you. Really. I think I might be getting more out of this than you are," he quips, and while I'm relieved that telling me about his father hasn't made him shut down, he is very firmly wrong about that. He straightens his posture, returning to the beginning of our conversation: the editing we have to do to our history. "We can start with what we talked about the other day. We fell in love as teenagers, and then reconnected."

"Love at second sight," I agree, the word *love* getting trapped in my throat in a way it didn't for him.

"You crashed your bike into me—we can keep that part."

"Do we have to?" I rub at the spot on my knee where the bruises have finally started to fade.

A half smile. "Probably best to stick as close to the real story as possible. Let's say that happened in the first couple days you were here, just to give us a bit of extra breathing room."

"Okay. So I crashed my bike into you, and we realized how much we'd missed each other all these years. And we got married quickly because . . ."

"We couldn't wait another minute. We'd been out of each other's lives for over ten years, and we didn't want to waste any more time."

"You think they'll buy that?"

At that, his gaze falls to the floor. "They . . . know how I feel about you. *Felt* about you. Back in LA."

I almost choke on my next sip of tea. "You told them? About us?"

I wasn't prepared for any of tonight's revelations, and this one stuns me more than it probably should. I assumed that after the breakup text, he hid me away like I was something to be ashamed of. By the time I got to college, I sometimes questioned whether any of it had been real, and the hookups I had freshman year, the greedy touches and desperate releases—none of them made that ache go away. All through my twenties, every casual relationship felt like something was missing. The guy who only texted me after midnight. The guy who hated foreplay. Jace. Maybe it was just the innocence of first love and the dry-throat, beating-heart adrenaline rush of discovery.

Or maybe I was broken.

They know how I feel about you.

I thought I did, too.

He nods, toeing a line in the rug with his sock. "Not everything, but some of it." A sip of his tea, another long pause. "What happened when I went back to Amsterdam, I want you to know— it's one of my biggest regrets."

When his gaze meets mine, it's almost wistful.

I try for a joke because anything else might take this conversation somewhere I'm not prepared for it to go. "So, what, they think I'm this charming, jaw-droppingly gorgeous American who was the love of your life?"

A quirk of a smile. "Precisely. Not that you aren't all those things, but—"

Now the joke is getting out of hand. "It's okay," I say quickly, still reeling but trying to spare us both. "You don't have to pump my ego."

"I'm not." His brow furrows, as though he's working out some complex equation. "Danika. It can't be some mystery to you that you're beautiful."

The uneven apartment floor seems to tilt at a more precarious angle. The sun went down hours ago, but in the amber lamplight, I can see the faint freckles dotted across the bridge of his nose. His facial hair isn't a single color but a whole spectrum, blond and reddish and that hint of silver. His sweet dog is asleep in his lap, and if I squint, there's the Prinsengracht reflected in his glasses. *God*, his face is a painter's dream.

Even if his family views me a fraction of the way he's describing, I can't help thinking they'll be skeptical. They know he needs to be married to inherit this place—they could see right through us.

Something else hits me then. Wouter is single—obviously he wouldn't be entering into this agreement with me if he weren't—but I don't want him to think he needs to stay that way.

"This whole thing," I say, putting a little more space between us on the couch. "It isn't going to infringe on your wild bachelor lifestyle? Because if you want to bring anyone home, I'm sure we could figure out an arrangement."

Wouter looks horrified by this. "There's no wild bachelor lifestyle, I assure you. If one of us feels the need for . . . companionship, we'll sort that out."

I hadn't expected that he'd want to respect the sanctity of our marriage, at least not in that particular way, and yet I'm relieved that we won't have to make this even more complicated.

"I should also ask what you're comfortable with in terms of . . . showing affection in front of my family," he says, a blush creeping back onto his cheeks. "Obviously, we're not going to be, ah, mauling each other in front of them."

If we're really going to sell this, he's right: we have to act like a couple so infatuated, they tied the knot after being back in each other's lives for only a few weeks. Real couples have their own language, sentences they punctuate with a hand on a shoulder or lower back. "I think I'm comfortable with just about anything? Short of mauling?" I say, phrasing it as a question because all of this is new territory. A nervous laugh slips out. "What about you?"

He stares down at his mug again. Waits a moment to speak. "When I'm in a relationship, I tend to be . . . a very touchy person. My family might notice if I'm not doing that with you. If I'm not . . ." A clearing of his throat, a dragging of his gaze back to mine. " . . . touching you."

Oh.

"I don't mind that," I say as a new set of memories rushes back to me. A hand on my ankle while we studied in my room. Brushing my hair away so he could kiss the back of my neck. He seemed addicted to that physical contact, and I loved it so much that my next boyfriend told me I was being too clingy when I wanted to hold hands or nudged him to put his arm around me. "We did plenty of it when we were teenagers."

If his voice sounds a little rougher the next time he speaks, surely it's only because it's so late in the evening. "What about you?" he asks. "How do you act in a relationship?"

"Your family won't really know the difference, will they?"

"But you might."

I consider this. "I haven't had many serious relationships," I admit, stifling a yawn with my elbow. "I'm not sure. Maybe . . . maybe it'll all be new to me."

What I don't say: that I haven't always liked the way I've acted in relationships, the closed-off girl so desperate to stay in control that she got her heart broken the moment she let someone in.

Now it's Wouter's turn to yawn, and we both agree to call it a night. He collects my mug and deposits both of them in the dishwasher, and once he's done in the bathroom—I insist he go first—I go through every step of my skincare routine for the first time in months. When George makes to follow me into my room, I laugh and urge him back toward Wouter, who shuts his door with a quiet click.

I guess I'm going to have to start acting, and that begins with pretending I am completely calm, getting in bed with my fake fiancé on the other side of the wall.

Ten

"SO THINGS WITH WOUTER HAVE ... ESCALATED," I TELL MY
sister a few mornings later.

Phoebe's half laugh manages to communicate both concern and
intrigue. "Elaborate."

With the phone pressed to my ear, I rummage through a drawer
for a pair of sweatpants. Fortunately, my sister's a night owl; these
early conversations are becoming as much a part of my routine as
hearing the front door open and shut every day at precisely seven
thirty, with Wouter's whispered *braaf, braaf—good boy*—to George
as they trot outside for a walk. I'm always hovering on that dream-
like edge before they come back inside, listening for the sound of
him pouring food into a bowl. The jingle of George's collar, a mug
of tea being placed on the counter. A few more hushed words in
Dutch to his dog before Wouter leaves for work. All of it so quiet,
and even so, he messaged me the first morning: I hope we didn't
wake you up.

What I wanted to say: that it's the best way I've woken up in
years.

"You cannot tell a soul," I say to Phoebe. "Other than Maya, because I assume you tell her everything anyway."

"Correct. Proceed."

Once I tell her, my Amsterdam life will collide with my American one, which feels, if mildly terrifying, like the necessary next step. I trust her implicitly; I know she won't tell our parents. And I can't fathom sharing this with anyone else—certainly not with the friends who've barely checked in since I left.

I've never been able to keep secrets from Phoebe for very long. She knew about my crush on Wouter even before I admitted it to myself, and I texted her about our first kiss minutes after I left his room. Right before I was hospitalized, those blurry few weeks in my mid-twenties I try not to think about, she was the first to gently suggest that I talk to someone.

No matter what I'm going through, she's endlessly supportive, with an underlying sense of sisterly worry.

"You know that startup sponsored my work visa, and I can't be here longer than ninety days without it." Somewhere in the low eighties now. "But there's actually an easy solution, and it's that I'm—well, we—Wouter and I—we're going to get married." My mouth trips over the words. I take a steadying breath, bracing myself for her reaction. "So I can stay in the country, and so he can inherit the building his family owns. We're obviously not in a relationship or anything—it's just for the visa. And by the time we get divorced, I'll be much more settled and we can both just . . . move on with our lives."

Those words, *get divorced*—I'm not sure anyone's ever said them as casually as I just did.

The other end of the phone goes silent. I pull on the sweats and sit down on the bed, wondering if the connection dropped.

"Phee? Hello?"

"I'm here, I'm here. I think I fainted."

"I know it's ridiculous," I say, aware of my quickening heart rate. I've never been so desperate for her approval. Her understanding. "But if you think about it, it makes a lot of sense. It'll give me more time to find a job without the stress of potential deportation hanging over me, and—"

"Oh, I'm thinking about it. And it might be the most ludicrous thing I've ever heard." Even though I can't see her, I can picture her: she told me when she answered the phone that she was wrapped in a blanket on the couch while Maya was asleep upstairs, and I hear what sounds like the blanket being pushed to the floor, Phoebe getting to her feet to pace. When she speaks again, it's more frantic. "Do you have any idea how much trouble you could get into? Like, internationally?"

"We're not going to. We have history." Without meaning to, I've echoed exactly what Wouter said to me. "We can pretend we're in love the same way we pretended we weren't back when he was living with us."

"Well, good. Sounds like you've really thought about it. Weighed all the pros and cons," she says. "And your plan is just that Mom and Dad won't find out? Because you know they'd absolutely lose it if they did, right?"

"They're on the other side of the world." I bite down on the inside of my cheek a little too hard. We've never fought about anything serious, only childish arguments that led to one of us slamming a door, only for our parents to find us an hour later singing along to vintage Britney Spears and painting our nails together. The hard edge in my voice is almost unrecognizable. "Phoebe. I'm doing this. I wasn't calling to ask for permission or for a voice of reason. I just wanted you to know."

There's another long stretch of quiet. "Okay," she finally says after blowing out a long breath. Her couch creaks as she sits back down. "I get it. You're an adult. If you're sure about this, if this is what you really want to do . . . then I'm not going to stand in your way."

"Thank you."

"And you're still living downstairs?"

The truth hovers right there on the tip of my tongue—but I swallow it back. "Right."

"Good. Probably smart to have that extra space."

With everything I'm telling her, I'm not sure why I lie about this. Maybe because the marriage is easier to grasp: we're connected only on paper, except in front of his family. Living together, the reality of navigating these tight spaces and darkened corners . . . I'm not sure I could describe it to her in a way that doesn't make it sound more intimate than it actually is.

Because it isn't. It's just practical.

Even when Phoebe tells me she and Maya want to visit before the baby is born and I say I can't wait, it dawns on me that I haven't yet planned the opposite: visiting California. It didn't cross my mind when I was packing up my life, and while I miss her and Maya and my parents, flights are expensive, and leaving and returning to this country might draw more questions at passport control than I'm prepared to answer. Another quandary for the expat crisis center of my brain.

After we hang up, I head across the hall to shower. We were talking for a while; Wouter must have left for work over an hour ago. I reach for the doorknob, push it open, and—

"*Oh*—"

"Sorry—"

"—shit—no—*I'm* sorry!"

Wouter's standing there shirtless, a towel wrapped around his hips, mouth open in horror. A razor dangles from one hand.

Fuck fuck fuck. I haven't even been here a week, and already I've fallen into my worst nightmare.

The scene registers in breathless snapshots: wet hair and a fogged-up mirror. The tang of shaving cream in the air. His chest, still glistening from the shower, and a flash of ink on his left shoulder I can't make out. That trail of hair I spied when he was working on the sink, dusted along his abdomen and disappearing somewhere beneath the towel.

Maybe most dangerous of all is the cherry-red shyness splashed across his face, like I've caught him doing something far less innocent than shaving. Our eyes lock for an instant longer than they should, our bodies frozen, neither of us lunging for the door.

He hitches the towel higher, tighter—but not before I get a glimpse of that suggestive V-line between his hips.

Finally, I snap back to my senses and shut the door, my heart still in my throat. It was only open for a few seconds, which was somehow enough time for me to map every detail of his half-naked body. Never let it be said that I'm not efficient.

Even though I can't see him anymore, I cover my face on instinct. Give my forehead a few light bangs against the wood. "I thought you left for work," I manage. "I'm so sorry. I shouldn't have just barged in."

I can still smell his shaving cream. His peppermint shampoo. Because we shower in the same place, I know exactly what's in his soap, an off-white bottle with a French name. Notes of green tea, citrus, sage.

"I had a patient cancel this morning. Should have locked the door." A cough. "Do you mind if—I didn't bring a change of clothes into the bathroom with me."

"Oh! Yeah. Of course. You're safe!" I call out once I'm in the doorway to my room. George is sitting there on the floor, wagging his tail at me, so I toss him the pair of my socks he's already almost chewed his way through. I have a feeling animals know exactly what ridiculous antics their humans are up to, and they are definitely always judging us. Lovingly.

Years ago, Wouter and I had an awkward bathroom interaction in my house, though both of us were fully clothed. And now I'm wondering if he's remembering it, too: me at the sink in pajama shorts and a Speak Now World Tour T-shirt, the door opening because I hadn't locked it.

"Oh—sorry," Wouter said, backing up.

"I'm just brushing my teeth." I held up my toothbrush. "You can stay if you want."

I was rarely so brazen with my flirting—was it flirting, telling him we could share the bathroom? There was a moment of hesitation, as if he didn't know whether he was allowed to say yes. Then he stepped inside, keeping the door wide open.

We'd seen each other in pajamas before, but something about standing next to him at the double sinks like that felt unbearably intimate. We brushed our teeth together, eyes catching in the mirror, and in all my teenage misguidance of how a girl should act around guys, I tried to make my spitting as dainty as possible.

Until my chest grew so tight I couldn't breathe, and I dropped my toothbrush into the sink.

He was quick with my inhaler, which was just in the medicine cabinet, helped me sit down on the toilet seat as I held it to my mouth. I'd felt the early stages of an asthma attack most of that day but chalked it up to wildfire smoke.

"You're going to be okay," he kept saying, but I could see the concern in his eyes that he was trying so hard to fight against. "You're doing great. Slow breaths, just like that."

It was impossible not to fall for him after the way he talked me through it.

Thirty-year-old Wouter reemerges from his bedroom a few

minutes later in jeans and a collared shirt. "Guess we should always lock doors from now on," he says, but there's a flash of amusement on his face. His hair is still damp, the scent of his aftershave clinging to my nostrils.

My face flames. "Great idea. Knocking, too—house rules one and two."

In the kitchen, he takes a kettle off the shelf and lifts his eyebrows at me. I give him a nod and he grabs two mugs.

For the most part, this is what living together has been like, a choreographed politeness not too dissimilar from when he lived with my family. I take George for walks during the day, and then I open my laptop and browse job listings until my eyes burn. I cooked dinner for us last night, an Albert Heijn meal kit with Dutch instructions I translated with my phone, figuring it was the literal least I could do with how much he's given me, and the night before he had a work dinner with some colleagues. He's already rented out the ground-floor unit to a friendly Serbian couple—which makes our cohabitation feel even more final.

When we were teenagers, we dreamed of something like this: no parents, complete independence. The ability to come and go whenever we wanted. A shared bed, which of course isn't applicable here. The reality of living together is much more tentative, neither of us wanting to encroach on the other's space, trading apologies when we pass each other in the narrow hall. He even made room for me in the bathroom cabinet, but a general fear of overstepping has me keeping most of my products on my desk, my antidepressants safely inside a drawer.

"What are you up to today?" he asks after I finish showering, joining him in the kitchen where the tea is steeping. When he reaches for the kettle, I try not to picture the way the muscles in his arm flexed when he held the razor, because that only leads to picturing his bare chest. And his shoulders. And the way water dripped from his hair to the hollow of his throat.

"My first Dutch class!" I say with genuine enthusiasm, in part to mask the fact that what I'm really up to is pushing all those images far, far from my mind. For some reason, this makes him laugh. "What? Should I be more morose about it?"

"That's the most excited anyone's ever been about learning Dutch." He passes me a mug of Earl Grey with its relaxing hint of lemon. "Amsterdam can be kind of a transient place. A lot of people stay here for only a short time before they move on, back to their home country or somewhere else. So plenty of internationals never learn the language, which I can understand. You've been here only a couple months, and you already want to make the effort . . ." A shake of his head. "I guess I'm touched? On behalf of my entire country?"

Now it's my turn to laugh as I reach for the bowl of brown sugar cubes, although the sound is quite in opposition to what's happening in my heart. "I was also wondering if maybe I could visit you at work?" When he gives me a perplexed look, I add, "Is it so weird that I want to see what you do before we're—married?" Even after a few days of this, I still trip over the word.

"It's just an office," he says, but tells me to come by after his last patient.

George trots into the living room with my socks in his mouth, determinedly not letting go even when Wouter bends to scratch him behind the ears. Then with a wave and a final sip of his tea, my almost-husband is out the door.

NOW THAT I'M TECHNICALLY UNEMPLOYED, I'M NOT USED to the freedom. I've only experienced this twice in my life: The first was in between my freshman and sophomore years of college, when

I didn't apply for an internship because Phoebe wanted to drive Route 66 together. The second was when I was hospitalized, though I didn't exactly feel very independent back then.

Every time I have a moment to contemplate my future, the same refrain plays in my mind: I should be doing something meaningful. Something that shows I'm taking full advantage of the life I wasn't supposed to have.

It wasn't just the fact that I was a micro-preemie, that strange term that's always brought to mind a delicate glass figurine instead of an actual human. Every few years when they had nothing else to report, some local newspaper or TV station would want to do an update on me. One of those feel-good stories about the insurmountable odds I surmounted and how I was doing now.

The last time this happened was part of a bigger story tied to the opening of a new NICU at the hospital where I was born. I was one of a handful of "miracle babies" they interviewed, twenty-six and working at a tech company that didn't have the best reputation. The other people they profiled had gone on to become a social worker, a civil engineer, a neonatal nurse. One was even a violinist with the Los Angeles Philharmonic. And there I was in my tiny studio apartment microwaving instant ramen, my latest casual relationship having just fizzled out, working on designing a drop-down menu for a corporation most people hated.

The night the story aired on TV, I crawled into bed and started shaking. Gasping for air. My lungs felt fragile, but my inhaler barely helped. Though everything in my body hurt, somehow I was certain what was wrong with me wasn't physical. It had been building for months, but I'd dismissed it as flu season or not getting enough sleep. I was just a little *off*, I always told myself, but how many people could say they felt truly *on* all the time, or even most of it?

Days later, when I'd still barely moved, so dehydrated it hurt to swallow, I called my sister and, when she showed up, asked her to take me to the nearest hospital. I wound up getting a referral to a mental health facility, where I voluntarily checked myself in, hugged Phoebe goodbye, and told her not to worry.

There I learned that I'd been hiding my symptoms for years. High-functioning depression and anxiety. I'd ignored so many signs—the endless fatigue, body aches I couldn't explain, an inability to focus. There were therapists and groups and medication until we found the right one and, finally, the ability to breathe again. When I was there, I didn't have to worry about work or meals or other people. My only responsibility was getting healthy.

I still can't believe I let myself get to that point, that I was so out of tune with my body and mind that I didn't realize I was on the verge of collapse until it had already happened.

Slowly, I got better. Not 100 percent, but the fog lifted, and I got stable enough to consider myself content on most days, though I still had some gray moments. I used all my vacation time and even some unpaid leave to figure it out, and when I got back to work, I lied and told anyone who asked that it had been surgery.

After I lost my job, even after the breakup with Jace, I was so terrified of another breakdown that I did everything I could to distract myself. There was the haircut, attempts at self-care disguised as expensive beauty products, spending as much time with my family as I could before I left. And then, of course, the international move. The great escape. If I could just run fast enough, then maybe the darkness in my brain wouldn't be able to catch up with me.

I'm aware that plenty of people no longer work in the fields they majored in. I just don't know what else I'm qualified for or what might make me happy, which makes me feel a bit like I'm having a quarter-life crisis.

A single dinner isn't enough to repay Wouter for this gift of time to figure myself out—it's a tremendous privilege, I realize that. But for now, all I need to figure out is how to pronounce the *eu* sound in Dutch.

I've always liked languages; I took three years of French in high school and had a brief Italian phase in college, because I had a brief everything phase. One semester and an application to a study abroad program in Florence, which my parents didn't think was a good idea. "It's just so far away," they said, and so I didn't go.

Here's my chance to start fresh with a new vocabulary.

Before class, the room is filled with chatter in a half dozen different languages, only some of which I recognize, and I trade smiles with my new classmates as I sit down and take out my textbook. Despite feeling very out of practice when it comes to school, I'm relaxed for the first time all day. We're all here because we want to be, because we're trying to soak up every bit of our new lives.

"Welkom in de Nederlandse les," says the teacher, a friendly middle-aged Dutch woman named Femke. "Laten we beginnen. Let's begin."

Eleven

· · · · · · · · · · · ·

AS I'M LEAVING CLASS, MY MIND SWIMMING WITH BASIC grammar and verb conjugations, I spot someone familiar exiting the room just across the hall.

"Iulia?" I call out, and she turns around.

"Dani!" she says, sounding delighted, an emotion I'm not sure I've earned. We stand off to the side to avoid disrupting the flow of students. "How are you? Are you taking a class here?"

"Just finished my first one. Slightly overwhelmed, but in a good way."

"I know the feeling. I'm in an advanced conversation class where we mostly talk about current events all in Dutch, because apparently I love pain." She slides her bag to her other shoulder. She's dressed casually, the way I've always seen her: joggers, boots, oversized sweatshirt, her long hair loose and wavy. I can admire someone who prioritizes comfort. "Good to see you're still in one piece."

Immediately I'm struck with embarrassment. "I should have reached out—after I moved. You were so nice to let me keep my stuff at your place." Then I chew the inside of my cheek, unsure how to navigate this. It's been years since I went from acquaintances to friends with someone, and I've never gotten the hang of doing it as an adult. In the end, I decide to go with honesty. "I thought maybe it would be annoying to hear from someone still stumbling their way along when you've been here for a while. I . . . didn't want to overstay my welcome."

Iulia's dark eyes grow wide. "Are you serious? *I'm* sorry. I was worried about overstepping if you had a million other things to stress about."

I have to bite back a smile, because maybe our anxieties are kindred spirits. "Do you want to grab coffee?"

We find a spot on the next block, where I learn that she has the coolest job I've heard of in quite some time.

"I'm a boat tour captain," she says after we sit down with our mugs. "Not for those giant boats down by the train station. We're sort of alternative—we take a max of ten people, and they can even bring alcohol if they want. And I'm allowed to swear." A sip of her coffee. "What about you?"

"I'm still trying to figure that out, actually." I fiddle with the wrapper of the biscuit that came with my latte—it's rare to be served coffee without one. "My company sort of fell apart, so I'm looking for something new."

She gives a somber nod. "Not easy sometimes, I'm sorry. And where are you living? Hopefully somewhere with better plumbing?"

"Oh—I found a place in the city center." And since that feels too Wouter-adjacent to discuss with someone I barely know, I change the subject.

Iulia Bojescu, I learn, came over here in her early twenties from Bucharest. She'd visited with a few friends and fell in love with the city, vowing to do whatever she could to make it work. She waited tables, bartended, and then took a boat tour that changed her life.

"I get to talk about what makes Amsterdam amazing all day,"

she says. "Even when it's pouring rain and I'm out on the water, I still can't believe someone's paying me for it."

It's impossible to miss the way her eyes light up, and there it is: another person who's found exactly what they're meant to be doing.

This time, though, it doesn't inspire any jealousy.

"Come on the boat sometime soon," she says when it's time to part ways, and I promise I will.

I break into a grin the moment she leaves, like my parents dropped me off at kindergarten and I just made my very first friend.

MY CONFIDENCE PEAKS ON MY WAY TO WOUTER'S OFFICE, when an older couple approaches me and offers up a shy wave.

"Excuse me," a woman with short gray hair asks in a heavy accent I can't place. Her husband is frowning at a paper map. "Do you speak English?"

Oh my god.

They think I'm a local.

I'm much too giddy as I reply, "Yes! I do!"

She and her husband look relieved. "We're trying to go to the Rijksmuseum. Is nineteen the right tram?"

I nod, even more thrilled that I know the answer to the question. "It's that stop over there, on the other side of the street."

They're effusive in their thank-yous, and I just give them a bright wave before I board a different tram to Wouter's office.

Once I sit down, my phone buzzes with a text from my mother.

How was your first Dutch class? Did you make it home okay?

I fight back a flicker of frustration. The last time we talked, my parents asked what time the class was, and I told them I'd let them know how it went. Apparently the fact that I didn't do it right away means something went horribly wrong.

I am thirty years old, and my parents are still checking up on me like this.

Great, just had coffee with a friend. I promise, I AM FINE.

The building is on a quiet street in Amsterdam's Oud-West neighborhood, just outside the city center. Dusk fell an hour ago, and while there are still a few bikers making their way home or to after-work plans, the streets are a bit emptier over here.

He's on the third floor in a practice with a few other therapists, the space tidy and well-lit, with a large plant in one corner of the waiting area that seems to be thriving. The receptionist is gone for the day and the whole place is quiet, so I'm guessing Wouter's the last one here.

When I call his name, he pokes his head out of his office, and I have to take a moment to process him here, like this. He's in a charcoal-gray shirt, the sleeves pushed past his elbows and the top button undone, his hair in slight end-of-work disarray.

Without meaning to, my eyes drop to his waist, just above his belt, where that deep V I noticed earlier is now swathed in denim.

File under thoughts I cannot be having about my future husband.

"You'll never believe what just happened," I say to him, hoping the giddiness in my voice will cover up anything else. "A couple of tourists asked me how to get to the Rijksmuseum. They thought I was a local!"

"Oh? What did you tell them?"

"I said to take the nineteen going to Sloterdijk."

Wouter's jaw tenses as he tries to fight a grin. And fails.

"What?" I ask.

"That was the wrong direction. Right tram, wrong direction."

"Shit. Is it too late to run out and find them?" Now Wouter starts laughing, so I give his arm a nudge with my elbow. "Nooooo, don't laugh! I feel terrible!"

"They'll figure it out," he says. "I promise you, they'll be okay."

We small-talk about my Dutch class, and I mispronounce my way through telling him my name, my age, and where I'm from. Then he leads me into his office, a medium-sized room with a desk on one side and a platform table in the middle, a stack of clean towels and a laundry bin on the other side. There's a rack of dumbbells, an exercise ball, and various stretching bands. His framed degrees hang on the wall alongside some artwork that looks like it came with the frame, the kind you're supposed to replace.

"So this is where the magic happens."

"If by magic you mean sweat and tears and muscle cracks, then yes," Wouter says, but I can tell he's proud of what he does. It reminds me of how he'd act after finishing a sketch or painting, never one to seek out compliments or disparage his own work. There was a quiet confidence there, a pride in completing it, whether it was a doodle or a detailed landscape, though he always preferred art with people in it.

In some ways, I'm still reconciling the wide-eyed artist with the logical physiotherapist. The boy who confessed his dreams in the middle of the night when it was just him, me, and the stars with the man who let go of those dreams long ago.

Then again, maybe this was always the person he was going to be, and I was just a detour on the way to some better destination.

Maybe it's a Pavlovian response to where we are, but I can't help stretching to one side, trying to soothe a stiffness in my back.

"Are you okay?" Wouter asks, mouth pulling into a frown. "You've been doing that a lot lately."

"Is it that obvious?"

"Maybe just because of my line of work."

"And it's probably because of mine that my posture is a nightmare." I extend my arms as far as they'll go, to one side and then the other. "It wasn't enough for me to be a hundred and fifty centimeters tall. I have to slouch, too."

"You should see a doctor. A physiotherapist," he says as his mouth kicks into a smile. "I could take a look if you want. Give you a bit of relief."

"Oh, no—you couldn't," I say, although *a bit of relief* sounds like the loveliest thing I've heard all day. "I'd feel bad, not paying you."

"I could charge you if that would make you feel better." He pats the table. "It's no trouble at all. Some of my friends have asked me to do the same, and I don't mind it if you think it might help."

I can't deny that it would probably help a significant amount, so I tell him yes. He lays down a fresh towel while I hang up my scarf and jacket.

"How does this work?" I ask, leaning down to unzip my boots. "I've had a massage, but I've never been to a physio or a chiropractor or anything."

"Well, you can keep most of your clothes on. That's a major difference."

"That's a relief, because I'm not wearing underwear."

The joke . . . does not hit the way I expect it to. Wouter immediately freezes as he's adjusting the towel.

"Uh—sorry, that was a bad joke," I say, fighting a full-body wince. "I'm wearing underwear. I promise. Not that it's a big deal either way, I guess plenty of people like the freedom of it, but—I was just thinking about this morning when I walked in on you, and you weren't wearing—you know what, now I'm making it worse. I'm just going to put my face in the face hole thing and we can forget I ever said anything!"

I climb on top and spread myself out. Wouter might be swallowing back a laugh, so at the very least, I'm glad my agony is entertaining.

With my head down, his voice sounds like it's coming from farther away than right next to me. "I typically start by asking my patients where they're experiencing pain and if they can describe what it feels like."

"My ego," I mutter.

"Sorry?"

"My lower back." I consider the question for another moment. "And my neck, and maybe also my shoulders? I wouldn't say it's a sharp pain, more of a dull ache. I only notice it if I really stop to think about it, if that makes sense?"

"Yes, it does. That's good to know."

I hear the sound of running water, Wouter washing his hands at the small sink in the corner. Then he comes closer, soft footsteps until I can see his shoes on the floor below. Though his hands aren't cold when he pats them along my back, I shiver at the lightest touch.

"How did you realize this was what you wanted to do?" I ask the floor.

"My dad had this excellent physio after his first stroke—that was what inspired me. He wound up mentoring me during my studies," he says. "The connection between the mind and body fascinated me. I went to as many of my dad's appointments as I could. I wanted to be able to help people in pain, to help them figure out how to be comfortable in their bodies, even when their bodies are working against them."

"That's really incredible," I say, entirely genuine. "I'm so glad your dad had that."

His hands travel up my spine, as though checking that each vertebra is where it's supposed to be. "*Wow.*"

"What? Is my back totally fucked?"

"No, no," he says. "It's just—I've treated a lot of injuries, but I don't think I've seen anyone this tense in a while."

"It's a gift."

"You must carry a lot of tension here, in your shoulders." His palms find my shoulder blades above my T-shirt, and I try my best to relax them. "If I gave you some stretches, would you practice them on your own?"

"Depends. Does our insurance cover this?"

And even though I can't see him, I'm certain he's rolling his eyes at me.

"Yes," I say. "If it would make you happy, I'll do your stretches."

"You shouldn't do it to make me happy. You should do it so you're not in tremendous pain by the time you're forty."

"Why do you have to be so reasonable?"

At this, he finally laughs, and that makes me relax a little. He tilts me to one side and then the other, guiding me through a couple stretches before returning to the massage.

As he continues his survey of just how stiff my muscles are, the fabric of my T-shirt seems to get in his way. "Is it easier with my shirt off?" I ask. "Because I don't mind—"

His hands pause. "Oh—only if you're comfortable."

"But most people do?"

"If I'm working on their back, yes."

So, because I want the full experience, I sit up and he averts his eyes as I tug off my T-shirt before giving him my back again. His hands settle on my bare skin, fingers warm. Practiced. Intentional. I thought maybe he'd avoid the band of my bra, that it would be too intimate, but he doesn't, like the professional that he is. He even stops for a moment and returns with some oil, and while the lavender scent calms my muscles a bit, my brain has not forgotten that I'm half-naked in his office. That slickness turns his movements smoother, makes his skin glide across mine.

What he said about being a physical person comes back to me—it makes sense, now, that his career would take this turn.

That this would be his something meaningful.

My mind wanders as I sink into the sensation. He lingers in certain places, repeats a movement when I let out a sigh of satisfaction. It makes me painfully aware of the fact that no one has touched me like this in so long, which is a sad thing to realize when someone is touching you in a wholly medical context.

"Good?" he asks.

"Very. Please don't stop."

This is a new peace between us, and while there's so much we haven't talked about, right now he feels closer to the boy I used to know—though the baggage we shared back then was significantly lighter.

Even once we're married, I can't imagine bringing up the past. Our relationship is too new, too easy to ruin by digging up a complicated history, and yet there's still that unanswered question: *Why?* Teenage immaturity, like he said? Or something else entirely, something that might hurt to hear all these years later?

"I've been wondering," he says, "how your parents reacted when you told them you were moving here."

"Well, they thought I was on drugs when I told them. My mom put her hands on my shoulders and looked me deep in the eyes and said, 'Danika, have you taken something? Do we need to go to the hospital?' It was so outside the realm of what they expected when I said I had something important to tell them. Then they asked if there was a small town in California also called Amsterdam that they hadn't heard of."

Now Wouter's laughing again, and yet his hands remain steady on my spine.

"They didn't understand it. They probably still don't. They were just concerned, you know. The way they always have been. That I'd fall into a canal or get run off the road by a cyclist."

"Or the other way around."

"Precisely." I close my eyes while Wouter's fingers massage deeper. "I have to admit, I'm a little nervous about your grandmother not approving of me."

"I don't think you have anything to worry about. Her English is a bit more limited, but she'll love you. She's loved all the girls I've brought home."

"All of them, huh? How many would that be?"

He turns sheepish—I can hear the new shyness in his voice. "Maybe 'all' wasn't the best word. All two. Is that better? My last serious relationship ended about a year ago and—I don't really do casual, so . . ."

He trails off, as though realizing he's gotten too personal. It takes me moment to connect the dots—if he doesn't do casual, that might mean he hasn't slept with anyone in a year.

Which is not something I need to linger on, especially not while I'm in his office in just a bra and jeans, my breasts pressed hard against the table.

"You know I've just had one, really. Unless you count you," I say, because the way he's loosening my muscles is apparently loosening my tongue, too. "Then that's two."

"It was that serious to you?" His surprise throws me off. I don't know if this means we were only ever superficial to him or that he never felt any remorse for ending it. *It's one of my biggest regrets*, he said the night I moved in.

I'm not sure which version of him is telling the truth.

"I—I don't know," I lie. "Everything feels intense when you're that age, I think."

"Hmm" is all he says in response, leaving me to interpret that single syllable in only a hundred different ways.

"Teach me some Dutch words," I say, eager for a subject change.

That seems like a much safer conversation. "I want to impress everyone in class."

"Well. This is de rug." He splays a hand on my back, and I repeat the word. "Some of these are very similar to English. De arm"—he touches my arm—"de hand"—grazes my palm with his fingertips—"de voet." With that one, he gives my foot the lightest tap.

I can't help laughing. "So I've been speaking Dutch my whole life."

Then he moves backward from de voet, up to my left ankle, touching the top of my sock. "De enkel."

"Now you're just fucking with me."

His voice is pure joy. "Oh, I'm very serious." His fingers move to my shin. "Het scheenbeen," he says, and it takes me a few tries to get the pronunciation right. "De knie," he continues, and even though it sounds almost the same as in English, suddenly I'm not laughing anymore. With my chest to the table, he has to reach around to find my knee, his fingers skimming along my jeans and drawing out a shiver. "Ticklish?"

I shake my head. "De knie. Keep going."

There's a pause on his end as he drops his hands, and it takes me longer than it should to realize why: the body parts directly above my knees are ones he's definitely going to skip.

"As we already covered: de rug." In one fluid motion, he whisks his thumb up my spine like it's made of silk. "De wervelkolom."

For a while my muscles demand his full focus, the heels of his hands chasing down an ache I've never been able to reach for myself. It's as though he knows exactly what's twisted and tangled up inside me, and if he could just find it, just wrap his hand around it, he could soothe it with a single stroke.

He's at my neck now, his breathing pattern growing steadily

quicker. Fingertips press in on either side as his exhale rolls across my skin. *Christ*, it's almost too good. He rubs me there for a long moment, until my lungs rush to keep up with his.

"What's next?" I ask, not expecting the rasp of my voice.

"Right. The back of your neck is, quite creatively, de nek. De hals: the throat." A clearing of his hals as he pushes back my hair to graze my ear, and even that brief touch drags a sigh up my throat. I muffle it just in time. "Het oor. And then we have het hoofd." The pat he gives my head does nothing to calm the thudding of my heart.

This game wasn't safe at all.

He works his way back down the column of my neck, down my spine, and it occurs to me that he could pull away at any moment. He could stop, and he probably should, since I'm not paying him and this can't possibly be a good use of his time.

But he doesn't. Either he truly believes my muscles need the attention or he wants a reason to keep touching me like this, a ridiculous thought when we've only just dipped a toe back into friendship. My body is simply broken, I conclude, just as his thumb digs into a spot between my ribs.

And *oh. Right there.* He dips in again, kneading the muscle back and forth until I have to grit my teeth against the sensation. *Fuck*, I'm not strong enough for this. I can't pretend I'm not slowly turning to putty with him working my body like every time he gripped a paintbrush was child's play compared to what his hands can do now.

His touch turns languid, like he could keep going and going, keep stretching my tightest spots until I snap. I'm shuddering, trying to keep my gasp locked away, but the pressure is so gorgeously intense, so unexpected—and then I can't fight it.

I *moan.*

"Was that okay?" he asks, a hint of concern in his voice. "Do you want it a little gentler?"

"No, it's fantastic." I'm starving for air, bracing myself for him to do it again. Desperate for him to. "Harder. Please."

With more force, he pushes deep into my skin as another throaty sound falls from my mouth. It's just this side of painful, but somehow that's even better, especially as he alternates between hard and soft, giving me a moment to catch my breath before he starts again, fingertips tracing some invisible map. The lavender oil should be stronger than any of it, but I'm still too aware of his scent. Peppermint shampoo, though it's been hours since he washed his hair. Something earthy. Something citrus.

Then I sense him leaning over me, his forearms flat against my back. There's a new heat, a new weight—all of that skin searing mine—and I've never been more grateful that he can't see my face. He even lets out a sound of his own—a rough grunt, like he's trying to keep himself from showing the effort of it all.

It shouldn't be sexy, that sound. It shouldn't rumble through my whole body, settling low in my stomach.

But *god*, the way it drags me back in time.

Now I'm remembering how quiet he used to be when we were together, even when we were alone. We both were, likely a combination of secrecy and the comfort we hadn't yet found in our own bodies. Only on rare occasions—the back seat of my car, for instance—did he let himself go. Velvet moans and my name murmured like a plea when I kissed down his chest, teased the waistband of his boxers. *Can I* and *are you sure* and *yes.* I'd never imagined how it would feel to undo another person like that, to get to see them at their most vulnerable.

Gently, he brushes aside my hair so he can give more attention to my neck, a sensation that has the effect of beaming a pulse directly between my legs. He's massaging behind my ears, beneath my jaw, but I can feel his hands on every outstretched limb. Every place that craves his fingertips.

For a moment, I let myself give in to the fantasy, because certainly there's no harm if it stays inside my head, where I want him *loud*. I want those expert hands on my hips and thighs. I want his weight on top of me, a hot mouth on my skin while he pushes my body to its limits.

He lets out another low groan, one I'm worried I may have conjured through sheer desire—and that's what makes me tremble back to my senses.

It's too much. Too intimate.

"You—you can stop," I say, the words shaky, and he instantly moves his hands away. "I think I'm good for now."

I'm newly self-conscious as I lift myself from the table too quickly, my head spinning. Without looking, he passes me my T-shirt, and I'm so dazed that I put it on backward. Once it's properly on and I give him the okay to turn around, his cheeks are pink with exertion.

The way that blush is spread across his face is downright sensual, as though he's the one who's been caught in the middle of a gasp. Sweat edges his hairline, and I picture him wrapped in that towel again, wondering if he blushes all the way down his neck. If I touched him the way he touched me, how hot his skin would be.

"How do you feel?" he asks.

Feverish. Trembling. My back, however, has never felt better. "Great," I manage. "Thank you so much. You are . . . extremely good at what you do." I reach for my scarf and jacket, feeling exposed in just a T-shirt, and grasp for a conversation topic that will throw cold water onto my indecent thoughts. "So. Friday's the big day."

Our appointment with city hall, more bureaucracy than romance, and thank god for that.

He nods. "And then I thought we could go to Culemborg to

have lunch with my family." Now his voice is steadier. Cheerful, almost, as though to confirm everything we did in this office was just part of his job. He tugs his sleeves down his forearms to rebutton them, and I try not to think about those long muscles flexing as he hovered over me. "Everyone will be dying to meet my wife."

Twelve

WHEN I IMAGINED GETTING MARRIED, I NEVER HAD THE clearest vision. I didn't have dreams of long white dresses or flower arrangements, but I did picture a kind face at the end of the aisle. Someone who loved me.

I certainly didn't picture the amount of paperwork involved, or that it would all be in Dutch.

The gemeente building, Amsterdam's city hall, is a modern structure that looks out of place in a neighborhood of canal houses, all glass and concrete. We take our place in the waiting area, and because we'll need two witnesses to sign the wedding certificate—who can be anyone at all—Wouter asks another couple if they wouldn't mind stepping in.

I bury my hands in the sleeves of my cable-knit sweater, probably stretching them out past the point of no return.

Four. Everyone knows this is fake.

Seven. The police are on their way.

Eight. I'm going to waste away in a Dutch prison and bring eternal shame to my family.

It's possible the therapist who taught me those exercises never accounted for this specific circumstance.

When it's our turn, Wouter translates for me. A middle-aged woman gives us a restrained smile as she conducts the ceremony, and I have to remind myself she's just doing her job, that she sees dozens of couples every week and can't tell that we're not madly in love.

The whole thing takes less than fifteen minutes, as anticlimactic as waiting in line at the DMV. The past month and a half tumbles through my head in a bizarre tableau. Moving across the world. Everything falling apart. Crashing into the man who was able to pick up some of the pieces.

Then there's the form we have to sign declaring this isn't a marriage of convenience. Standard procedure when a national is marrying a foreigner, the woman tells us, which only yanks my anxiety out of its hiding place. My chest is tight—either a symptom of an impending asthma attack or just the consequences of my actions coming back to bite me.

Marriage of convenience.

Schijnhuwelijk.

The Dutch even have a single word for it.

That's exactly what this is. Marrying him is extremely fucking convenient for me, and yet seeing it in such plain words makes the illegality sink in.

"You all right?" Wouter asks.

I keep my voice low, hoping my shakiness looks like regular wedding jitters. "I didn't expect there would literally be something we'd need to sign declaring this isn't a marriage of convenience."

He gives my hand a squeeze as though he knows I need not just the reassurance but some kind of anchor. "That's the beauty of it, though," he says. "We've been madly in love for the past ten years."

If only, I think, and then I sign my name next to his.

Gefeliciteerd to us.

"One last thing," he says, reaching into his jacket pocket and producing a small velvet box. "They're nothing special, I'm afraid. I didn't know your size, so I borrowed one of the rings you left by the sink. I hope that was okay?"

I've never been someone to fawn over a piece of jewelry. Even during a brief jewelry-making phase right before I was hospitalized—when I thought my exhaustion was because I needed a new creative outlet and figured I could open an Etsy shop and work for myself, and wouldn't that be the dream?—my heart was never really in it. I only wound up making one bracelet, which I gave to Phoebe.

Even though these rings are fake, even though they don't actually mean anything, they steal my words for a moment. They're simple gold bands, nothing fancy, but they manage to gleam even in the dim lighting of city hall.

"They're beautiful," I say, meaning it, my lungs still tight. "You didn't have to."

His face is so earnest, as though he's genuinely relieved I like them. "We have to look the part, right?"

And with that, he lifts an eyebrow, motioning for me to take his ring.

"Many Dutch people wear it on their right hand," he says. "But we can do whichever you want."

I go first, sliding the band onto the ring finger of his right hand, wanting this to be as authentic as possible. When we did this with the straw wrapper, he was the nervous one. We'd barely touched at that point, and now he's familiar with all the tightest muscles along my back. It should be less awkward, this kind of physical contact—and maybe it is for him. Because this time, when it's his turn to slide the ring onto my finger, he grasps my hand to steady it, and it's only then that I realize I'm still shaking.

"There." He extends his hand so we can admire both rings. "How does it feel?"

I turn my hand over a few times, getting used to the new weight of it. "Just like the real thing."

THE NERVES ONLY INTENSIFY AS WE GET CLOSER TO MEETing his family, a sense of breathlessness that follows me around the next week, enough to keep my inhaler closer than usual.

Culemborg is about an hour southeast of Amsterdam, and since Wouter doesn't own a car, it's my first time on a train. As we pass each platform at the station, dodging frantic travelers, I'm shocked to discover this is the same place you can board a train to Paris, London, Berlin, Zurich. All these cities suddenly at my fingertips, itching at a wanderlust that's been dormant for too many years.

The train ride is a pastoral postcard, the familiar quickly giving way to great swaths of green, farms dotted with cows and sheep, powerful old windmills in the distance.

"Welkom in Culemborg," Wouter says when we get off the train. "The city that feels like a village."

I slot my transit pass back into my wallet. "A city? Not a town?"

"Actually, yes. They may only have a population of thirty thousand, but they're very proud to have city rights."

His mom's house is only a ten-minute walk from the station, mostly through farmland. More animals graze behind low fences on either side of us. The roads are single-lane and unmarked, cyclists and drivers sharing them without effort. I wonder what would count as a traffic jam. I'm not used to this kind of quiet, but I can see the appeal, how peaceful it might be with all this space to hear yourself think.

Wouter's in jeans and a black jacket, his face newly shaven, and while I prefer the stubble, the clean-cut look isn't a bad one, either. I fear the man doesn't have a bad look.

Lately I've caught my gaze traveling to his hands when I'm not paying attention, imagining the way they pressed and stroked and worked out knots I didn't know I had. My libido was out of control, I deduced after the massage. The next day when he was at work, I locked myself in my room and held the vibrator between my legs until I was sweaty and spent. Yet each orgasm had felt unfinished somehow, grit-your-teeth just barely there—good, but not enough of a relief to fully take me over the edge. Almost more of a frustration than if I hadn't touched myself at all.

Wouter—innocent, clean-shaven Wouter, who knows nothing of what I do when he's not at home—leads me through a small neighborhood of modest homes with actual *yards*, which don't exist much in Amsterdam.

"I feel like I might need to say thank you a few more times, so really: thank you." He's stopped in front of a single-story home with tall hedges and a couple of trees in the front yard. A garden that looks like someone has lovingly tended to it. "Maybe I'm too sentimental, but I can't imagine ever selling that house, and if all of this means I never have to . . . it's going to save me a lot of sleepless nights."

A lump forms in my throat. "Now if *I* say thank you, we're going to be saying it back and forth forever." I square my shoulders, worrying my ring. That's one additional benefit: it's essentially become a fidget toy. "Any final words of wisdom? Faux pas I should avoid?"

"I didn't want to say this earlier, but they don't really like Americans." He's completely straight-faced. "Can you do any other accents? That might help."

And I just gape at him until he finally breaks into laughter.

"You asshole," I say, biting back my own smile as I give him a gentle whack with my purse.

"I'm sorry, I'm sorry, I couldn't resist. But you're relaxed now, aren't you?"

"A little," I say begrudgingly.

One more deep breath past the tightness in my chest, and then I'm ready to meet my in-laws.

The girl who opens the door is in her mid-twenties, with strawberry blond hair tumbling past her shoulders and huge blue eyes, wearing a linen blazer paired with wide-legged jeans. Though she's not quite as tall as Wouter, there's an undeniable resemblance in the angles of their features.

"Hi, I'm Roos!" she says, and given the sheer wattage of her smile, I'm positive no one else has been more excited to see me in the history of my life. What's more, it seems *genuine*. She needs to bend down for the customary Dutch greeting: three kisses on alternating cheeks. "So amazing to finally meet you. Wouter has told us . . . well, he used to talk about you all the time, but it's been a while!" An easy laugh as she pats me on the shoulder. "But I'm very much looking forward to getting to know you."

He used to talk about you all the time.

All Wouter told me was that his family knew about our relationship. That's not quite the same thing as talking about me all the time. Next to me, he rubs at the back of his neck, determinedly not making eye contact.

"Dani," I say. "It's great to be here. This might be one of the most charming cities I've ever seen."

Roos expertly raises one eyebrow. She doesn't have a reaction to my port-wine stain, either because she's seen pictures of me or because it really doesn't faze her. "I'll have to tell the mayor you said that. She lives on the next block."

Footsteps, and then Wouter's mother appears at the door. She has the same dark blond hair, thinner and streaked with gray; large glasses; an inscrutable expression. And the height—I've married into a family of giants.

Of course they're going to be suspicious. I'm the outsider, the American interloper. And even though this is fake, I desperately want them to like me.

"My apologies, I had a pot that just started boiling," she says, her accent much more pronounced than her kids'. When her eyes land on me, she gives a hesitant smile. My face heats up more than it usually does when I'm meeting new people, because now I'm intensely aware that she's assessing me, and I can't help wondering what she might consider a flaw. My birthmark. My slight stature. The way I'm dressed, or the way I speak.

I've never been as self-conscious about any of it as I am right now.

"Mam, this is Danika," Wouter says. "Or Dani, but I've always liked Danika. Sounds like it could be Dutch."

"You're still the only one who calls me that," I say, and somehow it manages to sound like this is an in-joke we've had for years. I even catch Roos biting back a smile.

His mom leans in for the three cheek kisses. "Aangenaam, Dani. I'm Anneke." Her gaze lands on the ring on my finger, and she gives a nod of approval. "Very classic. At least Wouter had good taste—that hasn't always been true."

Wouter lets out a dramatic groan. "Is this about the year I refused to wear anything but sweatpants to school?"

"Of course it is." Roos clasps my arm and lowers her voice to a conspiratorial whisper. "Don't worry, I have pictures."

Anneke gives Wouter a ruffle of his hair. "That was only a year? It felt so much longer."

"Fair warning," Wouter says to me, "this is going to be a *lot* of them teasing me."

"All the more reason to be excited," I say as we step inside and I unzip my boots. "Your house is lovely."

"Thank you so much." Anneke gestures to my skirt. "I like your . . ." She fumbles around as though searching for the right word. "Panty."

Panic flares through me.

"Sorry, my what?" I crane my neck over my shoulder, wondering if this is her way of telling me my underwear is showing. I guess it's not impossible I accidentally tucked my shirt into my underwear instead of the teal tights I paired with a black skirt, but surely the universe wouldn't do that to me today?

"Panty," Anneke repeats, louder this time.

Wouter has turned a deep shade of scarlet. "It's Dutch for 'tights,'" he says to me, motioning to my legs. "Pantyhose."

"Oh. Guess my class hasn't covered that yet." Then, to Anneke: "Dank je wel."

"'Panties' in English is underwear, Mam," Roos offers helpfully, and I'm grateful she's the one explaining it instead of her brother.

Then it's Anneke's turn to cover her hand with her mouth, muffling a laugh. "Ah. I assure you, not what I meant," she says as she takes our coats, hanging them in a shallow closet. "You're taking Dutch classes, Dani?"

I allow myself to relax as I tell her more about them. I love the rules and the pronunciation, learning which sounds you drop at the end of a word and which ones you emphasize. It's challenging, of course, but I think I've needed that.

Even if part of me is worried it's just another hobby I'm going to abandon a few months from now.

Wouter's grandmother is in an armchair in the adjoining living room, a cozy space with one wall painted blue and plants dangling from the ceiling. A tall bookshelf is filled with all manner of knickknacks, along with some framed family photos.

Wouter greets her with a gentle hug before introducing me in Dutch. I only catch a few words.

"Aangenaam," his grandmother says in a sturdier voice than I'm expecting, and then points to herself. "Maartje." She's small and soft-featured, her hair a cloud of white-blond wisps. A knitted blanket is draped over her lap, and on top of that, a sudoku book.

"So nice to meet you. Thank you so much for having me over." I lost both my grandmothers when I was very young and a grandfather just last year. My only remaining grandparent is in a retirement home in Sherman Oaks, and being here with Wouter's grandmother makes me want to call him up the moment I get home.

His grandmother says something in Dutch again, and Wouter translates. "She says this happened very fast. But she can understand sometimes that's how it goes when you're really in love, and she and my grandfather knew right away that they were meant for each other."

This is where we really have to sell it. Wouter slips his arm around me, though not before he lifts his eyebrows to confirm it's okay. I give him a slight nod as his hand comes to rest at my waist.

I lean in, placing a hand on his chest just long enough to feel the rise and fall of a single breath, wishing my lungs had that same steadiness. "Your grandson is very special, but I'm sure you know that," I say, and Wouter translates again. "We fell in love thirteen years ago and never stopped thinking about each other."

"Lunch in about fifteen minutes," Anneke calls, moving into the adjoining kitchen to finish up. A warm, savory aroma already fills the house.

Roos volunteers herself to give me a tour. She has this frenetic kind of energy, like if you touched her, you might get zapped—and her lack of judgment is so opposite what I was expecting that I probably wouldn't mind it at all. The house isn't large or showy; there are bedrooms for his mother and grandmother, a guest room for Roos or Wouter when they're visiting, and just one bathroom. I wonder if there's some strangeness there: Wouter took over his childhood home that no longer resembles where he grew up, while his family moved farther away, to this house that doesn't have as many memories in its walls.

"I wish I could see what the Prinsengracht house looked like when you were kids," I say, and the siblings exchange a grin before leading me back to the kitchen, where a photo wall separates it from the living room.

The collage is a burst of nostalgic joy: baby photos and awkward preteen years and vacations and everything in between. Wouter as a baby with tufts of strawberry blond hair, peeking out from a crib. Dragging a paintbrush along a canvas in the room that's now our kitchen. Roos dressed as a fairy, spread out on her back on the apartment's treacherous stairs. Their father holding a birthday cake. Kissing their mother on the cheek. A trip to Disneyland Paris, the kids wearing mouse ears and posing with Mickey and Pluto.

"This is precious," I say, pointing to a picture of toddler Roos and what must be a five- or six-year-old Wouter missing his two front teeth. "You two were the cutest kids."

"Here's his sweatpants phase, as promised." Roos gestures to photos of a ten- or eleven-year-old Wouter at a backyard party, goofing off with friends, giving a presentation at school—all in the same frayed pair of navy joggers. "And a series of increasingly bad haircuts to go along with them. Didn't Dad threaten to burn them?"

"They were comfortable," Wouter says in protest. "Oh—and here's our parents on their first King's Day together. Or I guess it was Queen's Day back then." He points to a photo of a twenty-something Anneke dressed all in orange, with Wouter's father next to her in a giant orange hat and a feather boa. Now that I'm seeing their parents this much younger, Roos looks more like Anneke while Wouter has his father's intense eyes and broad shoulders.

"I think it's my favorite photo," Roos says.

Wouter goes quiet for a moment. Reverent. "Mine, too."

I don't realize until he says it that this is what I wanted when I moved in. A deeper understanding of this family and their history.

Anneke says something in Dutch, calling Roos into the kitchen, leaving me alone with Wouter.

He inches closer, ducks his head. "You're doing great," he whispers with a palm on my lower back, as though he knows I needed the confirmation.

Then he strides into the kitchen to help his mother and sister set the table. It lingers, the phantom heat of his hand pressed to my sweater. The slight twitch of his fingertips.

"Is there anything I can do?" I ask, feeling slightly useless, but his mother just gives an adamant shake of her head.

When we sit down to eat, Maartje gestures to the ceramic baking dish in the middle of the table. "Stamppot. Very, very Dutch."

Anneke offers a more thorough explanation: "It's potatoes and vegetables mashed together—'stamped'—all in one pot, with sausage on top. I use kale, carrots, and onions. It's very wholesome in the winter, which always lasts longer than any of us want it to. Much more common for dinner, but we thought you needed to experience it."

"And I certainly can't cook it," Wouter says, which makes Roos nod vigorously in agreement. "Not the way my mom does."

I'm so touched by this that I could almost ignore the rush of guilt that comes with it. They're treating me so nicely, too nicely—and of course they are. They don't know the truth.

After a chorus of "eet smakelijk," we dig in. The dish is hearty and savory, something I imagine would be even better in the colder months, and I make sure to tell Wouter's mother how much I like it. Everyone else murmurs their approval, and for a couple minutes, the only sound is the scrape of forks on plates.

"We know so much and yet very little about you," Anneke says.

Now that we're all in the same room, it immediately becomes clear that she's more suspicious than Maartje. "We're all so curious. You've only been in Amsterdam since January?"

Wouter and I agreed we wouldn't mention my company's collapse in front of his family. "Yes. I'm a UX designer—a startup brought me over here." Technically not a lie.

"That's very interesting." Anneke dabs her mouth with a napkin. "It doesn't sound like the kind of thing you would need to leave the States to do."

Roos slants her mother a disbelieving look as she reaches for more sausage. "Are you serious? Companies here are always trying to poach talent from abroad. We just hired an American developer last month."

I give her a silent thank-you.

"She's very talented," Wouter says, his free hand coming up to rest on the back of my chair. If my hair were longer, he'd be touching it. "Has a great eye. Isn't that right, lief?"

Lief. A Dutch term of endearment, I'm guessing. Even without knowing the meaning, I can feel the sweetness there—or at least the performance of it.

He's good at this.

I force my lips upward, as though this is a game we play all the time: who can compliment the other the most. "Just as talented as you are at taking people's pain away."

Wouter's grandmother says something in Dutch, and the rest of them laugh.

"She said your hair is very beautiful," Wouter translates for me, "and that she hopes our children inherit it from your side of the family." He clutches the thinning patch of hair at the back of his head. "Low blow, Oma."

Anneke takes this opportunity to switch to Dutch for Wouter, too rapid for me to catch anything but a preposition here and there.

That furrow appears between Wouter's brows as he answers her before switching languages again.

"Can we keep it in English?" he asks, and his mother's mouth forms a harsh line.

"It's just so romantic that you two found each other again after all those years," Roos says, and then turns to her mother. "You remember how he used to talk about her."

Anneke nods, and if she's doing it begrudgingly, I can't tell. "His face would just light up. You know, I can't recall if he's ever reacted that strongly to anyone else."

"I'm sure that's not true," I put in, a little overwhelmed by all the attention. There's that tightening in my chest again, and I lift an arm to cough into my elbow. If I can just calm myself down, I can avoid the worst-case scenario. Hopefully.

But Roos won't let it go. "He said no one made him laugh the way you did. That you just *got* him. It always seemed cruel that there was too much distance for you to give it a real shot."

He told them it was the distance that split us apart? Even if that's likely what would have happened if we'd continued the relationship, something isn't matching up, but his mother and sister have no reason to lie to me about this.

They're painting a picture of someone lovesick, while I was on the other side of the world certain he'd forgotten about me.

I raise my eyebrows at Wouter. "Really," I say as he busies himself with his stamppot. "What—what else did he say about me?" It's a struggle to get the words out through a rush of breathlessness, and when I try to take in more air, I can't fill my lungs.

"That you were completely shameless," Wouter says. "Not a hint of modesty."

I try to laugh, but the pressure in my chest is getting harder to ignore. Heat rushes to my cheeks in a violent coughing fit, everyone turning to face me.

"Are you all right, Dani?" Anneke asks, and in that moment, it becomes apparent that no, I am not all right.

I am having an asthma attack. In the middle of lunch. At my fake in-laws' house.

I turn to Wouter, hoping the panic in my eyes is enough to communicate what my words might not be able to. "I—I can't breathe," I rasp out. I'm desperate for air, but it's as though I'm breathing through the thinnest straw, unable to suck in enough of it.

He drops his fork with a clatter. "Where's your inhaler?"

All I can do is helplessly point to the foyer of the house, where I left my bag. He shoves out his chair and makes a mad dash for it.

"Do you need some privacy? Take her into the guest room," Anneke says when Wouter returns, and he guides me down the hall and into the first room on the left with superhuman urgency, an arm around my shoulders.

Gently, he helps me onto the bed as I wheeze. Gives the inhaler a shake and passes it to me. I grip it with trembling hands, pressing down and trying to breathe as slowly and deeply as I can.

Wouter sits next to me while still giving me enough space, projecting a sense of calm. His breaths are steady, the slow, thoughtful inhales and the deepest exhales.

"You're going to be okay," he says softly. The same way he did in the bathroom when we were seventeen. "I'm right here breathing with you."

Thirteen years, and he still knows exactly what to do.

As I take another puff, he runs a hand down my hair. A quick motion, something he's probably barely thinking about, and yet it's more soothing than it has any right to be. Slowly, slowly, I feel my muscles relax and I can gulp in more air.

"That's it. You're doing amazing."

"At breathing?" I say when I can finally speak, and this makes his mouth quirk in the smallest smile.

Then he shudders out a long breath of his own, his shoulders leaping with the effort of it, almost as though he kept his anxiety at bay for my sake. I see it so clearly now, the kind of caregiver he must have been for his father.

I let out a groan as I bury my face in my hands. "I can't believe they had to see me like that," I say, peeking out from behind my fingers. "Terrible timing."

"Why would they judge you for having an asthma attack? You can't help it."

"I know, it's just—not the first impression I wanted to make." Another deep breath. Air is wonderful. Air is everything.

"We can go home, if you want. They'll understand." *God*, the concern is still written all over his face, from the crease between his brows to the slight downward turn of his mouth.

"No, no. I want to stay."

He nods as he stretches out his legs on the white duvet, and I let myself do the same. Husband and wife sprawled on a tiny bed and explicitly not touching.

"You scared me," he says with a lopsided smile. "I thought I'd stay calm if it happened here, but . . . for a moment there, it was really fucking terrifying."

"You *were* calm. You were perfect." This close, I can feel the heat buzzing at the surface of his skin. "You were so fast, too—thank you. And I'm fine! That's the first attack I've had in months."

Still, he's looking at me with genuine relief, and something about a six-foot man being frightened for me . . . it lands in a strange place in my heart. Aside from my parents, I've never experienced anything like this. Anyone this protective.

It almost makes me wish he'd stroke my hair again.

"What did your mom say to you in Dutch?" I ask.

"We don't have to talk about that."

"Oh god. I can handle it," I say, bracing myself for the worst.

"It's not bad. She's not unsupportive," he starts, "but she wants to understand. She said that if we did this just for us, without a ceremony or party, and if that was truly what we wanted, then she supports it. I told her we wanted something small, without any of the fanfare. We didn't want it to be a big deal."

"Right."

"So she's just a little sad none of the family could be there. That they couldn't celebrate with us."

I can understand that—I imagine occasions like this took on a different meaning after his father passed away.

"I'm sorry," I say around the guilt. "I hope I didn't make anything uncomfortable between all of you?"

He shakes his head, not quite meeting my eyes. "They just— they want to make sure you really care about me?" He says this with a laugh, even phrases it as a question, as though this part has never been important to him.

And then I can't stop myself—I lay a hand on his arm. Graze his elbow with my thumb. His skin goes taut beneath my touch, and I'm quick to move my hand away. Right. No one's watching us. We don't have to perform when we're alone.

"I do," I say gently.

That, at least, isn't a lie.

ONCE WOUTER'S CERTAIN MY LUNGS AREN'T GOING TO tense right back up, Anneke and Maartje ask if they can talk to him alone in the backyard while Roos joins me in the guest room.

She tells me about her job: she works in marketing for an Amsterdam attractions site. "So I basically get to pretend to be a tourist every day. If there's ever something you want to do, I can probably get you in for free." Then she wants to know all about growing up in LA. "Is it just like *The O.C.*?"

"Yes," I joke, "only everyone's even hotter in real life."

"I knew it. I knew they were only putting the uggos on TV."

"My parents weren't in entertainment, but plenty of my friends' parents were. The food is great, the beaches are great, but I don't miss sitting in traffic. And the air didn't agree with my lungs, so I tried to stay inside as much as possible during wildfire season." I gesture around the room. "You didn't mind it when they moved to Culemborg?"

"I love it, actually," she says. "I can relive my childhood at my brother's apartment, even if he's made some very boring decor choices, and when I want to relax, I come down here."

We hear the screen door open and shut.

"Should we go outside and see if they're gossiping about us?" Roos asks, and I fight a laugh because they're almost certainly gossiping about me.

On our way there, Roos swings by the kitchen for a bottle of champagne and a pair of glasses. Her mother is right behind her with three more.

"A toast!" Roos declares once we're all outside, popping open the bottle and pouring some for each of us. "To Wouter and Dani. Op het bruidspaar!"

Wouter turns to me, sheepish, and the expectation dawns on me a split-second later than it should.

They're waiting for us to kiss.

I am a colossal idiot for not anticipating this. For not preparing, though I'm not sure any length of time could prepare me for the tentative way Wouter bites down on his lower lip. We were able to avoid it at city hall because there were so many other people waiting to sign their own marriage certificates. After we exchanged rings, we fell into an awkward hug, and that was that. No one banged silverware against a champagne flute and demanded anything more.

Now he once again asks for my permission with a lift of his brows, even after we established we were fine with *anything short of mauling.* Which of course, of fucking course, would include kissing.

Still, it means something that he checks in with me. That he doesn't just go for it. I answer him by stepping forward just as he dips his head, my heart hammering against my rib cage.

Wouter van Leeuwen is about to kiss me for the first time in thirteen years.

With an audience.

He floods my senses—the soap I see in the bathroom every day, the peppermint shampoo—and because he is so *close* in this moment, my mind goes completely blank. There is only him, an overwhelming dizziness and his hand poised on my cheek as he tips my face upward.

His lips brush against mine so briefly that by the time I close my eyes, it's over.

All of them clap, and Roos holds two fingers to her mouth and lets out a whistle. I pull back, slightly dazed, my lips warm with the memory of him. It was only a peck, wasn't it? Barely a kiss. And yet it's enough for them to believe it, all of us clinking glasses and sipping champagne.

Maybe it's because, more than anything, they *want* to believe it. This family has already had so much tragedy, and all I want is to give them something good.

Even if it has to be wrapped in a lie.

"Maybe—maybe we could still celebrate," I say as an idea forms, remembering what Wouter said in the guest room. "Nothing big, just the immediate family and friends. A little party?"

Anneke's features soften, a new calm on her face. "That sounds wonderful," she says, and so much of the tension I've been holding on to since we left Amsterdam eases from my body. Wouter smiles too, that dimple showing up for at least the twentieth time today— and if his cheeks are flushed, it must be from the champagne.

If mine are, I'm sure his family will think it's just that newlywed glow.

Roos turns to me. "Dani and I could go dress shopping!" she says, and I wish I didn't love the sound of that so much.

"Is there any chance your parents would be able to join us?" Anneke asks.

"I'm not sure," I say, the lie bitter on my tongue. "It's not easy for them to take time off work. You know how Americans are with their vacation days."

"We'll take a million pictures," Roos promises, with a kindness that tugs at my heart. "It'll be very gezellig."

"What's that?" I ask.

Wouter's arm is around my back again, and it's too easy to lean into the solid heat of his chest. *I tend to be a very touchy person*, he said that first night in the apartment. Because this is just who he is. Because it doesn't mean anything.

"There's no direct translation," he says. "It's the relaxed time you spend with friends and family in a cozy, comfortable place. A feeling of togetherness."

Roos continues, "So a party can be gezellig, or an intimate gathering, or a night out at a bar with friends."

"Gezellig," I repeat, and she shakes her head.

"The Dutch *G* is not an easy one," she says, and then demonstrates. "It's more guttural, and it comes from the back of your throat."

Wouter gestures to his mouth, and I definitely did not need a reason to look at his lips again. "You have to blow out the air as you're saying it. *Gezellig.*"

"They picked the least cozy word to mean the coziest thing," Roos adds.

I say it a few more times, my tongue tripping over the *G* until both of them beam at me.

"Perfect," Wouter says, fingertips skimming up my spine. "Now you're really becoming Dutch."

Thirteen

· · · · · · · · · · · ·

I WAKE TO AN APARTMENT COVERED IN POST-IT NOTES.

Koelkast is scribbled on a yellow square stuck to the refrigerator. *Wasbak* on the sink. *Hond* on George Costanza's collar, along with dozens of others, tiny neon scraps of paper looking like it rained confetti.

All in Wouter's handwriting—small, precise letters.

"Wouter," I say, and then I can't think of any other words. Not in English, and not in Dutch. It's incredibly sweet, the fact that he did all of this for me, and he's leaning expectantly against the kitchen counter like he's worried I may not like it—when nothing could be further from the truth.

"I'm not quite done." He jots something on the pad of Post-its, peels it off, and sticks it right on the tip of my nose.

He lingers in front of me for a moment longer than he should, his citrus scent much too powerful for eight o'clock in the morning. That soap company really ought to change their recipe. I imagine him waking up early, getting the idea in the shower, tapping the

Sharpie on his chin while he decided which words to include in my vocabulary lesson.

Once he steps back, I reach to pull off the Post-it with a slightly shaky hand.

Vrouw, it says.

Wife.

"Ha," I say, trying to ignore the strange tug in my chest. "Believe it or not, that was one of the first ones I learned."

What happened in Culemborg threw my mind into chaos. Wouter coaching me through that asthma attack only made him more attractive, like learning the hot jock has a secret heart of gold. I need to see him doing something entirely unappealing. Kicking a baby lamb. Winning a hot-dog-eating contest. Losing a hot-dog-eating contest.

We haven't talked about the kiss, and the simple explanation is that it didn't mean anything. It was chaste. Brief. Just for show. Unfortunately, my lizard brain can't stop replaying those few seconds his lips were on mine.

We are a ping-pong game of off-limits—my house, and now his. And it isn't that I want him to be *on*-limits . . . it's that I can't figure out why I devote so much time to thinking about it. *He hurt you*, I always remind myself, begging that lizard brain to listen to logic, because our only-on-paper marriage has no room for complication.

I thought the heartbreak had healed, a wound scarred over by force and then by time. Now I realize all those years were just a temporary salve, because being in his presence, knowing how he makes his tea and where he stores his toothbrush, replaces all the mystery with a fierce ache—not of wanting him now but of wanting what we could have had.

Quiet weekend mornings like this: something I didn't even have the range to dream about.

Then, as Wouter warned, there's the fact that the apartment needs a bit of work. I set my mug on the counter and open up one of the kitchen cabinets—and the handle comes off in my hand.

"Ah, shit," Wouter says when I hold it up. "Fixed that a few months ago. I'll try to take care of it after work next week."

"I could do it, if you want."

He waves this off, passes me a mug of tea. "Nah, I don't want you to have to worry about it."

What I don't say: that I like this place, and I want to put the same kind of care into it that he does.

Then again, it isn't going to be mine forever.

I take a seat at the table and add sugar to my tea. Today I planned a surprise, wholly platonic outing for us, and later we're meeting up with his friends. He asked me a dozen times if I was comfortable with it—they've been badgering him, but he hasn't wanted to throw me to the wolves. The thrill of finally getting to know the people he spends his free time with was almost immediately canceled out by the fact that they don't want to meet the real version of me.

They want to meet Danika Dorfman, Wouter's wife. His long-lost love.

"You want some hagelslag?" Wouter asks, still rummaging around in the kitchen.

"Are those the little sprinkles?"

With his hair shower-damp and face unshaven again, he looks so soft, this side of him that isn't ready to face the world just yet. There's even a smudge of Sharpie on the side of one palm. "I haven't had them in years, but I was inspired at the market yesterday." He holds up a box and gives it a shake, mouth tilting into a smile. "I figured you wouldn't say no to sprinkles for breakfast. There's a lot of debate on the proper way to make it," he continues, pulling out two pieces of wheat bread Post-it-noted *volkoren* and spreading butter onto them with the utmost concentration. "But don't listen to anyone else. The butter is nonnegotiable—that's how the sprinkles stay put. And you shouldn't fold the bread, either, or it'll get everywhere."

He upends the box of hagelslag, raining chocolate sprinkles over the two slices. Then he passes one to me.

"Twelve out of ten," I say after biting into it. "Absolutely inspired. What will the Dutch think of next?"

"I'm almost scared to ask how your teeth are when sugar is seventy percent of your diet."

I bare them at him in my widest grin. "Never had a cavity."

AMSTERDAM-NOORD IS A NORTHERN SLICE OF THE CITY across from the IJ River—pronounced *eye*, and I know this only because I too-confidently said "I-J River" when we got off the ferry a few minutes ago. Ahead of us is A'DAM Tower, a skyscraper with a giant swing perched on the edge of the building. Not where we're going, but it's the closest I've been to it so far, and it confirms that you could not pay me enough money to do that.

This area used to be mostly industrial, but now it's more of an up-and-coming neighborhood, with unique restaurants and breweries in converted warehouses—and plenty of art.

"I've never been here," Wouter says when we get to the STRAAT Museum, mouth kicking up just slightly, like he's trying to hide his excitement. "Two months in Amsterdam, and you're already showing me something new."

The museum is devoted to street art and graffiti, murals splashed across concrete walls and suspended from high ceilings, and beyond-life-size sculptures made of found objects. We wander through the colorful first room, pausing to read the descriptions beside each piece, but Wouter looks a little uncomfortable, fidgeting with his hands. "Danika . . . you've been settling in okay here, yes?"

"A little late to take everything back if I'm not, isn't it?" I say. "Hopefully I'm not a terrible roommate?"

"Only when you didn't tell me my shirt was on inside out before I left for work last week."

"It was early! I was still waking up," I protest.

"I just wanted to make sure," he says, becoming serious again. "It's a huge change, and I've been worried that maybe I haven't been checking in with you enough. About . . . everything."

If there's anything Wouter's good at, it's checking in with me, and I'm never not grateful for it. "Obviously it's an adjustment, but the day-to-day isn't as hard as I thought it might be. Except for being away from everyone back home."

"You miss your sister."

"All the time." Somehow, saying it makes that stab of homesickness all the more intense, a visceral longing between my ribs. Until I got here, I didn't realize you could be homesick for a person. "It's the longest I've ever spent away from her, and I'm lucky that she's a night owl and we can talk with some regularity, but . . . it's not the same."

"Hmm. She sent you an American care package. What if you sent her a Dutch one? You could give her some stroopwafels, some tulip knickknacks, some blue-and-white pottery . . . and they have Gouda cheese in vacuum-sealed bags that's safe to travel." He coughs into his elbow. "Of course you don't have to replicate, ah, everything she sent. Unless you wanted to."

"I love that idea. Well—the first part. Thank you," I say, meaning it. "It's weird, though. I'll get the most ridiculous cravings for American food. Like, the other day I was randomly missing Pop-Tarts even though I haven't had them in years." We move forward to the next piece of art, a geometric black-and-white optical illusion. "But aside from Pop-Tarts, it's just hard not to feel like I left things . . . unfinished, I guess."

"With your ex?"

That is not at all what I was expecting to hear, and the laugh that bursts out of me is so loud, a few people turn to look at us. "Oh, no. No, no, no. That is most certainly finished. In the most disastrous way possible."

He lifts his brows as though urging me to continue, eyes bright behind his glasses, and I wish curiosity weren't so cute on him. I sigh, preparing to tell the whole sordid story.

"We worked together, and we'd been dating for almost a year. And then a few months ago, I got a screenshot from one of my sister's friends . . . who'd matched with him on Tinder."

"No fucking way."

I nod miserably. "When I confronted him about it, he gave me some bullshit about having forgotten to delete his accounts, even though it showed he'd been active within the past week. He had all these messages, these photos from other women, photos he'd sent them . . ."

I think back to the shock of those pictures of half-undressed strangers. He was always saying he wanted sexy pictures of me, but I was too afraid they'd end up somewhere I didn't want them. Even after a year of dating, I didn't fully trust him.

And yet I'd almost been ready to say *I love you*—not because I did but because it seemed like I was supposed to. I was pretty sure I *could*, if I had more time.

After I saw the photos, Jace thought we could still make the relationship work. *You said at the beginning that you liked to keep things casual*, he said. *Maybe we can just do that?* But he didn't understand. I couldn't go backward, not after I'd already broken all my rules. The cheating had confirmed I wasn't worth a serious relationship, that I'd been right to keep all the others at a distance.

"Maybe you don't want to hear all of that," I say to Wouter.

He takes a step forward, his gaze piercing mine, feeling not dissimilar to the way his fingers pressed into the back of my neck. "Why wouldn't I? We're friends."

We're so many other things: exes, roommates, husband and wife. Somehow *friends* feels the most foreign.

"My big fuck-you was sending around his emails to the whole office." Maybe it was out of character for me, but he'd made me feel so small, so insignificant. I hated that I couldn't fight back. "We probably shouldn't have, but we'd sent some . . . racy stuff to each other while we worked there." At that, Wouter blushes, and I drop my voice lower. "And then I got fired, while he got promoted last week, according to LinkedIn. The worst part," I continue, gaining more momentum now, "is that not even my friends were on my side about it. They thought I'd been stupid and impulsive, that I lost the job because of my own bad decision. And . . . fine, okay, maybe I was. I guess they've all grown out of their pettiness, but not me. Guess we're all supposed to be boring adults now," I finish, though of course there's a whole spectrum between boring adult and someone who doesn't mass-forward their ex's emails to their whole team.

"As a boring adult," he says, "I'm on your side here. You're allowed to be petty at any age."

"Nah, you're not boring. You're conning the Dutch government. If that's not badass, I don't know what is."

Though he allows a small smile at this, his jaw ticks with what I think might be anger toward this man he's never met. "What a piece of shit. You deserved so much better."

"Yeah, well. Half-true."

"You don't believe that?"

"I told you," I say, wondering why my voice sounds thinner than it did a second ago, "I haven't done serious relationships. Clearly I'm not cut out for them."

We're standing too close, and I'm sure it's only because I wanted to keep this conversation both quiet and private, and he needed to be able to hear me. I can see his strawberry lashes almost brushing the lenses of his glasses. And there's the scent of his soap again, invading my brain.

I back away. Clear my throat. "Besides," I say, with a flutter of my ring finger, "I'm married now. So I'm off the market."

We continue making our way through the museum. Not everything is designed to be aesthetically pleasing, and I like that—that messy, rebellious art has a home here. The abstract shapes and the realistic figures, the blocky text and the canvases that look like they're dripping paint. Wouter spends a while in front of a piece that features a man in gray scale pulling back a curtain to reveal a brightly colored wall of graffitied words bursting to get free.

"I was reading about this one online," I say, and without even needing to glance at the description: "Martin Whatson, Norwegian artist. He has a whole series of work like this, where he mimics the urban environment in order to contrast it with the vibrant nature of street art." A sigh slips out. "If only I could get a job spouting obscure facts about Amsterdam."

"The job search isn't as fruitful as you'd like?"

I consider this. Are there jobs out there that suit my skill set? Sure. Does a single one of them fill me with anything but dread? That's a harder question to answer.

"I had a phone interview a couple days ago." A big tech company based in the US that also has offices in Amsterdam. Maybe I was out of practice, but I stumbled my way through basic questions and ended the call uncertain how I'd ever been hired for anything. "Not sure how well it went."

"But you're still looking," he says, phrasing it not as a question but as a declarative statement. I'm still looking, because that's what I'm supposed to be doing. The reason he married me.

"Of course. I don't know, maybe I'm just burned out." I say this half as a joke, so I'm surprised when he responds with pure seriousness.

"You don't have to brush it off like that. Burnout is very real," he says. "Here we even have burnout leave."

I've never considered the word before, because the only extended time I ever took off from work was when I checked myself into the hospital. What I don't tell him is that sometimes I feel rudderless, that it's almost a scary amount of freedom I have here. There's nothing but a marriage certificate to catch me if I fall.

"I can tell UX design isn't your life's great passion," he continues. "You used to enjoy everything, though. You tried it all. I liked that about you, that openness you had."

The words scrape against my skin like gravel. Because maybe he liked that about me for a short time, but once he got back to Amsterdam, he realized that what he liked didn't matter or that he'd never liked it all that much in the first place.

I have to keep reminding myself he's no longer the carefree teenager who pushed me up against the wall to kiss me when my parents were downstairs, who showed me sketches of myself I couldn't believe could be that beautiful.

It's deeply unfair that all my memories of him are tender, hot, or both.

"When I studied it, I didn't imagine spending the next forty years doing it," I say. "For a while I thought I'd study something related to art, but it didn't feel practical. I mean, I still love museums, and I've always spent too much time deciding what to put on my walls, but I never let myself just *play* the way I used to. Maybe we both thought that we had to give it up and get serious about something else."

"I miss that." His voice is so soft, the draft in this warehouse could carry it away. "The playing. The day you moved in and asked about art and I said I had other hobbies . . . I went upstairs and racked my brain, wondering what other hobbies there really were. When we went to Van Gogh, I realized I hadn't been to a museum in years. Aside from walking George and getting drinks with friends, the occasional football match . . . it's possible I've been in a rut."

I wish that didn't make my heart ache—it would be so much easier if it didn't. He had been so starry-eyed and hopeful when I knew him, and the truth is that he returned to what I thought was this fairy-tale country and retreated entirely into himself. Spent his twenties taking care of his father, and when he finally came up for air, the grief must have been the heaviest weight.

Without overthinking, I place my fingertips on his sleeve, give him a quick brush of my thumb. This time, unlike in his mother's guest room, he doesn't pull away. "Maybe we could have some hobbies together," I offer, because I've certainly never been a stranger to them. Hobbies are safe. Hobbies are platonic. "We could make art without caring about whether it's good or not."

He smiles at this. "I think I'd really like that." Then he clears his throat, and I drop my hand. "Can I ask you something? I have this work conference next weekend in Bruges—Belgium. It's only a few hours away by train. I was considering canceling, but then I was thinking, you haven't been, and Roos is always begging to watch George more often because she's convinced, probably correctly, that she's his favorite person. Though you might be giving her a run for her money. And it's a beautiful city . . ." Now he's the one tongue-tied, whipping off his glasses to rub them against his shirt as though hoping it'll distract from his rambling. And it does, if only because of how soft his face looks without them. "Would you want to come with me?"

"Come . . . with you? To Belgium? For a physiotherapy conference?" The words rush out before I can overanalyze them. "Absolutely, yes. Let's go to Belgium."

"Great," he says, sounding relieved. "I really think you'll love it."

His gaze holds mine a beat too long while my pulse falls into an uncertain rhythm. I try not to think about the constellations I could draw in his pattern of freckles, or how much I like the faint lines on his face he didn't have at seventeen, the ones with stories I haven't been around to hear.

There might be something else between us, something either unresolved or wholly new. In this moment, I'm not sure I can tell the difference.

I'm not sure I want to.

WOUTER REACHES FOR MY HAND ON THE WAY INTO THE bar, and at first I'm so startled by it that I nearly yank my arm away. But then I understand: we're about to put on another performance.

"Just so you know," he says, "my friends are going to give me a lot of shit for not introducing you earlier, but that's just how they express their love."

"To be clear, I would also be giving a lot of shit if one of my friends got married without telling me."

It hits me again, that guilt, because he's the one carrying all the weight. I can't imagine lying to Phoebe if the situation were reversed. Then again, the real estate market is broken everywhere. Who knows what I'd do if a house like his was on the line?

I thread my fingers through his while we wait for a table with his friends: Sanne, a girl who also grew up on the Prinsengracht; Thomas, a close friend since grade school; Bilal, a college friend whose parents immigrated to Rotterdam from Pakistan when he was a toddler; and Evi, who became part of their friend group when she started dating Thomas.

Thomas, who's even taller than Wouter with a wave of slicked-back blond hair, claps him on the arm. "Can't believe you didn't tell us! We would have thrown you a bachelor party."

"It was a surprise to us, too," Wouter says. "But I'm so glad she hit me with her bike, because then we realized we're just as in love with each other now as we were when we were teenagers."

"Even more," I say, reaching for his chin and giving it a little shake in this over-the-top gooey way. *We can do this.* "I just can't get enough of this face."

"So you married me only for my looks?" Wouter asks, mock-offended as he holds a hand to his heart.

I bat my lashes. "What can I say, none of the American boys could do it for me." I drop his chin and clear my throat, turning back to his friends. "I'm going to apologize for not speaking Dutch. Or at least, for speaking very bad Dutch. I'm taking a class right now, and I could talk you through buying groceries or explaining various symptoms to the doctor, but we haven't covered casual pub chats yet."

"Wouter hasn't been teaching you? What a terrible husband," Sanne says, with this easy way of ribbing him that can only be achieved by someone who's been part of your life for that long. She's effortlessly chic in round glasses and a cropped black jacket, long hair parted in the middle.

"No, no, he's been . . . very helpful," I say, thinking back to the Post-its and the way he massaged his language into my skin. *De wervelkolom. Het oor.* I could live to be one hundred, learn a dozen other languages, and I'd never forget those words.

When we finally get a table, the booth only has room for four people with a single extra chair, even after we try our best to hunt down another one.

"She can just sit in your lap, yes?" Sanne says, and at first I assume she's talking to Evi and Thomas.

But her eyes are on Wouter.

She can just sit in your lap.

A normal suggestion for two newlyweds who are madly in love, and exactly the reason I black out for a second.

Wouter rubs at the back of his neck as his eyes find mine, asking with a lift of his brows if that's okay. If this is part of the ruse neither of us knew we signed up for.

And there is something so earnest about that expression, his forehead wrinkle on full anxious display, something that convinces me sitting in his lap can be a wholly innocent thing instead of the very bad idea it is.

"Right. Of course," I say, hoping the words sound breezier than they do in my mind, where it's all anarchy and flashing red lights.

So I slide into the booth and lower myself onto his thighs, about as gingerly as if his friends just suggested I sit on a box of live snakes. One arm comes around my waist, clutching me to him, while the other reaches for his drink.

And then I try to breathe. "You okay?" I ask, fully aware that *I* am not okay. Because I am in his lap, and nothing about this feels innocent. My ass in his crotch. His hand lightly curved around the wool of my sweater. And he's *warm* and sturdy and considerate, the solid wall of his body keeping me upright.

When he lets out a muffled laugh, his breath on the back of my neck makes me shiver. That doesn't feel innocent, either. "Alles goed."

I learn what everyone does: Sanne and Thomas both work at a tech company, Evi is an architect, and Bilal is a teacher—"but more importantly, a Feyenoord fan," he says, gesturing to the beanie he's wearing with the Rotterdam football club's logo.

"And for that, we're all deeply sorry," Wouter says to a chorus of laughs, and I assume there's a rivalry with his beloved Ajax.

I want a million more details about all of them, but they have just as many questions for me.

"I need to know how exactly this"—Sanne gestures to the two of us—"works. Wouter, you're, what, at least twenty centimeters taller?"

Evi gives a suggestive lift of her brows while I choke on my beer. "I love a height difference."

"We . . . get creative," Wouter says, and I can hear the bashful smile in his voice. "It's not as hard as you might think."

Bilal holds up his glass. "Nah, I thought that was the whole point?" he says, which makes Sanne and Evi groan.

At the very least, sitting in his lap means Wouter can't see me blush. *We get creative.* I wonder if he's remembering the two of us in the back seat all those years ago, how difficult it was to find a position that didn't have his head bumping against the roof of the car. The rare times we had the house to ourselves, he'd tuck me up against him in my bed like I was the perfect size. "I love the way you fit right here," he'd say.

If he can play the game, then so can I, so I give his friends my wickedest grin. "And it never seems to matter when I'm on top."

Given where I'm currently positioned, this sparks some laughs and a hoot from Evi. Even Wouter joins in, which means I can feel the vibrations against my back, the puffs of air on my neck.

Thomas holds up his hands. "Okay, okay, let's keep it family friendly."

"We're so curious about *you*," Evi continues. "We've heard about you from Wouter, of course, but what brought you to Amsterdam? And how do you like it?"

I give them the story Wouter and I decided on. I want to be the charming, fascinating girl his friends can believe captured his heart, but I'm deeply distracted by the fact that his thumb is a small swipe from my navel, and that two pairs of jeans is barely any fabric at all. Every time I shift, I'm aware of his sharp inhales and slow exhales, like he's trying to prevent a certain situation from rising up as a result of having a woman in his lap. Surely any attractive girl in this position might test his self-control.

And yet despite all the anxiety and the intense and unexpected glute workout, because I still haven't let my body relax—it feels *good*, sitting in his lap like this. To be this close after thirteen years.

"Sorry," I say when he takes another rough breath, and I wonder if I should recommend the 4-7-8 exercise. "Am I hurting you?"

"No, no," he says quickly. "You're fine, lief."

"What are the biggest differences between America and the Netherlands, do you think?" Sanne asks, and I'm grateful for the subject change.

"Wouter's going to get mad if I bring up the sinks," I say, which draws another round of laughter. I can feel him shake with it beneath me. "The public transportation, obviously. And the air quality here is much better."

It's true—with the exception of that stress-induced asthma attack in Culemborg, I've felt healthier than I have in ages. Long walks around the city don't aggravate my lungs the way short ones did in LA. I never imagined I could have this kind of lifestyle, and it's exciting to realize that I'm capable of it, that my personality wasn't set in stone. That even at thirty, I can change.

"The desserts aren't number one?" Wouter asks.

"I was getting to it!" I say, giving his ribs a gentle jab of my elbow. "I think poffertjes would break America. It's a good thing they don't know about them."

"Evi and I went to New York a few years ago," Thomas says, and she holds a dramatic hand to her heart.

"Still obsessed. It was an architect's dream," she says. "And the subway there was pretty great. Smelled awful, though."

"We have maybe three cities with decent public transportation, where you could legitimately get by without a car. But the vast majority are still car dependent—and it's not any single person's fault for driving one. It's just the way the cities were laid out."

"And everything is so big." Thomas rolls his eyes even as he says it. "Yes, I know that's a cliché, but it's a cliché because it's true. I couldn't believe the size of the portions you'd get at a restaurant."

"LA, too," Wouter says. "Every time we went to dinner with your family, we brought home leftovers."

"I do love leftovers, but you're right. The US always has so much of everything. You can get exhausted by the number of options." I take a sip of beer. "When I go to the grocery store here, sometimes there's only one brand of each thing. Like . . . diced tomatoes."

Bilal looks perplexed. "Why do you need more than one brand of diced tomatoes? You just get whatever they have at Appie."

"In America, you can't set foot in a store without someone rushing over and asking if they can help you," Wouter says. "It took me a while to get used to it. I thought it was sarcastic at first—but it really isn't. They genuinely want to help."

"Here we find that very annoying," Sanne says.

Evi nods. "If someone comes up to me and asks if I need anything, I'm like, 'Uh-huh, sure, thank you,' and then never ask."

"That's one of the stereotypes about Americans, isn't it? That they can seem a little fake?" Sanne says, but there's no animosity in her voice. "There's more small talk. We don't do that as much here." She clears her throat, putting on an exaggerated American accent that sounds more like Cher in *Clueless* than any actual American I've met. "Oh my gosh, how are you? I *love* your shirt. Where did you get it?"

I can't help laughing. "But what if I really do love their shirt?"

"Even the American chains are a little different," Bilal says. "It was a big deal when we got the pumpkin spice latte over here. People lined up for hours. It was madness."

"Look, we don't fuck around about pumpkin spice in the US, either."

This leads to a discussion about Starbucks' holiday drinks, and the ones they have in the Netherlands that they don't have in the US—like the stroopwafel latte, which I fully intend to order the moment it hits the menu. Then Sanne and Evi get up to use the bathroom, and Bilal and Thomas head to the bar for another pitcher and a couple more baskets of bitterballen.

With more space in the booth, I expect Wouter to relax his grip. The alcohol is already messing with me, amplifying some of my senses while muting others. So when he leans in close to my ear and brushes aside my hair, I feel his whisper in every part of my body. "You smell so good," he says, his breath tickling the small hairs on the back of my neck.

My eyes fall shut, my imagination running wild, and I let my muscles go for the first time all evening. If he can sense that I'm giving him my full weight now, he only reacts by sliding me slightly backward, as though to rebalance us.

If we were alone right now, I might test our limits, press myself harder against his lap. Tease him, lift my hips for a moment before sinking back down. I wonder if his hand around my waist would tighten. What other things he might whisper in my ear.

His mouth is so close to my neck, close enough to imagine the slick heat of it against my skin.

"You a lightweight?" I ask. "Because you're, like, eight feet tall, which I think is about five hundred centimeters. Give or take a hundred."

"Maybe." His nose grazes the top of my ear. "Or I'm just very, very stupid." Then, before I can process that: "Finally!" he says as Bilal returns to the table triumphantly holding up another chair. The outburst startles me to my feet, and Wouter practically leaps out of the booth with me. "I mean—Danika's probably eager to have her own seat."

"I was actually having a great time." I give him a suggestive look that might be just for his friends. As I hoped, they let out a whoop as his cheeks redden.

This isn't real, I remind myself. Whatever I'm feeling for him is warped by proximity and lies, nothing more.

To drown out any lingering doubts, I reach for the pitcher.

At the end of the night, after more drinks than I can count, I wave a wobbly hand around the group. "This has been . . . gezellig." I overpronounce it, giving each syllable far too much emphasis.

Still, all of them light up at the word, and Sanne mimes applauding. "Let's do this again soon," she says, giving me a hug. Then she whispers in my ear, "You two are so cute together. He seems absolutely *obsessed* with you."

All the way home, I marvel at how he must be a much better actor than I am to be able to communicate something like that when I'm not even looking.

Fourteen

· · · · · · · · · · ·

"HOW—DO YOU STAIRS—DRUNK?" I SLUR, MY HEAD SPIN-
ning and the hall seeming to grow tinier and tinier until it's almost
the size of a pinprick. My shoes are impossibly heavy. I let out a
long sigh as I cling to the railing. "How many more flights?"

Wouter places a hand on my shoulder to keep me from back-
sliding. "Just one. Can you make it?"

"No," I say honestly, and before I can even register what's happening, he's bending down, slipping one arm beneath my knees, the
other supporting my back, and it's with a ridiculous amount of ease
that he's able to lift me.

And then my husband is carrying me up the stairs.

I wrap my arms around his neck, hugging myself closer than I
probably need to. His tea-and-citrus scent. The thudding of his
heart. I'm not sure if he had more to drink than I did, but he seems
a hell of a lot steadier.

The rhythmic sound of his exhales as he carries me up, up, up
might be enough to lull me to sleep if every one of my other senses
weren't dramatically heightened.

"Thank you," I say when he places me down on solid ground, feeling somehow wobblier than I did before.

He gives me a goofy little salute, a gesture I've never seen him do sober. "Door-to-door service."

As usual, George Costanza acts as though we've been gone for four months instead of four hours, his tail a blur as he leaps to me and then to Wouter, letting out a garbled little cry of joy. Both of us bend down to give him the love he deserves, and Wouter even gets on the floor to have him roll over for some belly scratches—his favorite. The way they interact is always so pure. Give any man a small dog and he instantly becomes ten times more attractive.

"I know, I know, your parents made some bad decisions tonight," I tell him. "Nightcap?" I ask Wouter as we breeze into the kitchen.

He shakes his head. "No, no, no. We are getting you some water."

"Water. Wouter." In my inebriated state, this is hilarious to me. I repeat it a few more times just to make sure, and yep, still funny. "What does your name mean anyway?"

"It's the Dutch form of the English name Walter. 'Ruler of the army.' And my last name means . . . 'from Leeuwen,'" he says, passing me a glass of water. "Or 'of the lions,' whichever you prefer."

I take a long sip and then wave my glass, pointing it at his chest. "Ruler of the army of lions." God, he's tall. So very tall.

He gazes down at me, hazel eyes bright. "That's me."

George scampers into the living room, where he curls up on the blanket on the couch, despite the presence of his bed in the corner, and I notice a familiar sock tucked underneath the blanket. A few pairs of mine have gone missing, but he's too cute for me to steal them back.

It's late, much later than I've been out in a long time, and yet zero part of me wants to go to sleep. Given the way Wouter lingers in the kitchen, pouring himself a glass of water and leaning back against the counter, I imagine he feels the same.

"That was fun, with your friends." I place my glass on the counter opposite him, a little steadier now that I have some nonalcoholic liquid in me. "I really like them."

"They *loved* you. Evi already texted asking when they can see you again." He grins, rakes a hand through his hair. Somehow this only musses it more. "You know what I remembered the other day? That game we used to play. 'One day, when we have our own apartment . . .'"

"Ah, yes. Our domesticity kink."

One day, when we have our own apartment, one of us would say, and the other would finish the sentence with something we couldn't do at the time but desperately wanted.

We'll play music as loud as we want.

Kiss in every room.

Fall asleep next to each other every night.

"Is it everything you dreamed of?" he wants to know. "Our own apartment?"

Of course, nothing could live up to the fantasy. I mean, we wanted a Jacuzzi in the bedroom and one cabinet entirely devoted to chocolate. "Sure," I say. "At least for the next ten months."

This makes his giddiness falter. I watch his throat as he swallows down another sip of water. So fucking hydrated, this man. From what I can tell, he drinks at least four whole glasses when we're at home, probably that many or more at work. Then there's all the tea. And sure, maybe that's the amount you're supposed to drink, but I've never actually seen someone execute it, and it's a testament to my current mental state that I find this deeply fascinating.

"I know it was different back then," he says. "But what we had when we were seventeen—it was good, wasn't it? Even though it had to be a secret?"

This surprises me. Maybe he turns self-reflective when he

drinks. Back then, I'd been so certain we were on the same page. Those first *I love yous*—*ik van hou jous*—seemed entirely without anguish on both our parts, and maybe it was teenage recklessness, but I never once stopped to question my feelings. I knew in my bones that I loved him, so I said it.

"No. It was *great*. You were so kind. No one had ever made me feel interesting before you," I say. "I never wanted to tell you this because I didn't want you to think I was *too* obsessed with you, but I could have watched you draw for hours."

"I quite like the idea of you being obsessed with me."

"You're a very honest drunk."

He tilts his head, as though looking at me through some new lens. "You know I was obsessed with you, too. Completely smitten. This gorgeous American girl, with her slang and her driver's license. You were so glamorous to me."

This makes me bark out a laugh. "I was not!"

"You were," he insists, laughing too. He takes a step closer, and he must be warm, because he's rolling his sleeves up past his forearms, exposing those muscles that knew exactly what to do with me when I was face down in his office. "Now I have to know. You wore those little shorts just to get me to notice you, didn't you?"

I take an innocent sip of water. Press my lips shut. "I have no idea what you're talking about."

"You didn't have to do it." A final roll of his left sleeve to get the two of them even. "I'd already noticed you. I felt so tortured, having this crush on my host parents' daughter, who was such a fucking knockout."

"I hope I didn't peak back then." Sober Dani pretends she doesn't need compliments. Drunk Dani craves them.

"No. She's even more beautiful now," he says. "I'd get so riled up, knowing you were sleeping right across the hall."

"And I was feeling just as riled up."

God, I love this honest version of him. Now that we've broken the seal on our history, it's suddenly all I want to talk about.

I need to be eye level with him, so I plant my hands on the counter and hop up onto it, pushing scattered Post-its out of the way, *aanrecht* and *fruitmand* and *fornuis*.

"We were so innocent, though. Back then," he says. I lift my eyebrows at him, and he laughs. "Okay, maybe not always. So *young* is maybe what I meant."

"We were," I agree. But maybe *innocent* wasn't wrong, either, because there was a wholesomeness to experiencing all those firsts with him. Every touch felt like it opened up a brand-new universe, every one of his sighs like we were discovering a new star.

He changed his mind about you once, logic reminds me. *What's to stop him from doing that again?*

"If it's my turn to be honest . . ." I continue, because I left logic behind half an hour ago and the tipsiness makes me bold. "You set the bar way too high for my future relationships." All those bad hookups—men who were too aggressive, but I pretended I didn't mind because I loved feeling desired. Men who thought *casual* meant a complete lack of common decency. It was always rushed, rarely tender. "No one has ever touched me like you did."

The blush that spreads across his cheeks is an almost indecent shade of pink. "Oh?" he says, and there's a hint of pride in that single syllable. "How did I touch you?"

The alcohol pounds against my temples, reminding me that I was supposed to be different in Amsterdam, and yet here I am, desperate to fall into bed with a man I've already slept with.

It's been exhausting, pretending this attraction is nothing more than residual teen infatuation amplified by sheer proximity to the person who loved me during the most self-conscious time of my life. It's something new, I can tell. Something electric.

How did I touch you?

"Like you weren't just biding time until the main event," I say. "It felt like you wanted to know how I reacted to every single thing. Like you were memorizing all of it."

"I remember." Without dropping his gaze from mine, he steps toward me. Braces himself on the counter, one hand on either side of my hips. His voice is rough as gravel. "The way you'd hold yourself back sometimes, like you wanted to be quiet even though we were the only people in the house. The way you moaned into my ear—it was my favorite sound. You even bit me a few times, and I think you were shy about it, but I fucking loved it. That probably wrecked me for the next five years."

All the words that don't go straight to my heart land between my thighs with a pulsing want. I bring one leg around his waist to draw him closer, watching the way it plays across his face. A fluttering of his lashes. A heavy exhale. *Yes. This.*

Some of his hair has fallen into his face, and I reach out to push it back, the soft strands slipping through my fingers.

"Bedankt," he says. Slowly, one of his hands inches toward my thigh, dipping into the crease at my hip. The other hand follows, until he's gotten enough of a grip to drag me forward along the counter. The breath stills in my lungs as he pulls me flush against him, my center at his navel, both of my legs wrapped around his back now.

The very first time he touched me, hand inside my underwear, he let out a gasp before I did. I've never been able to forget it. I had my forehead pressed against his shoulder, overwhelmed by the sensation, and he was the one gasping—at least until my vocal cords started working again.

"Do you still do that?" He brings up his hand to rest a fingertip on my collarbone. Gently, as though he's still in full control of his body, he traces the column of my neck. Up to my ear, along my jaw, and then back down. "Bite someone's ear when they're touching you?"

"I . . . don't know." An honest reply. A shaky breath. "Maybe it was just for you."

He swears softly, maybe in English and maybe in Dutch. In this moment, I can't tell the difference. Suddenly it feels as though I haven't been touched in ages. Haven't been kissed. Haven't been properly fucked. My body doesn't care about our history, only the throbbing desire between us, buzzing at the surface of our skin.

When he dips his head, his mouth lands on my neck, warmth and pressure as he follows the path he just charted with his finger. He might as well be scalding me with a match, dragging the tip of it along my skin. A moan is trapped in my throat, one I'm too afraid to let out because *Jesus*, he's still barely touching me. His other hand finds my wedding ring, his middle finger circling the cool metal.

I can sense all the ways he's trying to hold back, because Wouter is not someone who lets himself have good things. He's been so immersed in work that he's denied himself simple pleasures. He's stayed away from art. From sex.

He gives and he gives, the physiotherapist who teaches people to feel good—and just this once, I want him to *take*.

My hands go to his hair again, but this time they dive into it, hard and eager. When I sigh at the heat of his lips on my jaw, I can feel the way it affects him, the effort of his muscles holding himself back. An immovable object taunted by an irresistible force.

I imagine ironing out his tightest spots. Finding all the places that make him moan. I want to know him all over again, use my mouth to map that flash of ink on his shoulder, and I'm no longer sure if it's the alcohol or the illusion of these fucking rings or the way he's looking at me.

He pulls his head back for only an instant, gaze burning mine before our mouths collide.

And *this* is what it's like to kiss him after all these years:

Inevitable.

We're remembering and learning at the same time, a honeyed urgency as we crash into each other again and again. Hands in hair, already breathless. The groan in his throat tells me exactly how good it feels to give in like this, and I tell him the same thing in the way I part my lips for him. He tastes my sighs. Swallows my gasps. I drag him closer by the collar of his shirt while his fingertips dig into my hips—because even with his body aligned with mine, he's not close enough. *More*, I beg with my teeth on his lower lip, and so he bites me right back.

This is nothing like the way we kissed in his family's backyard, a wholesome production that didn't mean anything. This one means something—I'm just not sure what.

With all of him pressed against me, I can feel his hard length through his jeans, a delicious friction as he rolls his hips to mine. There's no self-consciousness, just the rawness of that base instinct, the confession that he doesn't merely want to kiss—he craves relief the way I do. Mouth on my neck. Stubble scraping my skin. I spread my legs wider and rock against him, matching his want in every way I can. Chasing the ache only he can soothe.

Suddenly he draws back with a sharp breath.

"Danika . . . *fuck*." He grits his teeth. Pushes out a sigh, drops his hands from my hips and puts more space between our chests. Like he's going to drag us both away from that cliff's edge even if it kills him. Even if his mouth is still wet and swollen. "We shouldn't—not while we're drunk."

Are we? Is that the buzzy, electric feeling in my veins, or is it idiocy and unbridled lust?

"I'm not—" I start, unable to finish the sentence with *that drunk* because it's decidedly untrue.

"And I wouldn't want to . . . it's been so long . . ."

He wouldn't want to . . . what? Take advantage of me? Do something we'd both regret? Because he's not, and I wouldn't.

Unless he's the one who would.

"I—okay. Okay." This return to reality has my head spinning. He doesn't want me, or he's being a gentleman, or some combination of the two. Except I can only focus on the first option, the devastation of finally having him so close before he ripped himself away.

And yet neither of us moves, as though we're engaged in a silent challenge. Which one of us is going to break, give in, reach for the other?

Our breathing is still rough, his chest heaving with it in the semidark. His glasses are crooked. Hair mussed. That splash of maroon across his cheeks—I'd die to put my mouth on it. Beneath his belt, it's extremely obvious his body wants something different from his brain. He must have an astonishing amount of self-control.

Well, I can do that too.

With shaky limbs, I try to lower myself from the counter. But without anything to hold me up, I stumble, losing my balance.

"Careful." Wouter reaches for my arm, and the room tilts again, because evidently being this close to him is the equivalent of downing a half dozen tequila shots. "I can help you to your room, if—"

"Yeah—might be good," I mumble, slouching against him as we shuffle down the hall. He keeps his arm around my waist to steady me, bending in what must be an uncomfortable position for him given his height.

The exhaustion hits me as we reach my room. I slump onto the duvet in a sitting position, glancing back up at him. "I shouldn't sleep in jeans," I say, popping the button but struggling to do much more than that.

There's a flicker of tension in his jaw. Slowly, he inches forward. "Do you want—?" he asks, because we are only cut-off questions and awkward pauses now.

I nod.

He kneels down. Places a hand on either side of my hips and tugs. He's so close to me again, that heady scent of him, and once the denim is in a puddle on the floor and I'm in my underwear and a sweater, he makes every effort to keep his gaze above my waist.

"This, too?" I hold up my arms. Gently, so as not to stretch the fabric, he pulls at the sleeves, removing the sweater and folding it on top of the dresser. The bra I'm wearing is basic nude cotton, my underwear similarly casual if far less sexy: a pair of briefs patterned with tiny hedgehogs.

The moon and streetlamps cast shadows across his face, this cinematic dusky light making him look like he's from another era. In a way, he is.

With my last functioning brain cell, I force myself not to drag him down onto the bed with me. "You can look," I tell him. Softly, so as not to spook him.

"It's not a good idea."

He peels back the duvet for me to slip beneath it, and it's cozy and warm and *bed*. At first I think he's going to slide in next to me—but of course, he doesn't. My head is pounding and I'm going to feel like shit tomorrow, but Wouter van Leeuwen is tucking me in, and somehow that makes all of it worth it.

"Slaap lekker, Danika," he says, pulling the duvet all the way up to my chin. When he bends toward my face, his mouth lands on my forehead. Lingers there for only a moment before he backs away and leaves the room.

I hear the sink turn on and off. The hum of his electric toothbrush.

Then the house goes quiet, and I'm all too aware of the fact that he's on the other side of the wall. The first few nights here, I could barely sleep, worried about how much he might be able to hear. Then it became a comfort—I might have been thousands of miles from home, but I wasn't alone.

Now the knowledge of where he's sleeping makes me wired. Everything in me is tightly wound, craving release. I half expect him to rush back into the room, the top button of his jeans undone, shirt already tugged off. My hedgehog panties would be on the floor before he reached my bed.

But there's only a piercing silence and a closed door, no light coming from underneath it.

A frustration starts at the base of my spine and curls low in my belly, almost a physical thing I could snap with my fingers. I trail a hand down my neck, replaying the way he touched me. Measured at first, and then more reckless. I let my head sink into the pillow as I pinch one aching nipple and then the other. With my other hand, I push aside the fabric of my panties, already damp. When I find the slickness between my thighs, I let out a silent moan. I'm already close—he could have so easily tipped me over.

That's when I hear something on the other side of the wall.

A squeak of mattress springs. A rustle of bed sheets.

And then: the unmistakable sound of skin against skin.

My eyes fly open, my hand going still. There's another metallic squeak, followed by a bitten-off groan that drags my pulse into a manic rhythm.

I have no idea if he heard me and that's what made him reach for himself, or if he thinks I can't hear him, or if he *wants* me to hear him—but it's suddenly very, very clear what's happening in his room.

I imagine him sprawled out on his bed, muscles in his abdomen straining as he reaches downward, past that deep V. His hand on his cock would be an instant shot of relief, one that feels a little wrong at first, knowing I'm nearby, but too good to make himself stop. I want him to give in to every impolite urge he's ever had. Every dirty thought. I touch myself the way I'm desperate for him to touch me, circle my fingers closer and closer, *not too fast, not yet.*

A breathy gasp falls from my lips, one I'm almost certain he can hear.

And—maybe I want him to.

Maybe I want him to know exactly what I'm doing.

The next sound I hear is his. A low groan comes from somewhere deep in his throat, and I swear it makes my bed tremble. It's so fucking sexy, that sound. Raw. Needy. He must be beautiful when he's touching himself, no inhibitions as he surrenders to his basest instincts. I want to know if his free arm is triangled behind his head or resting on his chest. If his mouth is open, if his eyes are shut. If he likes it fast and rough or prefers to draw it out, making the pleasure last as long as possible. Just like the way he massaged me, stretching and stretching until I was right up against the edge.

I don't hold myself back as I picture him picturing me. I cup my breasts harder, tease myself with wet, insistent strokes. In his head, I hope I've never looked filthier. My panties are lost somewhere in the sheets and my thighs are shaking, a tight bundle of nerves slowly unfurling.

With every shred of self-control I can muster, I force myself to pause—I don't want it to be over just yet. It's the headiest surprise to hear his breaths slow down, too. His strokes must have turned languid, sweat glistening on his chest.

I'm not sure if he's waiting for my signal or I'm waiting on his, but when we start back up again, we keep pace with each other. There's a frantic slap of skin from the other side of the wall as he matches me breath for breath. Gasp for gasp. This is the only way he'll let himself have me, and right now that's enough.

He urges me faster. Shallow breaths now, neither of us shy about the noise we're making. My mind loops through all the ways I wish he would fuck me, with his hands and with his mouth and with his cock buried deep inside me. Until I'm begging for it. Until he is, too.

I'm dizzy and drenched, bucking against my hand like I've never wanted anything more. Back arched, chest heaving, that sweet release only seconds away. A whimper of bedsprings. Gritted teeth and hands fisted in sheets. We're so close—*so close*—

Then, two desperate syllables in the dark:

"Dani."

Oh—oh fuck.

I collapse into stardust the moment he does, loud and unapologetic as a gorgeous moan tears from his chest. That sound alone might be enough to push me over again, but there's nothing left in my body.

I am utterly, blissfully spent.

We're still breathing in sync, softer and slower—until we fall asleep, together, with the world's thinnest wall in between.

Fifteen

· · · · · · · · · · ·

ROOS VAN LEEUWEN IS WAITING FOR ME AT A CAFÉ—STILL not a coffeeshop—on a narrow street tucked behind a kitschy tulip museum in the Jordaan, Amsterdam's most picturesque neighborhood, where every canal looks plucked from a dream.

"I'm so glad you could do this," she says after we order. She's adorable in a blue plaid overcoat and short gray boots, a hip bag casually slung across her chest. "Your job was fine with you taking the afternoon off?"

I'm still wearing a turtleneck under my wool jacket in March, and I'm not even mad about it. Cold-weather clothing is simply superior. "It's a startup, you know. Weird hours sometimes." Then I force a smile, trying my best to brush it off. "I'm happy to be a tourist. As long as I don't have to get a T-shirt with, like, an anthropomorphic penis holding a joint on it." Unfortunately, this is something I've seen at numerous souvenir shops.

Roos feigns offense at this. "But that's our national uniform."

We exchanged numbers in Culemborg, but I hadn't expected her to reach out so soon. She was working on a list of Amsterdam's numerous canal cruise options, she said, and wanted to know if I'd like to try one out with her. I leapt at the chance to get out of the apartment, away from the monotony of job hunting.

Away from Wouter.

After that night of bad decisions, I woke up with a throbbing headache. On the counter was a spread of remedies for a hangover, or *kater*, according to a new Post-it note. A bottle of aspirin, a loaf of bread, a whole ginger root he'd peeled and chopped for me.

And then what I could only assume wasn't for the hangover but to combat the homesickness I mentioned at the museum: inside a bag from an American expat shop, a box of frosted cherry Pop-Tarts.

It was unfair that he could make me soft for him even when I felt this complicated.

That was only three days ago. Barely half a week since we kissed, since he tucked me in, since we did . . . *god*, I don't even know what to call it. And that's part of the problem. I have no idea where he's at with it or if he wants to forget it ever happened. To be perfectly honest, I don't know where I'm at with it, either—only that I don't regret it.

How could I, when it was one of the most intimate, freeing moments of my life?

So I've been avoiding him, taking my laptop to the library in the afternoon, "missing" dinner and texting him that I'm studying for class. Based on his early mornings and late evenings at work, he's been doing the same.

I just wish I couldn't hear him growl my name whenever I close my eyes.

Roos and I pick up our coffees and venture back outside. It isn't lost on me, the strangeness of getting space from Wouter by spending time with his sister. The area is mobbed with tourists, some of them dawdling in the streets, people with giant backpacks forcing the cyclists to dodge them. I envy their confidence—I've been too nervous to get back on a bike.

"None of this ever gets old?" I ask as we pass a tour group, a dozen white-haired people following a guide speaking in rapid Spanish. "The tourists, the bachelor parties, how busy it always is?"

"Never." Roos takes a sip of coffee. "Some Amsterdammers hate it, but I'm addicted to the energy. I don't know if I ever appreciated it until my twenties, though. I used to complain about the tourists as much as everyone else, but once I started traveling on my own, I realized—I was that tourist who gets in the way sometimes, too. I was the person wanting to get the perfect picture. Now every time I see a girl taking a photo of her friend in front of a canal, I can't help smiling. Even if it's the same shot as everyone else here on vacation." With a knowing look, she nods toward a couple doing this exact thing on the opposite side of the canal. "I'm like, 'Yes, you go for it, and do you want me to take one for you?' Because this city is beautiful, and I don't want to miss a moment of it."

I've never met someone like this, someone seemingly without a shred of cynicism. "You and Wouter have that in common. That deep love for the city."

"It's only the best place in the world," she says. "Plenty of people who grow up here never leave. They have Amsterdam in their veins."

I always liked LA well enough, considered myself a true Angeleno in the sense that I'd slept through a few earthquakes and always noticed when a movie was shot in LA but was supposed to be some other major city. But in my veins? I don't know if I ever had that kind of connection to it.

"This is going to sound strange," I say, "and don't take it the wrong way, but . . . you're being really nice to me." Given all those false friendships I left back in California, it feels like a gift, being let into the Van Leeuwens' world like this.

Roos almost chokes on her latte. "Are you not used to that?"

"Well—it depends." I try to backpedal, since I don't want to verge on giving the truth away. "I guess I thought you'd be more skeptical?"

"What can I say, I'm a little sappy. I know it was more than ten years ago that you two met, but I always wondered if anyone could ever be as special to him as you were. Even though I hadn't met you—I could just tell. And then fate brought you together again, and, well . . ." She punctuates this with a little shrug, gesturing to my ring. "It's kind of magical."

She doesn't ask me to defend it. She doesn't press me for details. It's not naivete—I can tell, and Roos isn't an idiot. She saw, once, how much he loved me, and she believes it's still there.

"And you love my brother," she says.

I swallow hard, the lie settling uncomfortably in my stomach. Wouter must be selling this harder than I've given him credit for, and I should be doing the same. Even if what happened in our rooms obliterated my capability for rational thought.

"I do," I manage, the words tasting far less acidic than I thought they might.

"Then that's all I need to know." She tosses her empty cup into a nearby trash can and steers us toward the dock. "He's just . . . he's been a little closed off, ever since our dad passed away. So focused on work, which isn't necessarily a bad thing, but . . ."

"I've noticed that." He admitted the same—and that he wants to change.

"Getting George was a huge deal. That gave him more of a reason to get outside, to go to the park. And he obviously has his friends, but I don't know how much *joy* he has in his life on a regular basis, you know? When I saw you together, I could tell right away—I hadn't seen him that relaxed in a while." She clutches my arm as we approach the dock, and I wonder if physical touch is a love language that runs in their family. "I'm just really glad he has you."

DAM FINE BOAT TOURS IS EMBLAZONED ON THE SIDE OF A little blue boat on the Keizersgracht. A perfect bit of kismet that Roos's assignment brought us to Iulia's company.

While we wait, Roos asks what kind of dress I might want for the wedding celebration, which the Van Leeuwens have planned for early May. It's only another performance, and yet when I imagine Wouter's broad shoulders in a suit jacket, a tie around his neck . . . I feel a little unsteady on my feet.

"I'm not sure," I tell Roos truthfully. The best summary of my current emotions.

"Don't worry, we'll find something. If you want to go less conventional, maybe a lavender or powder blue would look good with your complexion? Or even something darker, like a navy or forest gr—"

"Welcome, welcome," a familiar voice interrupts us, thankfully. "It looks like there was going to be a family of six with us, but they called to say they have food poisoning, so I guess it's just us three!" Iulia beams at us, looking casual in jeans and a utility jacket, hair in its usual ponytail.

After I introduce the two of them, Iulia tips her head toward me. "You have Dutch friends already? Very impressive."

Roos beams right back. "Well, she did marry my brother."

At that, Iulia's dark brows leap all the way to her hairline, this expression of sheer confusion.

Oh.

Oh, shit.

As it turns out, I left all my brain cells in North America. Iulia knows I'm out of a job. She knows I've only been here for a couple of months, and I can see her putting the pieces together right in front of us.

"It's, uh—very new," I manage. *Idiot, idiot, idiot.* "We dated when we were teenagers, and we just reconnected . . ." I stumble my way through the spiel, certain I'm giving myself away with every word.

To her credit, Iulia simply puts on a grin. "I had no idea—gefeliciteerd." Then she motions us toward the electric boat, flashing me a side eye that Roos can't see. I can only offer an awkward grimace in return. "Let's get on board and start this thing, shall we?"

She holds out her hand to help us climb inside. The boat rocks for a moment, adjusting to our weight, and then Roos and I take seats on either side of the captain's chair.

"Here at Dam Fine Boat Tours, we pride ourselves on being Amsterdam's alternative canal tour company," Iulia says with all the breeziness of someone who makes this same speech multiple times a day. "Which means you can drink, you can swear, you can ask all your burning questions about the underbelly of the city. Just keep it civil, okay?"

The boat's motor whirs with a soothing hum as Iulia starts it up and runs through some basic safety information. "At this point in the tour, I usually ask where people are from and what they've been doing in Amsterdam so far," she says. "But you both live here, so . . ."

"Yes, but we want the full tourist experience," Roos says. "Please don't hold back."

"Roger that." Iulia says something in Dutch into her radio and, with considerable ease, weaves us around a much larger tourist boat.

We glide underneath a bridge, bicycles locked to every available inch of space. The streets above us might be packed, but there's a distinct sense of calm here on the water. Sun on my face, wind in my hair—an ideal way to spend the afternoon. The canal houses look even more stunning from this angle, and I'm not sure how I ever thought the color palette was anything less than beautiful.

"I always start with some basic facts about Amsterdam," Iulia says after opening a cooler and telling us to help ourselves. "And it's more fun when this is interactive, so feel free to interrupt me at any time. This city was originally a small fishing village in the 1100s, then expanded to become a global power during the Dutch Golden Age in the 1600s. The Dutch East India Company was part of a vast trading network that turned Amsterdam into one of the wealthiest cities in the world. Amsterdam experienced huge economic growth at the time, but there's a dark history of colonialism and slavery there, too. Fortunately, that's something the country is starting to speak about much more openly.

"As you probably know, we're below sea level right now—most of the Netherlands is. The residents built small dikes about two thousand years ago to push back the water, and in the 1200s, they started using windmills to pump the water out. It's pretty incredible, actually, and it's a marvel Amsterdam even exists the way it does now," she says with a flourish of her arm. "Let's talk about the canals. Can anyone guess how many canals Amsterdam has?"

Roos's hand shoots up, and Iulia tosses her a smirk. "You're not allowed to answer."

"Oh god, the pressure," I say between sips of a pilsner. "Um . . . fifty?"

"Try a hundred and sixty-five," Iulia says. "Seventy-five kilometers. And fifteen thousand bikes are fished out of them each year."

"One year, two of those were mine." Roos lifts her beer in tribute. "Dark times."

"How clean is the water?" I ask.

Iulia holds up a finger, grabs a clear plastic cup, and bends over the side of the boat to scoop some up. "Pretty damn clear," she says, holding it out so we can see. "I wouldn't necessarily drink it, though. I used to take a sip every tour—after a month, I got sick."

Roos shudders. "You see enough people peeing into it, and you never want it to touch any part of your body."

"True. Guess I like to live on the edge." With a laugh, she throws out the water before turning back to me. "How long do you think you'll be here?"

"Well—I initially thought a year or two," I say, even though I never really thought about it, just took the job and leapt. The ring on my finger reminds me I should be giving a different answer. "But now that I'm married . . ."

"You know the expat joke, right? You say it'll be a couple years . . . and then you blink and it's been ten or fifteen," Iulia says. "You and your husband plan to stay here in the Netherlands?" If there's an extra emphasis on *husband*, Roos doesn't seem to notice.

"Yes. Definitely," I say, and Roos exhales with relief.

I probably deserve to be tossed into the questionable canal water.

We pass the school where I take my Dutch class, the Westerkerk, the Anne Frank House. Maybe it's just the fact that Roos is an Amsterdam native, but I catch her watching Iulia more than the scenery. Pink tinges her cheeks whenever the captain smiles at her. That's enough to distract me from all the lies—because here is something pure, something sweet.

Since I'm a tourist today and there's no shame in it, I take some photos for my parents. There in our chat is the one they sent yesterday from my favorite taco truck, a Jarritos raised in cheers. I know it's just their way of showing they miss me—but I can't help wondering if it's something else, too. A reminder of what I'm missing.

An attempt to lure me back.

We've fallen into a regular schedule of Sunday phone calls, evening for me and morning for them, and while they tell me it's the best way to start their day, I always hang up feeling a bit worse than I did beforehand.

"Maybe it's for the best," my mother said last week when I mentioned I'd stopped biking. "You should be wearing a helmet anyway. I still can't believe no one there does it."

"Babies do," I offered, and I could practically hear her rolling her eyes through the phone.

For most of my life, they've kept their leashes tight around my ankles. It was for my own benefit, wasn't it? That was what I told myself every time I thought about pushing back. They just wanted me to be healthy. Happy.

It's only now that I have space from them that I'm wondering whether I could have been happier without a leash at all.

"Now we're moving into what used to be the old Jewish quarter," Iulia says. The architecture here is different. Less charming. Most of these homes were destroyed during World War II and rebuilt as blocky apartments or office buildings, she explains. "The Netherlands had more Jewish victims than any other country. Everyone knows Anne Frank, and as devastating as that story is . . . it's only one person. One person out of more than one hundred thousand who were taken to camps, most of whom never came back."

Of course I knew there was a deep, complex Jewish history in Amsterdam. I was raised secular, and I've never been very religious. Never had a bat mitzvah. We belonged to a synagogue but stopped going eventually, when our after-school activities and other responsibilities started feeling more important.

It feels different here, being confronted by the history, and it turns me reverent for the rest of the tour.

"This was amazing," I tell Iulia as she steers us back to the dock. "Better than any history class. Thank you so much."

"My pleasure," she says. "This is the awkward part where I ask you to leave us a five-star review and mention my name."

Roos swipes around on her phone before holding it up trium-phantly. "Already done. My list will be up next week, and you're definitely going to be at the top."

Now Iulia blushes before returning her attention to the water, the first moment she hasn't seemed fully in control. "I always like to end my tours with this," she says, turning off the boat's engine. "Right over here, you can see seven bridges all at once, perfectly lined up. It's my favorite spot in Amsterdam."

Even though she's probably done this tour hundreds of times, she sounds a little mesmerized.

From this angle, I have a view of all seven for only a few seconds before the boat nudges one of them from view. Seven concentric semicircles, with the nearest canal framed by leafy green trees. The bikes and the tipsy houses, those Amsterdam trademarks, and the sunlight turning everything golden.

My breath catches in my lungs. It feels like magic, the way time stops for a moment in this city I thought had rejected me—when I only needed to give it a chance to truly come alive.

This place doesn't have to be an escape from a life that wasn't making me happy, I realize. It doesn't have to be temporary, a spot for me to pick up the pieces before moving on to something better.

It could be my home.

Sixteen

. . . .

WOUTER GIVES ME AN INSCRUTABLE HALF SMILE AS HE lifts my suitcase onto the rack above our heads. If there's any kind of grunt while he does this, it absolutely does not remind me of what we did in our separate rooms last week.

Then we drop wordlessly into our seats on the train, both of us too awkward to claim the armrest in between.

For a while I considered backing out of this trip, but maybe some time away from home will do us both good. We'll return with fresh perspectives and clear minds, because quite simply, there is no other option. Now that I know what this version of him sounds like when he comes, the way his moans slowly reach that aching crescendo—there's no comparison to our history. He had none of that brashness back then.

The thought comes with a quiet kind of heartbreak. We were so close that night, closer than I'd been with anyone in a long time. For those few breathless minutes, we understood each other.

Now we're only capable of small talk.

"Beautiful scenery," I say when the silence starts to get to me, pointing out the obvious. I check my phone, stunned to realize we've only been on the train for fifteen minutes.

He crosses one leg over the other, glances up from the book he's reading. "Really beautiful," he echoes.

Disheveled isn't a look I'm used to seeing on him, and yet that's the only way to describe him right now: deep lavender circles beneath his eyes, jaw and cheeks patterned with days-old stubble, and his hair messier than usual, as though he's been raking his hands through it. His shoulders are stiff, and what's ironic is that he looks like he could use a massage more than anyone.

I doubt it's the situation between us that's been keeping him awake at night—more likely it's a challenge at work, or some other stress—but for a moment, I let myself imagine I'm the reason he's this rumpled. That he can't sleep because he craves my mouth on his neck. That he can't make eye contact because of what we did in a daydream.

I broke a couple nights ago and called Phoebe, told her only about the drunken kiss and the emotions it had stirred up.

"Oh, Dani," she said with a sigh, and though there was some concern there, it wasn't judgmental. "Do you have feelings for him?"

"I don't know," I said in a quiet voice, and she sat with me in my confusion for a while.

Because it's so much more convenient if I don't.

Wouter tucks a bookmark into his paperback. Scans the train car. Midafternoon on a Saturday, the seats around us are empty enough. "I think we should probably talk."

"But the not talking was going so well," I say, hoping this will make him laugh. It only earns me a small puff of breath. Nothing like the reckless way he laughed that night in the kitchen, that dimple only disappearing when he tucked me into bed.

He waits a while before speaking again. "What happened last week—it was a good thing we didn't go too far."

Too far. What we did was already so fucking intimate that I can't even imagine what *too far* would look like.

"It would complicate things too much," he continues, a little quickly, like he's worried if he doesn't get it all out fast, he might lose his nerve. "If it ended poorly, and we're still married . . ." He runs a hand through his hair, and when a strand sticks out, I have to fight the urge to smooth it back into place. "I would hate for you to be uncomfortable living here."

All the logic is on his side—I know he's right. I can't fall into bed with Wouter, blur our boundaries even more, and have it mean nothing when we're tied together in so many other ways.

"I agree, one hundred percent. It would have been a mistake." I fold my hands primly in my lap, like I'm conducting a business meeting. A professional discussion of our unprofessional behavior. "We can absolutely just forget about it."

Relief washes over his face, as though he expected me to challenge him. As soon as my pulse returns to its regular rhythm, maybe I'll feel that relief too. Then he slips out a laugh. "God, I can't tell you how glad I am that you feel the same. It's . . . been a while for me. Since I was with anyone. I probably got a little carried away, and I apologize for that."

"How long is a while?"

His teeth bite down on his lower lip. "About a year."

A year. I had already assumed, but it still takes a moment to sink in. A year since he held someone that close. Sighed into their skin. Unraveled them with his beautiful hands.

It's almost unbearable, how badly I want to be the one he's unraveling.

"Well. All droughts end eventually," I manage.

He waves this off, as though the drought doesn't bother him, but there's a cord of tension in his jaw. "I'm glad we could get that all out in the open. Now we can enjoy the trip."

"I only want to eat chocolate and waffles for the next two days," I say.

"No arguments from me."

Wouter returns to his book, marginally less rigid, and I half-heartedly swipe through Duolingo on my phone, still waiting for that relief to hit. The hum of the train tracks is peaceful, though, and soon I'm drifting in and out of sleep, where my subconscious doesn't seem to agree with our decision to forget Saturday ever happened.

We're back in the kitchen, only this time, we don't stop. He teases and teases and teases, lips on my shoulder before he pulls away, unbuttoning my jeans before he inexplicably buttons them back up. All of it turns me wild, makes me plead, and in this dream, Wouter loves to hear me beg. Finally, he tugs me to the edge of the countertop, hands pressed to my thighs as he drops to his knees. The look on his face is all hunger.

"We're almost in Brussels," he says.

I wake with a jolt to his hand on my shoulder, telling me it's time to change trains.

These waffles better be life-changing.

"THERE SHOULD BE TWO ROOMS," WOUTER TELLS THE HO-tel receptionist. He uses English for my benefit, though Bruges is in the Dutch-speaking northern part of Belgium called Flanders. "One under Van Leeuwen and the other under Dorfman."

The woman frowns at her computer. "I'm sorry, sir, I only have one here. One of our best suites." She stage-whispers: "One of your colleagues told us you two were recently married, so we up-graded you!"

I've never forced a grin with as much effort in my entire life.

"That's so kind of you," I say, fumbling for the right words.

"You're sure there's nothing else available? My husband snores like you wouldn't believe!" I try to pass this off as some charming quirk. Just two deeply in love newlyweds who don't want to sleep in the same room!

"Unfortunately not. We're all booked."

Wouter accepts the two keys. Forces a smile to match mine. "Thank you so much."

We're quiet on the rickety elevator up to the top floor of the quaint historic hotel, white-knuckling our suitcase handles. Both of us try to avoid our reflections in the full-length mirror, but I can't help stealing glances. There he is, so much taller than me, his hands fidgeting in that trademark Wouter way. I wonder if we look like a happily married couple. If we look like we belong together, or if people wonder what we see in each other.

"Well," I say when he unlocks the door. "I guess we're on our honeymoon."

Because not only is there a bed scattered with the reddest rose petals forming the shape of a heart and two towels meticulously folded into kissing swans, there's also a bottle of champagne and a pair of flutes, a container of bubble bath, and a plate of chocolate-dipped strawberries. A large window looks out onto the city's medieval main square, lit up at night.

"I could sleep on the floor." Wouter drops his backpack. His cheeks are already flushed nearly the color of the rose petals. "Or in the chair?"

"This is your work trip. Your *physiotherapy* work trip. What would the other therapists say?" I give this suggestion a firm shake of my head. "We're adults. We can sleep in the same bed without it being weird."

But it's not just the fact of there being a single bed that's unusual for us. It's that we have *never* shared a bed.

When we were together, I always dreamed of it; nothing seemed more romantic to me back then. As an adult, the romance of it faded and I realized I needed my space, and on those rare occasions I spent the night with someone, I'd complain I was too hot when a guy tried to spoon me afterward. In reality, I hated the feeling of being caged in. The lights would go out and an arm would go around me, and suddenly I wouldn't be able to breathe.

"I'm sorry about that. The upgrade." He picks up the bottle of champagne. "Extremely nice, though."

I pop a chocolate-covered strawberry into my mouth. "We might as well enjoy it, right?"

I open up my bag, finding my toiletry case and bringing it over to the bathroom. Even though we share a bathroom at home, this one feels far more intimate. Maybe it's the curse of the honeymoon suite, or that this is a much smaller space. Or that we're about to be sleeping in the same bed. Either way, it turns my hands shaky as I remove my little bottles of shampoo and conditioner and prop them on the countertop.

As I'm doing this, my bottle of antidepressants falls out of my case and rolls its way out of the bathroom, into the suite.

"It's nothing," I say quickly, bending to snatch it up before it lands at Wouter's feet, my face burning. "Just—vitamins."

I hate myself the moment I say it. Because I'm not ashamed of the fact that I take medication, but the history there often feels too complicated to unspool. I've always been anxious about telling people, worried they'll wonder what made my problems so important I needed that kind of care.

Maybe I have some shame there after all.

My phone rings as Wouter starts unpacking. "Phoebe," I say, reaching for it. "Do you mind if I—"

"Go ahead. I'll take a shower, give you two some privacy." He knows I've told her about the marriage, that I fully trust her, but still I wait to pick up until he's carried a toiletry kit and change of clothes into the bathroom.

Phoebe's voice is almost too loud for the small room. "We're coming to see you!" she shouts, and Maya lets out a whoop in the background.

"What?" I ask, plugging my other ear so I can hear her better. The shower turns on in the bathroom. "You're coming . . . here?"

"Next month! For your wedding celebration thing. The dates matched up perfectly, and we figured, better to do it now, before the baby comes, and so . . . we're doing it! We're coming to Amsterdam!"

The grin spreads across my face like I've been waiting weeks for good news. "Oh my god, oh my god, I can't wait. I have so many places to take you, and only half of them are dessert-related. You're really coming?"

Phoebe lets out another squeal. "We really are. Free upgrade to economy comfort, so we're going to be living that extra-legroom life."

"You're way too fancy for me."

We talk more about logistics as my mind spins. "Before I go," Phoebe says after I've told her to bring her most comfortable walking shoes, a rain jacket, and a few more boxes of Annie's mac and cheese, "Mom and Dad texted wondering why you're in Belgium?"

"They . . . *oh*." I let out a groan as I run a hand down my face. "Shit, I don't think I ever turned off my location sharing." Something I only turned on for safety reasons because dating in LA was questionable at best. The water in the bathroom is still running. "I'm in Bruges for a physiotherapy conference. With Wouter."

Silence on the other end of the phone.

"It's a really good thing you're coming, Pheebs," I say with a defeated little laugh.

"We'll figure everything out," she promises, and we exchange *I love you*s before hanging up.

When Wouter emerges from the shower in shorts and an Ajax T-shirt, still drying off his hair with a towel, my heart twists. It's not the same T-shirt he wore when he lived with us, but the memory's still there.

"My sister's coming," I say, but I can only give him a wobbly smile. "At the end of April."

He lights up at this, tells me how fantastic it is, how excited he is to see her. "But—it seems like there's maybe something else?" he asks, mouth slanted in a frown.

"Just my parents. They're freaking out that I went to Belgium without telling them, because they don't realize how easy it is to just hop on a train. They still can't accept that I'm a wholly independent person, I guess."

He nods, gives his hair a final scrunch before hanging up the towel. "I remember. They've always been a bit overprotective. I hoped it would change as you got older, but . . . it sounds like it hasn't?"

The words rub me too harshly—I'm not expecting such a strong reaction. But goddamn it, he seems to remember *everything*, but he only lets on when it's convenient for him. We can't talk casually about my parents without acknowledging the gigantic thing we still haven't discussed. Our history is too tangled to pick and choose, and if I've been looking for another reason to guard my body and my heart, here it is.

He doesn't want to make things complicated? That's just fine with me.

"It's not a big deal. I should get ready for bed."

With that, I grab my pajamas and shut myself in the bathroom, urging my breaths to stabilize. *Four. Seven. Eight*, and a loud exhale through my mouth. Fucking stupid is what I am, thinking that this trip could be normal after everything we shared.

How could it be, when he's never offered a real explanation for the breakup?

I haven't thought about it in weeks, and yet there it is again, pounding away at my skull. I thought we were letting each other in, beginning a new kind of closeness. Maybe I was fooling myself about that, too.

Once again I use all my skincare products, delaying the inevitable that is getting in bed next to Wouter. Apparently the secret to glowing skin is inner turmoil, because mine has never looked better.

He's in bed when I exit the bathroom, sitting up with a book about the impact of stress on the body open in his lap, the sheets pooled around his hips. With his glasses and the soft light of a bedside lamp, he paints a painfully inviting picture. His hair is mostly dry now, and I wish I didn't remember how it felt between my fingertips.

"Everything okay?" he asks when I slide in next to him, trying to ignore the extra heat from his body even with a foot of space between us. His citrus-and-peppermint scent.

"Yep. Great."

Finally, he puts down the book and gazes at me over the top of his glasses. "Danika," he starts, but I don't want to hear where that sentence ends. I have a feeling we've been there before.

"I'm pretty tired from the trip. And you have a busy day tomorrow. We should probably just go to sleep."

He pauses, caught off guard by my sudden chilliness. "Sure. Okay. If that's what you want," he says, and takes off his glasses, folding them on top of his book before switching off the light next to his bed. "Good night."

"Fijne avond," I say, wishing I weren't such a fucking coward.

My chest tightens as I roll over to face the wall. In an alternate universe, we'd cross the invisible line in the middle of the bed and make up for so much lost time.

That's not the only way I want him, though, and that might be the scariest part.

Waffles, I remind myself with a fierce resolve. In the morning there will be waffles, and maybe I won't be thinking about all the ways this could be different.

Maybe I won't be missing something I never really had.

Seventeen

BREAKFAST THE NEXT MORNING IS SHEER PERFECTION. THE Belgian waffles are a toasty bronze and gloriously fluffy, their deep squares filled with syrup. It's possible I go overboard on the toppings: strawberries and blueberries and fresh cream, a dusting of powdered sugar, a dollop of Nutella. Truly, the Platonic ideal of a waffle. No notes.

The sugar rush is enough to lift my mood a little, along with the anticipation of some Bruges tourism, since we arrived too late last night to see any of the city.

Wouter, however, has barely touched his waffles. I can understand why—he opted for a bit of butter as his sole topping. He's wearing a slate-gray collared shirt with thin white stripes, the sleeves rolled to his elbows, and the furrow between his brows has made a reappearance. He was already showered and dressed when I woke up at seven o'clock, so clearly he's still barely sleeping.

"I have a dinner with some colleagues after the conference," he says. "It might go late. You're sure you'll be fine on your own?"

I take a sip of orange juice. "No problem at all."

Already this trip is undoing our progress. Turning us into friendly strangers.

"Wouter van Leeuwen!" calls an Irish-accented voice, belonging to a bald man dropping his breakfast tray on the other end of the table. "It's been ages!"

Though Wouter gets to his feet and extends his hand for a shake, the other man pulls him into a hug.

"Rory McDonagh," Wouter says, instantly seeming lighter. "Where are you working these days?"

"Went back home to Belfast for a while, but now I'm in Leiden. Got my own practice there. Fell hopelessly in love with a Dutch girl and now I fear I may never leave," he says with an amiable shrug, his brogue making it sound all the more charming.

"Well done, on both counts." Wouter turns to me. "Rory and I were in university together." Then he swallows hard, his hand wavering as though unsure where he should place it. Nowhere, he ultimately decides. "This is my wife. Danika."

The ring on my finger feels more like a lie than it ever has.

Rory gives me an enthusiastic handshake. "I didn't know you'd gotten married! Hey, congrats."

"Nice to meet you," I say as the three of us sit back down. "You must have tons of great stories about the two of you from college."

"Loads. Has he ever told you about the time we got absolutely jarred and decided to climb the tallest tower at school?" When I shake my head, Rory keeps going. "We made it halfway up. Stopped at a balcony . . . at which point this guy decided to take a nap."

"That was where the university police found me the next day," Wouter says. "Passed out with a Sharpie eye patch and mustache on my face to make me look like the world's least-threatening pirate."

I force a smile, wishing I could find this as endearing as it is.

Rory feigns innocence. "No idea how that got there, mate." He gestures to me with a cup of coffee. "You're not a physiotherapist too, are you?"

"No, I'm not. I'm . . ." I trail off, unsure what to call myself. A liar in a green-card marriage. A woman who has no idea what the fuck she's doing.

When I still can't decide how to end the sentence, Wouter speaks up. "She's a UX designer at a startup in Amsterdam."

"Very impressive! Must be an exciting environment," Rory says, perfectly jovial.

The floor goes wobbly beneath me as I process Wouter's words.

She's a UX designer at a startup, he said, like he was worried I might tell the truth.

Like he was worried how *unemployed* might sound.

"Actually, I *was* a UX designer," I correct, finally finding my voice. "But I'm in between jobs at the moment. Still looking for the right fit."

Rory gives me a reassuring nod. I'm not sure he's capable of anything but positivity. "We've all been there, haven't we? I'm sure you'll land back on your feet."

I don't register anything they talk about for the rest of breakfast. My waffles grow soggy, but I shove bite after bite into my mouth anyway, trying desperately to make eye contact with Wouter as he tries desperately not to.

I've never felt more seventeen, the girl without ambition he discarded all those years ago. It's a staggering realization that he might feel this way about me. *Still.* After all the reassurances that I could take my time.

I want so badly to believe this wasn't what he meant, and yet I can't rationalize it any other way.

"Right on," Rory says when we're finished eating, completely unaware of how the energy has changed. Then to Wouter: "Ready to go?"

Wouter nods, still not meeting my gaze as we all rise to our feet. "See you tonight?"

"Yep." I give the *p* a hard pop before clearing my throat. "Enjoy the conference."

All I hear is Rory saying, "Seems like a lovely girl!" before the two of them disappear into the hall.

Bruges is the most charming place, with Gothic houses and cobbled streets that make me feel as though I've traveled hundreds of years into the past. And the city's defining feature: the canals are full of swans. I've never seen this many all in one place, dozens and dozens of the elegant, long-necked birds.

I take a boat tour to get even closer, sending a few photos to Iulia with the caption Promise I'm not cheating on you, and she responds right away: Bruges is magical so I forgive you ;)

While I love the freedom of wandering a new city by myself, the conversation with Rory sits like a brick in my stomach. Amsterdam was supposed to be my second chance, but I'm no closer to figuring out what I want to do than I was when I got off that plane. In fact, I may be even further from it, since I don't have a steady paycheck.

Wouter and I promised nothing about our day-to-day lives was going to change, and yet there's been a massive seismic shift. Every day contains only more pretending, more mystery about how I'm supposed to act around him.

His simple presence in my life makes it dramatically different, and not just because we're married. I could feel all his disappointment when he mentioned my job, and I'm no longer merely sad about the shifting dynamic between us. I'm *angry* with him, and the emotion is such a strange, unexpected relief.

I know exactly how to be angry with him.

My day ends with a torturous climb up all 366 steps of the Belfry, Bruges's imposing thirteenth-century bell tower. I hear my parents' voices, warning me about my lungs and how unsafe these cracked stairs are, and how it's okay if I can't handle this.

"How many more steps?" the people around me ask other tourists on their way down, those who've successfully made the trek and lived to tell the tale.

"Almost there!" they promise. "It's worth it!"

But I pace myself. I take breaks, drink water, let others pass. It probably takes me longer than almost anyone else, and when I finally get to the top—

There's the city spread out beneath me, those tiny historic buildings and a Sunday market, orange roofs extending far into the distance.

I stay up there for a long time, not minding the wind that blows my hair around my face or the tourists who ask if I'll take photos of their families.

Because there's that wanderlust again, that itch at the back of my throat that quietly pleads: *more*.

I'M PRETENDING TO BE ASLEEP WHEN WOUTER GETS BACK to the room that night, the duvet wrapped tight around me. I haven't decided yet if I want to confront him or ignore him.

But he's being so fucking considerate as he quietly goes through the room, toeing his shoes off and carefully unzipping his suitcase, tooth by agonizing tooth, and it's downright infuriating. How dare he be polite about this when he was so quick to speak for me, when he made it clear that who I really am isn't someone he's confident introducing as his wife.

The rage wins out.

I throw off the duvet with such force that it startles him.

"Jesus," he says, holding a hand to his chest. "Didn't realize you were still awake."

He looks so soft in this nighttime lighting, the cathedral reflected in his glasses. That's infuriating, too, that I am all sharp edges and he has the audacity to look this touchable.

"How was dinner with Rory?" I say flatly, not caring about how pillow-warped my hair must look or the fact that I'm braless in a T-shirt and tiny shorts. "The one who just *had* to know that I was a UX designer. Because god forbid someone thinks you have a wife who's unemployed."

He gives me a bewildered look. "Danika," he says as he approaches the bed, holding up his hands. "Slow down, okay? Let's talk." The top two buttons of his shirt are undone. Another infuriating detail.

"You had to introduce me that way—why? So that I wouldn't jump in and tell him the truth? So I wouldn't . . . embarrass you?"

"*No*," he says, finally seeming to understand what I'm saying. "Because I didn't want you to feel pressured to explain yourself when you're still figuring it out. I don't care if my colleagues know you're not working right now."

I'm still too riled to be touched by this gesture, even if it was semi-thoughtful. I push my fingertips into my eyes, heave out a breath. "It's not just that. I'm just—I never really learned how to navigate the aftermath of getting yourself off while your fake husband does the same thing in the next room. My mistake." My face flames with the memory as red attacks his cheeks. "So we're back in this place where we don't actually talk about anything that matters, and you know what? I really hate it."

Now he looks properly confused. "I didn't even drink tonight and I'm still lost. Where is all this coming from?"

"Are you serious? It can't be a mystery."

"Enlighten me, then. Please."

It's too good to see him pleading, even if it brings back that vision of me at the edge of the counter, completely bare to him, his face between my legs.

I want this man on his knees either way—whether he's begging forgiveness or making me cry out his name.

"Enlighten you. Sure. Let's talk about the real problem, then," I say, thrusting aside the duvet so I can get to my feet, anger thrumming all the way down to my toes. "Thirteen years ago. The fact that we had a *plan*. We made it *together*. And then you went home and changed your mind. Decided I wasn't 'ambitious' enough for you and didn't even give us a chance to talk about it." I stomp over to where he's standing, wishing I were about three feet taller and wearing at least 30 percent more clothes. Still, it's an adrenaline rush, finally having the courage to say all of this to his face. "So what the fuck really happened, Wouter?"

I'm not expecting the words to hit him like a blow to the chest. He staggers backward, runs a hand down his face, jostles his glasses. He's less soft now. More wrecked.

"Oh my god . . ." He shakes his head as the reality sinks in. "That message. That stupid message. I had no idea you were still thinking about it. It—it haunted me for so long."

"Better to be haunted than dating a girl with zero ambition, right?"

He gives me this hollow, tortured look. "It was callous. I know. But there was a life waiting for me in Amsterdam I didn't think I could just turn my back on. I thought I was supposed to be this person with a clear path, even though I know now that I was too young to have any of it set in stone."

The room is too small and there isn't enough air. I snatch up one of the swan towels, ruining someone's hard work as I clutch it tight in my fist. "And I didn't fit into that life."

"Some part of me thought so. Yes. I'm not proud of it, but I don't want to lie to you," he says. "But there was more. I thought if I gave you a reason, if I told you I wanted to be with someone more ambitious . . . then maybe you'd hate me. And that would make it easier. The truth is, any reality where I wasn't with you sounded only marginally better than the pain of trying to make it work with all that distance between us."

I choke out a laugh. "So you told me 'bye, thanks for everything' to spare my feelings?"

"Because I didn't think I'd be able to get over you otherwise! Is that so hard to imagine?" His eyes are blazing, chest rapidly rising and falling. "If we're really talking about this, what about you? You sure didn't wait long before you moved on."

"I—what?"

"I saw on your social media. You were dating some football player a few weeks later. Soccer, whatever. I figured the breakup didn't even affect you if you already had a new boyfriend that fast. You just swapped me out for the next guy, someone more convenient."

I'm struck by this. He seems actually, genuinely *hurt* in a way I never anticipated. "Wouter—that wasn't anything real. It barely lasted a month. I was missing you, and I thought seeing someone else might help me get over you faster."

"Did it?"

"No."

What he said that first evening comes back to me, about the relationship not being what either of us thought it was.

"You knew I was all in with you," I say quietly, my teenage aching steeped in those words. "You knew I loved you. That didn't just change overnight."

He's walked to the edge of the room, and now he turns back and presses his lips together, as though trying to lock the emotion inside. The way he's been doing since I arrived. "That was what I thought, too, but I saw those posts and figured . . . maybe it was for the best. You'd go have the beautiful life that you deserved without someone on the other side of the world holding you back. I couldn't bear the thought of you holing up in a dorm room somewhere waiting for me. And I couldn't—" A deep, anguished breath. "I couldn't bear the thought of having a relationship with you where I couldn't see you all the time. Hold you all the time. *Touch* you." His voice breaks a little, and he shakes his head as he cuts his gaze to the floor. "A long-distance relationship would have made us miserable in the end. I thought I was sparing us both."

All of this rushes through me in fragments. A tidal wave of understanding, of finally being able to put the pieces together in a way my younger self never could.

"I wanted to talk to you all the time," he continues, voice still a little hoarse. I wish it didn't affect me the way it does, making itself at home inside my chest. "I wrote and deleted a hundred other messages. When I got into university. When my dad had his first stroke. When he passed away and I realized all the hard work didn't fucking matter if it was taking time away from the people I loved. Even stupid shit, like seeing a sunset I thought you'd really like. I thought, 'Maybe I'll send her this photo and take it all back.' But you were so far away that everything that happened with you felt like a dream."

"I thought—I thought you regretted it. Like I was some dirty secret you left behind in America." There's a fragile catharsis in finally being able to say these things. I'm unsteady on my feet, like one more truth from him could knock me over. "You broke my fucking heart, but maybe the worst of it was that I was convinced you thought I was some aimless loser, and over a decade later, that's still exactly who I am."

"*No.* I could never. Not then, and not now." With a cautious kind of strength, he strides closer. "I am so sorry, Dani. I really screwed up. What I told you when you first moved in, about this being one of my biggest regrets—I meant it." He's been worrying at the sleeves of his shirt, at his neckline, and the whole thing has become a wrinkled mess. I've never seen a man look more disheveled, and it's sexier than it has any right to be. Like he's been tortured keeping all this in, and now that he's letting it out, he doesn't quite know what to do with himself. "Your family had even talked about coming to visit, and I let all of them down. I held on to the guilt for so many years. I never thought I'd have a chance to make it up to you. And then you show up here, a hundred times more gorgeous than I remember, and I think: 'I am so fucked.'"

Despite everything, this makes me bite back a smile. Because I believe him—I do.

"You could have offered me a room in your house and asked me to marry you," I say as I drop the towel to the floor, and he fails to hide a smile too. I'm still stuck on the knowledge that I am the one who made him look this wrecked. I never thought I had the power to take someone apart like that, and it makes me wonder how else I could do it. Whether he'd let me. "God. This would have been so much easier if you told me all of this at the beginning."

He folds his arms across his chest and quirks one eyebrow. "'Hi, great to see you again. By the way, I liked you too much when we were teenagers to have any semblance of rational thought, so I broke up with you over text like a coward'?"

"So we were just idiots who didn't know how to communicate."

"Maybe we still are. I know I am. And I'm sorry," he repeats. "I'm so sorry you ever thought it meant you didn't matter. When I was in LA, you were just . . . everything to me."

Those words hang between us, so visceral that I almost believe I could pluck them from the air and tuck them away for safe-keeping.

"And now?" I ask, my voice wavering, almost afraid of the answer.

Maybe the question is too bold. Maybe he won't give me a real reply.

But slowly, slowly, I sense something in the room start to shift. My adrenaline has dropped to a low simmer even as my heart hammers. This time, though, it's with anticipation. He moves closer, until there's a couple feet of space between us, and with that wrinkled shirt and fierce longing in his eyes—how did I not see it before?

"You have to know I can't stop thinking about you. Every spare moment," he says, voice rough. "Tell me you haven't thought about it, too. When we kissed in the kitchen, and—and what happened after."

"I've thought about it a lot." A hard swallow. A step toward him. "Probably too much."

"No such thing." His gaze tracks my bare legs. Pauses at my hips before going higher, back up to my face. He lifts his hand at the same time as he lifts his eyebrows, as though asking for permission to touch me. Dazed, I give him a nod, his fingertips landing on the curve of my biceps.

"You said you wanted to stop. That night we were drunk," I say. "And yesterday, you wanted to forget about it."

"I didn't want us to make such a big decision when we weren't sober. And then you were avoiding me, and . . . I got scared. That you didn't feel the same way." He drags his finger down my forearm, taking his time before he speaks again. As though realizing we're on the precipice of something dangerous, and whatever he says next might seal our fate. For better or for worse. Till death do us part. "When we were in the kitchen . . . it had been so long. I didn't want to ruin it by not being able to remember every single detail." That fingertip sweeps upward, beneath the sleeve of my T-shirt, curving around my shoulder. "I didn't want to kiss you if my senses were the slightest bit impaired. Being around you already does enough of that."

"Oh," I say softly. Half relief, half awe.

"Tell me you think we're better off just friends," he says, and from the focused way his eyes hold mine to the determined tone of his voice, I can tell something's changed in him. He's finally giving in to the side of himself he's been so desperate to hide. "Is that better than me kissing you until neither of us can see straight? Because there are so many places I want to kiss you, Dani. *So many.*" He moves his hand to the side of my neck, thumb stroking along my skin. "You're so pretty right here." Up to my jaw. "And here." He grazes my hip bone with his other hand. "Here, too. Your hips. Your waist. Your perfect tits."

My throat is dry, the ache between my legs almost painful. Every place he's touched me feels singed. Electric. I take a final step, my toes aligned with his, wondering if the weight of his thumb is all that's holding me up. Just to be sure, I grip his arm. Savor the swell of solid muscle.

"Tell me right now if you'd rather ignore all of this," he continues. "Because all I've been able to think about, ever since you were on that table in my office, is ripping off those sweet little panties so I can feel how wet you are."

A whimper slips out. "*Please.*"

"Please what? Tell me, Dani." Now his hand is at the juncture of my thighs. He gives me the smallest amount of pressure, enough to have me gasping as he massages me through my shorts. "Tell me platonic is better than me getting on my knees and fucking you with my mouth all night long."

My chest is already heaving with the effort of holding back. There's nothing else. No more reasons not to do this.

So I press myself to him just as his lips crash down on mine.

His kisses are greedier than I remember them. They're reckless and unashamed, infused with the kind of urgency that makes it clear we've both been denying ourselves for far too long. He clutches me tight, his hands tangled in my hair, his tongue parting my lips so I can open for him.

I'm on my tiptoes, his hands traveling down my shoulders until he realizes the height difference doesn't make this particularly easy. So he picks me up in one effortless motion, my legs wrapping around his waist while he trails his mouth down my neck. *This*. This is perfect. Tongue and teeth. Sighs and gasps. I cling to the solid heat of him, fingertips in his hair. When he hoists me higher to kiss my breasts through the fabric of my T-shirt, I shudder against him, my head thrown back. His mouth finds my hardened nipples—and *oh*. It's almost too good when he gives them a few exploratory flicks with his tongue, making damp spots on the thin cotton.

Every touch feels like a small miracle.

He pauses for only a moment to look at me with wild eyes, breathing hard, glasses askew. "You're sure about this?"

"We're already married," I say, and suddenly it's so funny that I have to bite back a laugh. "Wait, wait, wait." I give his chest a pat. "Are you—? I have an IUD, and I was tested before I left the US."

"I got tested, too." The blush across his face deepens as his thumbs trace circles on my back. "Right after that night in the kitchen, actually."

He leans close to kiss me again, but I pull back with a grin. Hearing that is hotter than I can imagine—that he was preparing for something we swore we wouldn't do. "You wanted to be ready for me." I nip at his throat, kiss all of that warm, citrus-tinged skin, and beneath it an earthy scent that's wholly *him*. One that's been locked in time, stowed away in some kind of olfactory memory box for the way it ignites something in me.

"*Fuck*, Dani. It feels like I've been ready for years."

He uses my nickname, like he's so hungry for me that he can't bother with the extra syllable.

I grab his crooked glasses and place them on the nightstand as he lowers us to the bed, mouth fused to mine again. These kisses are somehow both frantic and sweet—because we have so much time to make up for.

When he pulls away, it's only to yank my shirt off just as I'm fumbling with his buttons, eager to get my hands on all of him. The broad expanse of his chest. The tattoo on his left shoulder, though I'm in too much of a rush to linger on it. He slides off my pajama shorts in one quick movement. In my dazed state, it takes an actual eon to undo his jeans, but finally they're tossed onto the floor and he's staring at me in panties and no bra.

I don't cover myself the way I might with other new partners. Obviously I look different than I did at seventeen, my stomach softer, my face rounder. But I let him take an extended moment to drink me in, the same way I look at him, at the angles of his chest and the tent in his boxer briefs and the trail of hair I mapped weeks ago. His mouth kicks into an awed, lovely smile that he tries to bite back before letting it go.

"Beautiful," he says as I tug him on top of me, savoring the weight as he presses me into the mattress. "Absolutely beautiful."

He buries his lips between my breasts, a thumb sweeping along one nipple. Slowly, slowly, back and forth until I'm aching for more. A gentle pinch. A little harder.

"During that massage in my office . . . *god*," he says on a hot breath. "I felt so fucking unprofessional, the thoughts I was having."

"Tell me."

"How incredible it felt to touch you again. How I couldn't believe you were letting me work your body like that." He sucks a nipple into his mouth while I grasp at his hair, and I let myself be loud about how much I love it. Then he releases me with a pop, blows cool air on my breasts before catching them with his lips again. "Every sound you made, I wondered if it was because of what I was doing to you."

"It—it was. I wanted you on top of me. Inside me," I admit as his teeth drag along my sensitive skin. "I locked myself in my room for an hour the next day, just . . . imagining."

He groans, rolling his hips into mine, kissing up to my neck again. "You"—mouth on my throat—"think about me"—tongue on my pulse—"when you touch yourself."

"Yes. Wouter. *God*." And even though I know the answer: "Do you?"

Somehow, there's a sheepishness in the way he bites down on his lip. Even though we're sweaty and half-undressed, he can still be shy. "Last week . . . wasn't the first time I've come with your name in my mouth."

His confession turns me wild. Now I'm the one pinning him, kissing down his chest as he grabs my waist, my hips. I have to get my mouth on the muscles that knew exactly how to stretch my body. The forearms that flexed over me. He laughs, even when I plant little kisses on his hands, but that only makes me kiss him more.

He's hard as steel beneath me, gripping my ass as I straddle him and rock against his erection, two agonizing layers of fabric separating us. *Fuck*, he feels good. My eyes fall shut at the sensation. I slide a hand between us to rub him over his boxers while he swallows a moan, growing harder in my palm.

"Not yet," he manages, and though I want to watch him come undone until every last muscle stops protesting, I lift my hand away. "Please. I need to feel you."

I have no objections to that. He kisses up the column of my neck, messy and open-mouthed, while he slips a hand into my panties.

"I'm not—I haven't waxed or anything in a while," I say. Jace always preferred it, almost as much as I hated doing it.

He gives me a bewildered look. "I want all of you. Exactly the way you are." He finds the coarse hair between my thighs and almost seems to relish it, letting out a growl as he parts me with two fingers. "*Dani*. You feel fucking amazing. Are you really this wet for me?"

All I can do is gasp in response. We never spoke like this back then—I'm certain we wouldn't have known how—and it takes my brain a second to catch up to the fact that Wouter van Leeuwen now has a filthy mouth.

Achingly slow, he works off my panties. Drags his fingers up my bare legs, mouth on my knees, my calves, my ankles. I'm already breathing hard at the anticipation of him filling me, but he takes his time relearning me, reacting to each new sound. A knuckle brushed down along my pubic bone. Two slick fingers stroking my lips. He teases my clit for only a moment before he slides a finger inside me, deeper this time.

When I bite down on his ear, I can feel the way it affects him, a tremor of his shoulders that makes me do it again.

Somehow it manages to feel like the first time and also like we've charted these paths before, but he's smoother now, more sure of his movements. Even after all these years, my body remembers how to bend for him, and yet still there's a question in the way he touches me, waiting for my eager *yes*.

"Good?" he asks as he returns to my clit, this time with the heel of his hand, pulsing there while I shudder beneath him. There's a thread of amusement in his voice, because he knows it is. "More pressure? Less? I'm a professional, as you know."

"More. I—I like a lot of pressure."

Instead of obliging, he keeps his eyes on me as he readjusts. He sits back on his knees, treating me to a spectacular view of his chest before he settles himself at my hips, tugging me upward until my head is on the pillow. He's gentle at first, planting soft kisses on my thighs, playing connect-the-dots with the freckles I have there. A bite. Another lingering kiss.

"Please," I croak out, because he's rendered me incapable of keeping my begging to myself. "Now you're just torturing me."

A broken-off laugh. "Going slow is more for my benefit than for yours. As soon as I start licking you, I'm afraid I'm not going to last long."

For a second, I'm convinced he's used the wrong pronouns, that he means *I* won't last long. But the moment he puts his mouth on me, I realize he was exactly right. His body tightens as he grasps my hips like an anchor, and the way he groans when I fist a hand in his hair is my new favorite thing about him.

He pauses to touch his damp forehead to my inner thigh. "You taste even better than I remember."

Then he takes the tip of his tongue to my clit and neither of us can speak. He licks me like he missed me, giving me all the pressure I need and more, until I feel that tension building at the base of my spine. My legs begin to shake, and he must be able to sense it because he quickens his pace. One hand keeps me spread to him while he flattens his tongue, flicking it against me in a firm, insistent rhythm that has me pulling at his hair, biting the back of my hand. Swearing his name.

Everything in me winds the tightest tight before my muscles go slack, a gasp yanked from my throat. The orgasm rolls through my body in waves of white-hot pleasure—thighs quivering, eyes shut, head thrown back. The neediest burst of relief.

Wouter holds his mouth to my forehead, brushing aside sweaty strands of hair as I come back to earth.

A laugh mixes with a sigh as I force my eyes back open. His hair is wild and a lovely scarlet spills across his cheeks, matching the marks on his neck where I left eager kisses, but it's not enough. I want this man to look fucking debauched.

"Come here," I say, tipping his mouth to mine and tasting myself on his lips.

Then I give my hand a long lick before I wrap it around him.

"You really thought you might come, just from going down on me?" I ask. "Before I could get my hands on you?"

He groans, buries his mouth in the side of my neck. With my thumb, I rub the head of his cock, spreading those drops of moisture along his shaft. And even though I'm desperate to go slow, to make this last as long as possible, I can't resist pumping him harder. Faster.

"*Dani*," he grits out. "I'm trying so hard not to embarrass myself here, but that's—that's so fucking good."

God, he's already about to fall apart in the palm of my hand, this gorgeous man who made me see stars. His fingertips travel up my back, inching upward, until he can spread them along my neck and up into my hair.

Just when I sense he's moments from the edge, I release my hand. He lets out a heavy breath at the loss of my touch as I move up to his face, kissing him slowly. Sweetly. His eyes are shut, long lashes looking so delicate.

Then I reach for him and start again.

The expletives that tumble from his mouth are more than worth it, especially when I lean down to close my lips around him. He's even harder now, heat and salt. I take him in slowly, swirling my tongue around the tip of his cock. Watching him watch me. I commit every single one of his reactions to memory: a fist gripping the bedsheets. Adam's apple fluttering in his throat. Abdominal muscles trembling with the weight of all the times he's held himself back.

"Oh fuck," he pants. "Just like that, lief."

The word slips out—I'm sure of it. He doesn't have control over himself like this.

Suddenly his eyes go wide, and he gazes down at me as though making sure I know I don't have to let him finish like this if I don't want to. But *god*, I want to. I give him a fierce confirmation as I suck him deeper, and within an instant, he's completely undone. Pushed over the edge with a brilliant moan and a rush of heat in my mouth, his fingertips still stroking the nape of my neck.

When our breathing calms down, he heads to the bathroom for a warm, damp towel, one of the ones that used to be shaped like a swan. I'm not sure why my heart squeezes when he cleans me up first—probably I'm not used to anyone taking care of me like that.

"Correct me if I'm wrong," he says, "but I don't think it was ever quite like that when we were seventeen?"

I laugh, nudging him with my elbow. "No, you've definitely picked up a few moves."

"As have you."

He props himself up on one arm to kiss me but hesitates, as though unsure how to navigate this new territory. I close the space between us and bring my mouth to his. I don't know what we are or what this means—just that I don't want to stop kissing him.

"How early is the train tomorrow?" I ask.

"Too early. I should probably set an alarm."

After fiddling with his phone, he slides an arm around my back and pulls me to his chest. His hand rests at my hip, my face in the crook of his neck. It's peaceful here, his pulse drumming against my cheek, probably the most peace I've had in months. The rhythm of it lulls me into a trance; my eyes are already starting to shut.

"We always wanted to sleep in the same bed together," he says, his words thick like he's already on the verge of it. "All those years ago."

I let his legs tangle with mine and stop short of telling him I'm not sure I can fall asleep with someone wrapped around me like this.

Until I do.

Eighteen

· · · · · · · · · ·

"IS THAT GEORGE?" I ASK ON THE TRAIN RIDE HOME, POINT-ing to an inky scribble in Wouter's notebook.

He's been sorting through his conference notes. "Oh—just a little doodle. One of the speakers was a bit less engaging than the others." He tilts the page toward me: a ballpoint sketch of George Costanza, the dog, watching TV with George Costanza, the char-acter.

Though he does his best to hide a smile, I can tell he's proud of it.

When we get back to the apartment early Monday afternoon, we're met with a surprise: a pipe started leaking in the bathroom while we were gone.

We stare at the puddle of water, Wouter silent for a good ten seconds. I can see his brain trying to work out a solution from be-hind his eyes. "Shit," he says quietly, scrubbing a hand along his stubble. "I was going to go into work, but . . ."

"Hey." I place a reassuring hand on his arm. "I'll handle it."

"Really? You'd do that?"

I'm struck with a flashback of suggesting this same thing only a few weeks ago when that cabinet handle broke off and he immediately told me not to worry about it. Because it's not that he's suddenly eager to give me a task.

It's that he trusts me. This apartment means the world to him, and he trusts me with it.

"Of course. I'm ahead on my Dutch homework, so I have the time."

"Thank you. I'll send you the info for the plumber I used last time." Wouter visibly exhales, then heads to the utility closet to shut off the water supply. When he returns, he's sorting through the mail he picked up on our way in. "Some good news, though." He grins as he presents a document to me, all in Dutch. "The title to the building. It's officially been transferred."

"Why do I feel like we should frame it?" I say, grabbing the title from him and scanning over it, even though I can only read some of it. "Right there, over the couch? Or maybe we just slap it on the bathroom mirror so we can see it every time we brush our teeth?"

Wouter glances down at my mouth, and a second stretches longer than it should. There are no rules for any of this, how you're supposed to act after you hooked up with your fake husband–slash–ex-boyfriend and former forbidden love. His smile softens into a look of uncertainty, and my heart drums against my rib cage in anticipation.

"Should we . . . talk about this?" he asks as he steps forward.

"I think we've done a lot of talking lately." I close the remaining space between us, wrap my arms around his neck. "Maybe we could just have fun, without worrying about the rest of it? Keep it . . . casual."

He pauses for a moment, seeming stuck in thought, but then brushes his lips against mine. "I can do that," he says, and then kisses me harder.

It's not long before he has me pushed up against the wall, mouth hot on my neck, my hands tugging at his hair. Even after last night, I'm still hungry for him. The way he touched me with tender desperation, unstitched me with those gorgeous filthy words . . .

With all my willpower, I pat his chest. "I should probably call that plumber." I'm going to guess there isn't a single sentence in either English or Dutch more likely to kill the mood.

"I know, but—" He groans and gives me one last kiss, and I pretend to swat him away. "Fine, fine. I'll see you later tonight. I'll pick up George from Roos on my way home."

"And then we can see who he missed the most," I call after him.

I meant what I said: I don't want to overanalyze what we are now, especially with my sister's visit and the impending faux-wedding. We can be casual; after all, I have plenty of experience with it. I didn't think I'd be able to do it with him, but I'm now certain it's the only option.

We can't have anything else—not when this is already going to end in divorce.

The plumber doesn't answer when I phone, so I leave a message and proceed to search online for someone else. Just as I'm about to make another call, a message from an unknown number pops up on my phone.

> **Hello Dani. This is Anneke, the mother of Wouter. I have an appointment in Amsterdam today and I would like to stop by the apartment to pick up something in storage, but I don't have a key. Are you there this afternoon?**

I fumble out a text letting her know that yes, I'm home, and that I'm happy to let her in—but that we have a leaky pipe and the apartment is in a slight state of disarray.

There's no reply, so I subject myself to the frustration of trying to find a plumber available today, because my basic Dutch—asking someone, *Do you like to eat bread?*—is not exactly useful in this scenario. I manage to talk to a couple people who can take a look at the end of the week, and I'm about to start googling some DIY fixes when the doorbell rings.

"Hoi, Anneke," I say, realizing I'd forgotten about her during my frantic search. "I'm so sorry—I didn't know if you'd gotten my text, or . . ."

"I was driving." That's all she says—curt, to the point. "Nice to see you again."

"You, too." I bite the inside of my cheek, unsure how to navigate this strangeness. I was not prepared to be alone in the apartment with my mother-in-law today—or ever. "Can I take your jacket, or get you anything to drink?"

It doesn't escape my notice that she seems a little stiff, a little wary, even though this is where she lived for much of her life. I wonder if she's looking for signs that I've changed anything, some obvious American influence.

"No, thank you," she says. "You said there was an issue with the pipes?"

I grimace. "Over in the bathroom. I was going to call a plumber, but I'm afraid I haven't had much luck."

"Mind if I take a look?"

I'm only slightly embarrassed by the mess of products on the counter. Without giving them a second glance, she kneels on the floor, inspecting the pipes beneath the sink.

"Ah, this shouldn't be too bad," she says. "It'll just take two of us."

There's some plumber's putty in storage, it turns out, because this isn't the first time this has happened. We dive in with latex gloves, and though we'll eventually have to get a professional to replace the pipe, this fix will hold for now.

And this time, when I offer her some tea, she says yes.

I've watched Wouter do this dozens of times now, but I'm still a little shaky with the tea infuser. *Thee*, reads the Post-it note stuck to the pot—I rolled my eyes when I saw that one.

Anneke picks one up that reads *keukenhanddoek*, and I think I catch her smiling as she places it back on the kitchen towel. "You seem to have really made yourself comfortable," she says after watching me move about the kitchen, setting two mugs down in front of us, a plate of cookies in the center of the table. It's not an admonition or judgment. Just a fact.

"I have. It's an easy place to feel at home."

"I remember Wouter and Roos used to love that window nook over there." She nods toward it. "One day they were boat captains, and the dogs or birds they saw down below were sea creatures. The next, it was a spaceship, and they were fighting aliens. There was never any arguing. No tears. Sometimes we couldn't believe they got along that well."

"They've always been close?" I ask, and she nods. "They're so lucky. I'm the same way with my sister, but—" I break off, unsure how personal I want to get with her.

"It's hard, being away from your family." She dips a biscuit into the tea and takes a small bite. "I studied in America when I was in school, too. Michigan—not quite as glamorous as LA."

"He was disappointed that we weren't constantly passing celebrities on the street. The one time we did see someone, it was an actor he'd never heard of, and he was so upset with himself. But he was such a sweetheart back then," I say, trying to think how a parent would like their kid to be described. "So polite, so easy to get along with. I mean—he's still all those things. We loved having him."

"I'm sure you did."

At first I don't realize it's a joke because she says it in such a nonchalant way—but then her expression cracks, allowing a smile through. I let myself laugh along with her.

"I adored his art," I continue, hoping this isn't a touchy subject. "He could capture people's expressions so beautifully."

Anneke goes quiet for a few moments, and I'm worried I've said too much. "You probably know we weren't very supportive about him studying it," she says. "I knew how much he liked it, but I worried so much. Sometimes I wonder—what if we hadn't pushed him as hard? Especially when his father got sick, I could tell he struggled to stay on top of his studies." That vision makes me ache, Wouter the college student up late cramming for a test while his father's future seemed so delicate. "Then there was all the time he spent taking care of his father, and after he passed . . . he thought he still needed to take care of the rest of us. Not that we wanted him to ignore us, of course, but Roos is plenty self-sufficient. And as for me"—she motions with her head toward the bathroom—"I picked up some skills from my husband as well."

"He wants to be needed," I say, and Anneke gives me a solemn nod.

What she said burrows deep in my heart as a crucial piece of Wouter suddenly becomes clear. He wants so badly to be needed by his family because he's afraid to want something just for himself.

Anneke's gaze flicks over to my hand. Without realizing it, I've been fiddling with the ring.

"I have to admit, I was a little concerned when he first told us you were getting married. But I was young and in love once, too. I can see how much you care for him, Dani, and I'm very glad you found him again." She reaches across the table, her hand covering mine. "And I hope we can keep getting to know each other, too."

The words nearly get caught in my throat. "Of course."

The guilt is an ugly, bitter thing. I give Anneke a tight smile, not unlike when Roos asked for confirmation of my feelings for her brother. Even if it took Anneke a little longer to warm up to me, the conclusion is the same: they both believe I love Wouter.

Wouter's devotion to his family is something I've grown to admire. He was willing to do anything to keep this place that holds his dearest memories—even lie, which I know must be very nearly killing him. All because he wants them to see that he's happy.

And he is, isn't he? He certainly was last night.

Maybe this is working better than we ever planned.

"How about your parents?" Anneke asks. "Have you talked to them more about our little celebration?"

"Oh—it's just so expensive," I manage, feeling like an idiot not to have anticipated this question. Obviously it would strike them as bizarre that my family wouldn't want to see me get married, even if on paper, I already am. "They wanted to. Really wanted to. They just . . . couldn't figure out a way to make it work. But my sister will be here! She and her wife found some cheap tickets."

"I'm very glad to hear that. We'll find plenty of ways to make it special, yes?"

I blow out a shaky breath. It occurs to me that despite all the stress of the pipe and Anneke's surprise visit, I haven't felt the need to count my breaths today. The anxiety isn't overwhelming. "Just the fact that all of you will be there—that's all we really want."

Then she gives me her most genuine grin yet. "Have you decided what you're going to wear?"

I TURN IN FRONT OF THE MIRROR, TRYING TO SEE THE BACK of the gown.

"I love that cut on you," Roos says from a plush couch in front of the dressing room.

Next to her, Iulia nods. "Kind of a vintage vibe."

"And we're all just ignoring the giant bow on my ass?"

Roos laughs. "I think it's cute!"

"Like your ass is a present," Iulia puts in.

I let out a groan, twisting to catch the zipper. "This is a no."

I tried to put off shopping for my not-wedding dress as long as I could, but I was no match for Roos's enthusiasm. If I were in LA, I'd probably have come here with a gaggle of bridesmaids, pressured to return the favor for the women whose weddings I'd been in. Even if it's been a while since I could call them friends.

So I take photos to send to Phoebe, because I'm not sure I can get fake-married in a dress my sister doesn't love.

Roos leaps up to help me with the zipper while Iulia waits nearby with the hanger.

"It's a bit anticlimactic, isn't it?" I say as I step out of a mess of chiffon and satin. "Since we're already married?"

"Maybe a teeny bit." Roos holds up her thumb and forefinger. "But how many times in your life do you get to shop for a wedding dress?"

I have to speak through partially gritted teeth. "Hopefully just once."

One thing I didn't realize is that this friendship with Roos, just like my marriage, has an expiration date. I have a feeling most people don't remain close with their exes' siblings, even if the marriage was fake. However close we get—that all ends the moment we sign the divorce papers.

It doesn't even end with Roos. Iulia, too—my guilt over the number of people we're fooling continues to climb.

As I sort through the rack of dresses, I catch Roos and Iulia laughing as they try on increasingly ridiculous veils. Iulia bats her lashes at Roos, dramatically attempting to cast off a long veil before her hair gets tangled and Roos reaches forward to help. I take longer than I should to put on the next dress, not wanting to interrupt them.

"That color completely washes you out," Roos says when I reappear in a ghostly white. "I like that silhouette, though. I think I saw it in a couple other colors—let me go grab them."

While Roos heads to the front of the store, I turn to Iulia. This is the first time she and I have been semi-alone since the boat tour.

"Iulia," I start. "I feel like I might need to explain some things—"

But she holds up a hand, gives me a swift shake of her head. "Maybe it's better if I don't know? Because . . . I really like Roos. And you, obviously. I don't want to have to lie to her."

I nod, swallowing hard. "And I don't want to put you in that position. I swear."

She must be able to tell how awkward this makes me feel, because she jumps to her feet and wraps me in a quick hug. "Hey. It's okay. No judgment from me, I promise."

"God, you're almost being too nice to me."

I mean it as a joke, but Iulia takes it seriously. "I know expat life isn't always easy," she says in her matter-of-fact way. "There were a few people who helped me out when I first got here, so I just . . . wanted to pass that along."

That only makes me hug her tighter.

A saleswoman sees us embracing and swoops in with a box of tissues. "I know it can be a very emotional time," she says, and Iulia and I fight a laugh as we each accept one.

Roos returns with her arms full of tulle, and Iulia tells us about one of her colleagues who just got fired for breaking into the Dam Fine office after hours and taking one of the boats for a joyride. Her manager found it crashed into the dock the next day, littered with liquor bottles. "So if you know anyone with boating experience or even someone who's a quick learner, let me know."

"I'm almost impressed," Roos says. "It's so hard to get fired here."

"I got fired. Before I left the US."

Both of them whirl to look at me. "Unexpected and intriguing," Roos says, tapping her nails on her chin.

There's a moment when I debate sharing it with them. It's never an easy thing, unpacking your trauma for new people, but I like this feeling of closeness. I want to cling to it as long as I can.

After I've told the whole sordid story, Iulia shouts, "Fuck him!" a little too loudly, drawing the attention of a few other women browsing the shop. A wince as she lowers her voice to a whisper: "Sorry. Fuck him."

This was what I wanted when I told my friends, I realize. How is it that people this far from home can understand me better than people who knew me for years? Is it just that I've already become someone different here, that thing I was aching to be?

"I can't believe you got fired for that. Everyone wants dirty details about their coworkers," Roos says, and when Iulia lifts her eyebrows, she amends: "Fine, most people."

"It wasn't my finest hour, but you know what? I don't regret it." When the words leave my mouth, I'm surprised to find that they're true. "Maybe it was childish, but I don't regret it."

"Because all of it brought you back to your one true love!" Roos says.

Iulia plucks another dress from the rack, a red so dark it verges on merlot. When I lift my eyebrows at her, she holds up a hand. "Don't judge yet! I know it's a bit nontraditional, but this one is speaking to me."

I decide to humor her. The dress is a light gauzy material over-laid with lace, a dramatic V neckline that's mirrored in the back, and though it'll need to be hemmed quite a bit, it instantly feels like the most elegant thing that's ever touched my skin.

Maybe in reality it's a shade or two off, but from a distance, it's the same color as my birthmark. It doesn't try to mask it or pretend it's not there. It emphasizes it. I bring a hand to my cheek, this part of me that I always wanted to hide.

All of us gaze at my reflection in the mirror. I imagine Wouter seeing me in this dress. The way it dips down low and emphasizes the curve of my hips, but most of all, how *happy* I look in it.

"That's it," Roos says on an exhale. "That's the one."

Nineteen

· · · · · · · · · · ·

THE GUY AT OUR FIFTH BIKE SHOP SIZES ME UP. SQUINTS.
"You're looking for an adult bike?"

"Maybe a frame size under fifty centimeters?" Wouter says.

This earns us an exaggerated grimace. "Something that small . . .
I'm afraid I only have bikes for children."

"Can I see?" I ask, and he disappears into a back room.

When I got home from Dutch class late last night after missing
my usual tram—a construction-related reroute—Wouter was on
the couch reading, George curled up beside him.

"It would be so much easier if I could just bike home," I said,
breathless.

"Then that's it." He snapped his book shut and sat up straight.
"We're going bike shopping tomorrow."

The bike the guy wheels out is secondhand and a little scuffed,
black with red and yellow flames swirled on the side. LITTLE
DEVIL is written in aggressive white letters.

I'm instantly obsessed with it.

"I just don't want to make any of the ten-year-olds in the neighborhood jealous," I say as he raises the seat for me.

I can tell even before I climb onto it that it's a perfect fit. My hands wrap loosely around the handlebars, and when I ring the bell, it lets out the shrillest little ding. I take it around the block a few times, getting used to the feel of it. It's older, and there's something comforting about that. Like this bike has seen a lot of kids through their most adventurous, carefree years, on their way to school and their friends' houses and out for ice cream.

Wouter just watches me, a ridiculous grin on his face that must match mine.

The sales guy looks thoroughly perplexed, but he just shrugs with a sense of finality. "I suppose it's less likely to be stolen."

"OKAY, LITTLE DEVIL," WOUTER SAYS WHEN WE GET TO Vondelpark, Amsterdam's largest park. "Show me what you got."

Before we left the bike shop, I had a basket added to the front, and while it doesn't satisfy my pastel Dutch daydream, I don't feel like I'm losing control with my feet on the pedals. My demon bike feels sturdy. Reliable.

In the early afternoon, the park is full of people enjoying the rare springtime sun, even if my weather app warns me it might rain later. As soon as it hits sixty-eight degrees—twenty degrees Celsius—everyone seems to rush outside, determined to get their vitamin D before it's gone. A few herons, those statuesque birds, dot the sides of a pond.

Once I hop on, it takes me a moment to gain full control of the handlebars, and I accidentally nudge Wouter's bike with mine.

"And one more thing," he says as I mumble a *sorry*. "You're not allowed to apologize."

"What?"

"You're learning. You don't have to apologize for that."

"Even if I crash through a shop window?"

"Nope."

"Even if I topple headfirst into a hot dog truck and bring you down with me?"

"Unlikely, but nope."

I start pedaling, wobbling a bit before I find my center of gravity. Every time we encounter a pack of people, I get too in my head, needing to get off the bike to go around them.

"Trust yourself," he says when I hop back on. "I've seen you make that turn without people around—yes! Like that. Goed zo." The pride in his voice sends a new kind of thrill down my spine. He wants me to be good at this—not just good but confident enough to do it on my own.

"I've been intimidated," I admit after a few more minutes. I hate saying it. The first few years of my life were marked by so much weakness that I always felt I had to prove I was strong enough, healthy enough, game enough. "I think that crash maybe left a bigger psychological wound than a physical one, and I've had this mental block ever since."

"I get it. When I was eight or nine, I hit a pole and flew off my bike, right onto the concrete. When my mom bandaged up my knees, I told her over and over that I was never getting back on a bike, and she just laughed. Because she knew there was nothing that could keep me from it—not in this country, not when that was how all my friends were getting around. And she was right. I was back on it the next day, scraped knees be damned." He cups my handlebar. "But getting over the mental hurdle is the hardest part. You're doing fantastic. Not to mention . . ." His voice drops an octave. "You look so fucking cute on that thing."

"Ridiculous, you mean."

"No," he says, and tosses me a smirk as he speeds off.

After a few more laps, we take a break to grab some döner wraps from a food cart, and Wouter spreads out a picnic blanket he had tucked away in his backpack. The first tulips are poking up out of the ground, yellow and pink and red with white tips. The sky has turned gray, thick clouds threatening to yield to rain, but for now, we're safe.

Mostly.

We got back from Bruges a few days ago, and the only reason I haven't begged him to take me to bed is that I have a Dutch exam coming up. I'm relieved my interest in the language hasn't faded. That I haven't given up, tossed it to the side when I wasn't instantly good at it.

Because I want this to work, I realize. *Because I want to stay here.* The closer I get to fluency—though I'm still many months away— the easier time I'll have finding a job, even if that brings back the uncertainty of what Wouter and I will become once we're divorced.

Do we simply . . . stay friends? Keep having casual sex?

Or is it that once we've each gotten what we need, his house and my visa, we'll have no reason to remain in each other's lives?

"There's something I don't understand," I say once we've finished eating, trying to avoid a thought spiral, "and I'm hoping you can enlighten me. You're obviously not terrible-looking—"

"Wow, thank you."

"—and you have some decent qualities—"

"Stop, I'm blushing."

I lean over to push against his arm, and with the way he's grinning, it takes all my willpower to keep from tipping him completely over onto the blanket and climbing on top of him. "If you knew you had to be married to inherit the apartment—I mean . . ."

Now he lifts his eyebrows. "Are you asking why I'm still single?"

This makes me groan, because it's such a cringe-inducing

question. The question no single person ever wants to hear. "I'm not *not* asking. But . . . yes."

"I did think I'd be settled down with kids at this point," he admits after a while, sliding a blade of grass between his fingertips. "When I was taking care of my dad . . . that became my whole life. I don't regret any of it, but my mom was always encouraging me to go out, and I did—sometimes. But I don't think I was a very present partner."

My heart breaks for him all over again, the ways he closed himself off because he wanted all the time with his father he could have. "What was your dad like? If you want to talk about him, I mean."

A slow nod, as though he's making the decision in this moment that he does want to talk about him. "He was a lawyer. That was how my parents met, actually—in law school. That might make it sound like he was this strict, very by-the-book kind of person, but he was only like that at work. He had the most booming laugh, one that I swear I could hear sometimes when I was outside turning onto our street."

"And—what was his name?" I ask, realizing I don't know, and it feels crucial.

"Joost. Very Dutch name," he says. "He was good with his hands, too. Always working on the apartment, because he knew how much it meant to my mom. When I was younger, I wanted to know everything he was doing. He humored me, getting me a little wrench so I could pretend I was fixing things up, too. And he loved American pop culture," he continues. "He'd seen everything, and he always knew the popular shows on HBO. I've never met anyone who loved *Entourage* more than my dad."

I can't help laughing at that, and Wouter's smiling, letting me know it's okay. "I really love that for him."

"He was a huge part of the reason I wanted to go to the US. Especially to LA."

"I am so sorry I couldn't help you live out your *Entourage* fantasies. You could have at least called me Turtle when I was driving us around. I wouldn't have minded." I squint one eye at him. "Were you more of a Vince or an E? Don't tell me you were an Ari."

"'They're all terrible in their own ways," Wouter says, leaning over to nudge my shoulder. Then he turns serious again. "Now you can understand why I hadn't dated anyone in a while. Sometimes I even wonder if I'd be a good partner. A real one," he says, tapping my ring with his index finger. "My family and my work have been my whole world for so long. It felt like I didn't have space for hobbies or for travel or for *fun*, really. My whole life has revolved around being practical, being logical, being available. I told you why I wanted to keep that apartment, even if it's falling apart—I used to imagine my parents growing old there, that I'd bring my kids to visit. That's changed, of course, and now I want so badly to raise children in the place I love so much." Another pause. "Maybe that's the problem. Maybe I want it too much."

I think back to what his mother said about his desire to feel needed. All of that caretaking he did for his father—and then when he passed away, he didn't know how to take care of himself.

My throat is dry when I speak again. "I have absolutely *zero* doubts that you'll be a phenomenal partner. For—for the right person."

Slowly he nods, and I wish I could explain why that cracks my heart in half.

"For what it's worth," I continue, "I don't think you want too much. At all." Because that's the truth—he deserves the fucking world, and whoever gets to give it to him is going to be indescribably lucky. "And . . . I'm trying to think of a delicate way to ask this, but you're doing okay?"

"I spent some time in therapy after my dad passed away. Just needed to talk to someone who could be gentle with me, and who could help me be gentler on myself."

"I've been in therapy, too. Not that I'm saying that my issues are anywhere near yours." The words come out too quickly, before I can second-guess them.

He frowns at this, and for a moment I'm worried this wasn't the right time to share it. "Why does it have to be a competition?"

"It's not. I just . . ." I take a deep, shaky breath. I hadn't planned on telling him any of this, not now and maybe not ever. But now it's out there, and he's already shared so much . . . "I had a bit of a breakdown. About four years ago." The way he's watching me doesn't make me feel as though there's a spotlight on me, like I'm onstage confessing this while sweat drips down my back. There's no pressure here. "I was in the same place I am right now, pretty much—no boyfriend, a job I didn't care about, and everyone else was doing great things and getting married and having kids, and I just . . . felt so far behind. Like I'd never be able to catch up. I've always had that. This worry I'm not living up to my potential. I mean—you know my whole birth story."

He nods, because he knows the basic facts. "There was a lot of trauma there for all of you. I remember the photos your family showed me. The news stories."

"God, those stories. I couldn't help feeling I was supposed to do something *good*, something that *mattered*, all because I'd survived. I was a 'miracle baby,' and therefore I needed to go out and do something miraculous. And my parents—I know they meant well, but they had me in a bubble, like I could get a paper cut and it would be a national emergency." I'm breathing hard now, my chest aching a little. *Four. Seven. Eight.* When I say it out loud, none of it sounds worthy of that hospital stay or the pills in my nightstand drawer. How could something that happened solely in my head measure up to everything he's just confessed? The horrible things he's been through? I'm such a fucking idiot, embarrassed to have brought it all up. With a trembling hand, I shade my eyes from his.

"It all just kind of caught up to me. I spent two weeks in the hospital with therapists, getting stable and figuring out the right kind of medication. It . . . was probably the best thing I could have done at the time."

Wouter's eyes are full of an emotion I don't think I've ever seen on him. Sympathy, but it's misplaced. "I'm so sorry, lief," he says softly, cupping my knee with his hand. "I wish you hadn't had to go through any of it, but I'm so glad you got help."

"It was a positive experience," I say honestly. "I'm grateful I was able to do it. But sometimes even now, it's like—what right do I have to depression?"

"The same right as anyone else," he says. "You don't have to feel any shame about asking for what you needed."

"But on paper, there was nothing wrong with my life. And yet I just couldn't make myself be happy."

"You took charge and prioritized yourself. You should feel the opposite of ashamed. You should feel . . ." He searches for a word, fingertips stroking along my jeans. "Strong. That's what I always think when I look at you."

I bite back a laugh at how ridiculous that sounds. "*Strong?* Me, the thirty-year-old woman who's learning to ride a child's bike?"

"*Yes,*" he insists, and there's something in his conviction about it that washes over me and makes me want to believe him. "You've always been brave. Ever since you were a baby—you're a fucking fighter. You moved here with no idea what it was going to be like. You didn't know anyone, didn't have a backup plan. You just took a leap."

"But you did the same thing."

"Completely different. I didn't have to worry about money or a job or where I was going to live." A crooked smile. "Although I probably should have worried about how I was going to keep my cool, living in the same house as you."

"Please. You were so chill, it took me ages to realize you liked me back."

He holds a hand to his heart in faux shock. "Me, chill? My seventeen-year-old self didn't know the meaning of the word." Now his hand finds mine, tracing along my knuckles, inching up my wrist. "There was something special about it, wasn't there? Sharing all those firsts the way we did."

"Stumbling through them, sometimes," I say, all my senses attuned to his fingertips. "Like the time we were fooling around in my car, and you smacked your head on the roof of it. I was so worried you had a concussion, even though you had zero symptoms, and I was going to have to explain to my parents that you got it from trying to take off my bra with your teeth."

"Suave, I was not." His hazel eyes turn soft, crinkling at the edges. "But you still stopped at a grocery store for a bag of frozen peas."

We sat in a park like this one until curfew, Wouter's head in my lap, me holding the makeshift ice pack to his forehead, feeling for a bump that wasn't there.

"I think my hand went numb," I say, laughing. I never thought I'd have the chance to do this kind of reminiscing with him, and it's healing something inside me I didn't realize needed closure.

"We had a couple disasters, yes, but I like to think we figured it out."

And we did, didn't we? For a while, we had something so precious. Maybe it ended in heartbreak, but the memories are still there, and finally knowing the truth about the breakup repaints them all with the rosiest lens.

He brings his hand to my shoulder, fingertips flirting with the edges of my hair. I lean into him—not overthinking, just accepting this kind of simple, tender touch for what it is. Now that he can be open about how he feels, he's letting out everything he's kept locked away. I close my eyes at the sensation, lost in thought while a beautiful man braids his fingers through my hair.

In so many ways, I still don't know what I'm doing here. I was supposed to find a new job, but I can't picture being stuck in another one of those corporate offices. I don't know what I want, but it's not that.

Burnout, he called it at the STRAAT Museum, and it seemed foreign to me. Probably I thought you had to be settled in a career to feel burned out, that you needed to have some kind of fire beneath you when all I had were a few sparks. I don't think he was wrong, though—between the job I didn't love and the constant yearning for more, my utter exhaustion and my stay in the psych ward . . . all of it added up to something that's only now becoming clear.

"I guess it just feels like I've never found my footing. A perpetual late bloomer." I glance up at him. "Is there a similar phrase in Dutch?"

"It's the same, actually. Laatbloeier." He considers this for a moment. "I get it. I can't decide if I'm too old for my body or if I'm something of a laatbloeier, too. Or maybe I bloomed, but not in the right way. Not in a way that my younger self, the self that you knew in LA, would be very thrilled with, I don't think."

"Then change," I say, as though it's so easy. As though it didn't take me stumbling halfway across the world to learn I was capable of it. "It's not too late. I promise."

It's only when we fall into a companionable silence that I realize he called me "lief" when no one else was around. I looked it up after Culemborg. "Sweetheart," "darling"—that's what it means.

Scattered raindrops have started falling, and some people are packing up their stuff. I'm not used to putting my insecurities on display like this. Even Jace didn't know much about my hospitalization or the residual miracle-baby anxiety.

We said this was going to be casual, but that doesn't account for all the truths I've already spilled to him. All the things I've never been able to share with anyone else.

I squint up at the clouds. "Should we get back on our bikes, or—"

It's at that moment the sky opens up, unleashing a torrent of rain unlike any I've seen before.

People shriek as they snatch up their belongings and head for shelter. We jump to our feet, Wouter collecting the blanket and stuffing it into his backpack.

"You okay to ride back in the rain?"

The ground is soggy beneath my feet, and even though I'm already soaked, I'm not in any rush to leave.

I tilt my face toward the sky, letting the rain wash over me. "In a minute?" I ask, and he laughs.

His hair is already slicked back in a way that makes me want to run my tongue from the hollow of his throat down to his navel. Rain dots his glasses, but I can still tell he's watching me as the downpour renders my thin T-shirt absolutely useless.

The pure yearning in his expression is enough to undo me. I can't resist—I crush myself against him, tipping up my head to catch his lips.

I don't think it's closure at all. It's something else, something scarier, and yet I can't help running straight toward it.

His mouth is wet and wanting. If I'm shivering, I'm not sure if it's from the weather or from *him*, the way he clutches my soaking body to his, the rumble in his throat sounding like thunder. I can't see with the rain in my face, but it doesn't matter—all I need to do is feel.

I don't know how long he kisses me there, urgent and unafraid.

"What do you think?" I ask when the rain starts to let up. He's still holding me by the waist, both of us breathless. "Should we keep biking, or . . ." I hook a thumb to one of his belt loops, hoping my intention in the *or* is clear.

A shake of his head. A crooked smile. "What I want right now," he says, fingertips splayed on my hips, "is to go home and fuck my wife."

Twenty

. . . .

WE'RE ALREADY A SLIPPERY MESS AS WE STUMBLE DOWN
the hall to the shower. His hands are on me before we make it
there, pinning me up against the wall, lifting my legs up around his
hips so he can kiss my neck, my collarbone, my chest over my see-
through shirt. I'm addicted to how greedy he is—because I feel it
too, the electricity pulsing between us as I grab his hair, moan into
his ear.

The ride home was still mildly treacherous. Water and mud
splashed up my legs, and every inch of me is soaked, but I don't
care. We locked our bikes and sloshed up the stairs, laughing, kicking off our shoes outside the front door. A moment to give George
some pets and a treat.

Once we get to the bathroom, Wouter flicks the knob of the
shower and takes his time undressing me in front of the mirror
while we wait for it to heat up, wet clothes clinging to wet skin.

Fuck my wife. Fuck my wife. Fuck my wife.

The words are stuck in my head on filthy repeat.

He stands behind me, pulling my hair away from my neck while he kisses me there, sweetly at first and then hard enough to leave a mark. One hand is spread across my waist while his thumb strokes the sunflower petals on my hip, and I press against him when his erection nudges the middle of my back.

"I love the way you look like this," he murmurs. He drags a finger up my jaw, toward my cheek. He doesn't shy away from touching my birthmark, and I realize that without even meaning to, I've been tilting my head slightly to the left.

"Naked?" I ask with a laugh, and the dimple appears when he smiles.

"Yes, but—specifically right now. All flushed and beautiful. I can see the anticipation on your face."

I reach a hand backward to circle his cock. "And I can feel yours right here."

I watch us in the mirror, the way that smile morphs to a groan, eyes shut while I stroke him. In retaliation, he cups my breast, teases my nipple like he knows this is the quickest way to turn me liquid.

Maybe this is how we reestablish a boundary. Sex is casual. Sex doesn't have to be emotional.

And once I have an employment contract, we won't need to be anything to each other anymore.

He spins me around and we tumble into the shower, our mouths fused together. For a moment I'm unsure whether he actually intends for us to get clean—until he reaches for a bar of soap.

He drags it along my skin and I let myself turn off my brain, focusing only on the way he lathers my arms, my neck, my stomach. Warm water pounds against my back. Washes away the grime. I catch plenty of it in my mouth—that's how much I'm grinning as he soaps up my breasts.

When he passes me the bar of soap, I start with his ankles. Move up to his calves. His knees. His cock is at perfect attention, and I can't resist giving him a few tugs again. *God*, he's so expressive when we're like this, and it might be my favorite thing about him—how every touch sparks a reaction. This time, it's his hand coming up to give the wall a wet smack.

I inch up his stomach, learning where he's ticklish, which turns out to be everywhere. Wouter fights back laughter as I run soapy water along his abs, then catches me around the waist and bends down for a kiss, as though he thinks it'll distract me.

And it does, because of course it does.

"Be shorter," I whine, as he dutifully crouches down for me to get his arms and shoulders. It's criminal how hot he looks like this, wild hair and suds dripping down his body.

He throws me a smirk. "And yet you never hear me asking you to get taller."

He doesn't just have the one tattoo, I realize. There's another, a swirl of roman numerals on the back of his calf—a date. And then the one I caught only a glimpse of last time, rendered in delicate black ink just above his shoulder blade. Small leaves and wide, flat petals, with a dark center.

A poppy.

The California state flower.

I swallow around a lump in my throat. It has to be a coincidence, or even likelier, I don't know anything about flowers. There must be some other symbolism there.

Before I can linger on it, Wouter is opening my bottle of shampoo. He beckons me closer and I shut my eyes, letting him swirl his fingers through my hair and along my scalp in these soothing, tender circles—

Too tender.

My eyes fly open and I have to blink shampoo out of them, wiping it away even as they're stinging.

"What you said in the park," I say, eager to turn this casual again. "Right before we left. I like—when you talk to me that way."

A slow, wicked smile spreads across his face. "That I wanted to fuck my wife?"

God, this man is going to turn me feral. "Yes. *That*."

Now he takes me in his arms again, pushes me against the wall of the shower. "Watching you come just once wasn't enough." He drags his tongue down the column of my neck while I fist a hand in his hair. "Fuck, Dani. The way you come is so gorgeous. How you lose control, bite your lip like you're trying to hold back, until you just can't take it anymore. The sounds you make . . ." As he's doing this, he slips a finger between my thighs, and I'm completely unashamed of how quickly he finds a slick, torturous rhythm. *"All* the sounds you make."

A cry escapes my throat. His gaze sparks with mischief as he gets to his knees to start kissing up my legs. It's such a beautiful sight, him kneeling in front of me, a privilege to see him this vulnerable.

"The number of times I've imagined your legs wrapped around my neck . . ." He grasps my thighs. Presses open-mouthed kissed to them.

In response I can only groan as he licks a hot stripe up my thigh, so close to where I want him.

He holds me steady as he parts my legs. "Tell me what else you like," he says. "How else does my wife want to be fucked?"

The parts of me that are still breathing stammer out a response. "I like—" Suddenly it's hard to vocalize. No one's ever asked me this before, just assumed whatever they were doing was one-size-fits-all, and I writhed around enough to make them believe it. "Everything you did last time."

A fingertip traces a line of freckles on my hip. "There has to be something else."

There is. Of course there is. "If you lick me while you have your finger inside me, that's—I like that. And then—" I swallow hard, wondering how far I can go. "You can put a finger in my ass, too. If you want."

He loses his cool for just a moment there, like maybe this was unexpected. But he makes no secret of how hungry it makes him, dragging his hands up to squeeze my ass. "Christ. Yes. I want."

Hearing him say that is an instant relief.

He hikes one of my legs over his shoulder, balancing me with the help of the wall. At first it feels precarious, but there's a sureness in his grip that makes me trust him. I'm completely bared to him like this—physically, and also with what I've just asked for—and yet I've never felt safer.

He starts slowly, slowly, a graze of his tongue along my lips. Teasing. Last time he found all the places I'm most sensitive, and he seems to have remembered them all. He fucks me with his finger, languid strokes that drag obscenities from my mouth.

Then he increases his speed. Adds a second finger. Even as my thighs shake, he keeps me upright. I am entirely at the mercy of his tongue, lapping at that sensitive bud of nerves. *Fuck*—I'm not going to last long at all, but he's doing his damnedest to draw it out. Every so often, he gives my clit a flick of his tongue or brush of his finger, but he knows better than to give it too much attention too soon.

And even though I've asked for it, I'm not prepared for him to slick a finger with my wetness before reaching around to my ass. That touch, that single gentle touch that must only last a couple seconds, as though he wants to make sure he gets it right before he keeps going—it electrifies all my nerve endings. He might as well have reached right inside my chest and yanked. I grab his hair so tightly, I'm worried I might hurt him.

He glances up at me with wild eyes. "Like this?"

Yes, I try to tell him. *You're amazing. You're perfect.* But the only sound that makes it past my mouth is a strangled moan.

"Good girl," he says, and then he does it again, balancing that soft stroke with his tongue's more fervent one against my clit. "Beautiful girl. Keep moaning just like that for me."

It's too much. Too good. I'm putty in his arms, feeling somehow weightless as I brace myself against his shoulders, against the wall of the shower. Pleasure pools low in my belly, and I can't look down at his face between my thighs or else I'll fall apart—but then I'm falling apart anyway, stars bursting behind my eyes, everything in my body letting go. I collapse against him, ungraceful, but he's got me. He's got me.

When I finally glance down as he eases me to my feet, he's grinning. Blown-out pupils. Wet mouth. Pure satisfaction.

"Bed," I say, my voice hoarse. "Now."

We bother with towels only long enough to make sure we're not dripping water everywhere. He gathers me into his arms again, one pair of damp footsteps over to his room, the part of the apartment I've spent almost zero time in, but I barely have time to register the details—

—because George is curled up in the middle of the bed, just staring at us.

I let out a startled yelp as Wouter laughs, gently setting me down.

"I'm sorry, buddy," he says, and the dog scampers out of the room, clearly unsure what's going on but sensing he probably doesn't want to be here for it.

"We'll make it up to him with a long walk later," I say right before my back hits the mattress.

The way he holds me feels different somehow. He plants a

lingering kiss on my ankle. My calf. The inside of my knee. That first time, we were frantic. This time, though it's grown dark outside, I make sure to switch on the bedside lamp before crawling back onto his lap and really letting myself *see* him. The angles of his chest, that red-blond trail of hair. How he has more freckles on his shoulders than anywhere else. His laugh, lungs shuddering beneath me as I press my face into his chest and inhale him.

"You said you have an IUD?" he asks, and I nod, skimming a hand over the head of his cock, knowing he'll feel so fucking *right* inside me. He pulses against my palm.

"I want to feel you. Just you. We've never—" When we were seventeen, we always used a condom. "I want it to feel like a first time."

"I know," he says softly. Reverent. "A second first time."

He holds my hips while I straddle him, taking my time teasing. With as much self-control as I can muster, I rub my center along his cock as he hisses out a plea.

"Need you," he murmurs. "*Please.*"

"Well. Since you asked nicely."

I sink my hips all the way down, taking his full length and drawing out a stunning groan. *Oh*—the instant heat of him, that exquisite pressure. I rock a few times, let out a shaky breath. *Just him*, nothing separating us as he stretches me in the most decadent way.

"You feel . . . absolutely unreal. *Jesus.* I think I could stay here forever," he says as we move together. Slowly, and then a little faster. His jaw clenches, as though he's trying to savor every inch. "This is good?"

"*Yes.* It's incredible." We exhale into each other, like this is some sweet relief we've been chasing for weeks. Months. With one hand he clutches my ass, fingertips brushing my lower back, and the other settles between us.

Somehow his gaze on mine is both fierce and tender.

Casual, casual, casual, I remind myself.

I need him deeper. I roll my hips up and then back down again, the fullness of him somehow a surprise every time. I love watching him like this, wholly surrendered to the sensation, content with me taking control. The sheen of sweat along his hairline and down his throat. The flex of his muscles.

"You just—you look so good at every angle," I say. "Like a fucking Michelangelo sculpture or something."

A choked laugh. "You're thinking about art right now?"

I move my hips faster, even as I'm biting out a gasp. "Just the most basic kind. Just for you."

Some part of me still can't believe this is happening. That this is the same boy who gave me my first orgasms with curious, determined fingers.

Still curious. Still determined.

His hand finds my sunflowers again, and for a second he looks like he wants to say something, but then he changes course and flips us around. His arms bracket my shoulders, my knees at his hips. Nails digging into shower-fresh skin.

I barely have a moment to ache for him before he's filling me again, perfect thrusts that have me spreading my legs wider and wider. Arching my back against the mattress. The sight of where we're joined, that primal smack of his body against mine—it's almost too much.

Casual. Casual.

"Can you come for me again?" he asks, licking his fingertips before dropping them back to my clit. Realizing the effect those words have on me, he continues: "Can you come on my cock?"

And *god*, I'm already almost there. I can tell he is, too, the way he tightens and lets out a rough exhale.

"Don't hold back," I beg. We couldn't be loud all those years ago, but nothing's stopping us now. "I want to hear everything."

The moment he finally lets himself go, his features struck with golden lamplight, the purest ecstasy on his face—*that* is the work of art.

Twenty-one

"I'M GOING TO ASK YOU A VERY SERIOUS QUESTION," MY sister says, and I sit up a little straighter, preparing for an interrogation. "Is he hot, or is he just tall?"

"Both. And that is part of the problem."

We're at a café in De Pijp, not too far from my first apartment—which, I saw when I pointed it out to her, had been completely boarded up.

It's so indescribably wonderful to see her that I can't stop touching her, as though needing to make sure she's real. I rested my head on her shoulder when I rode the train back with her and Maya from the airport, linked my arm with hers as we walked the streets, and even now, I have a hand on her elbow. Today she's in her indestructible patchwork cardigan, her dark hair in its usual messy bun, and she even managed to unearth that bracelet I made her years ago during my short-lived jewelry phase, with its blocky wooden beads. I could cry over how familiar these details are, this relief that she hasn't dramatically changed since I've been gone. There's an element of the surreal to it, my sister with Amsterdam's canal houses in the background. This merging of my two separate lives.

Maya returns to our table with a tray of pastries. I'm still getting used to the sight of her this pregnant, an empire-waist dress emphasizing her six-month bump, auburn curls hanging down her back. It's a staggering visual reminder of all I've missed since I moved here.

I couldn't help everything from spilling out as soon as they settled in a bit, at a hotel a couple blocks from the Prinsengracht, after they'd met Wouter and George and confirmed that my current living situation is far from dungeon-esque.

When Phoebe saw Wouter again, she dropped her purse, mouth falling open before she enveloped him in a fierce hug. Then, once she picked up her bag, she gave him a gentle thwack with it.

"I had to," she said with a shrug. "For the breakup. Sister loyalties."

He gave her a solemn nod. "I understand. Completely deserved."

Then he had a hundred questions about her bookstore, and she had a hundred more about his life here in Amsterdam. The kind of thirteen-year catch-up I've grown familiar with.

Maya takes a bite of a koffiebroodje, a swirl of sweet bread dotted with raisins, and her eyes fall shut for a moment. "Are all the pastries here this good? Because I think a few more would cure my jet lag."

"Unfortunately, yes," I say as I reach for a pain au chocolat.

Phoebe rests her hand on the back of Maya's chair as she downs her second espresso of the day. "If everything is finally out in the open between you two, the sex is fantastic, and you like spending time together . . . then what's holding you back?" She screws up her nose in confusion. "Sorry, am I missing something?"

My face heats with the memory of him hoisting me onto the kitchen counter a few days ago before dropping to his knees. Dragging me onto the balcony and asking how quiet I could be.

"I didn't come here just so a man could save me." Another few bites of pastry. "Not to mention, his family won't ever want to see me again once they find out the truth."

The statement is bitter on my tongue. I've never quite thought about it that way, but it's the truth, isn't it? As soon as we divorce, Roos and his mother and grandmother won't just be out of my life—they might even see me as a villain.

"I guess that does make it a bit more awkward than your typical forbidden teenage romance turned green-card marriage," Phoebe relents, and I'm grateful for it, because as much as I've craved her advice at times, right now all I want is to make it to the other side of this wedding with as little anxiety as possible.

"How's the baby's room coming along?" I ask.

"We're not quite done yet." As an interior designer, Maya's going all out, using as many thrifted materials as possible. "It's a bookish theme, and we have this friend working on an amazing mural combining some of the children's classics—*Goodnight Moon, Corduroy, The Very Hungry Caterpillar* . . ."

"Baby *Architectural Digest* or bust," Phoebe says.

"I can't wait to see it," I say, realizing with a lump in my throat that the first time I do, it may be with two phone screens in between.

KING'S DAY IS A LATE-APRIL HOLIDAY CELEBRATING THE king's birthday—but really, it's more of a countrywide excuse to party.

Just about everyone has the day off work, all the shops are closed, and the drinking starts early and goes late. Over the past couple days, the city's been setting up extra public urinals in preparation, and you can definitely smell it.

Outside it's a riot of orange, the Netherlands' national color.

Maya decided to take it easy, so Wouter and I meet Roos and Phoebe along the Prinsengracht, where Roos gives my sister a hug and drapes orange feathered boas around our necks to match the cheap orange sunglasses Wouter and I already picked up from HEMA earlier this week. We press our way through the thick crowd, Phoebe's jaw dropping every time we turn the corner. The streets are covered with blankets of knickknacks—vrijmarkten, free markets—because this is the one day a year yard sales are legal. There's a guy leading a group in the Macarena. A woman with cords wrapped around herself holding a sign that says MOBILE PHONE CHARGER. Every so often, there's a street too packed with people for us to freely pass through, so we have no choice but to dance along to whatever electronic track is blasting through someone's open window.

Phoebe grabs my arms and throws her head back as the horde sways with us. "This is *ridiculous*," she shouts. "I love it!"

When we pass more than a few people with their hair dyed orange, I reach up and ruffle Wouter's hair. "Where's your national pride?"

"I'm not sure my hair would survive the chemicals," he says with a laugh. His hand finds the small of my back, guiding me through the crush of orange shirts and face paint.

"We can stay married however long you need to," he said yesterday after a breathless morning in bed—all because I'd watched the way his forearms flexed while he was brewing tea and couldn't resist. Evidently, the process of making tea is foreplay to me now. "What's happening here . . . doesn't have to change anything."

There was some relief to that, of course. A year was the timeline we laid out at the beginning, but now that two months have passed since we signed those papers and he has ownership of his place, a year suddenly doesn't seem very long at all.

When we get to Dam Fine's dock, it seems everyone had the same idea; the canals are packed with boats, their passengers singing in Dutch and in English, orange confetti in the air. Even though the alcohol is flowing freely, there's an undeniable wholesomeness, too. An infectious energy.

"So it's always on the king's birthday, April twenty-seventh," I say once we take off. Iulia's at the front of the boat in her captain's hat, Wouter next to me, and my sister on the other side, along with Sanne, Bilal, and a couple of Roos's friends. "But . . . it's not always a king, is it?"

Sanne shakes her head, some orange hair glitter scattering on the deck of the boat. "It used to be Queen's Day. Queen Beatrix, she was the queen before Willem-Alexander—she kept it on thirtieth April because that was her mother's birthday. She was born at the end of January, which would have been a miserable Queen's Day." Then she breaks off, laughing. "The year it switched over to King's Day, a bunch of tourists came here to party on the thirtieth even though it was now the twenty-seventh."

"It was pretty hilarious, actually," Bilal says. "They completely missed it." He offers around a box of tompouce, a traditional Dutch sweet with—of course—orange frosting for King's Day. It's small and rectangular, two layers of puff pastry with cream in the middle.

"Super lekker," I say when I bite into it, accompanying it with the gesture I learned in Dutch class: a hand to the side of my face, waved back and forth.

"The lekker hand wave!" Roos exclaims, so enthusiastically that she nearly whacks her orange sunglasses into the canal. "I'm so proud." She cozies up with Iulia at the front of the boat, taking selfies, stealing her captain's hat.

Phoebe's gaze drifts from the chaos in the canals back to Wouter and me. "God, this is all so fucking weird. Amsterdam, the two of you . . . everything."

I nudge her. "That's what I've been saying for the past few months."

Wouter's arm comes around my stomach, pulling me onto his lap. "Weird at first, maybe," he says. "But now . . . it's really incredible having her here."

I thread my fingers with his as he leans his chin on my shoulder, and while this kind of gesture might typically kick my heart into panic mode, today it only sparks a warmth in my chest. We don't need to put on this kind of performance—not in front of my sister, not when everyone else on the boat is in their own worlds—but something about the way he holds me feels different now.

Real.

Almost terrifyingly so, and yet I'm not pushing him away.

"I feel like I'm getting a very specific picture of Amsterdam," Phoebe says to the group. "Dani keeps saying it's not like this all the time, but . . ."

"Maybe not quite this orange." I sit back, tipping my head toward the sun starting to peek through the clouds. "This place is unreal, though. I can't believe it's legal to just . . . live here."

"Yeah, we're absolute shit at keeping it a secret," Bilal says.

Wouter's thumb skims up my elbow. "They really just let anyone in here," he says, a hint of amusement in his voice that makes me squeeze his hand.

"Next year we should go to one of the music festivals," Sanne says. "There's a huge techno one that happens in Oost."

Next year. If anything could prick my King's Day bubble, despite my apathy for techno music, it's that.

Next year: when Wouter and I are divorced. When I'm no longer friends with any of these people.

"Does it ever get old?" I ask Iulia, eager for a distraction. "Being out on the water every day?"

"Honestly? No." She tips her bottle of beer toward me. "I'm sure most jobs start to feel boring after a while, but not this. Even if some of the facts I recite sound a little repetitive after a while, there are always new people, new questions, new ways to make it feel fresh. It's impossible to be bored when all of *this* is your office."

At golden hour, the light bends through windows and shimmers across the water, giving this weird and wonderful city an ethereal glow.

Days like this, I am certain this is the loveliest place on earth. There is something dramatically different about life not just on this side of the world but in this specific city, something that goes beyond the metric system and the public transportation and the weather. Despite how foreign all this might have seemed a few months ago, I finally feel like I *belong*.

Maybe this is what Iulia meant about expats staying here forever.

There's a sense of freedom out on the water that I'm not sure I've ever felt on land, but surely this isn't the something great I've been chasing. Unless "something great" seemed so radically unachievable that I set myself on the path of mediocrity early on, and now I'm too far down it to deviate.

I try to see beyond this marriage, once I've landed a solid job and proven to everyone back home that I can not only succeed here but thrive.

And I can't help wondering why the only person I've never tried to prove anything to is myself.

MY NEXT JOB INTERVIEW IS A COUPLE DAYS LATER, AND given the dwindling balance in my bank account, I couldn't turn it down. I steer Little Devil through narrow alleys until I can no longer avoid the busier streets and realize waiting for a crowd of tourists to disperse isn't as terrifying as I thought it might be. Especially when I'm ringing my bell.

When I lock my bike in front of the building, I have to fight the phantom urge to click my keys the way I'd lock a car.

The interview isn't with a startup but a big-name company I didn't know had an office here. This would be the same thing I did in LA, just for a competitor and on another continent. There should be some comfort in that, shouldn't there? If the lobby is a little soulless, that's just because everyone's already tucked away in their offices.

Keep an open mind, I tell myself as I smooth my slacks. *You are not special just because you don't love the idea of working in an office.*

"Danika, hi," says the interviewer when he meets me at reception, an American named Todd. "We're so happy to have you here. Come in, come in."

Over the next half hour, during which the phrase *core principles* is uttered no fewer than three times, I rattle off cardboard responses about my leadership skills and greatest strengths.

"One of the major selling points for people is that we serve lunch here every day." Todd seems stoked about this. "Plenty of gluten-free and vegetarian options. We definitely want to make this a fun, cool place to be!"

"Wonderful. I love lunch," I say, and although this isn't remotely funny, he laughs.

I even get a chance to experience it after the interview, and Todd's right: it's a solid lunch.

But it's not enough. It doesn't fill the existential emptiness, doesn't soothe the part of me aching to be out in the sunshine.

I've assumed my specific college degree qualifies me for this one specific thing, but even Wouter knew when he remet me: this isn't my passion. Halfway across the world, I'm still trying to force it.

I don't have to tie myself to those long-ago expectations imprinted on me before I had the words to fight back. Maybe during all those years as a serial hobbyist, I was looking for something I was good at when I could have picked something that made me *happy*.

Somehow that was never a priority, and now I can't under-stand why.

"You know what, I'm so sorry," I tell Todd as he's escorting me out of the building. "I'm so grateful for your time, but I don't know if this is the right fit for me."

He gapes at me. "Not sure I've had this happen before, but okay. I'm glad you figured that out sooner rather than later."

"Hope I didn't waste too much of your time. Thanks for the op-portunity."

A crisp handshake. "I hope you find what you're looking for."

I'm already unbuttoning my suffocating blazer as I head out to Little Devil. Then I hit the pedals faster than I ever have before, electric-charged with a false sense of urgency, because what if that job doesn't exist anymore and they found someone else, when the truth is—I might want it more than I've wanted anything in a while.

"Hi," I say, breathless, bursting into the office of Dam Fine Boat Tours.

Iulia is at a long desk with a couple coworkers, all of them whirl-ing to face me. "Dani, hi," she says. "What's up?"

I hold a hand to my chest as I try to catch my breath. "Are you still hiring?"

Twenty-two

MY NEW FAVORITE WAY TO WAKE UP: WOUTER, SOFTLY nudging me after spending the night tangled in my bedsheets. His nose in the crook of my neck, mouth on my shoulder. I'm already mostly lucid; now that we're closer to daylight savings, the mornings are much brighter. A dramatic difference from when I got here in the dead of winter. George is cuddled on my other side, having jumped on the bed sometime in the middle of the night.

"I have a surprise for you later," Wouter says into my ear. "Think of it as a pre-wedding gift."

"I thought we told your family no gifts," I mumble.

He kisses my temple. "But this is from me."

Dam Fine Boat Tours wound up interviewing me on the spot yesterday. It was just the first step of the process, but I left feeling giddy, like I'd said everything I wanted to. I admitted I'd never captained a boat before but I was eager to learn, and that I couldn't imagine a better way to spend my waking hours than showing people the most beautiful parts of Amsterdam.

The more pressing issue on my mind, though: the wedding is tomorrow.

I'm jittery about it all day as I pick up my port-wine dress, freshly altered. Phoebe and Maya took a day trip to a windmill village called Zaanse Schans, and I want to let them enjoy their vacation. Plus, my parents have been quieter than usual. They skipped our usual Sunday call, told me they were busy and that we'd talk next week.

Still, I could use a distraction.

So in the early evening, I meet Wouter at a pottery studio on the first floor of an old house in the Jordaan. Ceramic tiles are displayed in the front window, some of them in the traditional Dutch style, swirls of blue on white backgrounds. Others are more abstract, more modern.

"I thought we could paint our own tiles." He suddenly looks sheepish, a hand on the back of his neck, as though unsure this was a good idea after all. "It's time to redo the backsplash in the kitchen, and this way . . . the apartment could be a piece of both of us."

"That—sounds great," I say, swallowing back the emotion.

And in theory, it does. It's only about 15 x 15 centimeters, a small square of shiny clay. But this new backsplash, this imprint I make on the apartment . . . it's only temporary.

I was an idiot, thinking I could do casual without it amplifying my affection for him. It's too easy to close my eyes and let myself fall, no matter how high the cliff is.

The painting itself is soothing, but I'm still too stuck in my thoughts. I don't want the tile to represent me in any way, don't want him to be forced to think about me long after I'm gone. I decide on a teapot, since he loved tea long before he liked me, and that feels safe. Next to me, Wouter mixes blues and greens for water, darker hues for shadows. The view from the window in his apartment.

In the end, both our tiles are lovely but imperfect. The instructor collects our pieces to put them in the kiln and tells us we'll be able to pick them up next week.

After we leave the class, we wander the narrow alleyways, the unseasonably warm evening doing its best to soothe my residual nerves.

"It's going to be okay, right?" I ask, and I have to clarify because of course, Wouter does not live inside my brain. "The wedding. I know it's basically just a party, but . . ."

"They already like you," he says. Reassuring. Solid. "You don't have to prove anything. And you're feeling good about this job opportunity?"

"Better than I have in months." The honest truth. "Of course, I'd be lying if I said there wasn't a tiny part of me that worries I won't be good at it, but I'll cross that bridge if I get to it, et cetera. Literally," I say, gesturing to our feet.

"I have zero doubts that whatever you decide to do—because it's not just something that happens to you; you get to be in charge—you're going to be incredible at it."

"I don't know," I say, because my first urge is always to avoid accepting a compliment, even if it's something I desperately want. "Remember, I'm the girl who flooded her apartment and escaped a failing company within the same week."

But he remains steadfast. "You moved here and immediately wanted to take everything in. You're learning a hard language. You don't hold yourself back from enjoying something new. You think you don't have ambition? Because I think you have more than most people I know. You've always been looking for a passion that felt like *you*, and you weren't going to stop until you found it. What you were saying about this being your weakness, the way you've jumped from thing to thing? It's my favorite thing about you, the way you approach it all with an honesty and open-mindedness, this pure sense of *joy*."

Not aimlessness. Not wasted potential.

I've never heard myself described this way.

My voice is shaky when I say, "Like when I said yes to marrying you?"

"You can joke, but . . ." He waves an arm at the scene in front of us, the quaint bridge and tilted houses. There isn't a single street corner that isn't photo-worthy. "I love seeing this place through your eyes. Watching you fall in love with it makes me feel so fucking lucky to have a front-row seat."

I want to tell him it's so much more than that. Somehow he's seen me so plainly when I never meant to show that much of myself.

He moves closer, places a hand on mine. "I know you said you were a late bloomer," he continues, clearly determined to undo me with his words, "and obviously I am not an objective source, but . . . I think you're blooming at exactly the right time."

"Maybe both of us are." I go quiet for a moment, and then: "You know, for someone who proposed that spontaneously, you're a very good husband."

I'm not expecting this to affect him, but it makes him pull back, brows creased with concern. The moonlight illuminates the yearning on his face. "Is that all you want me to be?"

"No." I say it without hesitation, because it's been the truth for weeks, hasn't it? "I've been trying to rationalize it a hundred different ways, but . . ."

He gives me a soft smile. "I think I left rational behind a few months ago."

I close the space between us as he bends down, the two of us exhaling into each other. My nose bumping his. Lips brushing for a stretch of an instant.

Maybe it can truly be as simple as that.

"I have all the admiration in the world for you," I say. "And maybe that doesn't sound romantic, but I need you to know that it is. Watching you with your family and friends, with George, seeing what you do for work, the way you care for the apartment, even the way you make your tea—you just turned out to be a really wonderful person. It doesn't hurt that I'm a little obsessed with your hands, too. And your arms. And your mouth." I touch his lips as I say this, feeling them curve into a grin. "I'm just—I've been very good at denial," I say, which makes him laugh a little. "But it's been a while since it felt like pretending. Unless you're an even better actor than I thought."

"A terrible actor," he says. "This whole time. Absolutely terrible."

I let my eyes fall shut, trying to imagine it. The two of us, giving this a fair shot. I want to believe that we could be good at it, and even if I've never done serious, it has to mean something that I want him like this.

With him, I would try my fucking hardest.

He wraps me in his arms, holding me close. This time when he kisses me, it's not for anyone else. Not for show.

"Wouter," I say into his chest, "take me home."

"I LIED EARLIER," HE SAYS AFTER WE'VE WALKED GEORGE, a long one during which he tried to play with an aloof golden retriever and an overly friendly bulldog. "The tile painting—that was a backup panic surprise in case I lost my nerve with the real surprise."

I'm unsure what to make of that. "Then that was a really great panic surprise."

He beckons me to follow him into his room. Now he's a little more anxious, hands twitching. I wait while he rummages for something in a dresser drawer—a sketchbook.

We sit together on the bed while he passes it to me, keeping a hand on the cover for an extra moment. "I may have been a bit rusty. Try not to judge too harshly." He lets out a long breath. "But . . . it felt good, getting back to it. First it was just in between patients, and then when you were in class, or I was up late and couldn't sleep. And . . . well, you'll see."

When I open it up, I'm speechless.

There are sketches of Amsterdam, our little house and the Prinsengracht. The Van Gogh Museum. A field of tulips. George curled up in his spot on the couch, a pile of socks next to him.

Then there are the sketches of a woman—of *me*. Some are basic line drawings, and it's taken him a handful of tries to nail my expression, but as I flip the pages, the paper girl slowly becomes more and more familiar.

Before the pages of the book turn blank, there's a series of portraits that emphasize my birthmark. With paint and colored pencil and ink, he's turned it into an ocean. A map. A galaxy of glittering stars.

"You inspired me," he says as I gaze down at it, leaning in close to press his mouth to my neck. "I know they don't come close to the real thing, but—"

All I can do is kiss him, this man who's determined to wreck me.

A hand comes to my right cheek, and even though we've been far more intimate, he meets my eyes and softly asks, "May I?"

I nod. So, so gently, he runs the tip of his index finger along my birthmark. Beginning above my eyebrow, he follows the shape of it along the side of my nose. Over to my cheek, thumb coming up to graze my cheekbone. I might be holding my breath as he does it.

"You never touched me there. When we were teenagers," I say.

"I think I was nervous. I didn't know how you felt about it. If you were insecure."

"I'm not now—for the most part. I was for a long time, and I used to beg my parents to let me get it lasered, but there was a good chance it would have only lightened it a little." I cover his hand with mine, my heart in my throat. "I'd love it if people stared a little less, but I really am okay with it."

"I'm glad," he says. "Because I've always thought it was beautiful. All of you. Gorgeous Danika Dorfman."

"You know, they call it a port-wine stain because it looks like someone spilled wine over my skin. It's the same in Dutch, isn't it?"

"Wijnvlek. Yes," he says, but then he shakes his head, turning thoughtful. "I don't think that's what it looks like at all. More like . . . your face is a canvas, and someone was mixing all these colors of paint together to find the perfect shade." Another brush of his fingertips along my cheek. "And this is what they came up with."

He pulls me into his lap as his hands travel up my back and into my hair. I kiss him hard, my husband turned so much more, until I spot something bright yellow out of the corner of my eye.

The stack of Post-it notes on his nightstand.

I lift myself up to grab them and the nearby pen, scribbling a quick phrase.

Dank je wel, I write, and I stick it on his arm.

He glances down at it before reaching for the stack. I'm still in his lap, so I can see exactly what he writes: *mooi*, and then places it on my cheek. *Beautiful.*

I take back the pen and tap it on my chin, racking my Dutch vocabulary. *Geïnspireerd* goes on his hand. *Inspired.*

Proberen hun best, he gives my lungs. *Trying their best.*

Bekwaam, I put on his mouth with a sly lift of my eyebrows. *Competent.*

Meer dan bekwaam, he puts on mine. *More than competent.*

*Gevaarlijk—dangerous—*has me lifting up his shirt to stick on the trail of hair beneath his navel, and he has to bite back a smile.

*Oneerlijk—unfair—*goes to my cleavage.

We must already look ridiculous, the Post-its flapping every time we laugh or shift positions.

I borrow his word for me, *lief,* and I don't even hesitate before placing it on his heart.

Mijn, he writes, and puts it on my upper thigh.

We kiss in a burst of yellow, scraps of paper fluttering around us as I tug him down on top of me. Somehow it just feels *right* every time our bodies come together, like we started something years ago and trusted our future selves to finish it.

"I can't believe how much time we wasted not doing this," he says, lips trailing down my neck, a hand braced on either side of me.

"Thirteen years?"

"Well, I was thinking ever since you moved in here, but sure. Yes."

"Last time, you asked me what I like. And then there was the panic surprise, and the surprise surprise . . . so I need to know. What do *you* like?" I run my hands down his chest, lingering on his belt buckle. "And don't just say 'everything.'"

A twist of his mouth as he considers this, rolling to one side, propping himself up on his elbow. "There's a full-length mirror on the back of my door. I've wondered . . . what it might be like to watch ourselves."

I remember how he took his time undressing me in the bathroom mirror. The hitch of his breath. I can't tell him yes fast enough.

He unhooks the mirror, and there's a bit of maneuvering as we position it, ultimately propping it up against a chair so both of us can see our reflections.

"Sit here?" he asks, nudging me in front of him on the bed once we're both undressed. He slots himself behind me so that the mirror gives him a full view of my body. One of his hands comes around to palm my breast, the other rubbing circles on my hip.

Tracing the petals of my tattoo. "I want to see what you look like when you're touching yourself."

My throat goes dry at his words, but there's no hesitation as I spread my legs wide. I want him to see everything he wants, at every angle. "Only if you tell me what to do," I say, and he hardens against my lower back.

His reflection grins. Wicked. "I can do that." As I settle myself against him, he turns thoughtful, as though choosing his instructions carefully. "Lick your fingers," he says in a low voice. "And start teasing yourself. Slower—I know you can get greedy."

I can't resist a little whine at that, but I make myself pull back. With my middle finger, I stroke gently along my lips, that slight back and forth already drawing out a shudder. "Like this?"

In the mirror, he gives me a nod. Presses a kiss to my shoulder. "Fuck, this view. Look how pretty your pussy is."

His legs are bracketing mine, and not unlike when I was in his lap at the bar—but so much better—I can feel every vibration of his body. Every breath. It's incredible to be this open with him. There's no part of myself I'm trying to hide, and maybe his fantasy is mine too, because there's something intensely erotic about being ready to watch ourselves like this.

He nudges my head to one side to expose my neck, mouth landing in the soft skin there. "God, you're perfect. Put your finger inside. Tell me how wet you are."

"So wet." I gasp at the slippery sound between my thighs. "Dripping. Just for you."

He groans, sucking at my neck while he watches me in the mirror, pink and swollen and glistening. I lift my hand away for just an instant, panting and already missing the heat, but it's worth it for the way his eyes flutter shut when I bring a finger to his mouth.

"Can you handle two fingers?" he asks, a new confidence in his voice. "Can you fuck yourself with two fingers for me?"

For me. Those two words somehow do more than any of the others. There's something undeniably tender about having him this way and knowing it doesn't have to be an either-or. Dirty and sweet. Wholesome and depraved. Everything in between.

It occurs to me in this moment that he could ask me for anything and I'd do it. I'd get absolutely filthy for him and love every second.

I slide two fingers inside, nearly arching off the bed with the pleasure of it. I'm gripping his arm gripping my thigh, a deep flush spreading across my face, down to my neck, between my breasts.

"So goddamn sexy. I could watch you like this all day." He sinks his teeth into my shoulder, and I cry out at the sensation. "Rub your clit. You're dying for it, aren't you?"

"*Yes,*" I manage, feathering my touch exactly where I need it.

With his cock shoved against my tailbone and his teeth in my skin, I'm not sure how much longer I can last—or how much longer I can wait to undo him. My legs are shaking, fingers quick, head thrown back.

"I—I'm going to come."

"Yeah? Let me hear you."

Everything tightens, my vision shrinking to the size of a pinprick before I fall apart with a delirious gasp, a burst of incandescence as he crests the wave with me, kissing my neck and my shoulder and the back of my head. He murmurs words like "beautiful" and "perfect" and "Dani. *Dani.*"

But we're not done.

I push forward just as he grabs hold of my hips, helping me down onto all fours. His knees press hard into the mattress. In an instant, he's filling me, burying himself between my thighs, and here's another first: this position.

"Good?" he asks, slowly moving himself backward before plunging in again.

"*Very.*"

He watches my breasts bounce in the mirror while he fucks me from behind, an awed but fiercely determined expression on his face. *Stunning.* I flex my back to take him deeper. Slant my hips backward. There's a hard line of tension from his jaw to the hollow of his throat, and I'm still so dazed from my orgasm that every thrust feels explosive. It's almost too much, in the best possible way. I close my eyes before realizing I don't want to miss a moment of it—not when he sucks on a finger before teasing it along the seam of my ass. Not when he reaches around to stroke my clit with his other hand, yellow squares of paper in complete disarray all around us.

Just like that, I'm close again. And he knows it.

"Come with me, lief," he says, and our eyes meet in the mirror as he takes us through the final motions, our reflections crazed and sweaty and *vulnerable*, maybe most of all.

It's never been like this.

Once we've recovered, our bodies sprawled out on the bed, he gently runs his hand through my hair and plucks out a sticky note. *Gevaarlijk.* Then he continues down my back, landing on my left hip. "Ah. We have to talk about this."

"I'm surprised you held out this long," I say, biting back a smile as I turn to face him. "I was drunk and stupid. End of story."

He can hear the truth in what I'm not saying: that he made such an impact on me that I couldn't help but immortalize him on my skin.

"Nah, I'm not buying it." He examines the orange and yellow flowers, slightly faded with age. "You have a Dutch tattoo."

"As you know, Van Gogh's art really transcends cultur—"

He cuts me off with his mouth. "You have a Dutch tattoo," he repeats, and then moves down to kiss it, his lips tracing the ink.

"Then we have to talk about yours, too."

"This date—my parents' wedding." He gestures to the roman numerals on his calf. "I wanted to get something when my dad passed, and I liked the idea of picturing them at their happiest."

"That's really lovely." I give his hand a squeeze before skimming my thumb along the petals on his shoulder. "And this one?"

He swallows hard, eyes not leaving mine. "The California poppy. A few years after I got back. For . . . what I imagine are obvious reasons." He covers my hand with his. "Even if I wasn't ever going to see you again, even if I thought I'd ruined things forever . . . I wanted a way to remember it all."

"Did we really each get a flower that symbolized the other person?" My voice nearly breaks.

"In all seriousness," he says, "you probably should have gotten a tulip."

It evolves from there, the two of us telling stories of the scars and marks on our bodies, some from the past ten years, some from long before that. There's this joy in relearning each other as adults, giggling like the teenagers we used to be, those versions of ourselves locked in time and yet still so plainly present. I'd put a concrete wall between myself and joy for so many months that it's a relief to break it down and let myself fall.

George jumps up into bed, planting himself right between us, licking our arms and our faces like he overheard us laughing and didn't want to be left out. I love that, too, this little dog who's whittled my sock collection down to a precious few. "I warned you," Wouter said a few days ago when I was getting dressed and couldn't find a matching pair.

When I pull Wouter in for another kiss, my hand lands in the thinning patch on the back of his head.

"It's true," he says. "I'm going bald, and I'm no longer in denial about it."

Without missing a beat, I stroke him there, letting him know it doesn't bother me. "For what it's worth, I don't think you'd look terrible bald." I pretend to examine him, squinting one eye and framing my fingers like I'm taking a photo. "You have the right head shape. I think you can pull it off."

He laughs. "Thank you," he says, dropping his forehead to my bare shoulder and kissing along the pink marks he left earlier. "I've gone through my whole life assuming my head shape was completely normal, nothing to brag about. But now that I know it's special, this changes everything."

"You're ridiculous."

"You bring it out in me."

"Are you trying to tell me you never sit around with your friends discussing the shape of each other's heads? Because that goes against everything I know about Dutch culture so far."

"Danika," he says, his tone serious, indicating he's no longer joking. "I mean it. I love being ridiculous with you. I love being *anything* with you. I think . . . I think I'm the brightest version of myself when I'm with you."

In that moment, the words I've been running from for thirteen years cross my mind without hesitation.

I could love you again, I think. *Maybe I already do.*

LATER, ONCE WE'RE ON OUR THIRD CUPS OF TEA, AFTER we've showered and dressed in our coziest pajamas, we settle in on the couch with a couple flickering candles on the table next to us, just about as gezellig as I can imagine. Even when he accidentally sips from my mug and nearly spits it out.

"This is how much sugar you've been putting in your tea?" he says, incredulous but amused, and I give him my most innocent smile.

When he reaches for the remote, I'm shocked by how comfortable it feels, watching TV with my boyfriend—if that's what he is. We haven't put words to it, but maybe since we're already legally bound, there's no need.

"What do you think?" he asks, lingering on *Seinfeld*. "For nostalgia's sake?"

"I haven't watched any of this . . . since you lived with us."

He gives me a sheepish smile. "I've watched a bit over the years."

"Because you missed me," I say in a teasing lilt.

"Because it was funny," he insists. "And because I missed you." He scrolls through the seasons, the titles blurring together in a mix of laugh tracks and iconic lines. "Which episode?"

I point at the screen when he gets to season five. "That one. 'The Marine Biologist.' One of George's best."

As though summoned by his namesake, George Costanza leaps onto the couch.

And then the three of us watch this very American sitcom in this very Dutch apartment.

Twenty-three

PHOEBE WRAPS MY HAIR AROUND A CURLING WAND while she blasts a nostalgia playlist in her hotel room. The dress looks redder beneath the harsh bathroom lighting, my makeup the kind of natural-but-not look that requires at least seven products to achieve, especially after I anxiety-sweated through the first two layers and we had to start again.

"I don't know why I'm so nervous," I say as my sister frowns at a strand of hair that won't cooperate. Maya slipped out to get coffee and give us some privacy. Today doesn't truly *mean* anything, not really, aside from Wouter's family meeting two of my favorite people on this earth and my fierce desire for all of them to like each other.

"Please. Do you remember right before my wedding? I was such a wreck, you had to spoon-feed me cereal because my hands were shaking so badly. Then again . . . I hadn't already married her for a Dutch visa."

"Minor differences."

In the mirror, Phoebe's eyes meet mine as she drops her chin to my shoulder. "My little sister's getting married," she says, and I'm not expecting the break in her voice. "Kind of. And next week I'll be home and missing you more than ever."

Her words hit me like a blast of ice. I've loved having her here, but after the baby's born, and given how expensive flights are . . . there isn't going to be an easy time for them to come back. I'll visit, of course. As much as I can, once I have a steady paycheck—but will that ever feel like enough when I have to go through immigration on both ends? When I need a passport to see my family?

Everything in California will continue to go on without me, and even if that's always been true, I've never been confronted with the reality of it until this moment.

There's a knock on the hotel room door. "Maya must have forgotten her key," Phoebe says as she goes to unlock it.

But it's Wouter, holding a bouquet of tulips and sunflowers and poppies.

My knees turn to melted butter.

A navy suit clings to his broad shoulders, sunlight from the open window catching the auburn undertones in his blond hair. From his cornflower blue shirt to his polished cognac shoes, from his paisley-printed tie to the gleam of his belt buckle, he is an absolute dream in formalwear.

It makes me ache for all the school dances we never went to. Too risky, we decided, opting instead for an innocent night of bowling or arcade games.

"You don't want to find out if prom is really like a John Hughes movie?" I asked him once, after we toasted with milkshakes and watched the sunset at Venice Beach. "I'd hate for you to miss out on the quintessential American experience."

We both knew it was corny when he leaned in and said, "*You* are my quintessential American experience," the sky's reds and purples reflected in his glasses, his eyes lit with the purest admiration. It's the same way he's looking at me now, with all the wisdom of an adult and the awe of seventeen.

"Are you trying to kill me with that dress?" he asks, failing to bite back a smile.

An instant calm washes over me as I smooth down one of his lapels. "It's a good thing we never went to prom together. I don't think we'd have been able to behave."

"Do I need to leave the room?" my sister asks.

"We'll be good," Wouter says as he guides me into a spin to show off the dress, though the quirk of his brow promises something else entirely.

It's one of the last perfect moments of the day.

MAYA RETURNS AND WE ALL DOWN OUR COFFEES, AND then Roos shows up with George, looking dapper in a little bow tie. Wouter rented a car for us all to drive down to Culemborg, and he plays us some Dutch pop music on the radio as Maya balances a hand on her belly and says, "This is more than I've ever felt her dance."

Wouter's mother wanted us to be the guests of honor, the last people to show up, and the house is ready for us: a few other cars in the driveway, GEFELICITEERD spelled out in a banner above the front door. There's some noise from the backyard, and I wave to Sanne and Thomas and Evi and Bilal through the fence. Iulia's there, too, along with what I'm guessing are some family friends.

"Welkom, goeiedag," Anneke says when she opens the door, looking chic but not too overdressed in a sweater and long skirt. Wouter's grandmother Maartje is next to her, her white hair a little curlier than last time, as though she's just returned from the salon. After a flurry of introductions and some treats for George, they wrap their arms around my sister and coo over Maya's baby bump.

"So good to meet you both. We're honored that you're here." Then, to Wouter and me: "Everyone's out back, but take your time. There's no rush—I'm still getting snacks out of the oven."

"Thank you so much. For everything," I tell her in Dutch.

Anneke squeezes my hand. "Wat mooi, Danika," she says, and in that moment, I can't believe I was ever nervous. She's a proud mother, hugging her son and kissing his cheeks, trying to sneak in a ruffle of his hair. "I didn't know he had anything this nice in his closet," she adds with a laugh, and the rest of us join in. "Clearly you're a good influence."

The doorbell rings as we're moving into the living room, and when George barks, Roos gives him a half-hearted shush, as though trying to convey that she is fully in charge of the dog today.

"But you're still my perfect boy," she whispers.

"Isn't this everyone?" Wouter asks, craning his neck to see who's in the backyard. "Maybe it's a neighbor concerned about the noise. You told the group chat we were having a party, right?"

His mother checks her watch. "We're expecting two more."

And then I think the ground might give way beneath me.

Because on the other side of the door, looking all at once baffled and furious and jet lagged, are my parents.

No fucking way.

I have to blink a few times to make sure it's really them. That my anxiety hasn't conjured up some worst-case scenario. But no, Sharon and Bill Dorfman are standing on the Van Leeuwens' front steps, my father in the LA Dodgers cap he's had for at least ten years, and my mother similarly casual in jeans and a white blouse.

"What are you—" Panic rises in my throat. Wars with the tightness in my lungs. "How did you—"

My parents are here. In the Netherlands.

At a celebration for a marriage that isn't real, even if it's started to feel that way.

I've never really liked end-of-the-world movies because I couldn't ever picture that intermediate step, what happens before our world becomes a wasteland incapable of supporting human life.

In this moment, I understand them completely. Because this, I am certain, is how the apocalypse begins.

Phoebe is just as shocked, reaching out to grab my hand and holding on a bit too tight. "Holy shit holy shit holy shit holy shit," she says under her breath. On my other side, Wouter's been stunned into silence.

My father locks their rental car while Anneke beckons them inside. They look the same as they did when I waved goodbye to them in January, if a little ruffled by the travel. Maybe when he takes off his hat, I can see my father's hairline has retreated a bit more, and my mother has a new dye job, but they've brought with them the scent of my childhood home. *Familiar.*

And terrifying.

"Sweetheart, we missed you so much," my mother says as she wraps me in a hug. "You look fantastic."

"Sharon. Bill," Wouter says, finding his voice before I do, and I can tell he's trying his best to stay calm. His palm finds my lower back—a reassuring warmth. "It's so good to see you again."

The strained smiles they give him in response make me wistful for our alternate timeline, the one where my family visits him in the Netherlands the way we always planned. The one where we all remain close. They've certainly never regarded him with this much trepidation; they only ever welcomed him with open arms.

We're supposed to treat him like a member of the family.

"Wouter. Did you get even taller?" A classic dad joke, and yet there's no amount of humor in it.

Anneke shines her brightest grin before launching into the explanation I've been waiting for. "We invited them! Roos and me. We thought, this is such an important day, they ought to celebrate with us." Then she stage-whispers to me: "We told them it was going to be a surprise for you. Isn't that exciting?"

"I snooped through your phone for your parents' number," Roos puts in. "I hope you don't mind! Also, you should really change your password."

There's too much chaos between my ears. All the nerves feel like they might finally burst from my chest in some kind of anxiety confetti, and Wouter's hand on my back is probably the only thing keeping me upright.

My mother's knuckles tense on the strap of her purse, one of those RFID-blocking bags with industrial locking zippers that she uses only for travel. "I'm sorry to do this when you've clearly put so much effort into this party, but we need to have a word with our daughter." At first I assume this means she wants a quiet moment, but she turns to me with the same intensity as when she demanded my schools let me waive gym class, or when I slept over at a new friend's house and she wanted to make sure their parents knew about my fragile lungs. A fierce protector—or so I thought.

"Danika Hope Dorfman," she says, my middle name the eternal reminder of my first few months in the hospital, "you are not getting married."

An earsplitting silence rings through the house. Even the people chattering out in the backyard seem to stop, a dozen curious pairs of eyes swiveling toward the scene inside.

As though to protest the quiet, George lets out a low howl, and Roos scoops him into her arms.

My chest tightens, everything taking far too long for me to piece together. Wouter's mother contacted my parents. Told them about the wedding they had no idea had happened. Invited them to this party.

And now they're here, though obviously not to celebrate—to drag me back to my senses.

"We didn't want to do this," my father continues. "But as soon as we heard from Wouter's mother, we thought it might be the only way. We had to get on a plane and make sure you heard from us in person."

With a Pilates-toned arm, my mother grips my shoulder with enough strength to tug me away from Wouter, like we're some modern-day Jets vs. Sharks. "Was this what you planned all along? Was this why you picked Amsterdam?"

"What—*no*," I say emphatically. "We only bumped into each other back in January. We hadn't been in touch."

Her voice turns pleading. "We're just trying to stop you from making the biggest mistake of your life. I know you were going through a rough time at home, and maybe this seems romantic . . . but for Christ's sake, you can't—you can't just run off to Europe and get *married*."

Then, as though she's understood the whole conversation or at least the most important parts, Maartje declares in her accented English, "They are already married."

Everything feels suspended in time for a long, painful moment—before the room erupts into noise.

The horror on my parents' faces matches the confusion on Anneke's and Roos's as they hurl shouts and accusations, none of them having the whole truth but all of them eager to conjure their own versions of it. I shrink back against the wall. Count breaths like my life depends on it, because maybe it does. *Four. Seven. Eight.* Fuck, I need more numbers.

With everyone talking over one another, Wouter bends to rub my back again. "We're going to figure this out," he says softly, and the concern on his face is underscored with something else. A steady determination. "We'll be okay, lief."

I lean into his touch, wishing it could be as simple as he makes it sound. I find anchors to ground myself: the circular motion of his fingertips. My sister's familiar clean-linen perfume. "What if we just run away? Right now? We could catch a train to France. We'd be there in, what, three hours?"

"As tempting as that is," he says, "I think they might notice we're gone."

Then my mother reaches for my hand, holding it up to inspect the wedding ring and looking as though she might faint.

"Mom. Dad," Phoebe is saying, keeping her voice level and trying to play peacemaker. "Maybe we should all just take a moment and calm d—"

"No, I don't think it's time to calm down at all!" my father says. His jaw is set, arms crossed over his chest. "Tell us you aren't married, Dani. Tell us you didn't rush into this gigantic decision without telling anyone. Please."

"I . . ." This wasn't how they were supposed to find out. They weren't supposed to find out at all, and that was the beauty of it. "It wasn't rushed. We spent a lot of time talking about it," I say feebly, though it's not exactly true.

"You barely know him! You two were kids when he lived with us," my mother says, and the word stings. *Kids.* As though nothing we did back then could be considered serious. "That was almost fifteen years ago. He might as well be a stranger!"

Anneke places a hand on Wouter's arm. "What's wrong with my son?"

"Nothing. I'm sure he's grown into a fine young man," my father says. "But our daughter doesn't know what she's doing. She clearly wasn't thinking when she decided to marry some guy on the other side of the world."

"It wasn't just her," Wouter says, coming to my defense, because my father makes it sound like I tripped and stumbled into marriage. To *some guy*, and not the kind and caring Dutchman who used to be our foreign exchange student. "It was both of us. She didn't do anything wrong."

"Your parents didn't know? But I thought—" Roos's strawberry hair whips around her face as she shakes her head, unable to process this, and George stretches up to lick her cheek.

"Roos," I try, my heart aching. "I'm so sorry—"

"This is nonsense." My mother whips out her phone, as though Google has a simple solution to the problem. "You're an American citizen. Was it even legal?"

"Yes, it was entirely legal," Wouter assures her. "I wouldn't get Danika in any kind of trouble. Not intentionally."

"Then there has to be a way to undo it," my father says, and then he's swiping through his phone too. "Oh—I'm not connected to the Wi-Fi . . ."

At any other time, this would endear me to my boomer father—the fact that he didn't account for the nuances of an international phone plan when they decided to storm the castle and save their daughter.

"I was uncertain about it at first, too." Anneke might be in the worst position of all, needing to defend her family in her own home in front of these complete strangers. The mother-in-law I thought was starting to like me. Except she was never my mother-in-law at all, was she? "They're young—maybe they're a little impulsive, but I trust Wouter. They rekindled their relationship, fell back in love, and then got married."

And if that doesn't make me feel even worse.

So I do the only thing I can think of. The one thing I'm convinced will calm my parents more than the thought of their daughter getting married without telling them.

I wave my hands frantically to try to get everyone's attention. "No—we didn't," I say, and they all whirl to face me. "I mean, yes, we're married, but only on paper. That's all it was ever supposed to be."

It's a desperate rescue, poorly planned but entirely necessary.

We've kept this up long enough.

The phone slips from my mother's hands. "Danika. What are you saying?"

I swallow hard, aware of eight pairs of eyes burning into me. "We're not—we're not in love." My gaze flicks to Wouter for just a moment, long enough to clock his reaction: an almost imperceptible recoil before he steels himself once again. As though needing physical proof, I hold out my hand and give the ring a few tugs before it slides off my finger. "It's a green-card marriage. All of this is fake."

Twenty-four

· · · · · · · · · · · · ·

INSTANTLY I WISH I COULD TAKE IT BACK. MAYBE I COULD
handle my parents assuming I made a spontaneous decision in the
name of love—but I'm not at all prepared for them thinking I've
committed an international crime. Anneke and Roos are frantically
translating for Maartje, and Phoebe's and Maya's faces are all concern.

And Wouter—I can't even make eye contact with him as I stand
there in his mother's house, the ring in my trembling hand.

The guests in the backyard make no mystery of the fact that
they're listening in. Sanne and Evi have hands pressed to their
mouths, and Iulia's giving me a somber nod, this revelation con-
firming what she suspected all along.

That I am a huge fucking liar.

Roos is the one to speak first, in this shaky gut-punch of a way.
"You mean . . . you and my brother aren't really together?"

I want so badly to reassure her, to tell her there *is* something
between Wouter and me, even if I don't have the words for it—but
my parents' panic is more urgent. My mother scoops up her cracked

phone and drops into a chair, like she just can't take any more surprises while standing up, and my father shoves up the sleeves of his
shirt, because he's not used to a home without AC and it's grown
balmy in here with all of us yelling.

"I don't understand," he says. "Is this . . . some kind of immigration scam?"

"I . . . wouldn't use those exact words." I'm too warm in this
dress, the lace and tulle too delicate for this conversation. "I lost my
job. A couple weeks after I got here. The company went under, and
I was here on a work visa. If I didn't find another job, I wouldn't
have been able to stay in the country."

"And you never told us?" There's some amount of sympathy in
my mother's voice, the kind that drags me back to those dark moments when I imagined crawling home to them.

I didn't want you to think I couldn't handle it, I don't say.

"Danibear. You know you could have come home. We would
have paid for your ticket," she continues, as though the cost of the
flight was all that was holding me back. There's no way to rationalize this in their minds, not when they've wanted to protect me from
every bad thing that could be waiting for me out there.

Next to us, Wouter's speaking in rapid Dutch with his family,
so quick I can only catch a couple words here and there. *Apartment*
and *grandmother* and *wife*. Anneke's expression of shock, a hand
held to her heart.

My mother turns to Phoebe. "Did you know about this?"

She grimaces, eyes flicking over to me as I shrug, giving her
permission to tell them the truth. "I might have. Yes."

"And you didn't think to let us know that your sister was making
such a careless decision?"

"It wasn't careless," I insist. "We didn't just get drunk in Vegas
and decide to get married because it sounded fun."

My mother lets out a sarcastic snort. "Well, that's a relief."

Maya, who's been watching everything from the Van Leeuwens' couch, hoists herself to her feet, and Phoebe rushes to help her the rest of the way up. "Phee, maybe we should go for a walk? I could really use a walk."

"Go ahead," I say, and squeeze her hand to let her know I'll be okay.

"I wonder—" My father pinches his lips together after my sister and her wife leave, as though unsure whether he wants to say this at all.

"Go ahead, Bill," my mother encourages.

"I wonder if we should have put our foot down when she told us this cockamamie Amsterdam plan."

This ignites a new flare of frustration. "I didn't ask for your permission," I say. "I'm thirty years old. Even if you'd chased me all the way to the airport, I still would have left."

At that, Wouter extricates himself from the conversation with his family and faces my father. "With all due respect, sir," he says. "Dani isn't some kid who doesn't know what she's doing. Maybe it seemed ridiculous to you, but I think she's truly happy here." He meets my eyes, as though wanting to confirm it's true, and I nod while my heart swells with affection for him.

"And with all due respect to you," my father counters, because now he is no longer former host to an exchange student, he is the belligerent father of the bride, "you barely know her."

"I've gotten to know her quite a bit over the past several months." Wouter straightens to his full height, towering over both my parents. "She's one of the most headstrong, spirited people I know— who I'm lucky enough to know—and she's more than capable of making her own life decisions, no matter how big. In fact, maybe she *needed* to do this, to prove to herself that she always had this kind of independence in her. She didn't do it on a whim, and neither did we."

"I appreciate your sincerity. You obviously still care about her, but this isn't your battle."

Wouter's jaw tenses, as though there's more he wants to say but he knows he probably shouldn't. "Let's talk outside," he says to Anneke instead. "Give Dani's family some space."

On his way out into the backyard, he grazes my arm with a few fingertips. *I'm right here*, that simple touch seems to say. *You're not alone.*

I hear Wouter and his family in the backyard, telling the guests the party's over. His friends don't look angry, at least—just deeply perplexed as they file out through the gate.

Then it's just me and my parents in a house that isn't ours. Part of me is waiting for someone to tell us we're no longer welcome here, but when my parents head for the kitchen table, I follow along. Once we're seated, my mother fans herself with my father's Dodgers cap while he pours everyone a cup of iced tea, and the three of us silently take a sip.

When I speak again, I attempt a level, rational voice. "It's not as if we don't know each other," I say, and then with a grimace: "We . . . dated. When he lived with us."

"You and Wouter?" My father is softer now, he and my mother exchanging an amused smile. "Kiddo, we already knew about that. You weren't as sneaky as you thought you were."

Heat rushes to my cheeks. I'm not sure if there's anything more embarrassing than realizing your parents knew you were hooking up with your foreign exchange student.

"We were so sad that he never reached out once he went home. I always wondered if we'd done something wrong, or if life had just taken him in a different direction." My mother takes another sip of tea. "But you've been in contact all these years? I didn't know that."

"Not exactly." Another deep breath. "Not at all, actually. We ran into each other here right after everything fell apart for me, and he couldn't inherit his apartment without a spouse. When he suggested that we get married to solve both of our problems . . . it just made sense."

"You're not together," my mother says, as though needing to confirm it once and for all.

I shake my head. "No. We're not. We're . . ." I grasp for the right word. We might be sleeping together, but I'm not sure I have a parent-appropriate label for that. "He's just a friend. A friend who did me a tremendous favor."

"What I don't understand," my father says, "is why you didn't just come home, if everything was going so wrong? What was so bad about that?"

"I wanted to get away. It just felt like—like LA was holding me back, maybe. And now that I'm here . . . I love it more than I ever thought I would."

My mother looks hurt by this. "I had no idea."

"Hold on," my father says, his eyebrows shooting to his hairline. "Does this mean you're not coming back to the US?"

"I—I don't know yet," I backtrack. "I haven't thought about it beyond the next six months or so."

My father sets his empty glass of tea down on the table with a little more force than he needs to. "This is just a vacation, Dani. You have to come back to reality sooner or later. Think of everything you're missing at home—think of how much we miss *you*. Your sister's about to have a baby, and the family won't feel whole without you there."

Maybe it's the kind of manipulation only a family member can be good at, because it works. I imagine Phoebe and Maya's baby growing up without an aunt, never recognizing me when I come home to visit. I imagine birthdays and Hanukkah and Passover with an empty chair at the table.

A vacation—is that what this has been? I haven't been working. I've been indulging, making my way through tourist attractions and savoring my free time.

Maybe this isn't real life at all.

"I miss everyone too. Obviously I do," I say quietly. "But I have a final interview for a job next week. One that I'm genuinely excited about."

"So what's the plan?" my mother asks. "You'll get a job and get divorced? The choices you make here have consequences. What you did is *illegal*, and in *Amsterdam* of all places . . ."

"What the hell is wrong with Amsterdam?" Now I'm on the defensive again, fist tightening on my glass. "It's a beautiful fucking city! Every house in the city center is UNESCO protected!"

"It's not about how beautiful the city is." My mother holds up a hand in an attempt to get me to lower my voice. "Dani, what if—what if you have another episode?"

There's something in her gaze I don't recognize, and it takes me a moment to pin it down. *Fear*—that's what it is.

She's always seemed so strong to me, the person who would do anything to protect her kids, and it's rarely manifested in emotional ways like this. When she visited me in the hospital a few years back, she was all business, sharing updates about work and pop culture, since I'd gladly handed over my phone at the beginning of my stay, certain it was doing more harm than good.

"You'd be so far away from us," she continues, and I'm shocked when her voice breaks. "How could we be sure you're okay?"

"You'd just have to trust that I could handle myself," I say, a pressure building behind my eyes. "You knew I got a job here. You knew there was a chance I'd stay long-term."

In one quick motion, my mother turns her head away, her shoulders shaking. She doesn't want me to see how emotional this is making her. "We never thought you would."

My father runs a soothing hand down her arm. "Sharon, maybe we should go back to the hotel. Give everyone a chance to cool off," he says. "We can discuss this again tomorrow. I'll call Stan and see if he has any ideas on how to get you out of this."

Stan. Their friend who works in entertainment law and surely has a vast understanding of the Dutch legal system.

This seems to relax my mother. Stan is the solution. Stan can fix me. "Good idea."

In the backyard, Wouter's deep in conversation with Anneke and Roos and Maartje. I don't want to disturb them, and I'm not sure I can bear any more judgment from the people I was growing to like so much.

My mother has a vise grip on her purse as we head out to the car, where I inform them I'm going to take the train back to Amsterdam. Phoebe and Maya are waiting in the front yard; they haven't gone far.

"You're sure we can't drive you?" my mother asks. "Is that even safe, going by yourself?"

Of course they don't understand that this is part of daily life here. That this is one of the safest countries in the world.

"I prefer the train."

PHOEBE KEEPS HER ARM AROUND MY SHOULDERS ON OUR walk to the station, Maya on my other side. I feel raw. Scraped out. I'm squinting into the sun because I left my sunglasses at the house, and I'm not about to turn back and get them.

"They can't stay mad forever," Phoebe is saying, doing her best to lift my spirits. "Remember that time I crashed Dad's new car into the garage door? I'd never seen someone's face turn that color red before."

"I appreciate you. So much." I pause to sniff, to run a hand over my eyes. "Even if that feels like a very different situation."

Once we reach the station, a voice calls out from behind us.

"Danika—wait."

An out-of-breath Wouter is running toward us, his tie flapping in the wind.

He came after me.

"We'll give you two a moment," Phoebe says gently before she and Maya find a bench on the other side of the street.

And then, before Wouter speaks—he hugs me, a soul-deep hug that could make me forget anything else exists. In our formalwear in front of the train station, I inhale him, trying my best not to cry into his chest and failing. He cups my head to his heart, strokes his fingers through my hair.

When we pull back, there's a damp spot on his cornflower shirt. His face is beautifully flushed, glasses askew.

"I'm sorry I told everyone," I say around a hiccup. "It just— came out."

"I know, lief. I know. I'm not upset about that." He touches a thumb to my cheek, my right cheek, to catch another tear. "I didn't want it to end like that today. I don't want to ask if everything's okay, because obviously it isn't, but . . ."

A humorless laugh tumbles out. "Pretty sure my parents would ground me for life if they still could. What about your family?"

"My grandmother didn't understand why I'd do this just to in-herit the apartment," he says, turning sheepish. "She said I could have discussed it with her, and she would have transferred the deed to me. But they all understood that I wanted to help you out. They knew it was coming from a good place. And you saw them—they were ready to welcome you into the family."

Guilt wraps around my heart and squeezes. "We lied to a lot of people."

"Yeah. We did."

"I thought it would feel like more of a relief to finally come clean, but . . ." I trail off, biting down hard on my lower lip until I taste copper. Anything to stop feeling numb.

"I need to know." He glances down at his tie to straighten it—or to avoid my gaze. "What you said in there, about all of this being fake. Did you mean it?"

Oh.

I shut my eyes, trying to recall the exact words. I'd meant the marriage, didn't I?

"Because yesterday," he continues—and *god*, was that only yesterday?—"it felt like we were on the same page. And I don't want to be the idiot who hasn't realized you've changed your mind."

The fierce vulnerability in his eyes is enough to tear me in half.

"You're not—you're not an idiot," I say quietly. "I feel it too, okay? Whatever this is between us—I feel it too. And it's really fucking terrifying. Because there's too much we haven't talked about, and I don't know what we're supposed to do right now."

"Why can't we be terrified together, then?" He reaches out to thread his fingers with mine. "It's complicated, sure, but we'd figure it out, wouldn't we?"

"And our families?" I ask, because it's impossible to avoid the topic. "Maybe yours was quick to forgive, but I'm fairly certain mine isn't going to do the same. I just . . . I can't see a world in which they'd accept it."

"We'd talk to them. I think if they got to know me again, they might realize I'm not actually that terrible." One side of his mouth kicks upward, and while it's adorable when he's this optimistic, there's no way he can be this naive.

I drop his hands and rake a frustrated hand through my hair, ruining all of Phoebe's hard work. "Wouter, *stop*. It's not a question of whether they like you or not. It's that they treat me like I'm this doll who could break at any moment."

"And you let them."

"*What?*"

"Come on, Dani." Now his arms are crossed, fabric straining over taut muscles. "Have you ever really stood up to them? I saw it when I lived with you, and I thought they were a little overprotective, but it seems like nothing's changed. They might put you in bubble wrap, but you're not exactly clawing to get out."

You're wrong, I want to spit back at him—but the gruesome truth is that I'm not sure he is.

I've ignored it for years, letting myself be quietly frustrated, pushing back only gently. Maybe I was worried there'd be nothing out there to protect me if I let them go. Maybe I didn't realize I could protect myself.

Now I'm getting another surge of adrenaline, one that's raw, ugly. We're lucky this is a small town, that there's no one else in front of the train station to watch this play out. "What would this relationship even look like?" I fire at him. I snatch up the hem of my dress so I can put more space between us without tripping over it. "We'd date for a while and eventually break up, and then what?"

"In my mind, I guess," he says, "we wouldn't break up."

"Oh, okay, sure. We decide to stay married, because why the hell not, we like each other? And then it just magically works out?"

"Maybe! Is that so fucking awful to imagine? Someone loving you enough to want to stay with you long-term? Someone wanting to spend forever with you, because they never thought they'd see you again and by some miracle, you came back into their life?" His voice is hoarse now, and the amount of pleading in it could bring me to my knees if I'm not careful. "I'm sorry if that seems like the worst thing to you, Dani, because to me, it sounds pretty damn wonderful."

Something foreign works its way up my throat, something I'm

not sure I could name if I tried. *Someone loving you enough.* In all our late-night hookups and conversations, we never said that word. We haven't, not for thirteen years.

"I don't even know how long I'm going to be here," I say at last, because maybe my parents were right. Maybe the smart thing would be to get a quick and simple divorce, just like we promised we would, and go back home. "Or if I'm going to get that job."

"Then you'll get a different one."

"Because it's that easy? I've been trying for months, and I've barely gotten further than a first interview. And maybe I needed that time to cope with burnout, but—I didn't come here thinking this would be permanent. It was only ever supposed to be an escape. A change of scenery."

"Ah. I get it. You got what you needed, and now you're done?"

I don't say anything. I want to rewind to ten minutes ago, when he was holding me to his chest and the rest of the world seemed to stop. I want to be able to take a breath before time starts back up again.

During the few months I've been here, I've gained so much. Learned so much. There are too many places I haven't traveled, languages I haven't heard. The idea of packing up my life again sounds absolutely brutal.

But so does the inevitability of this relationship falling apart, the way it was always meant to.

"You were right," he continues. "There's a lot we haven't talked about. If you really want to go back to California, I won't stand in your way."

"Wouter." I stop just short of telling him I'm not going back to California—because even if I know in my soul that I'm not, I can't force the words up my throat.

I'm not sure what I want: for him to cling to my dress to keep me right here, or for him to let me go. Either way, he'd be making a decision for me that I've always needed to make on my own.

"What, Dani?" He yanks at his tie to loosen the knot, but there's a resignation in the way he grabs at it. It takes a few tries before he can get it undone. "I'm not going to try to convince you to feel for me the same way I feel about you. If you don't—it's as simple as that. Even if you decide you want to stay here, we don't have to be anything to each other. Just like you said."

The hurt that knifes through my stomach is so intense, I have to fight the urge to clutch at it. *I do feel the same*, I try to say. *I'm just scared of what it means. Scared of doing this again, when the first time went so horribly wrong.*

"I don't know what to say." Somehow it's the most honest sentence I've uttered all day, after a full afternoon of mistakes. The three words he must want from me are buried somewhere deep, rusty from lack of use. I want so desperately to be brave the way he told me I was—"a fucking fighter," he said.

Maybe the truth is that I never have been.

He presses his mouth together in what might be surrender. The way his fingertips start fidgeting yanks me back in time. This is the guarded Wouter from when we first reunited, the man I barely recognized.

Then he reaches into his pocket to pass me the sunglasses I left at his mother's house. "Let me know when you figure it out," he says. "I'll be here."

The words are curt, but they're not cruel. There's only heartbreak on his face, that thing I thought I had full ownership of when it came to us.

This time, though—this time I'm the one who put it there, and it aches all the way down to my toes.

Fight, I urge myself. *Fucking* fight. Because I can still say it. I can keep him from leaving. Just *I* and *love* and *you* in exactly that order, and he'll be mine again.

"I—I'm sorry I couldn't be what you wanted," I stutter out instead, mouth tripping over the words.

He looks at me for a long moment. "No," he says before he turns around. "You were more."

Twenty-five

THE FIRST TIME WOUTER AND I BROKE UP, IT FELT LIKE A BE-trayal.

That text arrived the week after summer vacation started, a sun-drenched day like so many other sun-drenched days. I'd meticulously planned out the whole week, determined to keep myself occupied with Wouter gone: beach, bowling, movies, parties. I was going to be a social fucking butterfly.

Instead I read the message over toast and eggs, dropped my phone into the butter dish, and got into the car in my pajamas. I drove straight to Phoebe's USC dorm, where she was staying for summer term, every minute I was stuck in traffic feeling like a personal attack.

"That *asshole*," she said after she wiped butter off my phone, rubbing my back, letting me cry. "You deserve so much better." At seventeen, a miserable mess of self-esteem and forehead acne, I wasn't sure if I did.

She said all the right things, those things you're supposed to say during a breakup that the person who's been broken up with might pretend they understand but never actually believe.

This time she doesn't say any of them, but she still holds me while I cry on the train.

I think we both need some space to process everything, Wouter texted when I got back to Amsterdam. I'll stay in Culemborg this week. Take as long as you need.

I wondered if it was implied that the space he's giving me is to move out. If that's the case, I'm not sure why I haven't been able to start packing.

This isn't a breakup, not exactly, and only in part because we made such a mess of the marriage, never putting a label on our relationship. And yet I let him know me in a way I haven't done since . . . well, since *him*.

The apartment is too quiet without Wouter and George, and I can't understand how he lived here on his own for so many years. We've marked every square inch—centimeter—of it, all the places where we laughed and drank tea and shared our deepest secrets. The places where we touched and moaned and murmured each other's names.

I convince myself that if I go to bed early, the memories won't be able to find me. But they keep me awake half the night anyway, because my brain is cruel and there was never a timeline in which Wouter would make anything less than the deepest imprint.

It isn't that I don't know what he wants from me.

It's that I've never been able to successfully give it—to anyone.

There's nothing I want to do less than see my parents the next morning. I texted Phoebe, begging her to help me with an excuse. Rip off the band-aid, babe, she wrote back. The anticipation is much worse than whatever you're picturing. I promise.

I meet them in their hotel lobby, praying she's right.

Despite the shock of yesterday, they look much more well-rested. My mother's in a patterned shirtdress and isn't gripping her RFID-blocking purse nearly as tightly. My father, still in his Dodgers cap—which I should probably tell him is a dead giveaway for a tourist—gives me a tentative smile as he adjusts the strap of his camera bag. Because of course he brought a real camera, certain his phone wouldn't be able to do Amsterdam justice.

They flew all this way, I remind myself as we awkwardly hug hello.

"How's the jet lag?" I ask.

"We've been up since four," my father admits, fighting a yawn. "Do you know what they have on the TV at four in the morning? Phone sex commercials!"

I'm fully prepared to defend the city by saying this surely can't be just an Amsterdam thing, but the two of them just laugh, like it's another quirk on a long list of them.

We head for breakfast at a nearby café with terrace seating, tables propped up along a canal. There's no better way to dine in Amsterdam, and if we're going to have this conversation, we might as well have it somewhere beautiful.

"Isn't this picturesque," my mother remarks once we're seated, and then asks the server, "Could we get three glasses of tap water, please?"

"I remember that from our last trip to Europe," my father says. For their thirtieth anniversary, they went on a Danube River cruise. "They don't always give it to you when you sit down. Maybe California could learn a thing or two, what with all the droughts."

We fall into silence while three glasses and a carafe of water are placed on the table.

"So," I begin after taking a sip, "yesterday did not go well."

"It's possible we all could have handled some things better." My mother reaches across the table, brushing her fingertips along my arm. "How did this happen, Dani? That's what I want to understand. Not just the marriage—all of it."

They're less combative today. Ready to listen.

I take a deep breath. "I guess . . . I guess it started a long time ago. You remember all those articles that came out when I was born?"

I swear I see the headlines, the photos play across my mother's face. No matter how fierce a mask she puts on, that trauma has never quite left her. "Yes," she says quietly. "I don't think we could ever forget. You were our miracle baby."

"Right. And for the longest time, I've just felt like . . . I had to do something great in order to live up to that."

Her brow furrows. "That's not what anyone meant at all. The fact that you're alive, that you're here with us—that's always been more than enough."

"Theoretically, I understand that. But those follow-ups that happened, the reporters checking up on me, looking for a feel-good story—it was overwhelming," I say. "Everyone around me seemed to find what they were good at so easily. It felt like I could never find it, and that created all the more pressure to achieve something. Even in college, I really just fell into UX design, and sure, I liked it . . . but I always expected I'd have this great passion. Something so uniquely *Danika*."

When I say it out loud, I can hear the ego in it. Because isn't that what everyone wants, really? To be lucky enough to spend their lives doing something that makes them happy?

On the bridge in front of us, a group of college-aged girls ask a stranger to take their photo. "Make sure you like it," the stranger says after snapping a few. "I can take more if you want!" The wholesomeness of it reminds me of Roos, her lack of judgment when it would be so easy to roll her eyes at scenes like this.

Sometimes you're the tourist; sometimes you're the photographer.

"You felt that pressure from us?" my mother wants to know.

"Not directly," I say. "But your jobs have always seemed so meaningful—public health, teaching. And Phoebe adores her bookstore. It was impossible not to wonder . . . why not me?"

With the hem of his shirt, my father polishes the lenses of his sunglasses before putting them back on. "You know it took me a while to find teaching, right? I had plenty of aimless years, plenty of jobs that didn't lead where I thought they would, until I went back to school for a teaching degree. For those people who find their passion immediately, that's fantastic. But it doesn't happen that way for many, many more of us."

"I guess I'm starting to understand that. The company I'm interviewing for—it's a boat tour company." I wait for some kind of outraged response, but it doesn't come. "I'd be a tour guide. It doesn't have to be my forever career—just something I'd like to do right now."

Neither of them answers right away—but only because the server's returned to take our order.

Once she leaves, a slow smile spreads across my mother's face. "That sounds like a lot of fun," she says. "Think of all the different people you'd get to meet every day, from so many different places. And I'm sure you'd learn even more about Amsterdam, too."

"It *is* a beautiful country," my father agrees. "Don't get me wrong—a weird country. I still can't get over all the bicycles! They really are everywhere, aren't they?"

"So fast, though," my mother says. "Like they could come out of nowhere. I hope you're careful when you're crossing the street."

Here we go. "That's another thing we should talk about." I straighten in my chair, though I'm surprised to discover I haven't been slouching through this conversation. I've said exactly what I've wanted with as much confidence as I can muster—I can't backtrack now. "I know you think I'm still that fragile baby who wasn't supposed to survive, but I'm not. I don't need to be coddled. I don't need to be protected from the big, bad world. I might be flailing sometimes, but I'm figuring it out. At my own pace."

My mother's jaw tenses. "It's just hard," she says, with that unfamiliar wobble in her voice that I've now heard twice in twenty-four hours. "You were *so* tiny, Danika. When I saw you on that ventilator, I thought—*I'll do whatever it takes to protect her. Anything at all.* And we tried our absolute best. Now, well . . . you're an adult. You don't need as much protecting, even if that's always my first instinct."

"I'm grateful for all of it," I say, my heart squeezing, and for the most part, I mean it. I believe that they did their best. "I know my health has been precarious, but I'm in a much better place than I was four years ago. I take my medication, and I've started researching therapists, and . . . I can talk about it now. I'm not in denial about it, and I can breathe easier than I ever have." They don't protest any of this—they let me keep speaking. "There's more. We can keep having regular phone calls—maybe every other week once you get home. And obviously we can text. But I don't want the constant check-ins about my health, or where I am, or how long I'm going to be there."

"I think we can handle that," my mother says, and my father echoes his agreement.

"I need to learn how to be truly independent," I continue. "And that's part of why I moved here. I know it was drastic, and that I probably didn't need to go this many miles to do it—but I wanted to do something fully on my own for the first time. Whatever does or doesn't happen with Wouter . . . that's completely different."

They fidget uncomfortably in their seats, as though this is the part of the conversation they've been dreading the most. Our plates of eggs Benedict and pancakes and French toast arrive, but no one makes a move to dig in.

"We didn't realize it was so serious between you and Wouter," my mother says. "When he was living with us, I mean. We thought it was just a teenage infatuation—not that those can't be strong. Maybe we should have intervened, but it seemed innocent enough, especially with him eventually going back to Amsterdam, and we trusted you to be safe."

A teenage infatuation. That's what it was, in the plainest terms, but even looking back from over a decade later, it never felt that way. We were young and overly optimistic, but the love was real. Weighty, like something you could hold in your palm.

"We thought we could make it work after he went back. But obviously it didn't, and then now . . ." I trail off, my throat tight, trying to keep the emotion from shuddering out of me.

"Oh, Dani." My mother starts to get out of her chair. "You still have feelings for him, don't you?"

I nod into her shoulder, welcoming the comfort of my mother hugging me—even in public, in another country, after I just told her I don't need her protection. Turns out, I still need *this.*

And that's okay.

"We were always going to get divorced," I say. "It was never supposed to be long-term. I know it was impulsive, but I don't think it was a mistake. And if it *was* a mistake—then it's my mistake. Our mistake."

"Now that we've all had some time," my father says, "I guess we've all probably done some absurd things in the name of love."

Love.

There's that word again, the one that shouldn't be as foreign as it was when Wouter said it yesterday.

I think back to all the times he called me "lief" when no one was around. At first I thought it was a slip of the tongue, but it happened too frequently, didn't it? Was that his way of telling me, even then?

"I don't know what I'm going to do yet," I tell my parents once we've started eating, and I'm irrationally proud of my city when they rave about the food. "If I'm going to stay, or for how long. There's obviously a lot I have to figure out, both with him and on my own. But I want you to know that whatever choice I make, I'm serious about it. And it doesn't mean I won't come back and visit as much as I can."

They exchange a long glance, communicating in that silent way couples do when they've known each other for years and years.

"Then that just means we'll have to come back and visit, too," my father says.

My mother gestures toward the canal with her fork, because of course this place has captivated her, too. It would be impossible for it not to. "Already looking forward to it."

I SPEND THE REST OF THE WEEK PLAYING TOUR GUIDE FOR my parents and Phoebe and Maya, showing them my favorite spots, the best stroopwafel that isn't the overpriced Instagrammable one with the long line but the one at an open-air market, the blink-and-you'll-miss-them museums hidden in old canal houses.

Then we spend hours browsing Amsterdam's bookstores. We go see the tulips, and Phoebe and Maya pose for some pregnancy photos in the vast fields of red and yellow that are entirely too lovely.

I still haven't taken out any of my suitcases, and I find every excuse to stay out of the apartment. When I'm home alone, I try to relax with a bubble bath. A mug of tea. My breathing exercises.

And then I make an appointment with a new therapist.

"How are you holding up?" Phoebe asks gently as we lock our bikes in Vondelpark. They rented a couple and thought I was kidding when I showed them Little Devil. My parents are flying back early in the morning, and Phoebe and Maya leave tomorrow night. I'm still in denial about all of it.

I'm not quite sure how to answer her question. No matter how many times I try to picture it, my vision of Amsterdam without Wouter is all gray scale. I should be moving on, shouldn't I? Preparing for my interview and viewing apartments?

"Do you think it's ridiculous for me to stay here?" I ask, realizing I'm not answering her question. "Indefinitely? Assuming I get a job and can fully support myself?"

The three of us accept cones of gelato from an ice cream truck. "Why would that be ridiculous?" Maya says. "I studied in Edinburgh for a year during undergrad, and it wasn't enough. If I ever had the chance to live there again, I'd hop on it right away. No looking back."

Phoebe nods her agreement as she dodges an e-bike, a guy steering haphazardly while a girl clings to his back. "We've talked about it, how we might want to do something like that one day. Seeing you here makes it seem all the more possible."

The truth is, it *was* ridiculous when I first got here. A complete disaster. I may have fucked things up with Wouter and his family, but before that . . . it was *good*.

"Then I think about everything I'd miss out on if I stay. Like the baby being born. I want to be there, okay? No matter where I'm living, whenever you want me—I'll get on a plane, and I'll make it happen."

Phoebe licks her own cone, then tries Maya's, and without even discussing it, the two of them swap. "We appreciate that. Maya's mom is going to be living with us for the first month, but after that, if you wanted to . . . we wouldn't say no."

I take out my phone, already searching flights. Phoebe laughs. "You don't have to do it right now!"

"It's just different, not being able to see each other whenever we want to."

Over her gelato, Maya lifts her thick eyebrows at Phoebe, who sighs.

"Dan, that was always going to change once we had the baby. You know that. I'm not going to disappear, obviously, but it's unavoidable," she says. "Think about it this way. When you were in LA, we'd have dinner, or coffee, or we'd go to a yoga class. A few hours, tops. When you come to visit, that's a week of solid, nearly uninterrupted time. Maybe it won't be as consistent, but it can be just as deep and just as meaningful." I do love the sound of that. Then she dabs her gelato on the tip of my nose. "And now we have to figure out what's going on with Wouter."

"If he wants to see me again."

Maya snorts at this. "The moment I saw you two together, I knew he was down bad. That doesn't go away overnight. I was silently pining for Phoebe for a *year*—"

"Eleven months!"

"—before I got the courage to tell her," Maya finishes. They met through mutual friends, in a book club Phoebe started and Maya kept going to, not because she liked the books Phoebe selected but because she liked *her*. Only once they were together did she finally admit she wasn't a huge reader, and Phoebe made it her mission to find something she'd love. Turned out, that thing was audiobooks, and now they often listen together while driving or cooking dinner.

"I like him so much," I say in a small voice after polishing off my hazelnut cone. "But I'm not sure that's enough for him. Obviously, it didn't end well the first time, and I don't know what it looks like, being in a relationship with him as adults."

Phoebe tosses her napkin in a trash can with a little too much force. "Bullshit."

"Excuse me?"

"You think anyone automatically knows how to be in a healthy relationship? No. You fucking practice. You communicate. You figure out the hard shit together," she says. "Some of those guys you dated in LA? They were really into you, Dani! They wanted to take you to brunch and meet your parents and go on weekend trips with you. But you ended it because you decided you didn't do relationships. *Couldn't* do relationships. And you know what? It's a self-fulfilling prophecy. You tell yourself enough times that you don't do something—eventually you can't.

"You think we're not afraid of bringing a kid into the world? An entire human with a whole set of needs and wants?" Phoebe shakes her head. "Just last week, I learned that newborns don't have knee-caps. Kneecaps!"

"Not until around six months," Maya confirms.

"Just because it's scary doesn't mean it's the wrong thing. Just because it's hard—doesn't mean it's not worth doing."

When my sister finishes speaking, she's a little out of breath, her cheeks pink, to the point where Maya has to give her a pat on the back.

Maybe it's not the reassurance I wanted but the tough love I needed. The older-sister wisdom.

"I—*wow.*"

Phoebe calmly clears her throat. "I can't tell if you want to slap me or hug me."

"Both at the same time?" I say, and she laughs.

"It's okay to let yourself want this." She places her hands on my shoulders, looks me straight in the eyes. "I promise you."

That permission slowly works itself through my bloodstream. Rearranges my molecules. I didn't need it from her, but maybe I needed it from *me*. If I allow myself to truly want this, to peel back the layers of *I don't do* and *I'm not ready*, then maybe what I'm afraid of most is that all my uncertainty will have pushed him away.

Now I'm picturing it, the two of us living in that apartment I've come to think of as my home, too. Staying up too late and not even regretting it when we need to wake up early. Taking George on long walks. Making fun of Wouter's complicated tea process when I've loved it from the very beginning.

I want all of it.

It was wrong to expect Amsterdam to change me, as though I could sit back and let it happen when I had to be the one making the first move. I am not the girl I was when I landed here, and it's a relief to realize that the process doesn't have to be over.

I can change. I can find myself a thousand different times, and I'm not done yet.

"Amsterdam looks good on you," Phoebe says at the end of the day, giving me a tight, linen-scented hug. "I love you and miss you to pieces—but I really hope you decide to stay."

After I drop them off at their hotel, a family of tourists flags me down.

"Do you know how to get to the Albert Cuyp Markt?"

And I can't help grinning as this time, I point them in the right direction.

Twenty-six

WHEN YOUR ENTIRE WORLD IMPLODES AROUND YOU, sometimes the only option is to figure out where everything went so disastrously wrong.

You study up on the history of Amsterdam so you can ace your final job interview.

You spend an entire day cleaning the apartment, until the uneven floors glisten and you can see your hopeful expression on every gleaming surface. You organize the tea collection and tidy up the dog toys, ignoring what this does to your heart.

You grovel your way into some face time with your semi-sister-in-law and her mother and grandmother, because even though you are absolutely terrified, you know you need to make things right with them.

And you may not be able to make things right with your husband until you do.

We meet at Roos's apartment because she thought it would be better than returning to *the scene of the crime*, as she put it over text. The studio is a colorful, well-lit space in De Pijp, not too far from my old apartment. Vintage-style posters of Amsterdam cover the walls, leafy plants hanging from the ceiling. I wouldn't be surprised if she has names for all of them.

I told Roos I wanted to talk to all three of them at once, and she had no reason to give in. Part of her must have hated to leave things unfinished, or at the very least, she was curious about what I might say. Either way, I'm immensely grateful. I'll do whatever I can to make it up to this family I crashed my way into.

If I left the Netherlands, I wouldn't just be leaving Wouter behind. It would be Roos and Iulia—who took me out on a Dam Fine boat for a few lessons before my interview—and the tiny community I'm starting to build here, if that community decides to forgive me. So far Iulia's the only one who has, acknowledging she might have considered the same thing if her visa was in jeopardy.

Everyone's already there when I arrive, arranged on Roos's thrifted bright yellow couch with tea and cookies.

"I'm not late, am I?" I ask as I step out of my shoes.

Roos shakes her head. "No, no. We were just talking about how miserable the weather is."

She isn't wrong. We had a bit of a false spring while my family was here, and now it's back to gray skies and wind and the occasional downpour. "That's Amsterdam," the locals say with a shrug.

I greet everyone in Dutch and take a seat in the armchair opposite the couch, my hands too shaky to handle a cup of tea. For the first few minutes, we are all forced smiles and awkward pauses. I fidget with my ring, spinning it around, nudging it up my finger and then back down, wondering if I shouldn't have worn it. Somehow, it feels like if I take it off, that means it's really over.

"Did your parents enjoy Amsterdam?" Anneke asks.

"They did, yes. I'm so sorry you may have gotten a terrible impression of them. They're . . . not usually like that."

"Upset because their daughter got married without telling them, and that the marriage wasn't real to begin with?"

Heat rushes to my face.

"It just made me question whether any of it was real. That's the part I've been struggling with. Not just you and Wouter—but you and me, too." Roos glances down as she says this, an unusual shyness coming over her.

"*Yes*. Are you kidding? I loved spending time with you," I say with as much emphasis as possible, scooting to the edge of my chair. "You've all been so generous, and keeping this secret . . . it's been hell, if I'm being honest." I turn to Maartje and say in Dutch, "I hope you'll still let Wouter keep the apartment."

She gives me an incredulous look. "Why would I take it back?"

"Because the marriage was fake," I tell her, grimacing at the fact that this is something I know how to say. "Schijnhuwelijk."

Maartje says something in Dutch, and although I catch some of it, Roos translates for me.

"She says she knows the stipulation was a little old-fashioned," Roos says. "She thought encouraging him to find a partner might help him get out of his shell a bit, so he wouldn't be as stuck in his ways. And maybe it was a strange way to go about it . . . but it seemed to work." Roos takes a sip of tea. "I think she speaks for all of us. Wouter was so much more *himself* with you than he's been in a while, and learning it wasn't real . . . we're just disappointed that he's going to lose that. A bit of a grieving process, really."

"That's the thing." I worry the ring again. "Even if it wasn't real at the beginning . . . my feelings for him are."

The three of them lean closer, Roos not even trying to hold back her smile.

"I'm so sorry about everything," I continue. "How it happened, and the way we lied to you."

"Wouter has been apologizing all week," Anneke says. "The funny part is—I know my son. The way he was with you, even when we first met you—it wasn't acting. I know that in my soul."

"I know that now, too," I say quietly. "I probably should have known a long time ago. Maybe some part of me did, because I—I love your son." I can say it with full confidence now. In English, and in Dutch. "I think I have for a while. The marriage complicated everything, but I really want a chance to make it right. For all of you."

"It may be unconventional," Anneke agrees, "but I'm happy to know you. I'm happy for you to be part of this family, for however long that lasts."

The next time Maartje speaks, I can understand her perfectly. "Whether you're his wife, or his girlfriend, or whoever you are— I'm just glad you can speak Dutch!"

After Anneke and Maartje head back to Culemborg, Roos drags me over to the couch and lets out a squeal.

"I've been dying to tell someone, but I have news about Iulia. I rented out the whole boat yesterday, so it was just the two of us. And I spent the first half of the tour worried that I'd trapped her or something, and if I confessed my feelings and she wasn't into it, would one of us have to go overboard?" A shake of her head, a slight grimace. "Anyway, that was extremely not necessary, and as it turns out, we have our first official date tomorrow."

I grin right along with her, hugging her and telling her how happy I am to hear it. "Whenever you need a wedding dress . . ." I say, and she just rolls her eyes and nudges me.

"And what about *you*?" she asks. "Any boat-related news?"

"My final interview was yesterday." I had to give a tour to the owner of the company and a few other higher-ups, and I felt as confident about it as I could. "I should hear back soon."

She holds up both hands, crossing her fingers.

As I'm leaving Roos's apartment, I get a message from Wouter. *Okay if I stop by to pick up a few things?*

My heart thuds in my chest, because as much as I want to see him, I don't want it to be an ambush. *Give me an hour*, I write back, and then I race home.

When I get there, I try to tidy up a little before realizing we've made much bigger messes together. Then I grab the familiar yellow stack from his nightstand and head into the bathroom.

My bottle of antidepressants is right there on the counter. I don't bother putting them away, the way I would have at the beginning, when I was overly concerned with him having an image of me I thought was the right one.

Now I only want the real one.

I stick a Post-it note in the center of the mirror, where he can't miss it.

> LOCALS-ONLY AMSTERDAM
> TOUR TOMORROW
> 10 A.M. SHARP
> Our first meeting place

ALL THAT NIGHT AND THE NEXT MORNING, I WORRY HE won't show up. It's not a significant intersection by any means, and I even panicked that maybe he wouldn't remember where it was.

The sight of him makes the breath stall in my lungs. This is springtime Wouter, almost summer, and even if we've had just as many gray days as clear ones lately, his wind-ruffled hair looks like it's been touched by sunshine more often than not. A deep green jacket, a heather-gray V-neck, every part of him looking softly touchable.

And the band of gold around his finger, catching the light.

"Hi," I say when he's finally in earshot.

"Hi." The sound of his voice, that single syllable, threatens to make my knees buckle. "This is where the tour starts? I see I'm the only one here . . ."

I have to bite back a smile. "Ah, this is actually a private tour. Did you not read the brochure? Costs *way* more than a regular tour, but the benefit is that you get some quality one-on-one time with the guide."

"Sounds worth it to me."

"How . . . have you been?" I ask, awkwardly jamming my hands in the pockets of my jeans. "You've been commuting in to see your patients?"

He nods. "I don't mind it. George has fully bonded with my grandmother, though. I'm not sure I'm going to be able to drag him back."

I imagine Wouter waking up in a room that's only half his, desperate to tell him I've missed not just a warm body next to me in bed but *his* warmth.

"Well. This first location is a really crucial one, because it's where everything began." The pavement isn't wet and the sun is bright in the sky, but there's the spot he locked our bikes, and on the next street, the café he took me to. "Or, depending on how you look at it, how everything began *again*. This is where I crashed my bike into my ex-boyfriend, because the bike was too tall for me and I didn't know how to properly ride it, and I was quite frankly not paying as much attention as I should have. And you wouldn't believe how shocked I was to see him again after thirteen years— because of the way he broke up with me when we were seventeen."

"Sounds like a real asshole."

"Yeah, well. Everyone's capable of growth," I say. "Keep up, we have a lot to cover."

I swear I hear a laugh as we continue walking.

"This is the place where my husband proposed to me." I wave my arm with a flourish. "It may look like any other canal, but if you look closer, you'll see that this one actually had to be completely rebuilt recently, just because of the sheer amount of drama that occurred on it."

"You know, I read about that," he says, craning his neck to see over the bridge. "I thought it was an urban legend."

"Nope. One hundred percent real."

"Dani." Wouter lets out a deep breath, runs a hand over his stubble. I'm already aching to touch his face. "I don't want to disrupt the tour, but I have to tell you—I was so nervous I'd get home and all your stuff would be gone. You have no idea how relieved I was."

I lean back against the bridge, drumming my hands along the railing. "I don't think I would have been emotionally capable of lifting my suitcase."

He waits a moment before speaking again. "I know you talked to my family. You didn't have to, but it meant a lot to them. And to me."

"They mean a lot to me, too." It's the truth. In such a short time, I've come to view them if not as in-laws, then at least as friends.

"Just them?" he asks with the smallest quirk of his mouth. Not begging. Not prodding. Just an innocent curiosity.

"That's for a little later in the tour," I say.

That quirk gives way to sheer amusement. He must realize I'm drawing this out, and I'm going to make it worth it for him.

"I talked to mine, too," I say. "Not just because of what you said—it was long overdue. And . . . it was not a disaster."

"I can't imagine that was easy." If there's a way to grimace empathetically, that's what his looks like. "I'm sorry for the way I said that to you."

"No, you were right. It was necessary, and I think things are going to be a lot better between us. It might take a while, but we'll get there. Eventually."

"And you feel good about it?" he asks, because even now, he's thinking about me. If I'm comfortable. If I'm content.

"I do. I really do."

Next, we hop a tram that drops us at the Van Gogh Museum. There's a line of people spilling out the front door, because there always is, and I'm hit with a pang of nostalgia for the morning we spent dodging each other.

"We're not going chronologically," I inform him, "because we've always had some trouble getting the timing right." He nods, and I clear my throat. "This right here is where you tricked me into going to a museum with you."

His mouth drops open. "I absolutely did not. I assumed you saw it was a two-for-one ticket!"

"Nevertheless," I continue with a firm lift of my eyebrows, "it wound up being the first time we really connected after I moved here, and I realized there was a chance we could have something new. And . . . that something new was better and more unexpected than I ever imagined."

"I loved that day," he says. "It felt like I was finally starting to get to know you again, and it was such a relief that we could start over like that."

"And because you finally admitted you love Van Gogh just as much as the rest of us."

A soft smile. "That, too."

Finally, I lead him to the dock of Dam Fine Boat Tours. One of their electric boats is taking off, and a tour guide I met the other day gives me a wave.

"This," I tell him with a grin, because I've been struggling to hold it in since I got the news first thing this morning, "is where I work."

The expression on his face is sheer delight, eyes lit up behind his glasses. He takes a step closer, arms lifting as though to hug me. "You got the job?" When I nod, he only hesitates for an instant, giving me a moment to back away if this isn't something I want— but it is, so I exhale as he pulls me flush against his chest.

This. I missed this.

With my face against his heartbeat, he's familiar and novel all at once. Citrus and warmth and an immediate sense of comfort. One hand on my waist and the other in my hair, tucking a strand behind my ear with his thumb. When he clutches me tighter, I can feel him trembling.

"So—I think that means you can divorce me now," I say when we move apart.

The hug turned his glasses crooked, but he doesn't even bother to fix them as he pins me with a heavy gaze. "Is that what you want, lief?"

With every ounce of courage I have, I shake my head. "Wouter . . . I'm sorry. I've always been the one breaking up with people before they could get too close. I've spent all these years sprinting in the opposite direction of a real relationship so no one could hurt me the way—the way you did, when we were seventeen. But the truth is, I'm tired of pretending to be your wife." I swallow hard, urging myself to keep going. "Because if I really were, we'd get to come home to each other every day, and you'd be in bed next to me every night. I wouldn't be running away the moment it got hard, just because I was scared."

The longing never leaves his eyes. "I've been scared, too. I'm still terrified that you'll leave, that you'll decide you miss where you're from, which is entirely valid, of course. But then I've been wondering . . . maybe it's unfair to expect you to stay here with me when your whole life is on another continent."

"That's the thing," I say. "I don't know if it is anymore. And what I'm realizing is that I don't have to have everything figured out at thirty, or forty, or fifty, or ever. Isn't that the whole point of being human? To always be growing and learning and changing?" I stretch a hand toward him. Graze his wrist. "I've never done anything permanent. Jobs, relationships, even hobbies. But with you . . . I want all of it. You make me feel like everything about me is on purpose. Like I'm not just flailing through life."

"You most definitely aren't," he says, threading his fingers with mine.

"Maybe a little. Sometimes," I say with a half smile. "The one thing I'm certain of is that you're the person I want next to me while I'm figuring it all out. No lies, no rules, no contracts. Just you."

He told me I was brave. I finally feel like I am.

His eyes flutter shut as he takes all of this in. I watch his chest rise and fall, this beautiful man who showed me we could be vulnerable together. "I know I fucked up once," he says, pulling me closer with the hand that's holding mine, "but Dani . . . I'm not going to let myself lose you this time. I'd stand in front of a moving vehicle if it meant keeping you from getting hurt, I swear to you. Maybe it's ridiculous to feel this way after less than six months, but god, I don't know what my life was until you came in and painted it neon. I know this marriage was never supposed to be real, but you're it for me." His other hand is on my waist now. His mouth hovering above mine, his nose nudging my cheek. "I think you always have been."

When he kisses me, there are thirteen years of yearning poured into it. Teenage firsts and misguided texts and the cosmic coincidence of finding our way here after all this time. The swish of the water beneath us and the ever-present *plink* of bicycles.

I breathe him in, and it feels like coming home.

Wouter. Home. At some point, the two became inexorably entwined.

"You fucking ruin me," he says in a choked voice. A tear slips down his cheek, and I reach to catch it on my thumb. "You ruined me when we were seventeen, and then somehow I got lucky enough to get ruined by you again."

"Lucky," I repeat, the word thick in my throat. The next time I kiss him, I taste salt, and then he's the one carefully swiping at my tears.

"Danika. Dani. I want to paint your face over and over. Learn all the curves of your body so I can try to do them justice. I want to know everything that drives you wild, all the things I can do to get you to scream my name. And then I want to wake up and make you breakfast. I want to know what you like on your pancakes, and I want to make sure there's always enough sugar for your tea. I want our whole lives to be too much, because that's how I feel when I'm with you. I want to make art together—messy, imperfect art." He strokes the ring on my finger. "I think I love being married to you."

"Ik hou van jou," I say, and the look on his face could light up the whole sky on a cloudy day. After all this time, it's that simple, isn't it? I run my hand up his rough cheek and into his hair. "Ik hou van jou."

He surprises me when he shakes his head.

"Am I saying it wrong?"

"No, no," he says. "It's just—it's not enough, I don't think. Maybe . . . ik hou het meest van jou. 'I love you the most.'" Another soft slide of his mouth against mine. "Because I do. The absolute most."

I repeat the words, committing them to memory as he kisses me again and again. I say them when he takes me back to his apartment, *our* apartment, where we don't come up for air for hours. I say them when we fall asleep together and the moment we wake up, love-dazed and drunk on each other.

I say them, and I say them, and I say them.

This isn't our hazy, romantic daydream from long ago, those wishes we made when we thought we had all the time in the world to keep wishing—it's something entirely new. Cozy and true and glowing with warmth.

Gezellig.

Epilogue

. . . .

"... AND IF YOU TAKE A LOOK AT THESE HOUSES, YOU CAN see that a lot of them are tilting slightly forward," I say, motioning to the row lining the Spiegelgracht. "Most of these used to belong to merchants who lived on the top floors and worked downstairs. They had hooks attached to the tops of the houses so they could bring up their goods with a pulley system, and the houses were built this way so that those goods didn't smack into the building on the way up. And over the years, the leaning got more and more dramatic until we have . . . this."

"They're beautiful," says an American tourist with short blond hair. "Is the pulley system still used today?"

"Actually, yes," I say. "Although most of the time, they use elevators, but you can always tell when someone's moving house because there will be an electric contraption out front. When you have incredibly narrow stairs and no elevator inside the building, you have to get creative. And that's really where the Dutch have excelled, in everything from architecture to water management."

The blond American leans back against her husband, a ginger

guy who looks strikingly familiar—a little like this actor from a werewolf TV show I watched years and years ago. Probably just a coincidence.

In the off season, when it's chillier out on the water, my tours aren't always full. Six months after I accepted this job, I still love going to work in the morning. Every day, I get to see this awe on people's faces, and I don't think there's anything that could fill me up in quite the same way.

"Where in the US are you from?" the American asks, and when I tell her LA, she and her husband exchange a grin.

"Small world," he says. "We've spent quite a bit of time there— I lived in Los Feliz for over a decade."

The woman nods, giving his hand a squeeze. "And I flew back and forth between LA and Seattle before we realized Seattle was a better fit for our personalities."

"You'd probably be able to handle the weather here easier than I did at the beginning," I say with a laugh, and then gesture to the gray clouds above us. "We're going to be drenched in about ten minutes."

When the guy triumphantly holds up an umbrella to show that they're prepared, I'm almost certain it's him. I wonder if there's a casual way I can ask for a photo. "What brought you to Amsterdam?" he asks.

This question comes up on just about every tour, and my answer is always the same:

"I fell in love," I say.

With a person, and with a place.

Ultimately, Wouter and I decided not to get divorced, and the reality of dating while married wasn't as awkward as we worried it might be. We were both in it for good, and if the worst-case scenario happened, we figured we'd deal with that when we got there. His friends still tease us all the time, because though they easily forgave him for the lie, they could tell we were madly in love when we couldn't yet see it.

We've made marginal progress on the apartment, enough for it to feel like ours. Along with the backsplash in the kitchen, we've added more art to the walls—some of it his, some of it mine—and we converted my bedroom to a combination guest room–slash–office. The remodel is an ongoing process; one of these days, we'll get around to the floors, but we aren't in any hurry. The apartment will wait until we're ready.

A few months ago, Wouter and I traveled to LA and visited my niece, Hazel—who is so adorable I could have watched her sleep for hours—and Phoebe and Maya were more than happy to let us take over so they could have a date night. I brought her too many tulip-printed onesies and enough tins of stroopwafel to get me flagged at security, and I've been sending home Dutch picture books whenever I find one I fall in love with—which is often, since I only just moved beyond that reading level. It was Wouter's first time back in the US since his foreign exchange, so we filled it with trips to In-N-Out and long afternoons at the beach and at the Getty.

And this time when we stepped inside my parents' house, we held hands.

AT FIRST WE JOKE THAT IT'S BECAUSE NEITHER OF US CAN resist the sight of George Costanza in a bow tie.

But then I find the dress, a sunflower-patterned sheath staring back at me from the window of a vintage shop, and it's not very hard at all to find Wouter a matching tie.

It still isn't white, but then again, we've never gone the traditional route.

We wait until the summer to rent a house for all of us in Zeeland, a coastal province in the southwest of the Netherlands. Hazel is almost a year old, and everyone coos over her, though she spends most of her time chasing after George on the sand.

A gauzy tent sways in the breeze, and flower arrangements mark every row of chairs. I'm in my sunflower dress, waiting at the back of the beach house for my husband—because we decided we want to walk down the aisle together.

Wouter appears in his floral tie and a charcoal suit, unable to hide his smile when he sees me. And I wouldn't want him to.

"You've got to be kidding," he says. "I can't believe I get to look at you for the rest of my life."

My cheeks grow warm at his words, because somehow we've never run out of ways to make each other blush. "Hopefully more than just look."

Even in my heels, I only come up to his collarbone, so he still has to lean down to kiss my right cheek. "So much more." But before he gives me his hand so we can head toward the tent, he pauses. "Wait. Something's wrong," he says, brow furrowing.

I hoped it wouldn't be obvious, but he's always been able to read me. "I'm nervous," I admit. "We haven't done this before."

"Nervous . . . because of me?"

"*No*. Never." I tug him closer by his tie. He's stubbled and messy-haired, thanks to the wind, and that's exactly the way I like him. "Everything was such a secret last time that it's hard to believe we can be completely out in the open."

"Completely," he confirms, his hands landing on my waist while his mouth slides to my ear. "And by that, I do mean I am going to maul you on the dance floor later."

"As long as you save some mauling for the honeymoon."

We're spending two and half weeks as tourists in our own country, from charming bed-and-breakfasts to remote cabins. We'll explore a bookstore nestled in a medieval church, a town where boats are the primary method of transportation, a village shaped like a star.

"I understand what you mean, though," Wouter says. "Part of me is worried some government official will be sitting in the audience waiting to object."

"I'll share a jail cell with you."

When he smiles, it drags out his dimple. "Danika—it's unreal how much I love you. I never imagined I'd be so lucky to do this with you twice."

"And this time, we don't have to do any of the paperwork," I say. "All we have to do is stand there and look pretty, which you're already excelling at. And then eat cake." He lets out a low hum of a laugh as he holds me closer, fingers linked with mine while his chin rests on my hair. "Ik hou het meest van jou."

For a few quiet seconds, we take it all in. We inhale the present, exhale the past. The innocence of first love, the crushing heartbreak, the thrill of rediscovering each other as adults. Sometimes this journey felt endless, spanning two continents and a decade and a half, and maybe what's most surprising is that I wouldn't trade it for anything. This will probably be the last moment we have tonight, just the two of us, but that's okay—none of it has to be hidden anymore.

I glance toward the beach, where all our favorite people are waiting for us.

"What do you think?" I ask. "You want to marry your wife?"

Then he gives me the look that I love more than anything else in this country, more than every sugar-dusted pastry or the sun glinting off the canals at golden hour. "Yes," he says, bringing my hand to his mouth and kissing my wrist, my palm, the shimmering gold band that I never feel whole without. "I do."

Acknowledgments

First, I have to thank the Netherlands book community for being the loveliest, most welcoming group of people. This book—my tenth, which feels absolutely surreal to type—would not exist if you hadn't been here to help make this new country feel more like a home. Hartelijk dank to Sanne Zwart (again), Destiny Stapper, Borre Boluijt, Monique Oosterhof, Julia Pennington, Dilayra Verbrugh, and so many more.

Everyone at Luitingh-Sijthoff I've had the pleasure of working with, both past and present: Rianne Koene, Hedda Sanders, Vivian Leandro, Sanne van Leeuwen, Bou Laam Wong, Joyce van Vliet, and Tonny Klaassen.

My editor, Kristine Swartz, always sees through to the heart of my books even when they hit her inbox in slightly scruffy states. At Berkley, I'm also so grateful to Mary Baker, Jessica Plummer, Kristin Cipolla, and Petra Braun for the gorgeous cover. At Penguin UK, thanks in particular to Madeleine Woodfield and Mylene van Musscher for handling my books on this side of the pond.

Elizabeth Bewley, you are a rock star of an agent, and I'm perpetually in awe of you.

To my dear friends and early readers, Alicia Thompson, Tarah DeWitt, Jessica Joyce, Carlyn Greenwald, and Kelsey Rodkey—I'm sending all of you virtual stroopwafel. Thank you to Veronika Zaytseva for the stairs and for the moral (and occasional physical) support. I recommend starting with chapter 14.

To my Seattle friends and family, who are always with me even five thousand miles away.

And to my husband, Ivan—sometimes I worry I'll run out of words for you, but not this time. Thank you for asking the question that changed everything. You know the one.

What Happens in Amsterdam

RACHEL LYNN SOLOMON

Discussion Questions

1. Have you been to Amsterdam? If so, what were your impressions of it? If not, did you have any preconceived notions of it before starting the book, and how did they change by the end?

2. When Dani and Wouter reconnect, they're both reluctant to dig up the past. Why does it take them so long to have an honest, vulnerable conversation about their history?

3. Dani notes that when it comes to Amsterdam's reputation, "the stereotypes are this mix of wholesome—tulips, clogs, windmills—and indulgent—weed, mushrooms, the Red Light District." After reading the book, do you think those stereotypes are accurate? Are there other cities that have similarly opposing reputations?

4. Do you think Dani and Wouter would have found their way back to each other without the marriage of convenience?

5. Why do you think it takes Dani such a long time to realize she's been struggling with burnout?

6. Toward the end of the book, Dani is surprised to realize that she's capable of dramatic change. In particular, she believes the move altered not only her worldview but her personality, too. Have you experienced a similar seismic shift in your own life? What caused it?

7. If you could read this book from Wouter's point of view, what do you think his character arc would be?

8. Cities such as London and Paris are familiar settings when it comes to romance, but Amsterdam hasn't had many moments in the spotlight. Why do you think this is, and where would your ideal destination romance take place?

Keep reading for an excerpt from

Business or Pleasure

THIS BOOK WAS A REAL LABOR OF LOVE," SAYS THE WOMAN seated behind a table of hardcovers sporting her makeup-free face, scrunched mid-yelp as she attempts to drink from a garden hose. "I can't believe it's something I can finally hold in my hands! And the cover's not too bad, either."

The audience laughs right on cue. In the back row, I can practically feel Noemie cringe beside me. "I've made bowls of cereal that were more a labor of love than the effort she put into that book," she whispers.

She's not wrong—I experienced it firsthand. Still, I give my cousin a nudge. "Be respectful."

"I am. To the cereal."

I press my lips together to keep from reacting and focus on the stage, where Maddy DeMarco commands the room with a warm, practiced confidence bordering on emotional manipulation. The bookstore is filled with just a fraction of her 1.6 million Instagram followers: mostly women, mostly white, mostly dressed in sustainable linen they bought using her discount code MADSAVINGS10. At first I thought it was a cult, and to be completely honest, I'm still not sure. Her brand of saccharine positivity doesn't quite do it for me anymore—whenever I need self-love, it's more likely to take shape as something handheld and battery-operated. Which Maddy has devoted tragic few (read: zero) social media posts to.

She's built her career on empty affirmations and obvious advice. Case in point—the book is called *Go Drink Some Water: A Guide to Self-Care, Self-Discovery, and Staying Thirsty.*

"People often ask how I turned one viral post into a lifestyle brand," Maddy says, crossing one linen-clad leg over the other. Her natural waves are shined to perfection with an expensive oil I'm ashamed to admit I tried before chopping my ash-blond hair into a pixie last year. "And the answer is simple: I don't sleep." This gets a few more laughs. A muted groan from Noemie. "No, I want to be real with you guys. I was one of those people who never had their shit together—wait, can I say that? Are there kids here?" She makes a show of squinting out at the audience before barreling onward. "I would get so stressed that I literally forgot to drink water! It wasn't until I got so dehydrated that I ended up in the hospital that I real-ized I'd stopped doing things just for myself. I'm talking *basic*, keeping-yourself-functioning kind of things. Like drinking water. And I knew something needed to change."

I wrote three chapters of her book on that hospital visit, poring over her Instagram to make sure I was capturing her voice. Every fourth comment swooned over how relatable she was—and this is someone who sells wall hangings that say LIVE LAUGH GIRLBOSS.

All through the writing process, I tried to keep Maddy relat-able: when she insisted on communicating with me only through her team, when that team sent me photos of notes she'd scrawled on compostable napkins, when she said the writing needed to feel *a little earthier.* I wanted to like her so badly, wanted to believe her posts were inspiring people to live their best and most carbon-neutral lives. Because the thing is, back before the book, I did like her. There was something both aspirational and authentic about her that had compelled me to hit "follow" a few years ago, long before the wall hangings and the constant #ads that clutter her feed these days.

Ghostwriting isn't a glamorous job, and even if nothing about this finished product screams *Chandler Cohen*, I've been strangely giddy over the idea of finally meeting Maddy—because some part of me is still a little starstruck. The book came out a few days ago, and I've made myself wait to get a copy until her Seattle tour stop, convinced her signature on the title page will cement this as a collaboration. I didn't even open the box of hardcovers that showed up on my doorstep last week.

In my wildest dreams, I've wondered if maybe Maddy will ask me to sign a copy for her, too. An inside joke between the two of us. And somehow, that would make up for all the eleventh-hour rewrites and irreversible, anxiety-induced damage to my cuticles.

Chapter 6: Harness Your Inner Optimist. Maybe the book really did make an impact.

Maddy lifts one arm in the air. "Can I get a show of hands—who here has ever posted a photo of themselves smiling when they were so far from happy, hitting the submit button almost felt like a lie?" Nearly every hand goes up. "There's nothing to be ashamed of. I've done it plenty of times. But it's not the photos of my smiling face that have enabled me to connect with so many of you—it's the photos of my crow's-feet. My frowns. Even my tears." She slips her phone from her pants pocket, scrolls through her own feed. "The next time you post something, think about how much it's representing your authentic self. And then don't just hit submit. Take a new photo. Write a new caption. Let your inner beauty do the talking."

"Then she's going to love my event recap," Noemie says.

A woman in front of us turns around, shoving a finger to her lips. Noemie goes silent and blinks wide, innocent eyes at her.

"You're going to get us kicked out," I say. "And then what am I going to say to my publisher?"

"You can tell them I'm living my truth and speaking my heart. Isn't that what chapter twelve was about?" Unfortunately, yes.

After another half hour of Maddy's sweeping proclamations about our on- and offline lives, infused with no fewer than four references to brands that sponsor her, she gets a signal from her assistant and claps her hands once. "I'm afraid that was all the time we have! I can't wait to sign these beauties for you, but before I do . . . I want you all to do something for me." A sly grin spreads across her face. "If you reach under your chairs, you'll find your very own bottle of water."

There's a flurry of eager, electric energy as those who didn't notice the water bottles when they came in discover them for the first time.

"Now I want you to open that baby up"—Maddy uncaps her water bottle, raising it high in a toast to the audience. I tap my recycled plastic against Noemie's with an exaggerated lift of my eyebrows—"and take a big, delicious sip."

"DOESN'T IT BOTHER YOU," NOEMIE ASKS IN THE SIGNING line, running a hand along the book's glossy cover, "not seeing your name on it?"

It did. At the beginning. But now there's a sense of detachment that accompanies a book release. As a celebrity ghostwriter, I'm not hired to be anyone's coauthor—I'm supposed to write from their point of view. To *become* them. My first author, a *Bachelor* contestant who infamously dumped the guy on national TV after he proposed, was an utter delight, and she still emails asking how I'm doing. But I quickly learned that wasn't the norm. Because then there was Maddy, and the book I just finished for a TikTok-famous personal trainer with his own line of protein shakes that really stretches the definition of literature.

Maybe there's some satisfaction in clutching these several hundred pages I churned out at record speed, a tangible conclusion to all those late nights and canceled plans. And yet I can also completely divorce myself from this book in a way that's either great or terrible for my mental health. Maybe both.

"It's not my book," I say simply, taking another sip from my Maddy DeMarco–branded water bottle. It's like, weirdly good water, and I'm not sure I want to know why.

The signing line crawls forward, people asking Maddy to pose for photos before they head off to pay at the register. I can't fault any of them for loving her the way they do. They want to believe that changing their lifestyle can change their life—after all, it worked for her.

"Thanks for waiting with me," I say, and Noemie's eyes soften behind her tortoiseshell glasses, her cynical exterior cracking for a moment. "I know this isn't your ideal Friday night."

"Considering I spent last Friday explaining to a client why we couldn't guarantee them a cover story in *Time*, this is a definite upgrade." She's still dressed in her PR professional best: tapered slacks, daisy-patterned peplum top, a blazer draped over her arm. Long dark hair straightened and frizz-free, because she's not Noemie if she has even a single flyaway. Meanwhile, in my cords, faded Sleater-Kinney tee, and a black denim jacket that's too warm for early September, I must look like I haven't seen the sun since 1996. No vitamin D for me, thanks.

"Can't argue with you there." I pick at a speck of silver nail polish, a tell my cousin will be able to see right through. "And hey, the longer we're here, the longer I can pretend everyone else isn't at Wyatt's housewarming."

Noemie grimaces in this familiar way I'm never sure whether I learned from her or the other way around. Noemie Cohen-Laurent is both my only first cousin and my closest friend. We grew up on the same street, attended the same schools, and now even live in the same house, though she owns it and I'm paying a deeply discounted monthly rent.

We both studied journalism, starry-eyed about how we were going to change the world, tell the stories no one else was telling. The economy pushed us in different directions, and before we graduated, Noemie had already been hired full-time at the PR firm where she'd interned during her senior year.

"I'm guessing that means you decided not to go?" she says.

"I can't do it. You can go if you want, but—"

Noemie cuts me off with a swift shake of her head. "Solidarity. Wyatt Torres is dead to me."

My shoulders sag with relief. I haven't wanted her to feel like she needs to pick a side, even if there's no risk she'd pick his. Still, she's the only one who knows what happened between us a few weeks ago: one incredible night after years of pining I thought was mutual, given the desperate way his hands roamed my body as we tumbled into bed. I'd helped him unpack his new apartment, and we were exhausted and tipsy and just seemed to *fit*, our bodies snapping together in this natural, effortless way. Wyatt's dark hair feathering across my stomach, tanned skin shivering where I touched him. The way he dug his nails into my back like he couldn't bear to let me go.

But then came the *Can we talk?* text, and the confession, during said talk, that he wasn't looking for a relationship right now. And I was a Relationship Girl, he said, with all the distaste usually reserved for that one person who replies-all on a cc'd email. He valued our friendship too much, and he didn't want either of us to get hurt.

So I pretended I wasn't.

"We would have been good together, though," I say quietly, forcing my feet forward in line.

Noemie places a gentle hand on my shoulder. "I know. I'm so sorry. We'll have a much better time tonight, I promise. We'll go back to the house and order way too much Indian food, because I know how you love being able to eat leftovers for five days afterward. And then we can watch people on Netflix making bad real estate decisions with partners they absolutely should not be with."

Finally, it's our turn, one of the booksellers beckoning us forward. Maddy's smile has barely slipped, an impressive feat after all those photos.

"Hi," I say, thrusting my copy forward with a trembling hand, which is only marginally embarrassing. I wrote pages and pages pretending to be this woman, and now that she's three feet in front of me, I can barely speak. Someone take away my communication degree.

"Hi there," she says brightly. "Who should I make it out to?"

"Chandler. Chandler Cohen."

She squeezes one eye shut, as though trying to remember. Any moment now, it'll ring a bell. We'll laugh about her takedown of internet trolls in chapter four and roll our eyes at all the people-pleasing she used to do, documented in detail in chapter sixteen. "How do you spell that?"

"Oh—um," I stammer, every letter in the English alphabet fleeing my mind at once. "Chandler . . . Cohen?" Maddy gives me a blank, expectant look.

No. It's not possible, is it? That she wouldn't even remember my name after all the back-and-forth? All her demands?

"You don't know Chandler—" Noemie starts to say, but I silence her with an elbow to the ribs.

Sure, I communicated mostly with Maddy's team . . . but my name was on the contracts. The rough drafts. The endless email chains. I wrote this fucking *book* for her, and she has no idea who I am.

I must mumble out the spelling, but my vision blurs as she swoops her magenta sharpie over the title page, sliding in a bookmark and passing it back to me like a seasoned pro.

"Thank you," I manage as Maddy waves us away with a sunshine grin.

Once we're safely in the picture-book aisle, the one farthest from the stage, I let out a long, shaky breath. It's fine. This is fine. Obviously, she wasn't going to ask me to sign our book.

Her book.

Because that's the whole point of a ghost—no one is supposed to be able to see me.

"You should have told her who you were," Noemie says, one hand gripping her quilted Kate Spade and the other white-knuckling the water bottle. "I would have, if you hadn't viciously attacked me."

"It would have just made it more embarrassing." I clutch the book tight to my chest because if I don't, I might hurl it across the store. "Maybe she's not great with names. She meets a lot of people. I'm sure she just gets . . . really busy girlbossing."

"Right." Noemie's stance is still rigid. "Well, I'm still going to unfollow her." And to prove it, she takes out her phone, only to have something else catch her attention. "Shit, it's work. The wrong draft of a press release went out and the client is *livid*. I might have to . . ." She trails off, her fingers flying over the screen.

Every so often, it hits me that there are only two years between us, though Noemie's life is wildly different from mine. When The Catch laid me off five years ago and eventually folded, unable to keep up with BuzzFeed and Vice and HuffPost, she was buying a house. When I was struggling to sell freelance articles about new local musicians and the evolution of Seattle's downtown, she was juggling high-profile clients and contributing a respectable monthly amount to her 401(k). She's twenty-nine to my thirty-one, but it's almost shocking how much better at adulting she is.

Only two years, and yet sometimes it feels like I'll never catch up.

"Go," I say, nudging her with the book. "I get it."

If I told her I needed her, she'd probably find a way to do both: comfort me and save her client. But most of the time, when work and anything else are fighting for Noemie's attention, work wins.

"Only if you're sure," she says. "You want to go back home, fire up DoorDash, and save me a couple samosas for when I'm done?"

"I actually might stay out a bit longer."

She gives me a lingering glance, as though worried there's something I'm not telling her. It's the same way she looked at me when I learned about The Catch slashing its staff. My onetime dream job forcing me to find a new dream.

"Nome. I'm *fine*," I say, with so much emphasis that it sounds more threatening than reassuring.

She gives me a tight hug. "I'm proud of you," she says. "In case I didn't say it before." She did, when I turned in my draft and my revisions and then on the book's release day, when she had to go into work early but had a spread of donuts and bagels waiting for me when I woke up. "You wrote and published a *book*. Two of them, in fact, with another on the way. Don't let her take that away from you."

I'm not sure I can put into words how much I love her in this moment, so I just hug her back and hope she knows. Clearly, I'm not the best at words today.

One great thing about this bookstore is that it has a bar, and I hate that on my way over, I have visions of Maddy sitting down next to me. I'd offer to buy her a drink and then tell her something that only someone intimately acquainted with *Go Drink Some Water* would know. She'd gasp, apologize, gush about how happy she is with the book. She'd confirm that all those months weren't just a paycheck—they *mattered*.

Except this isn't really about Maddy DeMarco at all.

It's the bundle of self-worth tangled in the sheets on Wyatt's bed, in the paychecks that don't always arrive on time, in the lovely bedroom in my cousin's lovely house that I'd never be able to afford on my own. It's the persistent tapping at the back of my mind that sounds suspiciously like a clock, wondering if I picked the wrong career path and if it's too late to start over. And if I'd even know how.

It's that every time I try to move forward, something is waiting to tug me right back.

The two bartenders are immersed in what looks like a very serious conversation, so I have to clear my throat to get their attention. I order a hard cider that's much too sweet, and before slipping Maddy's book into my bag, I open it up to the title page.

If I weren't already gutter-adjacent, it would sink me even deeper.

For Chandler Cone, it says in magenta ink. *Drink up!*

EMERALD CITY COMIC CON

SEPTEMBER 8–10,
WASHINGTON STATE CONVENTION CENTER

Meet Finn Walsh, better known as Oliver Huxley
from *The Nocturnals*! We're delighted to welcome
everyone's favorite nerd to ECCC once again.
Here's where you can spot him this weekend:

PANEL:

Every Hero Needs One: Familiars, Friends, and Sidekicks
Friday, September 8, 6 p.m., Room 3B

SIGNING BOOTH:

Saturday, September 9, 4 p.m., Hall C
AUTOGRAPHS: $75 · PHOTO OP: $125

AT FIRST, I INTEND TO DO EXACTLY WHAT THE INSCRIPTION tells me to: become heavily intoxicated, which is probably not what Maddy meant and also might not be possible with this too-sweet cider. I snap the traitorous book shut, letting out a sigh that draws the attention of the man a seat away from me.

I meet his gaze and give him an apologetic look, but instead of the judgmental frown I'm expecting, he nods toward my bottle of cider. "What are we celebrating?"

"The disintegration of my self-esteem, sponsored by my complete mistake of a career. And the funeral of a relationship that ended before it even began." I lift the bottle and take a sip, trying not to wince. "It's a wake, actually. I have a front-row seat to watch both those things implode. Spectacularly." Or at least, Chandler Cone does.

"Those aren't easy tickets to get." He holds his hands together, then bows his head as though paying his respects. "Dearly beloved, we're gathered here today to—"

In spite of everything, I burst out laughing. "I think that's what you say at a wedding. Or at the beginning of a Prince song."

"Ah shit, you're right." His mouth curves into a smile. "Good song, though."

"Great song."

In the most discreet way possible, I take a closer look at this stranger. I don't think he was at the signing, but then again, the room was packed. He looks older than me, though probably not by much—auburn hair, shorter on the sides and floppy on top, graying a bit at the temples, which I discover in this moment is something I find very attractive. He's in dark jeans and a casual black button-up, one sleeve unbuttoned at the wrist, as though he got distracted when he was putting it on, or maybe had a long day and the button simply gave up.

"I'm sorry, though," he says. "About your work, and your relationship."

I wave this off. "Thanks, but it'll be okay. I think." *I hope.*

I could easily turn away, tell him to have a nice evening. Down my drink in silence and stumble home to takeout, trashy TV, and wallowing. I've never chatted someone up at a bar before—I'm usually too busy avoiding eye contact with other humans—but something about him compels me to keep talking.

Because full honesty: maybe my ego needs a little boost tonight.

"What about you?" I say, picking up my bottle and gesturing toward his glass. "You're drinking alone because . . ."

When I trail off, I watch his face, catching a split-second flinch. It's so brief, I'm not sure he's aware he's doing it—maybe I even imagined it. But then he collects himself. Seems to relax.

"Same as you. Career-related existential dread." He motions to the pair of bartenders, dropping the volume of his voice. "I was going to head out twenty minutes ago, but then I got too invested in their personal lives."

He taps a finger to his lips, and I strain to hear what the bartenders are saying.

"*Those guinea pigs are not my responsibility. If you're going to insist on keeping them in our apartment, you need to clean up after them.*"

"*You could at least call them by their names.*"

"*I refuse to call those little beasts Ricardo and Judith.*"

"*Just like you refused to do the dishes after that party you threw last week? The one with a build-your-own-chili-dog bar?*"

"I want to call you out for eavesdropping, but I can't blame you," I say. "This is quality entertainment."

"Right? Now I can't leave until I know how it ends." Then he raises an eyebrow, squinting at the water bottle I stupidly placed on the bar next to me. "Is there a reason your water bottle says . . . 'Live Laugh Girlboss'?" He holds up his hands. "Not judging, just curious."

"Oh, this? I'm part of a hydration-based MLM. I'm in really deep. They'll be running the docuseries any day now."

Without missing a beat, he calmly places his glass back down. Flicks his eyes around the bar. When he speaks again, it's in a whisper. "Do I need to call someone for you?"

"Afraid it's too late." I give the water bottle a shake. "But if I can sell you a thousand of these babies, I might be able to get off with minimal prison time."

"The thing is," he says, drumming a couple fingertips on the bar, "I could probably find a use for three hundred. Maybe four. But I don't know what I'd do with the rest of them."

"You'd just have to find other people to sell them to. I could hook you up, give you all the training you need to become your very own boss."

"I'm not falling for that one." He's grinning at me, his teeth a brilliant white. The longer I study him, the cuter he is. It's all in the details—a dusting of reddish facial hair, the warmth of his rich hazel eyes, the freckles spiraling across his knuckles, up onto his left wrist where his shirt is unbuttoned and bare skin peeks through.

And the way he's looking at me might feel better than I've felt all day. All week. All month since Wyatt.

"I'm Drew," he says. "I completely understand if you can't tell me your name, though. For legal reasons. What with the show and all."

I try and fail to hold in another smile. God, he's charming. "Chandler," I say. "I was at the book signing over there." I drag out the book, as though the introduction necessitates some additional shred of truth. "What do you do? When you're not trying to rescue women from MLMs drinking at bookstore bars?"

"I mean, jeez, that's practically a full-time job." Then he takes another sip of his drink before tenting his fingers together. "I'm in sales. Not very interesting, unfortunately."

"I disagree. That depends entirely on what you're selling. For example, tiny rain boots for dogs? Fascinating, and I'll need to see photos immediately."

"Tech sales," he elaborates with a little sigh that makes him seem eager to change the subject. Which, fair—tech sales doesn't sound like the most edge-of-your-seat career. "What about you?"

If that isn't the million-dollar question. "I'm a writer. A journalist, I guess, but I haven't written anything I'm proud of in a while." I take a sip of my cider, remember it's too sweet, fight a grimace. "The whole capitalist machine really sold us lies about becoming an adult. I was under the impression that each of us was supposed to flourish into this perfectly well-adjusted, impressively accomplished person. That was what they told us all throughout school, right? That we could be anything we wanted. That we were special. But now I'm just . . ." *Writing books without my name on them. Struggling to pay my reduced rent. Floundering.* "Being a millennial in your thirties is a trip and a half," I finish.

"I'll drink to that."

He takes a long sip before setting down the empty glass, then splays a hand on the table, index finger tracing the wood grain. As though he's carefully considering what he wants to say next. A dim light bulb catches the swirl of freckles along his cheeks, down his neck, tucked into the hollow of his throat. Not the exact shade of his hair, I'm noticing—some darker, some lighter. A whole beautiful constellation.

"I've got to preface this by saying that I don't usually do this, but . . . Do you want to get out of here, Chandler?" At that, he winces. "Wow. That sounds like a really bad line. I swear, I'm genuinely wondering if you're interested in leaving this place and going to a different place. One that has more food, because I'm kind of starving and the 'loaded totchos' on the menu don't look very appetizing."

I could tell him I have plans. That the loaded totchos actually sound fantastic and I've been debating ordering a basket ever since I sat down. And yet.

Drew saying it sounds like a bad line could fully be a line, I realize that, but maybe I'm not ready to go back to Noemie's house and feel sorry for myself. This isn't something I'd ever do, and yet in this moment, that feels like exactly the reason to say yes. I could toss my half-empty cider and get drunk on his attention alone.

I grab my wallet, throwing a few dollars down on the bar. "Let's get out of here."

Author photo by Dennis Heeringa

RACHEL LYNN SOLOMON is the *New York Times* bestselling author of *The Ex Talk*, *Weather Girl*, and other romantic comedies for teens and adults. Originally from Seattle, she's currently navigating expat life in Amsterdam, where she can often be found exploring the city, collecting stationery, and working up the courage to knit her first sweater.

VISIT THE AUTHOR ONLINE

RachelSolomonBooks.com

𝕏 ⓘ RLynn_Solomon

Ready to find
your next great read?

Let us help.

Visit prh.com/nextread

Penguin
Random
House